# The Morrow Secrets
## Trilogy

Book Three

Sweet Cherry Publishing Limited
Unit E, Vulcan Business Complex
Vulcan Road
Leicester, LE5 3EB
United Kingdom

First published in Great Britain by Sweet Cherry Publishing 2015
This edition first published in the UK in 2015

Printed and bound by Thomson Press (India) Limited.

Title: The Dark Spell
© Susan McNally 2015

ISBN: 978-1-78226-247-3

Illustrations © Luke Spooner, Carrion House 2015

Find out more about the Morrow Secrets trilogy by visiting:
http://www.themorrowsecretstrilogy.com
www.facebook.com/morrowsecrets
www.twitter.com/morrowsecrets

For my mother Ellen and her spellbinding tales of family
history that kept me gripped for many happy hours

*Deep into that darkness peering,*
*long I stood there wondering, fearing,*
*Doubting, dreaming dreams no mortals ever*
*dared to dream before*

Edgar Allan Poe - *The Raven*

# The Dark Spell

# One

**B**ecky Lind was daydreaming again. She was sitting at the kitchen table, idly snipping the tops off the late summer gooseberries, humming to herself and making a half-hearted attempt to prepare the fruit for Frieda to bake into tarts.

'Watch it girl! Sprinkle them goosies with sugar and be sure to get all the stalks out!' the cook snapped as she inspected Becky's work. 'You're makin' a right old mess. Look, do it this way.'

Frieda grabbed the paring knife and demonstrated her trusted method to an indifferent Becky. The girl rolled her eyes with frustration.

'Yes, I've got the hang of it now,' she replied half-heartedly.

'Then get on with it! You've more to do today than just that fruit!' Frieda hollered bad-temperedly as she made her way down the back steps and into the kitchen garden.

Becky sighed, pushed her messy hair under her cap and stared forlornly at the mountain of gooseberries piled up before her. It was going to be such a very long and tedious morning with no one to keep her company. It was at moments like this that she yearned to be back home in Small Grovell, playing with her friends in the warm summer meadows. Instead, she was stuck on this miserable island with an endless list of boring jobs to do. So Becky reluctantly continued to snip, gouge and flick the sticky gooseberry stalks into the slop pail. Most of them missed and landed on the floor.

'Bother,' she grumbled, kicking the sticky stalks under the table and bemoaning her luck.

But as fate would have it, on that particular morning, Becky Lind was quite wrong. It was not going to be a boring day after all.

Suddenly a terrific noise roared down the chimney and landed with an enormous gust in the fireplace. The force scattered the smouldering cinders over the floor, taking the girl unawares and filling the kitchen with a plume of smoke and soot.

'Goodness!' Becky cried, coughing and leaping to her feet.

She scooted across the kitchen, grabbed the fire tongs, waving the smoke out of her eyes and attempted to pick up the cinders before they scorched the rugs.

Then she heard it again! A deafening sound that ended with another blast of thick, acrid smoke billowing out of the fireplace. This time, the dreamy-headed girl recalled what Plum, the housekeeper, had told her again and again, and the awful realisation began to sink in. It had to be HER!

Becky stopped dead still, raised her head and gazed warily in the direction of the mysterious Moon Tower.

'Oh my,' she whispered fearfully, dropping the tongs with a clatter.

The awful noise could only mean one thing! The Grand Witch had returned!

Becky had been warned by the housekeeper to be on the lookout for the dreaded signs; the thunderous noise and the blasts of billowing smoke – and now the worst had happened! The Grand Witch Selvistra Loons, the wicked sorceress from the Larva Coven, had come home, back to her remote sea palace on the island of Stack End, flying in on the tail of the westerly wind, after a long and tranquil absence.

Becky's heart thumped in her chest! She darted to the kitchen window, flung the lattice wide open and called out to the other servants who were working in the kitchen garden at the far end of the island.

'Plum! Trillie! Oh please come quickly! You have to help me! The Witch, s-she's come home!' she spluttered.

Becky waved and shouted to attract their attention but the sea winds were strong that day, masking her cries of distress so that when the servants' bell rang urgently, again and again, Becky knew she would have to go up to the Grand Witch's apartments, to the very top of the sinister Moon Tower, all on her own. The awful thought curdled like sour milk in the pit of her stomach and filled her with dread.

Becky Lind had never dared venture up to the Grand Witch's quarters before. The entrance to the eerie Moon Tower radiated fear into the younger servants who shunned any chore involving the Grand Witch's inner sanctum.

The blackened door was carved in the shape of a claw, positioned under a hideous cluster of stone ravens – an *unkindness* of ravens they were called – with their sharp beaks protruding viciously and their bejewelled beady eyes scouring the corridor for any intruders.

'Mind that horrible Witch and just serve your time,' her mother had cautioned as Becky departed some months earlier from the hamlet of Small Grovell. 'Keep to the kitchen and do your job, like a good girl. That terrible sorceress has caused havoc with her curses round 'ere and she'll not think twice about turnin' you to stone or inflicting you with a nasty curse.'

Becky bit her lip as her mother's warning came back to haunt her. The sound of the hollow bell clanged insistently again and again. What was she to do? If she didn't obey the summons, the Witch would seek her out and turn her to stone for ignoring her command!

So Becky Lind picked up her skirts and ran through the servants' hall. She stepped gingerly up the narrow steps and out into the corridor that lined the sea wall. Fierce winds tore through the open windows and lashed the curtains across her face, creating a ghostly spectre as she hurried towards the Moon Tower.

As Becky approached the entranceway, the unkindness of ravens turned their evil gaze upon her, as six pairs of jet-black eyes scrutinised the girl. Becky hovered uncertainly, on the verge of turning back in fright, when suddenly the door creaked open and an unseen force bundled her over the threshold. She landed with a sickening thud on the other side. The heavy door clanged shut behind her and the bolt shot home.

'Oh my,' she trembled, peering upwards into the gloomy stairway of the Witch's Tower. Now there was no way back! Becky was on her way to meet her sinister mistress.

Up she climbed, winding her way to the top of the Moon Tower in search of the infamous Spell Chamber; the Grand Witch's room of magic and mayhem that had often featured in scary stories from her childhood.

In the fleeting half-light, dagger-like shadows lengthened and shuddered across the grey pock-marked walls that were tinged with a reddish glow. The air smelled rancid, laced with the odour of rats, of long-caged animals and ancient spells, their power all spent and forgotten. Becky crept along the corridor, following the ebb and flow of the shadows as the sound of vermin scuttled away before her, their nails pitter-pattering across the flagstones. At the end of the passageway a solitary lantern flickered menacingly, drawing Becky further into the darkness and closer to the witch's lair. There before her a puddle of orange-red light seeped ominously under a closed door. She had found the witch's Spell Chamber.

'Is anyone there?' she asked tentatively, turning the handle and peeping inside.

As soon as Becky stepped into the room she saw her; a

dreadful and luminous creature bathed in a dancing red light. The Fire Witch was stretched across a winged armchair surrounded by flaming garnet sparkles that shimmered disconcertingly whenever she moved, like a thousand angry fireflies.

'Please, my Lady,' Becky muttered in astonishment, 'I-I'm sorry I took so long in answering your call - but I've never been up here before.'

The Grand Witch jerked her head in Becky's direction. A flaming bejewelled sorceress; she had a beautiful, yet monstrous presence.

Becky had come face to face with the Grand Witch of Stack End!

Selvistra Loons had not aged one day from the portrait that hung in the hallway. Her hair was golden-red, long and lustrous, encrusted with sparkling jewels and fine sea pearls. Her eyes, deep pools of chestnut in certain light and flashing orange when enraged, bore hot and menacingly into the servant's face.

'Why is my chamber not ready for my return? Where are all my potions and spell books?' Selvistra demanded, stabbing her long finger at the empty cabinets.

Becky shuddered as the witch's thunderous words reverberated around the room. It felt as though the ground was swallowing her up. Her legs trembled uncontrollably and her mouth was as dry as sand. The reply stuck in her throat.

'Well?' barked Selvistra, her eyes flashing fire-red.

Becky licked her lips. 'P-Please my Lady, the Mistress Plum locked them away for safekeeping. You were gone so long this time,' she replied.

Many months had passed since Selvistra last visited the

Moon Tower, but the Grand Witch still expected everything to be exactly as she had left it.

'And where's Orgen, my Hag-beast?' the witch snarled.

The wretched fetid odour of rancid fur was the smell of the beast.

Becky's colour heightened and she shook her head. 'I-I don't know about him my Lady,' she muttered gravely.

Becky wanted nothing to do with the enormous half-man, half-wolf that roamed the island after nightfall. When she had first arrived on Stack End she had heard the Hag-Beast's blood-curdling howls night after night. Now, she slept with cottonwood pressed into her ears and the blankets pulled tightly over her head.

'What's your name?' demanded Selvistra, smoothing down the folds of her black robe and turning her unendurable gaze on the miserable girl.

Becky wrung her hands, desperate not to cause offence.

'Becky Lind, my Lady. I'm the new kitchen m-maid from Small Grovell. I replaced Petra Givenns,' the girl stuttered, dipping her knee.

Selvistra sneered at the wretched servant. They were all the same, these children from the villages; sent to Stack End for a few years to fulfil the bargain that had been struck. Selvistra would not burn down their houses or kill their offspring on the condition that they paid their dues in servitude. The witch's blood-red eyes smouldered and her snake-like body portrayed every ounce of the wickedness that pumped through her veins.

In an instant she sprang from the chair, leaving a coppery dust in her wake.

She rose up, towering over the servant.

'Tell Plum that her Mistress is back,' she shouted angrily. 'I want my bed made with the finest goose feather quilts. I want grilled fish for lunch and then, - ALL MY MAGICAL POTIONS AND INSTRUMENTS!' she screamed, 'MUST be returned to their proper place, do you understand?'

Becky's mouth hung open and her cheeks burned. The Spell Chamber shuddered at the witch's rage; the glass-fronted cabinets shook and clattered as her towering form convulsed with fury. The room grew darker and Selvistra burned brighter and brighter as her anger intensified.

'And another thing!' Selvistra shrieked, grabbing Becky roughly. 'Don't ever look at me in the face again or I'll turn you to stone!'

Becky gasped and quickly averted her gaze as a slither of cold sweat trickled down her spine.

'Y-Yes of course, my Lady, I'll do just as you ask,' she stammered, turning quickly on her heel and flying from the Grand Witch's sight.

Selvistra Loons purred with wicked delight at the fear her rage had instilled in the servant. She slithered back to the nook by the fireplace, sprawled across her armchair and stretched out her smouldering body in the feathery gloom. The Grand Witch had old scores to settle. Her crimson eyes rolled back in her head as she revelled in her evil thoughts and the devastation that her spells would wreak on her enemies at Hellstone Tors.

It was the night of All Witches' Eve. The longed-for end was in sight at last!

All her scheming and plotting was nearing its end!

As Selvistra sprawled in the eerie darkness a menacing leer crawled across her perfect face.

*

The Grand Witch's sea palace was a tall square tower, built of iron-grey stone, turned moss-green with the onslaught of the sea that lashed the northern perimeter of the fortress with an unrelenting force. The Moon Tower was the only dwelling on the rocky island, jutting way up into the sky, far out into the Viridian Sea. The remote island was surrounded by the churning ocean and perched amid a nest of steep petrified rocks. Stack End was Selvistra's stronghold, protected by a web of intricate spells. No one visited and no one left without her permission.

Becky fled back to the kitchen, almost tumbling down the back staircase in her haste.

'Oh, Plum!' she wept, falling in a heap amongst the fruit baskets and scattering apples in her wake.

'Whatever is the matter?' cried Amy Plum, jumping to her feet.

'She's back! T-The Grand Witch!' Becky spluttered, pointing nervously to the top of the Moon Tower. 'Now I've met her, I never want to see her again! She scared me half to death, surrounded by that terrible red glow she was, with shooting flames and burning, hateful eyes,' she snivelled into her apron.

'Pull yourself together! What did she say?' asked Plum, shaking the wretched girl.

'She wants goose feather pillows and … and fish for lunch and I'm not to look at her ever again,' she cried. 'But Plum, why is she on fire?'

'I will see to her – now do stop blubbering, child!' said Plum, beckoning to the other servants. 'Selvistra Loons is a Fire Witch. The flame-coloured glow is her magic. All the Grand Witches are marked out by their magical light.'

Becky continued to weep. 'She asked me about that hideous Hag-beast, but I want nothing to do with him!' replied the distraught girl. 'My mother warned me about that witch. Told me to keep away from her and she was right!' she bleated, burying her head in her apron once more.

The servants gathered round, trying to calm the distraught kitchen maid whilst Plum issued orders to ensure that all her mistress's demands were fulfilled; the preparation of her lunch and the making of her perfect bed. There was one task, however, that Plum knew she must carry out alone. It was the unchaining of Orgen, the witch's Hag-Beast. He was a mad, wolfish creature with a vicious temper and needed careful handling.

Plum changed her apron, climbed to the top of the Moon Tower and entered the Spell Chamber.

'Do you expect me to wait forever?' Selvistra hissed as Plum approached.

'Of course not, my Lady, and welcome home to Stack End,' Plum replied whilst averting her gaze from Selvistra.

The witch paced the chamber, gesticulating towards her empty cabinets.

'All my magical instruments must be returned to their proper place. It is All Witches' Eve and I have magic to perform,' she said, choosing a red velvet dress from her closet. 'And Plum,' she added sharply, 'that numbskull kitchen maid looked straight into my face. Whenever a new servant arrives from the mainland it is your job to teach them the rules. She is lucky that I am weary from my travels or I would've spiked the silly mare!'

'Yes m'Lady, and I'm sorry she offended you,' replied Plum, keeping her eyes cast down as she fastened the buttons on her mistress's cuffs.

Amy Plum was well versed in the demands of the Grand Witch, with her nit-picking likes and the long list of her dislikes. She had served Selvistra Loons since she was a girl, trained by her own dear mother, Venetia Plum, hidden away on Stack End for the whole of her life. She had been promised to the witch as a child from one of the villages on the mainland, like all the servants on Stack End but for Plum, it was a lifelong debt.

'Now bring the Hag-Beast to me.'

Plum dipped her knee, returned to the dark corridor, stepped down a narrow flight of stairs and unlocked an iron gate. The Hag-Beast, Orgen the Wild, was kept in a stone cell at the end of the passageway. Plum was the only servant who ever entered the cell, letting the monster free at night to scale the tower walls and roam Stack End while the servants were sleeping. The Hag-Beast was a lumbering, lupine creature covered in silky black hair with black-diamond eyes and razor-sharp claws, half-wolf, perhaps half man – no one knew his origin.

Orgen leapt onto his hind-legs when Plum entered, panting in eager anticipation.

'Come, Orgen, your Mistress is home,' she announced, unlocking his chains.

The Hag-Beast growled as he skulked along the corridor, making dull thuds with his large clawed feet. Plum could smell his sour breath as he clamped his jaws behind her, slavering and chomping.

'He looks well,' crooned Selvistra, stroking the beast when he entered her chamber.

Orgen the Wild bowed his wolfish head for the Grand Witch to pet him.

'He has missed you, my lady,' said Plum.

'We shall have fun tonight,' Selvistra murmured in the Hag-Beast's ear. Then she turned abruptly to Plum. 'Tell Tench to visit me at dusk. He must prepare the Moon Tower for All Witches' Eve.'

Amy Plum dipped her knee and hurriedly departed.

# Two

Later, as the fire crackled on and the Hag-Beast slumbered by the hearth, Selvistra searched the nooks and crannies of her Spell Chamber.

'You're in here somewhere,' she said, removing stoppers from potion pots and turning empty flasks upside-down.

Through the arched window the evening sky was beginning to turn red, tinged with the eerie glow of the moon as the magic of All Witches' Eve stole in upon them.

Suddenly a tiny urchin, the size of a mouse, poked her head out of a large brown flask. Her sandy-eyed sleepiness made her yawn and she screwed her fists into her eye sockets. Picker, the witch's Feykin and her magical touchstone, had been hibernating for many months, awaiting Selvistra's return.

'There you are,' said Selvistra with delight, plucking the creature from the flask like a cork from a bottle with a loud *pop*.

Picker, the dark haired elfin creature, was dressed in a

flame-red costume to match her mistress. She unfurled her tiny form before settling down in Selvistra's palm, yawning contentedly and stretching out her arms.

'Wake up, my little Feykin,' Selvistra murmured. "Tis All Witches' Eve and the sky has begun to bleed its fury. You have an important task to perform.' The Feykin regarded the witch with eager anticipation. 'You must choose a nasty spell to rid us of the Swarm,' said Selvistra, placing Picker inside the dusty spell cabinet. 'It must be a hideous curse to crush the warlocks and witches of Hellstone Tors.'

Picker a silent creature by nature scrambled in and out of the enormous books, running her tiny fingers over the covers as she searched for the perfect spell. Finally she pointed to a worn, dog-eared volume. The witch opened the book as the Feykin jumped onto the spine and pointed excitedly to a spell written in an uneven hand. As she did so, the page began to seep with a thick black mist.

'Black Drop!' cried Selvistra, reading the spell as evenlight descended. '*Cressillita mentol mori!*' she announced delightedly as Picker thrust her finger towards the list of ingredients.

'Made from the rare stinging petals of the Devil's Heart Barb and the deadly Scarab plant. Come Feykin, we have work to do,' said Selvistra.

Picker leapt amongst the potion bottles as her mistress upended flagons, surrounding herself with mounds of blackened blossoms and vines. She dropped handfuls of petals into a wooden vat, twisting the handle of the vice and squashing the pungent flora into a steaming liquorice-coloured pulp.

'Squeezed from a thousand poisonous Scarab leaves,

squashed from the Devil's Heart Barb, crushed with revenge on my breath, hatred in my heart and pulverised into a foul-smelling syrup!' Selvistra cried, beaming at the Feykin.

Selvistra's fingers dripped with the black liquid as she held the phial to the candlelight and the elixir danced and swirled and ebbed.

'Those were dark days of heady magic,' she reminisced, turning and petting the Hag-Beast, 'when I toiled for that betrayer Edwyn Morrow, plying my spells so the banished Lord could capture Hellstone Tors. I taught those Hellstone witches secret curses and deadly magic. I plundered to fulfil their desires, cast spells to quell their enemies – and now it is my turn to reap the rewards!' Picker listened intently and Orgen paced the room as Selvistra's face shone with deadly anticipation.

'With this spell, the beautiful Bone Room will be mine and Kastra Micrentor will be no more.' The Grand Witch lifted the Feykin onto the palm of her hand and whispered her evil plan into the Hag-Beast's ear. 'Besides, the long rule of the Neopholytite is coming to an end and who better to break that Dark Spell than that Morrow girl from Wycham Elva,' she added cruelly. 'Then when it is finished – and the Swarm are vanquished, I will kill her too.'

The Feykin jumped up and down with delight.

'T'will be a gruesome end,' Selvistra crooned, stroking Orgen, 'for every Morrow witch and warlock!'

The Hag-Beast grunted and licked his fangs.

Selvistra blew a witch's kiss to the Feykin and the elfin

creature, bathed in a magical glow, slipped back into the warmth of her flask to sleep fairy dreams until she was needed once more.

*

As even-night approached on All Witches' Eve, a violent storm blew up and the blood-red skies raged over the island of Stack End. Tumultuous waves crashed against the rocks and peels of thunder cracked the heavens that bled with a heavy, pumping rain.

Selvistra Loons and the Hag-Beast, peered out of the arched window as the lightning zigzagged through the darkness, splitting the skies. The night wore on as the fierce crimson storm clouds battled the heavens with thunder, meeting out their fury across the raging seas.

At the appointed hour Tench lumbered down the gloomy passageway towards his mistress.

'I believe it is time, m'Lady,' he croaked. 'The storm will pass soon and the skies are turning red. All Witches' Eve is upon us.'

'Have you prepared the hexing-space?' Selvistra asked, gazing at the blood-soaked heavens. 'This is a perfect night for casting.'

Tench, a tall thin man with hunched shoulders, dressed in a long-tailed jacket with a thatch of grey hair over his furrowed brow, bowed to the Fire Witch.

'The hexing-space is ready,' he answered and ambled towards the staircase.

The old retainer, a stiff and awkward man with a sombre countenance looked as though he had just stepped out of an undertaker's parlour.

'The day is fast approaching when we will rid Hellstone Tors of the Swarm forever and then that castle shall be mine.'

Selvistra summoned the Hag-Beast and he sprang up the staircase, bounding onto the rooftop and sniffing the damp night air. The witch joined Orgen and Tench at the top of the tower as the moon shone down and bathed them in an eerie glow, glimmering through the last of the angry storm clouds as a trail of silky sea bats swooped and darted. A solitary tall black candle stood on a circular table prepared for the witch's rite of deadly piercing.

Selvistra Loons took a bundle of long black-headed pins from her cloak, testing the sharpness with her finger. The point pierced her flesh, a splash of blood fell on the table and she smeared her blood down the stem of the candle.

'I plunge this spell-stinger into the heart of Hellstone Tors to seek revenge against the Morrow Swarm,' she chanted impaling the stinger deep into the candle wax. 'Each stinger will spike a member of the Swarm – I plunge them all home!'

The Fire Witch skewered her black-headed pins into the core of the candle and cast her spell by the light of the moon.

'*Cressillita mentol mori, Cressillita mentol mori!*' she cried, lighting the black candle. 'The beautiful Bone Room shall be mine. Then I will strike dead that meddlesome child, the girl named Tallitha Mouldson.'

The flame burst forth and sucked in the air all around them, burning fiercely, casting flickering shadows across the rooftop as the thick black wax dripped over the spell-stingers, encasing the tops of the pins.

'Then, when Hellstone is mine I will take Wycham Elva! The Winderling witches are no match for my magic!' she raged.

But as Selvistra cast her spell, revelling in her evil curse, the hair on Orgen's back bristled; he raised his wolfish head and let out a terrifying howl.

'What is it, Orgen?' demanded Selvistra, running to the beast's side, her fierce eyes scouring the darkness for intruders.

The Hag-Beast snapped his jaws and growled, leaping onto the parapet, racing along its edge and baying into the night.

Suddenly a beam of slippery light skirted the Moon Tower, sliding over the castellated edge like an eel and whipping across the rooftop, snuffing out the black candle and plunging the hexing-space into darkness.

Selvistra felt a sudden cold breath against her face and a thin reedy voice whispered in her ear.

'*I will never forgive you Selvistra Loons!*'

Ice-dead fingertips slipped down Selvistra's cheek as the face of Arabella Dorothea, with coal-black, red-rimmed eyes, sprang before the witch; a grisly spectre in the darkness.

'You!' Selvistra cried.

The Grand Witch stifled a scream, hid her face in her cloak and cowered to the floor.

'What is it m'Lady?' gasped Tench, hobbling to her aid.

'I-It's that Morrow child!' she wailed, her voice laced with dread. 'That terrible child has come to take her revenge!'

Orgen the Wild bounded across the rooftop, lunging towards the slippery light as it wound its way over the parapet but the spectre was too quick. The Hag-Beast followed, leaping over the edge and scaling the tower wall, scouring the night as the Morrow child soared past him in a pearl-white blur. The ghostly presence outflanked the Hag-Beast and vanished into the darkness with a dreadful moan.

'I felt her frozen fingers and saw her blistered eyes! It's a dreadful omen!' Selvistra wailed, anxiously touching the spot where Arabella's icy fingertips had stroked her cheek. Orgen pounced and snarled at every fleeting shadow, panting and howling vainly into the darkness.

'Tench, quickly! You must turn the black candle, first to the left, and then to the right, and I must do the Widdershins before it is too late. This spell will rid the hexing-space of that damned spirit! That dead child shall not spoil my revenge!'

Tench dutifully twisted the black candle as Selvistra cast the Widdershins spell, turning thirteen paces to the left, and then, thirteen to the right.

Selvistra had the look of a haunted creature.

'What else shall I do, m'Lady?' Tench asked desperately.

He had never seen the Grand Witch so alarmed.

'You have done well, Tench. I won't let her frighten me!' she gasped. 'I will banish that spectre, Arabella Dorothea, forever,' she called out into the night.

The Grand Witch wrapped her cloak about her shoulders and scoured the rooftop for any last sighting of the Morrow Child, but apart from the blood-red streaks that criss-crossed the heavens on All Witches' Eve, the night was clear of ghouls and spectres.

And so it was that that the Grand Witch shook off the haunting image of the dead child and finally cast her spell, clutching the phial of syrup.

She would wait until the Wycham girl had stolen into the Witch's Tower, wait until she had destroyed the Morrow pact and then she would strike her dead!

Then the Swarm would be vanquished.

The Bone Room would be hers forever!

The meddlesome Winderling girl would be crushed and Hellstone Tors would be hers at last!

But the ghostly spectre of the Morrow child, with its blistered coal-rimmed eyes and dead-white face, still invaded Selvistra's darkest thoughts and pierced her deepest slumbers. At times the Grand Witch could still feel Arabella's dead fingertips, like cold spiders, running across her cheeks …

# Three

In the darkness of the Leaden Riddles, Quillam pressed his full weight against Tallitha's chest, pummelling her lifeless body again and again.

'Tallitha! Please!' he sobbed desperately, shaking her, 'you must come back to me!'

The girl's face was ashen, lashed with strands of her soaking wet hair. Her lips had a death-grey pallor where her life was slowly ebbing away. Quillam hurriedly crossed Tallitha's arms over her limp body, turned her over and knelt down heavily on her back. He held her shoulders and pushed her ribcage into the ground, willing her to breathe, waiting for any sign of life.

'Breathe, Tallitha! Breathe!'

Again and again he crushed her body into the wet rock.

Suddenly, she convulsed. Tallitha retched and spewed a sickly green liquid across the ground. Her glassy eyes flickered and she groaned.

'Oh Quillam,' she moaned, retching again, feeling the tightness in her chest.

Tallitha curled into a ball and covered her face, shivering from cold and terror.

'It's okay,' he said gently, taking her hand in his. 'The Vault Glimmers have gone – for now.'

He looked warily into the pitch darkness and listened intently. All was silent. Tallitha touched the spot where the Glimmers' talons had split her flesh – the gashes stung and oozed blood.

'You saved me from the Leaden Riddles,' she whispered hoarsely, casting her frightened eyes towards the turbulent stream.

'We have to get out of this desperate place.' His voice was edgy and tense. 'Do you think you can climb?' he asked. 'The Glimmers could return at any moment.'

Tallitha needed no more persuasion. She was soaking wet and terrified, but apart from the lacerations inflicted by the hideous Vault Glimmers, she was unharmed. She clambered to her feet, stumbled across the rocks and within seconds they were scaling the cavern walls. All around them, the honeycomb of caves echoed with the piercing shrieks of the Murk Mowl stampeding through the tunnels, waiting for them to emerge from the depths of the Leaden Riddles.

'Give me your hand,' Quillam urged in the darkness, struggling to keep a foothold.

He was afraid that the Mowl would discover them with every slipping second.

Tallitha reached out, still coughing up the foul water, clawing at the rock face as Quillam roughly clasped her arm. His strong grip slipped and he burned the skin on her wrist. She yelped out in pain.

'Put your feet there,' he said firmly, pointing to a small ledge. 'I've got you.'

Tallitha gripped the crevasses with her fingertips and edged upwards into the unforgiving blackness.

'My legs are like jelly,' she cried desperately.

Her face was streaked with grime and tears. In the distance they could hear the hideous grey hoard hollering to one another, reverberating through the dark passageways.

'Not much further,' Quillam replied, coaxing Tallitha upwards, 'then we'll be out of this tomb.'

Tallitha clambered onto a narrow ledge and Quillam held her tightly. She sobbed with exhaustion and fear.

'They're going to catch us,' she whimpered.

'No they're not!' he answered determinedly. 'Look, we're nearly there,' he said, pointing upwards.

Through her tears, Tallitha saw a thin streak of light leaking down the dismal shaft. If only she could hold on for a little while longer, then they would be free of the claustrophobic darkness.

'I'm coming,' she hissed through gritted teeth. 'I will do this!' she said over and over to herself, focussing all her strength on the climb ahead.

Tallitha took a gulp of dank air, steeled herself and with tremendous effort clambered up the remaining ridges and hauled herself out into the waxy grey light.

'Got you!' cried the youth, grabbing her shoulders.

Quillam heaved Tallitha's weary body out of the black pit. She lay gasping for breath in a heap on the ground. She blinked and her tender eyes, used to the pitch-black of the Bitter Caves, stung with the onslaught of daylight.

'Come on, let's get out of this place!' he shouted.

They had emerged at the foot of a steep incline of crags and tors that loomed high above them.

Tallitha stumbled up the hillside, falling and tumbling, her lungs heaving, desperately trying to put as much distance as possible between them and the Murk Mowl. Quillam's muddy boots pounded the earth in front of her, racing up the cliff path as he tore ahead.

'You can do it, come on!' he kept calling out, looking hastily over his shoulder.

But Tallitha was falling behind. She clawed at the earth, soil lodging beneath her fingernails as she clambered up the mud splattered slopes. Each intake of breath cut through her lungs like a knife.

'Where are we?' she cried, dropping to her knees and staring ahead at the bleak terrain.

The wind caught his voice but at last she heard, '*on the Barren Edges*' buffeting towards her through the pounding gale.

She bowed her head. She couldn't move.

'Tallitha!' he cried, but she didn't respond.

Quillam raced back and pulled her to her feet. 'Keep moving!' he yelled. 'You can't stop now! They'll kill us if they catch us!'

So Tallitha, willing herself onwards, stumbled after Quillam.

She snatched at clumps of bracken with her bloody fingers, dragging her ravaged body up the hillside, handhold over weary handhold, her face smeared with mud and blood, tears and the strain of exhaustion.

Dark heavy clouds swept across the sky threatening a storm. Layer upon layer of broken slate rose before them as if some long forgotten giant had crushed the mountain in a fury, shattering it into a thousand pieces. Then, from above, the bellow of rolling thunder spilt the sky with a deafening crack as huge drops of rain spilled from the heavens onto Tallitha's dirt-stained face. She raised her head and let the raindrops trickle through her hair and down her face, forging clean rivulets through her grimy skin.

Quillam climbed to the highest point of a rocky precipice and surveyed the terrain.

'That's where we're headed,' he said, pointing towards the rolling hills in the distance.

Tallitha slumped to the wet rocks, her head resting on her knees and her chest heaving. The stark emptiness of the Northern Wolds spread out before them, a remote expanse of lavender dales and grey-green moorland, a colour palette of purple heather and yellow gorse interspersed with trickling streams and undulating hills. Overhead, the beseeching cries of moorhens and curlews filtered through the grey-sodden skies with their intermittent weep-weary calls.

'What about the Dooerlins?' she gasped, staring nervously over her shoulder. 'Any sign of them?'

Tallitha could still hear the piercing screeches of the Murk Mowl pounding in her ears. Quillam peered over the rugged terrain to the point in the distance where they had escaped from the Bitter Caves. The sheeting rain marred his view but he could see no sign of the grey hoard.

He shook his head. 'I can't see anything but they could still be tracking us,' he insisted. 'Come on Tallitha, we must keep going.'

On and on they trudged, over the slate-grey hills of the Barren Edges and across the desolate lands of the Northern Wolds. Tallitha's head throbbed and her feet ached but she kept on running, slipping and stumbling across the wet slate to evade the Mowl. Slowly, the pale washed-out skies turned into a sickly yellow twilight.

'We'll make camp under that outcrop of rock,' Quillam said, pointing to a promontory above them. 'One last push and then we can rest.'

Tallitha stared at the hard climb ahead of her.

'Wait for me!' she called out, grabbing Quillam's hand.

Over the mounds and hollows of the Barren Edges, Quillam dragged Tallitha behind him, willing her onwards. At the top she fell to the ground; wet, starving and exhausted. Tallitha rolled onto her back and stared breathlessly at the bleak, drizzly skies. Somehow they had made it to a place of safety and had out-manoeuvred the evil brood … for now.

When the rain stopped, they foraged for mushrooms and Quillam made a fire in a dry nook inside their shelter. They ate the warm, greasy mushrooms, mixed with wild garlic and herbs as the juices ran down their fingers.

As dusk fell Quillam covered the entranceway to their hideout with branches to keep out the worst of the cold weather and fashioned a bed of leaves. It was going to be a damp, chilly night. They snuggled down with their backs next to each other to keep warm.

'How will we ever find Kastra?' asked Tallitha, shivering.

She tucked her legs up to her chest and buried her hands deep into her pockets.

'In time she'll find us,' he replied. 'Her spies from the Northern tribes will be out there, watching us. Now try and get some sleep.'

Tallitha closed her eyes and listened to the sound of Quillam's breathing as she imagined all that awaited them, out there on the slopes of the Barren Edges.

*

Over the next few days they foraged for food as they tramped northwards across the wild escarpment. Intense hunger soon got the better of Tallitha and she overcame her squeamishness, eating every last scrap of the rabbit that Quillam trapped and cooked. Each night they slept in makeshift shelters and followed a path across the Northern Wolds, skirting over the Barren Edges and climbing ever higher into the remote lavender-grey wilderness.

Quillam was right. Kastra had enlisted the help of the Black Sprites to spy on the travellers and track their progress through the northern lands. The Black Sprites, thin, horny creatures from the Northern tribes with ravaged faces and blackened stick-like bodies had pursued them across country, always just a few steps out of sight. But at certain times of the day, when the light was just right, Tallitha thought she saw a flicker out of the corner of her eye, like a streak of smoke, jumping, leaping and then darting out of sight.

'What was that?' she cried, scanning the landscape for any sudden movement 'I definitely saw something – over there.'

Tallitha pointed to where the Barren Edges sloped away into the distance.

The youth had seen something too, a fleeting shadow leaping over the dips and hollows of the rugged terrain.

'Whoever they are, they're in allegiance with Kastra and they're following us,' he added guardedly.

'I wish they'd just get it over with and …'

At that moment, a thin, dry hand went over Tallitha's mouth as four Black Sprites pounced on Quillam and bound his hands. Suddenly, they were surrounded by a group of the jumpy creatures.

'Untie me!' Quillam yelled, struggling to get free. 'We wanted you to find us – we've been searching for Kastra for days. We desperately need her help.'

Their leader, a willowy sprite named Flametip, sprang next to Quillam and put her blackened, stick-like finger up to her lips. Nervy, like quicksilver, her head bobbed from side to side.

'You may think we've been biding our time, tracking you across the Wolds, but we've had our hands full distracting the Dooerlins from your trail. My sister Rucheba has been leading the grey hoard to the west of here, out into the wilds of Lethland.'

Quillam strained against the ropes. 'Then you know I'm not your enemy. Set me free!' he cried.

'Blindfold him, Scoot!' Flametip instructed another sprite, ignoring Quillam's demands, 'and the girl too,' she said gesticulating towards Tallitha. 'You're strangers here, and the way into Kastra's world is a closely guarded secret,' she added mysteriously.

In a flash, Tallitha and Quillam's eyes were covered and the Sprites led them across the slate edges to where the ground became soft and springy underfoot. Tallitha could sense a change in the landscape as she breathed in the luscious aroma of heather and the sweet scent of wild flowers. It was the beginning of a long march across the moorlands of the Northern Wolds. The Sprites directed them over stepping stones and across gurgling streams, taking them on a winding path through the hills. Tallitha felt the warm sun on her face as the blissful drone of honeybees, heavy with pollen, sang in the air.

The Black Sprites were cautious folk, well versed in the treacherous ways of the Murk Mowl. They had left two of their party to follow on behind and to be on the lookout for any sign of trouble. As their journey continued, a Sprite named Dipper came leaping across the moors with another, called Fleet, at his side.

'Trouble's coming!' Dipper shouted. 'Take cover!'

'Horses and riders from Hellstone,' added Fleet sharply.

'Quick – hide!' cried Flametip.

The Sprites fell on them, bundling Tallitha behind a boulder and pushing an argumentative Quillam down beside her.

'What's going on?' he snapped. 'Untie me!'

'Keep quiet,' growled Flametip, gripping Quillam by the arm. 'Those dark riders are almost upon us. We must avoid them at all costs.'

In the distance Tallitha could hear the sound of hooves pounding across the moors, then the riders began calling out to one another. The Black Sprites were agitated, springing up and down, peering round the boulder to spy on their intruders.

'It's two of them on horseback,' murmured Dipper guardedly.

'Evil is here,' announced Fleet.

'But who are they?' asked Tallitha, tentatively reaching out to the Black Sprites. 'Please remove our blindfolds, just for now,' she pleaded.

'It can't do any harm,' urged Scoot, 'they're not going anywhere.'

So Flametip lifted their blindfolds. 'Those riders are the hated Spell-Seekers, Redlevven and Yarrow,' she replied gruffly.

'Do you think they saw us?' asked Quillam, quickly taking in his surroundings.

They were lodged between two boulders with the nervous sprites on the lookout for danger.

'They can't see us!' laughed Flametip. 'We change colour in the sunlight,' she explained. 'We become almost invisible, like a wisp of light, a mirage to anyone looking directly at us.'

'And don't worry,' explained Scoot, 'if they'd seen you they would have been over here in a flash.'

'This is border country; the divide between our lands and the Swarm's domain. It's dangerous, ripe with old spells,' said Dipper.

'But what're they doing?' asked Quillam warily.

'Checking their Stinkwells for prey,' replied Flametip,

Dipper peered round the edge of the boulder. 'Now that evil sorceress is climbing down one of the wells. Pity we can't trap her and finish the witch off.'

Tallitha gasped - *so Yarrow was a witch too!*

'Redlevven is following her,' Fleet told the others.

'Keep watch,' said Flametip, 'and warn us when they emerge,'

'But what are the Swarm doing so far away from Hellstone Tors?' Tallitha asked.

'Spell-seeking, of course and trying to catch unsuspecting souls in their accursed wells,' answered Dipper.

'Yarrow and Redlevven are devils,' explained Flametip. 'Stealing spells for the Neopholytite, and foraging for magic all the way from Lethland to Hegglefoot.'

Tallitha's stomach lurched. She remembered hearing about the Spell-Seekers from the Shrove, Embellsed when he had shown her the Swarm's palaces in Hellstone Tors.

'What happens – down in those wells?' asked Tallitha apprehensively.

'Terrible things,' murmured Fleet.

'The Stinkwells are traps,' explained Flametip. 'The Spell-Seekers lace them with magic to lure any passer-by on their way to Breedoor.'

'A bewitching aroma percolates from the heart of the well just like a flower,' explained Scoot.

'Then, anyone who enters is caught like a fly in a spider's web,' added Dipper.

'Not only that, the walls are laden with jewels – makes it hard to resist,' said Fleet.

'There's the promise of great riches, so curious travellers climb down to steal the jewels. Then the Stinkwell puts out its feelers and catches the unsuspecting visitor,' replied Flametip. 'They're stuck down there until the Spell-Seekers return.'

'To hand them over to the Murk Mowl,' added Dipper, twitching with revulsion 'To store in their turrows.'

Tallitha shivered at the memory of the grisly Murk turrows buried deep within the caves, woven with their hideous cargo of rotting flesh.

'Sometimes the prisoners are handed over to the Neopholytite,' said Fleet darkly, 'and if they're young girls, they end up in her Emporium of Lost Souls.'

Tallitha shuddered.

'Can the wells be destroyed?' asked Quillam.

'They're connected by a magical thread, a spell-line along the border,' Scoot replied. 'There's only one way to destroy them, a Grand Witch must enter and break Yarrow and Redlevven's spells.'

'And that's nigh on impossible,' Dipper said pointedly.

'The Spell-Seekers are leaving,' interrupted Fleet, peering round the boulder. 'They're riding back towards Hellstone,' he added.

'Come on,' Flametip replied. 'We must get out of here. We've a long trek ahead of us.'

Tallitha rubbed her hand. It was tingling. The Morrow stain was reacting to something – perhaps it was the potency of the Stinkwells, redolent with the Swarm's magic.

'First, you must help me!' said Tallitha, desperately. 'I-I have the Morrow stain upon me.'

'How did you come by that terrible blemish?' asked Flametip.

Tallitha explained about the Raven's Wing and the bloody cobwebs that had clung to her. She pointed to the spot where the stain had taken hold. Flametip took a phial from her pocket and rubbed a cool green liquid over Tallitha's hand.

'It will give you protection until you meet Kastra, only she has the power to remove the stain completely.'

Once Yarrow and Redlevven had departed the Sprites blindfolded their captives and led them to the edge of the moors to a track that meandered into a forest. Branches scratched at Tallitha's face and twigs snapped beneath her feet. The breeze dropped and from under her blindfold Tallitha sensed that evening was drawing in. The sound of a bustling campsite met her ears and the delicious smell of supper wafted in the evening air. Then an edgy Sprite suddenly sprang beside them and removed their blindfolds.

'Where are we?' asked Quillam, searching the woody vale that lay all around them.

'In a magical place,' replied Flametip mysteriously.

'Waiting for Kastra,' added Dipper.

'Will she come soon?' asked Tallitha excitedly.

'The Grand Witch will come when she's ready and not before.'

'Eat now and then rest. Kastra may come later tonight if she's a mind to,' explained Flametip as she handed Quillam a bowl of forest fare.

'Or she may come tomorrow night,' said Fleet with a rueful smile.

They ate their supper, an oat pudding mixed with forest fruits and lemon balm, washed down by a heady blackberry cordial.

The luscious sweet drink made Tallitha sleepy and she longed to lie down on the soft bed that the Sprites had prepared at the base of a hollow tree. The springy, darting creatures had placed a bowl of bubbling sweet-smelling oil by their bed, filling the night air with the strong scent of lavender.

'Why isn't she here yet? When will she come?' asked Tallitha, sleepily.

'It's time to rest now,' Flametip said, coaxing Tallitha towards her bed, 'Kastra never comes when she's expected. She's a Grand Witch and she does as she pleases. The time will soon pass and until then, you should get some sleep.'

It was a conundrum. *Grand Witches are a complete mystery, a law unto themselves,* thought Tallitha.

Soon Tallitha and Quillam were snuggled beneath a layer of cosy blankets, lying on a bed of moss and pungent heather. The scent of the aromatic oil wafted lazily about the hollow and in no time Tallitha tumbled into a deep sleep, so full of fanciful, turbulent dreams that she imagined she had entered another realm of magic and make-believe.

She dreamt of Tyaas and their wild adventures at Winderling Spires, of exploring the abandoned floors in the old house, of running over the rooftops and of climbing into their secret tree house. Then she saw Ruker flying through Ragging Brows Forest with the wind streaming through her hair as the dream suddenly shifted and Tallitha was creeping through the dark castle at Hellstone Tors, frightened and alone.

Then the dream dissolved once more, slipping and swirling into an extraordinary fantasy of light and shadows where a dark figure moved stealthily, in and out of Tallitha's slumbers.

A magnificent and dangerous presence had disturbed her sleep.

# Four

Tallitha whimpered and clutched her arm. Something sharp had pierced her flesh whilst she lay dreaming of the dark passageways of Hellstone Tors and the windswept rooftops of Winderling Spires. As she stirred, Tallitha noticed a trail of dark red blood trickle across her pale skin.

'You have been looking for me,' said a woman's voice.

Tallitha peered beyond the hollow, to where the night was no longer dark, but appeared to be a lustrous fantasy of iridescent colours, a palette of watery purples, of lavenders and pinks, like oil glistening across water, forming the surface of a luminous bubble. From within this pocket of glistening light, Tallitha heard whispering in the Ennish tongue.

'*Sante letherin, temistra vielle,* 'Tis a spell to ward off an unwelcome presence,' the woman declared, raising her head and searching the heavens.

Tallitha's hand tingled and her head throbbed, befuddled by the magic that surrounded her. The woman's face, obscured by the dazzling light, leant closer and Tallitha felt her warm breath brush against her cheek.

'Tallitha,' she whispered enticingly. 'Leave the youth and come with me. Enter my Charmed Wood and I will tell you all the things you long to hear.'

Tallitha rose and followed the woman into the heart of the mulberry wood, all the while cocooned in the shimmering bubble. The starry night, flimsy and imaginary, like the stuff of wild chaotic dreams, was shrouded in vapours, and the aroma of night-scented stock and moonflowers filled the air. Long-tailed dragonflies hovered and buzzed, their fragile wings fluttering past Tallitha's face, leaving a trace of lavender dust in their wake. But the haunting dreamscape, like so many dreams before it, made the task of walking arduous, like wading against the tide, waist high through water.

The strange woman, illuminated by a sapphire light, floated through the undergrowth, her dress swirling about her feet, turned every once in a while to beckon Tallitha further into the wood. The bubble glistened, reforming its shape to avoid the thorny branches from puncturing its fragile surface. Above, gnarled misshapen trees and warped black branches were tangled together with bulbous purple vines, rich in the succulent mulberry fruits, woven into nature's bizarre web. Tallitha hauled her body through the treacly night, flailing her arms to propel herself through the clawing mist.

'Step onto the wind,' the woman urged, draped in a cloak of midnight blue.

She parted her lips and a strong gust enveloped Tallitha, propelling her swiftly through the wood. *She is shimmering blue gossamer, unreachable, flimsy, a will-of-the-wisp,* thought Tallitha, as the woman came into view and her periwinkle eyes danced across Tallitha's face.

'Who are you?' asked Tallitha in wonder.

'I am the Grand Witch Kastra,' she replied, her gaze penetrating the girl before her. 'Come closer,' she insisted.

But as Tallitha approached, Kastra drew back, as if scalded.

'What trickery is this?' she hissed. Kastra's eyes darkened as she breathed in the bitter perfume. 'The Morrow stain!' she cried, spitting out the words.

Tallitha scratched the florid skin where the stain tingled the most.

'I can't get rid of it,' she gasped. 'It has plagued me since I visited the Raven's Wing in Winderling Spires, where the cobwebs clawed at me and stuck to my skin.'

Kastra blew on the spot where the Morrow stain had left its mark. At once, the sensation vanished.

'Now you're free of that terrible bloodstain. The Swarm will not be able to track you so easily,' said Kastra as she lifted her head and searched the night sky. Without warning, her face darkened. 'There's another Grand Witch abroad tonight! I can smell her magic.'

The Grand Witch muttered an incomprehensible babble of words and cast a spell to keep the entity at bay. The silver-blue pod of light closed in all around them as thunder split the sky and a lightning bolt flashed across the heavens. Their protective sphere shattered into a thousand shards of spinning light, flying through the trees and disappearing into the dark reaches of the wood. The warm night vanished in an instant to be replaced by a cold desolate forest: a dank, infected mire; a tangle of hoary branches; a cloister of sickly smells and an odour of rotten fruit.

'The spell has broken! Come, we must hurry!'

'Where are you taking me?' Tallitha cried as the witch dragged her through the forest.

'Why, to my Unimaginable Palace, of course,' she announced, handing Tallitha a cloak of midnight blue. 'This will protect you from prying eyes,' she said as she wrapped Tallitha in its folds. 'Now imagine you are flying, like an eagle!' she commanded, spreading her arms.

The witch's breath settled on Tallitha, then she threw back her head and waited for the magic to take hold. Tallitha's stomach jolted, the sound of rushing air filled her ears and a thousand pinpricks of light spun before her eyes. Suddenly her feet left the ground and a sharp blast of cold air enveloped her, propelling her upwards. Then she was spinning through the branches, bursting through the darkness, holding onto Kastra as they darted through the clouds, clinging to the tail of the wind, flying through the heavens with the air rushing past their faces. High above, the night was a beautiful blue-black, clear, starry and bright, where huge grey-winged hawk moths fluttered past their faces and the sky felt like quivering silk against Tallitha's skin.

'Am I dreaming?' she asked, staring at the spectacle of stars in the blackberry-coloured sky.

Down below, the earth shrank away.

'It is a dream of sorts,' answered Kastra, her hair shining raven-black against the moonlight.

The witch arched her body to catch the next surge of wind, effortlessly riding the currents like a bird, taking Tallitha into the slipstream and flying ever northwards.

'See that light, down there,' exclaimed Kastra, 'it points the way to my Unimaginable Palace,' she said, darting towards the light source.

An ice-blue light flashed amongst the fir trees illuminating their way like a beacon. Together they spun through the night air, riding the crest of the winds.

'Now, imagine diving like a swallow and soon we shall be home!' instructed the witch, breathing her magic over Tallitha once again.

Tallitha's stomach lurched and a terrific rush of wind enveloped her body and propelled her downwards through the clouds. For a moment she closed her eyes and revelled in the magical feeling of flight, of streaming through the night with the air rushing past her face. It was exhilarating; she was free! At last, Kastra reached for her hand and together they dropped towards the ice-blue light.

As they approached, the light source opened like a flower, taking them into its centre and closed safely around them. They flew into a cavernous hallway, spun from thousands of spiders' webs, woven into tangled vines and twisted branches. The sapphire witch landed with the lightest of steps, guiding Tallitha to the ground as a party of Black Sprites rushed to welcome them.

'Come Tallitha, let me show you my Unimaginable Palace,' said Kastra.

The Sprites removed their night cloaks, brushed Kastra's raven hair and replaced her boots with velvet slippers.

The witch's palace was a place of wonder and mystery. A cobwebbed entranceway meandered into the white-tiered castle, where spindly turrets and topsy-turvy balconies hugged the side of a mountain precipice. Tallitha could make little sense of her bizarre surroundings; she felt giddy and disorientated, running to keep pace with the witch who strode before her. The maze of narrow stairways stretched and twisted, merging into ever-vanishing hallways, where beautiful rooms melted into strange dark chambers. Doorways shrank, suddenly disappearing into walls as the view from the windows vanished into brilliant sunshine or into absolute darkness, cleverly concealing the location of the witch's hideaway. Kastra's white palace was a bewildering, ever-changing edifice and a conundrum of sorcery that aroused vivid hallucinations, clouding Tallitha's senses into a muddle of confused and disconnected images.

Suddenly, Kastra rounded on Tallitha, stepping suddenly towards her and fixing her with her piercing eyes.

'This will wake you from your befuddled dreams,' she said, jabbing a needle into Tallitha's arm.

One prick from the black-headed needle aroused Tallitha from her stupor. A large octagonal turret room came into focus, filled with looms and embroidery, tapestries and lacework, just like Great Aunt Agatha's grand sewing rooms in Winderling Spires. Yet, time for Tallitha had elapsed in an unfathomable way. She clutched her head. Had hours gone by? Had days passed? She could not tell.

'What is this place?' she asked, staring at the vaulted chamber and mirrored walls.

The reflected light from the sapphire witch bounced from one looking glass to another, as it dazzled into a thousand fragments of light, mirroring her blue-brightness.

'This is my sanctuary, my private roost, high up in my Unimaginable Palace. No other witch will find you here, for this palace is the stuff of dreams,' she whispered enigmatically.

It was a conundrum. *There are always witches*, thought Tallitha, *in this turbulent land of sorcery and magic*.

'How long have I been here?' she asked.

'This is a timeless place,' Kastra replied enigmatically. 'Time shrinks and time stretches and some things unfold in the blink of an eye. Come closer, Tallitha,' she said, beckoning to the girl.

Tallitha marvelled at Kastra's beauty. 'You're not like that other dreadful witch,' she said.

'Did you imagine I'd be old and wizened like the witch in the Bone Room?' asked Kastra laughing. 'That witch has become twisted and ugly in her cell of bones!' She took Tallitha's face in her hand and stared into her eyes. 'Tell me, is my cabinet still in the witch's lair?'

'Y-Yes,' Tallitha faltered.

'You want something from me, don't you, Wycham girl?' the witch teased.

Tallitha fumbled with her hair, twisting it in and out of her fingers.

'Please tell me how to destroy the Morrow pact,' she answered, hesitating for a moment, 'and how to find the Morrow child.'

Tallitha noticed the witch flinch. 'That child is dead,' Kastra replied coldly. 'She perished at the hand of Selvistra Loons.'

'Then how shall I break the pact?' asked Tallitha anxiously.

Kastra turned her awesome beauty on Tallitha. 'You must summon the child back from the dead, of course.'

Tallitha's heart sank. It was the last thing she wanted to hear. Magic was one thing but meddling with the occult filled her with dread. 'And what about Selvistra Loons? How will I defend myself against her?'

'That dark witch means to capture Hellstone Tors. She will do everything in her power to crush you. In time the Grand Witches may be forced to fight again,' Kastra said ominously.

'But will you help me?'

'If I do, Wycham girl, I will demand something in return.'

*She may be beautiful,* thought Tallitha, *but she's still a witch!*

'Be careful of your dark thoughts! I can read your mind!' Kastra snapped.

'But I must know if you're on my side!'

'I'm on no one's side!' the witch replied sharply, focusing her unendurable gaze on the girl. 'But when it is finished and the pact is broken I will return to Winderling Spires. I have yearned to be back in the magical stillness of my Raven's Wing.'

'But it belongs to the Grand Morrow!'

'The Raven's Wing is mine and always shall be!' Kastra shrieked 'That cursed pact has robbed me of my home and kept me from returning all these years!'

'But the Grand Morrow will have to agree –'

'I don't bargain with mortals, even those with magical powers,' Kastra sneered, 'besides, it was mine long before the Morrow sisters lived there.' She stepped towards Tallitha and her face darkened. 'Why should those sisters spend their days in the Crewel Tower and why should the Lady Agatha sit sewing in her grand apartments when I am prevented from returning!'

'Have you been spying on us?' asked Tallitha.

Kastra's mouth twisted into a sneer. 'Sometimes I watch you,' she replied with a sinister note in her voice, 'I gaze at you through the spell-ripples.'

'How is that possible?'

Kastra looked askance at the naiveté of mortals.

'I watch the sisters through my spell-catcher,' she announced, stepping towards an intricate loom and plucking at the muddle of silken threads. Tallitha peered into the depths of the complicated interwoven structure. It looked like a spider had spun hundreds of cobwebs and woven them together. 'Spells are delicate,' explained Kastra mysteriously, reaching down and tugging on the threads. 'Whenever a witch is casting, if a word is spoken out of place, then the spell can tear. That's when I can peek through – the spell-catcher is my gateway.

'But how does it work?' asked Tallitha, 'how can you see us?'

'Perhaps I'll show you one day,' the Grand Witch answered enigmatically. 'The Morrow sisters are out of practice so they sometimes make mistakes – and when they do, I am ready. Then I am able to see inside my beloved Spires,' she replied.

This was the moment Tallitha had been waiting for.

'If you tell me how to break the pact,' she said quickly, 'then you can return home to Winderling Spires, once I have destroyed it.'

The Grand Witch pounced on Tallitha.

'What do you know of spells and magic?' she answered aggressively. 'You're just a girl from Wycham Elva!'

'My Lady, she's more than that,' said a voice form the shadows. 'Perhaps Tallitha is the one who can rid us of the Swarm.'

A woman with silver hair and a timeless face stepped forward.

'You warned me not to enter Hellstone Tors! Then you came to me during my shadow-flight!' exclaimed Tallitha.

'This is Ferileath,' explained Kastra, ushering the woman into the room. 'I sent her to help you.'

'Why did you do that, if you don't think I can destroy the pact?' asked Tallitha sarcastically.

Kastra laughed. 'Don't be so prickly, Winderling girl. I intend to discover if you have the power.'

'She has courage, my Lady,' answered Ferileath, coming to Tallitha's aid. 'She left the safety of Winderling Spires to travel across the wilds of Breedoor; she braved the Murk-infested caves and faced the Swarm in their evil castle.'

'Courage is not enough! Does she have the magical power to confront the Dark Spell?' cried Kastra.

'Please let me try,' pleaded Tallitha, 'that's why I've searched for you! With your help it may work.'

Kastra looked doubtfully at the girl standing before her.

'Do you really think you can hoodwink the Swarm, steal into the Bone Room and destroy the power of the Neopholytite?' demanded the Grand Witch, searching Tallitha's face.

'Why did you bring me here?' Tallitha snapped haughtily

'To test you, little girl,' said Kastra menacingly, staring deep into Tallitha's eyes. 'Like this!'

The Grand Witch began to hex Tallitha, bewitching her so that her body shuddered and her head ached as a crimson aura glowed around her. Kastra dipped her fingers in amongst the aura and a knowing smile played across her lips.

'This is the sign we have waited for,' said Ferileath excitedly.

'If you truly are the one to save us Tallitha I will work my magic to keep Selvistra Loons at bay. But first you must pass the challenge of The Witches' Knot and read my Wall of Spells,' announced Kastra.

'Tell me, what must I do?'

'Let the magic flow through you,' explained Ferileath, 'use your senses, search deep inside yourself and set the power free!'

Ferileath bound Tallitha's wrists in a silken twine. She tied the first knot for magical intent; Kastra knotted the twine twice to forge the spell and then thrice for sealing the magic tight.

'The fourth knot will release your power,' explained Kastra pulling tightly on the twine.

The silken thread cut into Tallitha's wrists as a surge of energy soared through her with a tremendous force. Suddenly all the colours of the rainbow burst forth in an aurora of red, orange, yellow, green, blue, indigo and violet.

'See the colours, my lady! Tallitha has inherited an abundance of magical powers!' cried Ferileath.

'Magic is turning somersaults and racing through her blood,' announced Kastra with passion, placing a bloodstone pendant around Tallitha's throat. 'This talisman will give you some protection against the dark evil of Selvistra Loons,' she added. 'Now, if you're ready, my mirror will reveal its secret; it will show you how to shatter the Dark Spell.'

Tallitha's stomach lurched. This was it!

'Now, watch my mirrored walls,' said Kastra as the mirror shuddered and shimmered like quicksilver. 'See how it slips and slides. If you really are the one my mirror will reveal how to destroy the pact.'

The mirror bubbled and hissed as the words burst forth, scorched and etched in flame.

'I-I can see it!' Tallitha blurted out.

'Then read the words,' demanded Kastra.

Tallitha stepped forward and read the words that hissed on the surface of the mirror.

'The pact is protected by the Dark Spell,' she announced, her voice shaking. 'The Morrow pact is sewn on fine linen, embroidered with magical stitches, woven with the blood curse of the Morrow Clan, kept safe in Micrentor's cabinet – Your cabinet!' exclaimed Tallitha, turning to Kastra.

The Grand Witch led Tallitha closer. The heat seared her skin.

'What else does it say?' asked Kastra.

Tallitha stared at the blistering words.

'In order to break the Dark Spell, I must do three things,' answered Tallitha. 'First, I must destroy a hair or lash, a nail or a tooth, skin or blood from she who weaves her evil threads of bloody darkness.'

'Is that the Neopholytite?' she asked warily.

'Indeed, she is the one,' answered Kastra. 'It is the darkest spell of them all.

Tallitha read the words as they flared across the mirror.

'To break the spell, fling the pact into the whorl-pit with a piece of the witch.' She felt panic rise up inside her.

Tallitha looked at the shimmering surface and willed the mirror to show her more.

'Finally the Morrow child must renounce the blood-soaked words of Edwyn Morrow, then – and only then – will the Dark Spell be broken and the Morrow pact destroyed.'

The full horror had been revealed at last. The task ahead was daunting.

'The pact can only be destroyed in the Bone Room, nowhere else, do you understand?' said Kastra.

Tallitha nodded as the words of the Dark Spell spluttered one last time and melted back into the mirror.

There were so many unanswered questions! How would she get inside the Neopholytite's tower? How would she steal a piece of the witch? What if the Swarm caught her? But uppermost in her mind was how to make contact with the Morrow child. The dead girl was the key; without her, the pact was indestructible.

'But who is the dead child?' asked Tallitha.

'Arabella Dorothea Morrow; she is the child of Edwyn Morrow, who fled to Breedoor,' Kastra replied.

It was the child that Suggit had told her about when they had been travelling to Stankles Brow.

'But how will I contact her?' asked Tallitha apprehensively

'You must use supernatural powers,' said Ferileath.

It was too much to take in.

'How will I persuade the Morrow child to enter the tower at the right time?' Tallitha felt her stomach tighten. 'Is there a spell I can use?' she asked.

'The dead cannot be controlled by magic,' Kastra answered flatly.

'Then what shall I do?' asked Tallitha

Kastra smiled knowingly. 'The sisters at Winderling Spires understand these dark machinations – they know how to make contact with the spirits.'

So the truth was more sinister than Tallitha had imagined.

'The Morrow sisters understand the ways of the dead-ones,' explained Ferileath.

'What do you mean?' asked Tallitha apprehensively.

'The dead talk to the sisters.'

Tallitha shivered. Her thoughts turned to the old house in Wycham Elva and the sinister secrets it contained – secrets she was only just beginning to comprehend.

Her next step was becoming clear to her.

'Then I must go back to Winderling Spires,' she said finally, 'to persuade the sisters to show me how to make contact with the dead!'

But would her grandmother and the aunts reveal their powers? Great Aunt Agatha had always been so guarded about such sinister things.

'B-But I'm a long way from home,' she mumbled. 'How will I find my way back to Wycham Elva from here?'

'Take the winding route beneath the Green Gorge. My Black Sprites will show you the way.'

'What if I should need you?' asked Tallitha.

'Hold the bloodstone tightly and I will come to you.'

Tallitha felt the stone becoming warm against her skin.

'It's time to return to the Charmed Wood, the Black Sprites will awaken soon,' said Kastra, observing the night sky becoming tinged with the dawn.

The Grand Witch pricked Tallitha on the arm and the Unimaginable Palace dissolved into a muddle of light and shadows. Tallitha found herself flying by Kastra's side once again, soaring up through the heavens where the blue-black night kissed her cheeks and the grey-winged hawk moths fluttered idly by. Then Kastra and Tallitha raced headlong through the forest to the place where Quillam lay slumbering on the mossy bed.

'Sleep tight, witch-child,' Kastra said.

Tallitha nestled amongst the leaves and fell into a deep sleep.

Then the Grand Witch swirled her cloak about her body, spun round in a circle of ever increasing sapphire light and vanished into the liquid-blue night.

*

'Tallitha, wake up,' said Quillam, shaking her.

Next to Tallitha's sleeping form was a snail-trail of sapphire blue.

Tallitha woke with a start. Her head throbbed.

'I saw the Grand Witch, Kastra, or perhaps it was a dream,' she said touching her head. 'She told me many strange things.'

'It wasn't a dream. Kastra was here,' replied Flametip, pointing at the bloodstone pendant hanging around Tallitha's neck.

'What does it mean?' asked Quillam.

'Kastra pricked Tallitha with a dreaming spell and took her to the Unimaginable Palace,' explained Flametip.

'I remember now,' Tallitha mumbled sleepily.

Her fingers reached for the bloodstone pendant. It was cold to the touch.

That morning an uneasy presence pervaded the wood. A

smell of rotten fruit wafted towards them. Witchcraft and old magic filled the air.

'This place reeks of danger,' the youth said warily. 'What did the Grand Witch tell you?'

So Tallitha told Quillam about the Unimaginable Palace, about Ferileath and the mirrored wall and all that Kastra had revealed.

'We're one step closer to destroying the pact,' she said, feeling at once uneasy and excited. 'The Morrow sisters are skilled in the supernatural and know how to make contact with the dead – with the Morrow child.'

'So what happens next?' Quillam asked apprehensively.

'We must go home to Winderling Spires!'

# Five

The next morning Tallitha and Quillam said farewell to the Black Sprites and followed an old shepherds' pathway down the steep valley and out into the wide Green Gorge. The day was hot, and Quillam, tired from the night before, was edgy and tense. He had spent a restless night, waking fitfully and brooding about his past.

Tallitha sensed his mood.

'What is it?' she asked, turning to face him. 'Something's wrong, isn't it.'

He was distracted. She watched as he clenched his jaw.

'I-I have to know the truth,' he said finally.

'About what?'

'My past, Tallitha. You have to help me,' he urged. 'Use your special powers! Magic and the supernatural – whatever they are - but you have to find out where I'm from.'

Tallitha's heart sank.

'B-But –'

'No excuses, Tallitha. I must know what happened to me when I was little,' he cried, his eyes meeting hers.

'What if I can't help you?' she whispered.

He reached out and grabbed her arm tightly.

'You have to! You made a promise, remember?' he said desperately.

'Okay,' she replied, pulling away from his grasp. 'I will do all I can to help you – but I can't promise it will work.'

'You're the only chance I've got,' he glowered. 'I've waited all my life for answers – now my only hope is you!'

For as long as he could remember, Quillam had harboured a desperate yearning to discover his birth family, but now, for the first time, he felt afraid. What if he found out something terrible about his past? About who he really was and why he had been abandoned? A feeling of dread and excitement swirled in his guts.

'Here, this place will do,' he said.

Quillam pointed towards an overhanging rock that would give them some protection from the glaring sun.

Tallitha cast her eyes over the shaded area and nodded. They settled down beneath the rocky overhang.

'What happens now?' he asked, watching her every movement.

'I will need something from your past. A memory or an object – both would be good.'

He fumbled in his pocket and drew out a velvet pouch.

'This was fastened around my neck when the Grovellers discovered me wandering about Hegglefoot.'

The pouch contained several bloodstones set in golden cases. Tallitha took them out one by one and gazed at them, positioning them in the sun's rays. The blood-red veins ran in swirling patterns through the deep green gemstones.

'It's curious,' she said to the youth, turning the bloodstones over in her hand. 'These stones are in the same setting as the one Kastra gave to me.'

She lifted the pendant from underneath her shirt.

'Then it wasn't a dream after all,' said Quillam ominously.

Tallitha twisted the pendant, placing it in the direct sunlight and watching as the rays flickered through the red and green streaks.

'It was a sort of waking dream,' she replied. 'I-I was aware of what was happening but time had no meaning.' She raised her eyes and regarded Quillam's face. He had a wolfish glint in his eyes; an untameable quality. 'I'll need a memory too,' she said, gently touching his arm, 'the earliest one you can remember.'

'I-I remember being with Lutch and Buckle in the village,' he stammered. 'I was young, a small kid.'

'It must be an earlier memory than that,' she said encouragingly.

His ochre eyes flashed.

'But that's all I can remember,' he said.

Tallitha realised she would have to tread a darker path to get to the truth. Quillam wouldn't like it.

'I want to try something else,' Tallitha said gently, eyeing Quillam from beneath her tangled hair. If he wanted to unearth his past, this was her best shot. 'I want to hypnotise you, to take you back to earlier memories, to those hidden beneath the surface, beginning with the day the Grovellers found you.'

Quillam shot her a wary glance.

'Is there no other way?' he asked.

Tallitha shook her head. She had never hypnotised anyone before, but Quillam didn't need to know that. She would have to follow what she remembered of Essie's method.

'What will I have to do?' he asked guardedly.

'It will be okay, don't worry – I won't let anything awful happen to you,' she said soothingly. 'You trust me, don't you?'

'Of course,' he mumbled, blushing slightly. 'Let's get on with it.'

Tallitha placed the bloodstones in a circle, just outside the overhang in the sunshine.

'Concentrate on the sunlight as it dances across the stones,' she said enticingly. 'See how the red streaks shimmer and glow brighter against the vibrant greens. Watch the light, Quillam, and think back as far as you can. Remember how you felt when you were a child. Can you remember any sounds or smells? Think back to an earlier time and relax.' Even as she uttered these words, Tallitha's voice had taken on a mesmerising quality. 'Close your eyes, Quillam. Give in to their heaviness,' she said in a soft voice. Quillam's eyelids flickered. 'Go back to that day when the Grovellers found you.'

Quillam's breathing became deeper. Tallitha could see his eyes moving beneath their lids, searching for the memories that lay hidden.

'Tell me, what do you see?'

'I'm wandering along a path,' he replied in a monotone voice. 'I can feel the sand between my toes. I am wild, with a dirty face and tangled hair.'

The hypnosis was working. Tallitha bit her lip and watched Quillam's rapid eye movement tracing his past, following the path that would lead him to his future. But what if she couldn't bring him back? She wouldn't think about that now.

'Go further, Quillam, to before that day – relax and let your mind wander. Your memories are like buried treasure, like these beautiful bloodstones. Only you can unearth them,' Tallitha urged, gently placing his fingers amongst the warm dry stones. 'Remember how you felt as that child. Where are you Quillam? What are you doing? What are you feeling?'

Tallitha watched Quillam's body shiver. Something had unsettled him.

'What is it?' she asked.

'It's dark and I'm so cold,' he moaned, rubbing his arms.

'Tell me where you are – what you see.'

His voice sounded younger, frightened and lost.

'I'm deep underground in a dark, scary place. T-There's a woman but she isn't friendly and I don't like her … I-I am hiding my head – trying to keep away from her.' He whimpered. 'She's frightening – her hair is the colour of flames and she has piercing orange eyes,' he cried out. Quillam lifted his hands to protect himself. 'I-I want my mother,' he wailed. 'It's so dark!' He sobbed and put his head in his hands. 'I want to go home, please let me go home!'

'Don't be afraid. I am here with you,' Tallitha replied with tears in her eyes.

She held his hand in hers.

'Snowdroppe is here and she wants to take me away,' he whimpered.

Tallitha's shoulders tensed at the mention of her mother and her hand tightened on his. What had her mother to do with this? She steadied her breathing and replied calmly.

'Where are you now?'

'I-I'm still underground and – t-there are Groats and many hounds - it smells of rancid meat. But the dogs are friendly to me, they are wagging their tails; they are licking my hands and taking care of me.'

Tallitha felt a huge lump in her throat. Quillam's harrowing story was beginning to fall into place. After the Dooerlins had stolen the boy from Winderling Spires, the Grand Witch Selvistra must have handed him over to Snowdroppe, who had left him to be cared for by the Groats and the wild dogs.

'What happened then?' she asked, her voice breaking.

Tallitha wiped a tear from her face.

Suddenly, Quillam pulled away and hurriedly raised his hands to shield his face.

'The frightening fire-woman is leading me out into the

sunshine. I-I've been in the dark for a long time. '*Please don't leave me!*' I shout. I am scared. I cry out and grab hold of her but she pushes me away! Then she leaves me all alone on the path … that's where I feel the sand between my toes,' he sobbed. It was a wrenching sound, from deep within him. He buried his head in his hands.

Tallitha reached out to comfort him, taking his hand in hers. 'What happened next?'

'Then Lutch finds me wandering about. She picks me up and I am safe.'

Tallitha's face was streaked with tears. She dried her eyes. Her mother was an evil creature.

'Quillam, it's time to come back to me now. Wake up,' she said gently.

When he opened his eyes Quillam pulled his hand away from Tallitha's grasp.

'I-I can't remember anything,' he cried, his voice breaking with emotion. 'What happened? What did I say? Did you find out who my mother is?'

Tallitha shook her head.

'But I can piece together what happened after you were taken,' she replied.

'You must tell me – I have to know.'

She hesitated, watching his reaction. 'You spoke of a dark place. It must have been the caves, of the dogs that took care of you and of a frightening woman.'

Quillam shivered. 'I-I remember her,' he said slowly, 'not

what she looked like, but the feeling of dread when I was in her presence. What else did I say?'

'You spoke of Snowdroppe and of her wanting to take you away.'

'What then?' he asked.

'The frightening woman left you alone with the Grovellers.'

Quillam bit his lip.

'I remember being scared for a long time,' he said slowly, 'I remember wanting my mother.' His voice stumbled over the words. 'I-I must know who she is.'

'Then I'll continue,' Tallitha said.

It was in that moment, thinking of Quillam's abandonment as a child, that Tallitha realised that she had always been loved, by Cissie and of course by Tyaas and even by her Great Aunt Agatha. She felt a pang of regret. Why had she taken so much for granted?

'To unravel your past I must travel to another place in time.'

'Sounds ominous,' he answered nervously.

'You must recite a spell with me.'

Quillam hesitated.

'Okay,' he muttered.

'Repeat the words after me and remember whatever I discover is only the past. It can't hurt you anymore,' she said gently. 'Ready?'

Quillam nodded.

Tallitha recited the words of the time-span-rhyme. '*Lythin weche, lythin weche wetherwynde, ower wetherwynde, tore weche.*'

The Wetherwynde Spell sounded like a hundred tinkling bells as Quillam repeated the words. They tripped from his tongue and danced into the air.

'Say the words again,' she said.

'*Lythin weche, lythin weche wetherwynde, ower wetherwynde, tore weche*,' Quillam said.

As Tallitha held the bloodstones the Wetherynde Spell darted inside her mouth and stuck to her tongue like confetti. She concentrated on the warm, sun-baked stones as they lay in her hand. They felt warm and round, warm and round … and then she felt the familiar *pop-popping* sensation; a tremendous force engulfed her – and *whoosh!* The stones fell from her hand and landed on the earth. In the next moment she was sucked from her body, up the bright tunnel and far, far away.

Tallitha tumbled headlong into a pool of fragmented images that flashed before her eyes. She saw Tyaas grinning in one of his makeshift dens, then the sisters in the Crewel Tower, and of Cissie sewing in the sitting room at Winderling Spires. Then everything went black. A powerful force gripped her body and dragged her to a cold, dark place beneath the earth – somewhere that chilled her to her core.

The darkness was overpowering. In the corner, a light flickered and Snowdroppe came into view. She was stroking a child's head and talking to a figure in the shadows.

'Let me have him,' she demanded. 'You can abandon him in the Groveller village and when he is a little older and much less trouble I will take him for my own child.'

A fiery figure stepped forward. Her hair was the colour of flames and her eyes burned with an orange light. It was the same witch that had been with Great Aunt Agatha when the spell had gone so badly wrong. It was the Grand Witch Selvistra Loons, agreeing to hand over the child to Snowdroppe. A young Quillam was cowering and crying bitterly, pulling away from her, but in this dark place there was nowhere to hide. Selvistra led him deeper into the caves and left him alone with the Groats and the hounds. The dogs licked the child clean and nuzzled him until they settled about his shivering body, offering some warmth in the cold caves.

Tallitha felt her stomach lurch and tighten as her body began hurtling through the middle plane. Disconnected images spun past her, flinging her this way and that and suddenly transforming into a vision she had witnessed once before. Cissie and a dark haired- child were running happily through Winderling Spires, laughing and playing together. Then, the scene blurred and brightened. Tallitha watched, bewildered, as Cissie stepped towards the child's bed, bent down and whispered, 'Goodnight my boy,' to the child. She called him, 'Danny, my sweet Danny!' Then she kissed the child on his head, repeated an old Wycham saying and touched the pouch that hung around his neck. The boy looked up.

'*Goodnight, Mother,*' he whispered.

Tallitha stared from the boy to Cissie and finally back to the dark haired child. Cissie was the boy's mother!

Then, as quickly as the image had appeared, it abruptly

vanished. Tallitha shivered in the foggy-grey light and watched as the final image began to take shape before her. She was in Winderling Spires, but in a different part of the old house and it had taken on a deathly stillness. From out of the seeping darkness she saw the Dooerlins steal one by one into Winderling Spires. They crept along the shadowed passageways, broke into the small bedroom and snatched the dark-haired child away.

That child was Danny. That child was Quillam!

Tallitha cried out and repeated the *Wetherwynde* spell, the air filled with the sound of tinkling bells and she slipped back into her body with a shudder.

In the depths of the Green Gorge, Quillam stared at her, open-mouthed.

'What happened?' He asked desperately. 'You were shivering uncontrollably and making a terrible moaning sound. Are you hurt?'

Tallitha shook her head. How was she to tell him what she had just witnessed? Her dearest Cissie had borne a child called Danny, and now this child was the young man who was sitting before her, desperately seeking the truth.

'Tell me what you saw!'

Tallitha sat nervously twisting her hair in and out of her fingers.

'T-They – I mean, Snowdroppe and the witch, the one they call Selvistra Loons, left you with the Groats and the wild dogs in those terrible caves,' she answered breathlessly.

'Yes,' he answered slowly, 'I remember that,' he replied, as though waking from a dream. 'The hounds looked after me like an abandoned puppy. Perhaps I would have died but for them.'

Tallitha shivered as she recalled the pitiful image of the child, left alone with the dogs. Did that explain Quillam's wild, untameable ways?

'What else did you see?' he asked nervously.

Tallitha bit her lip. 'I-I know who your mother is,' she said quietly, 'and I know where you're from.'

Quillam's eyes flickered.

'Who is she?' he asked hesitantly, his ochre-coloured eyes shining.

'S-She's the one who gave you the pouch with the bloodstones. They were meant to protect you from the Dooerlins, they were meant to protect you from being secreted away,' Tallitha said sadly, her voice faltering with emotion. 'But Quillam, no matter what your mother did, she couldn't protect you from that terrible witch, Selvistra Loons, and she couldn't protect you from the Dooerlins. Please don't ever forget that. That witch's magic is too strong.'

He reached out for her.

'Please, you must tell me! I have waited so long to find out!'

Tallitha warily met his eyes.

'Cissie Wakenshaw is your mother's name. She's my dear friend and nurse from Winderling Spires. You're just a boy from Wycham Elva!'

*

72

Quillam, or Danny, Tallitha didn't know quite what to call him, was the happiest she had seen him since the day they had spent together in the Groveller village.

'But are you certain it's her?' he asked.

Tallitha nodded.

'You called her mother,' she replied.

'But was it definitely me?' he asked, 'can you be sure?'

'Yes,' she whispered, 'you had the pouch fastened about your neck.'

Quillam touched the soft velvet pouch, smiling to himself. Maybe it was true. After all this time, he had finally found his mother.

'What's she like?' he asked after a long silence.

'Kind, loving, straight talking,' she replied.

Quillam's face darkened.

'Then why did she never mention me?' he asked wistfully.

'I-I don't know,' she answered, catching sight of his wounded expression.

The revelation had come as a complete surprise to Tallitha but as with most things in Winderling Spires, it seemed that everyone kept secrets, including her dear Cissie.

As they tramped further down the gorge, Tallitha answered Quillam's questions, telling him everything she could remember about her nurse; about Cissie's family at High Bedders End and about the myths and legends of Wycham Elva. She recounted every folk-tale that Cissie had ever told her, about the Dooerlins and the terrible events that led up to Quillam being taken away.

'I have to meet her,' he said with a tinge of apprehension.

'Once we're back in Wycham Elva, you will.'

'But what will she be like?' he asked nervously, 'will she have forgotten about me after all this time?'

'Cissie is a wonderful woman with a good heart. She has kept a terrible secret all these years but believe me she will not have forgotten you,' Tallitha replied.

'Then why did she never mention me – not even once?'

Tallitha didn't have an answer to his question. In many ways, Cissie's secret was just another layer to add to the subterfuge that festered in the old house.

'Come on,' she said encouragingly, 'I don't know why she never spoke of you, just as I don't know why Great Aunt Agatha never told me about Asenathe's disappearance, or the Swarm, or about having supernatural powers. She must have had her reasons though.'

He cut her short.

'Families and their secrets,' he replied with a sorrowful look. 'I kind of understand that now.'

*

The entrance to the cave was at the bottom of the Green Gorge, under a round flat stone with a series of rope ladders leading down into the dark abyss. The Black Sprites had told them which route to take to avoid the Old Yawning Edges and the Throes of Woe, but there was no way of bypassing the Sour

Pits and the Shrunken Butts. Quillam was keen to journey through the caves as quickly as possible – because somewhere, out there, his mother was waiting.

'I can't keep up with you.' Tallitha called out to him.

Quillam raised his head and smiled.

'Sorry, I'm excited, I guess.' His voice sounded more animated than usual. 'We're nearly at the bottom, I can hear water.'

He flashed his lantern over the well of the shaft. A torrent flowed beneath them.

'Here, take my hand,' he said, helping her onto a rocky ledge.

'I wonder what's ahead of us.' She replied apprehensively.

The caves smelt bitter with the odour of aged stone, of rock rubbing against ancient rock; it was a cold, sharp smell that stung her nostrils and sat heavily in the back of her throat.

'Come on,' he urged.

Together, with Quillam's fingers clasped around hers, they edged forward into the inky blackness.

# Six

Cissie clutched Danny's old boat wherever she went, smoothing down the tattered sails and running her fingers over the faded blue lettering that picked out her child's name. The toy gave her some comfort but deep down the unanswered questions about her son's disappearance still remained. She went over in her mind the day when Danny was taken, trying to remember the sequence of events. Why had the Dooerlins stolen into Winderling Spires? But more importantly, who had let them in?

Since Snowdroppe had vanished like a lightening bolt down the Shrove tunnel, the Skinks and Cissie had been hiding out in the attics of Winderling Spires, watching and waiting for the right moment to follow her to Hellstone Tors.

'Are you ready?' Ruker asked, disturbing Cissie's thoughts.

She poked her head through the trapdoor and studied Cissie's forlorn expression. She hadn't been the same since the night they had slept in the Spider's Turret. She was uneasy and on edge.

'Coming,' she replied and slowly rose to her feet.

The night was quiet on the attic floors, apart from the mice scampering about behind the skirting boards. Moonlight streaked through the dirty windowpanes, the beams dancing through the dust motes that floated weightlessly along the dark and endless corridors. Cissie tucked the boat into her pocket and ventured into the labyrinth of unchartered passageways, leading the Skinks down unfamiliar staircases and meandering corridors and through the vast expanse of the empty wings and abandoned floors.

'So are we agreed on our plan?' asked Neeps, glancing nervously at Ruker for confirmation.

Ruker nodded. The Skinks had not stopped talking about the sinister Shrove tunnel since they had witnessed Snowdroppe's amazing disappearance; moving like a whirling dervish, spinning forward into the dark space and vanishing into the bowels of the earth in a burst of magical mayhem.

Ruker had considered the risks of following Snowdroppe's route underground.

'She must have used it many times, going backwards and forwards to the castle,' she explained.

'But is it safe?' asked Cissie, her eyes widening with apprehension.

'All we have to do is follow the tunnel, make our way to Hellstone Tors and rescue Tallitha and the others.'

'You make it sound so easy,' Cissie replied cautiously, 'but it won't be as straightforward as you think. I for one am uneasy about going down into that black hole. Anywhere those Shroves go is bound to be a wretched place, dark and terrifying! Who knows what will be lurking in wait for us.'

Cissie muttered an old Wycham saying, shaking her head at the foolhardy Skinks. Since finding Danny's boat she had felt more wary of the old house and its secrets. She no longer had the stomach for such an adventure. The tiny boat, with its tattered sails and faded blue paint, reminded her of the dark, lonely months after her son's disappearance. It was all going to end badly and no mistake.

As they crept along the fourth floor Cissie could stand the tension no longer. She tugged on Ruker's shirt.

'I'll never make it through that tunnel. It's the darkness and the memory of my poor boy,' she faltered, her face crumpling. 'I'll come as far as the kitchens and then I'll slip out the servants' door and go to our Rose's.'

'No you won't,' replied Ruker firmly, 'you're coming with us. We'll look after you, won't we Neeps? After all, everything may not be lost with your son. He may be out there somewhere, just waiting for you to find him.'

'Ruker's right. You're coming too, no argument,' added Neeps, pulling his hair into a ponytail, 'we're all in this together.'

'In any case, what about finding Tallitha and Tyaas?' added Ruker, touching Cissie's arm sympathetically.

The Skink had a point. Cissie felt she couldn't argue with

them any longer. She was being selfish and she felt guilty for being afraid of the darkness. After all, she was the one who had let the children leave the Spires and embark on their dangerous adventure.

So the wary band carried on creeping down the corridors, hurrying into the shadows whenever they heard a creak coming from the old house, ever vigilant in case one of the Shroves should discover them.

*

Marlin was on edge. He had awoken early that same morning in a foul temper; there was an odd smell in Winderling Spires and he didn't like it. Something told him there was an unfamiliar presence in the old house, and the odour wafting down from the upper floors only sharpened his sense of foreboding. Then Florré returned from his duties and announced that he, too, had experienced a queer feeling since breakfast. It had started in his toes and had run all the way up his spine.

'I came over all peculiar,' he whined, taking a good draught of berry juice to calm his nerves. 'It was when I was below the attics in the South Wing. There was something up there – ferreting about. It sent shivers all down my body.'

So Marlin's suspicions were confirmed.

'There's trouble afoot,' he replied, hopping about and wringing his hands, 'seems to me that we might have some nasty visitors on our patch.'

Florré nodded in agreement and greedily quaffed more of the fruit cordial.

Marlin was in a blither and scratched his whiskery chin. After so many years of secret visits to Hellstone Tors and duplicitous meetings with the Swarm, no one was going to spoil his long awaited plans! So the Shroves went about their business that morning on high alert, ostensibly completing their household duties, but taking every opportunity to scuttle into the locked rooms and abandoned wings, investigating the darkest corners of Winderling Spires for any intruders. Marlin caught the occasional whiff; it was an uncanny scent that lingered in a disturbing way and Florré was unusually twitchy, looking over his shoulder whenever he ventured above the fourth floor.

'There's summat wicked goin' on,' muttered Grintley, shuddering and hopping about. 'I smelled critters, up at top o'the house.' he growled. 'It smells like those dratted Skinks, I'm certain of it.' He muttered, finally naming the problem.

'Skinks!' hollered Florré, 'that's it! Oh my, how I hate those woodland rats! What they doin' inside the Spires?'

'Mayhem and mischief, I'll be damned! You leave them to me,' growled Marlin.

With that, he scampered up into the enormous house, searching the dusty rooms and scouring the dark empty hallways up to the very top of the Spires until eventually his trail led him to the disused attics. Silently, he crept into an adjoining storeroom, nestled next to the wall and overheard Ruker and Neeps discussing their plans to follow the Shrove route to Hellstone Tors.

'Got 'em,' he hissed, his beady eyes sparkling with wicked delight, 'and that Cissie Wakenshaw an all, the devious old shrew!'

Later that night, Cissie, Ruker and Neeps crept from their hiding place and began edging down the gloomy passageways. Marlin was on their tail, moving assiduously like a slippery fox, waiting for the moment when he would scurry off and inform the Grand Morrow all about their unwanted guests. The sneaky Shrove rubbed his whiskery chin and chuckled viciously. He would destroy that Cissie Wakenshaw for good! He would spike her so that she would never dare set foot in Wycham village again. She would hang her head with the shame. No one in the village would ever give her the time of day again once he'd finished with her!

As Marlin hid in the dark recesses, spying on the Skinks, Ruker leaned over the bannister and peered at the fleeting shadows in the hallway, glimmering softly in the candlelight. The old clock tick-tocked its melodic sounds and the smell of beeswax and lavender filled the night air; not a soul stirred below them.

'There's no one about,' Ruker whispered hoarsely to the others. 'Come on.'

They sneaked down the staircase like a band of wary mice, with Cissie alerting them to every creak and groan on the stair treads.

'Move over there, watch that step,' she murmured, pulling the Skinks to the left and then to the right.

Meanwhile, Marlin was ready to put his devious plan into action. He scuttled up to the Fedora Wing, all the while rehearsing what he would say to the Grand Morrow.

'I'll tell her there's burglars – that Cissie Wakenshaw has broken in and is stealing from the Spires, takin' the Morrow family's precious jewels,' he chuckled malevolently.

The door to the Grand Morrow's bedroom creaked open and the Shrove slunk up to Agatha's bedside. He coughed loudly and gingerly prodded his Mistress, feigning fright and pretending to be alarmed.

'Oh my Lady, there's trouble tonight! Wake up, I say!' Marlin called out, giving the Grand Morrow another dig in the ribs.

Agatha woke with a terrific fright. Her heart was thumping in her chest.

'There's mischief afoot,' Marlin rasped. 'There be burglars in the Spires, rapscallions and villains!'

'What the Devil is going on?' Agatha screamed as the Shrove's weaselly face loomed above her.

'Devils indeed!' cried the Shrove. 'M'Lady, there's trouble! That Cissie Wakenshaw and a band of no-good Skinks have come to steal your treasures and take revenge on us all!'

Marlin hovered in the candlelight, hopping from side to side, his wet lips slavering and his oily hair smelling of grease. Agatha reeled from the proximity of the Shrove and sat bolt upright, pulling the bedclothes up to her chin.

'Of all the nerve!' Agatha cried.

Marlin had invaded her bedroom!

'Are you sure it's not the Dooerlins?' she asked tremulously, eyeing the twitchy Shrove. 'Heavens, if those hateful creatures have managed to creep inside the Spires again, no one is safe in their beds!' she cried.

'Nay, it's that awful Cissie Wakenshaw! Back to take her revenge!' he replied venomously 'I always said that woman couldn't be trusted and I was right!'

Agatha glowered suspiciously at the Shrove in the candlelight. His mouth was slavering. He was beside himself with glee.

'Where are my sisters?' Agatha bellowed, grabbing her dressing gown. 'Wake them at once and meet me back here. No, not that way!' she shouted at Marlin as he made for the door. 'You can use the secret staircase,' she said, gesticulating towards her bed canopy.

Marlin slipped behind the tapestry and scampered up the hidden staircase. On the way to the Crewel Tower he woke Florré, who was snoring in one of the Shrove holes.

'We've got 'em!' Marlin gloated as his eyes glowed with menace. 'Wake those weird sisters and meet us in the Missus's bedroom and be quick about it. I can't wait to see Cissie Wakenshaw's face when I dump her right in it.'

Florré leapt from the Shrove hole and bolted into the sisters' apartment so fast that he slipped on the polished floor and landed with a crash against Edwina Mouldson's four-poster bed.

It seemed to Edwina, when she awoke with a terrific fright, that the damnable Florré had pounced on her bed in the middle of the night.

'Get out of here at once!' she cried. 'What is the meaning of this! Sybilla! Sybilla! Come here this instant. This Shrove has gone berserk!'

Edwina sat up in bed, holding the quilt up to her nose. Her wide, startled eyes peered over the edge, blinking at the frantic Shrove.

'Please m'Lady, I've been told to fetch thee by the Grand Morrow,' he explained, hopping about. 'It's a dire emergency!'

'At this time of night! Have you gone batty?'

'No ma'am, there be burglars,' he hissed, 'nasty Skinks prowling about the house, stealing your precious jewels, in league with that Cissie Wakenshaw!'

Edwina leapt out of bed, wearing only her cotton nightdress, trying desperately to wrap herself with the quilt.

'Don't just stand there! Fetch my dressing gown!' she barked at Florré.

At that moment Sybilla padded into the room accompanied by Marlin. Her long hair was wound in rags, twisted on top of her head in order to give her hair a curl in the morning. She looked a fright.

'Come dear, it's true. Apparently we have burglars!' Sybilla said excitedly. 'Marlin has told me all about it, we're going to apprehend the criminals,' she said clasping her hands together with glee.

The two sisters were flushed with a mixture of excitement and stomach-churning apprehension as they followed the Shroves down the back staircase and into Agatha's bedroom.

'Be quick sisters, apparently we have some nocturnal guests,' said Agatha. 'Here, you'd better take these,' she said offering Edwina and then Sybilla a large brass poker and a silver candlestick. 'To strike the varmints,' she instructed, whereupon she waved a pair of fire tongs in the air for dramatic effect. 'Onwards!' she cried.

Agatha Morrow marched the vigilant group downstairs, clutching candles and make-shift weapons but when they arrived in the hallway, it was quite empty. Agatha stared about her, peering underneath the grand staircase and inspecting the dark recesses by candlelight.

'Marlin, are you sure you saw these so-called burglars?' she remonstrated.

'Yes m'Lady, they were just here!' he said, pointing towards the servant's entrance. 'Look there! Mrs Armitage's door is ajar,' he added. 'And it's always closed at this time of night. They must 'ave gone down there!' he announced, making for the doorway and dragging Florré behind him.

The eager Shroves scurried down the steps into the darkness, beckoning to the others to follow them.

Agatha Morrow abruptly raised her hand and stopped her sisters from following. In her opinion, there was something decidedly odd about the Shroves' behaviour. Although she had been upset by Cissie's involvement in the children's disappearance, the old servant was certainly no thief. No, there was certainly more to Marlin's story than the Shrove was letting on.

'All is not as it may seem,' she said mysteriously. 'Sybilla dear, say nothing, whatever you may witness down there, and always follow my lead,' instructed Agatha.

'Y-Yes dear but what's going on? Where are the burglars? I was getting quite excited at the prospect of catching them red-handed!'

'Hush, dear. Just do what I say and keep close,' whispered Agatha.

Sybilla searched Edwina's face in the candlelight as her sister nodded gravely.

'Follow Agatha and do what she says,' said Edwina sagely, deferring to her elder sister.

'If you say so, dear,' said Sybilla, shuffling behind Agatha.

Edwina was altogether a little shaken. She was still recovering from the shock of finding Florré in her bedchamber at the dead of night!

'Horrible old Shrove,' she muttered with a shudder.

Agatha took hold of Sybilla's hand whilst a trembling Edwina brought up the rear. Together, they began the chilly descent into the dark kitchens.

# Seven

Ruker crept inside the pantry and peered down into the dark, black hole; all was deadly quiet. Step by step, she edged down into the Shroves' lair with her back against the wall, lifting her lantern and scouring the gloomy recesses for any sign of Marlin and the others. The Shrove hole was a mess, littered with half eaten kitchen scraps and old clothes mingled together into squalid piles. Ruker surreptitiously searched the Shroves' fetid sleeping burrows, gingerly lifting their smelly blankets, turning over their rancid clothes and picking over the remnants of their last meal. It was a grim sight and smelled unpleasantly of old socks.

'There's no one here,' she called, hearing Cissie's footsteps behind her.

'But what if they're hiding?' asked Cissie warily.

'The varmints have hovels all over Winderling Spires, chances are they'll be somewhere else,' answered Neeps, creeping beside Ruker. 'But I'll be happy to take them on. I'll make them pay for what they've done,' he sneered, brandishing his dagger.

The smell of old Shrove greeted Cissie's nostrils as she picked her way through the mess of food scraps and discarded rubbish. She reared back as the stench hit the back of her throat. There before her, winding away into the darkness, the Shrove's tunnel remained as it had on their previous visit, sinister and uninviting. Cissie lifted the candle, shuddered and stared down into the cold, black void. *Drip-drop, drip-drop* the water splashed from the roof into rivulets, trickling away beneath the old house. The tunnel walls glistened black-bright in the candlelight, stained a mossy-green with the years of seeping water.

'Let's get going,' said Neeps urgently, tightening his backpack. 'We have a way to go underground and who knows what we will find down there.'

Cissie's eyes widened. The deepening darkness of the tunnel, splashed with fleeting eerie shadows, made her stomach churn with dread.

'I-I'm not sure I can go through with this,' she replied, edging back towards the steps.

Suddenly there was the sound of muffled feet as the strong smell of greasy Shrove overpowered her. In the next moment, Marlin roughly grabbed Cissie and sunk his teeth into her neck, lacerating her flesh.

She screamed as the blood trickled down her skin.

'Let go of me!' She cried, trying vainly to escape.

'No you don't,' Marlin yelled, 'you're not going anywhere, Mistress Wakenshaw!'

He raised his head, licked his lips and his beady eyes revolved with pleasure. He had tasted her blood once before.

'Stop those Skinks!' Marlin shrieked. 'Grintley! Florré, grab them!'

From out of the shadows the Shroves leapt on Ruker and Neeps, biting and sinking their yellow fangs into their flesh.

'Get off me,' Neeps yelled, whacking Florré over the nose with his fist.

Ruker clubbed Grintley on the head and grabbed a fist full of hair, dragging the Shrove's fangs, dripping with blood, from her punctured arm.

Grintley yelped and staggered to the ground; stumbling, he got back to his feet and lurched at the Skink once more. Neeps lunged and stabbed Florré in the leg with his dagger. The Shrove's eyes bulged, he yelped and limped into the shadows to lick his wounds.

But Marlin still held Cissie by the throat. He pressed his gnarled fingers around her neck, tighter and tighter. His stinking breath filled her senses and made her retch. She was slowly losing consciousness. The Shrove's eyes closed with wicked pleasure. He had her now. He would crush the life out of her! He squeezed again, this time more tightly.

'Let go of her at once!' commanded Agatha Morrow as she stepped down into the Shrove burrow, followed closely by her sisters.

Marlin was so taken aback at the sight of the Grand Morrow entering their lair that he relaxed his grip. Cissie fell to the floor with a thud. Neeps hurried to her aid.

'M'Lady!' Marlin cried, bowing obsequiously. 'Look, we've caught the villains with their plunder.'

He buried his hands in his pockets and brought out a silver teapot, a bunch of spoons and a handful of sparkling ruby necklaces and bracelets.

'Why you lying maggot,' shouted Ruker, 'we've never touched a thing in this house!'

Ruker lunged at Marlin as the Shrove spat and screamed a torrent of abuse. The Skink kicked Marlin's legs out from under him as they wrestled each other to the floor, fists flying, rolling amongst the debris, scratching and punching.

'Stop this at once!' Agatha shouted as Ruker continued pummelling the Shrove with her fists.

Edwina and Sybilla stood anxiously on the steps, candles in one hand, their weapons poised in the other, staring at the spectacle unfolding before them with wide, staring eyes.

'Enough! This fighting will stop,' Agatha bellowed, 'pull them apart!' she shouted, pointing at Neeps.

Despite Ruker's protests, Neeps hauled her friend off the Shrove as Marlin scurried to safety. Breathlessly, the two adversaries glowered at each other across the Shrove hole.

'I have my suspicions about who the real villains are here!' She turned and pinned her eyes on the Shroves, looking from one miserable specimen to another. 'Is it you

Marlin? Have you betrayed us to the Swarm?'

Sybilla gasped and clung desperately to Edwina. For a moment she thought she would faint.

'B-But surely Agatha, they're our Shroves,' she cried, looking desperately at Florré. 'They would never…'

'Be quiet, Sybilla!' interrupted Edwina. 'Don't interfere!'

'I –I'm –,' Florré stuttered, bowing his head.

The Shrove flicked his eyes fleetingly at Sybilla as he inched towards the tunnel.

'Florré?' Sybilla muttered, bewildered by what had occurred.

'Don't speak to him,' shouted Edwina, 'the Shroves are in league within the Swarm!'

'But I trusted him,' Sybilla whimpered.

'He wormed his way in when you were off your guard, sister. Then tonight, they tried to trick us into believing Cissie and the Skinks were up to no good,' replied Agatha, glowering at Marlin.

The Shrove was hunched like a cornered cat, ready to bolt. He panted breathlessly and his beady eyes flicked madly from one Shrove to the other. He knew their game was up. In the next moment, he muttered something incomprehensible in Shroveling as Grintley and Florré rushed to his side. The Shroves crept into a huddle, slinking towards the tunnel entrance. Then with a sudden hiss and a scuffle, they high-tailed it out of the Shrove hole and sped off into the darkness.

The Skinks made to follow but Agatha called them off.

'Let them go to their evil masters, there's no sense in following them just yet.' She announced, holding them with a stern gaze. 'Besides I need to talk to you about Tallitha and the others. I have something important to say.'

As Agatha climbed the steps, she turned and her eyes strayed over Cissie's face. She coloured and turned quickly away, making her way up through the kitchens to her sitting room. She needed time to compose herself.

'What shall I do?' asked Cissie, getting to her feet, 'the Grand Morrow is still angry with me for not telling her about the children's plans. I-I should have warned her!'

'Let's see what she has to say,' added Neeps, tending to Cissie's wounds.

'Come on, Cissie, it can't be any worse than confronting those Shroves,' said Ruker, her face beginning to darken and bruise from fighting with the Shroves.

So, a reluctant Cissie followed the Skinks out of the darkness of the Shrove hole, fearful that the traumas they had endured that night were not over yet.

*

In the grand sitting room, Agatha and her sisters were waiting anxiously for the others to join them. Sybilla was fiddling with her black-headed pins while Edwina fanned herself, muttering all the while about betrayal and underhandedness. The sisters had suffered a ghastly fright, being woken in the middle of the night and having to endure the appalling altercation and revelation in the Shrove hole.

'Shall we have tea?' asked Agatha, calming herself and summoning the maid.

There was a moment of silence and neither sister answered the Grand Morrow.

'Oh my,' muttered Sybilla, biting her lip. 'Agatha dear, I-I believe I have done something dreadful.'

'What now?' asked Edwina, sounding flustered.

'I'm afraid that I told Florré …' she hesitated. 'I told Florré certain things that I shouldn't.'

'What did you tell him?' asked Agatha, distracted momentarily as the Skinks and Cissie entered the room, hovering uncertainly by the doorway.

Sybilla sat anxiously wringing her hands.

'I told him all our plans!' she blurted out. 'That we were going to break the Morrow pact and that we were going to rescue Tallitha and the others.'

'Did you tell them how we intended to do that?' asked Edwina.

'No dear, I didn't,' she hesitated, 'I don't know how we are going to do it.'

'That's all fine then dear, and you mustn't fret,' replied Edwina.

'Sybilla, the Shroves are not our trusted servants anymore - if indeed they ever were.' Agatha's face darkened. 'It seems that that they have betrayed us to the Swarm,' she added.

Sybilla closed her eyes tightly shut. The tears squeezed from under her eyelids and ran down her cheeks.

'It's too much to bear,' she sobbed, 'everything in our world is changing.'

'It will all be better once we get the children home,' said Agatha stoically, handing Sybilla a handkerchief and gesticulating towards the others to join them.

Cissie hung back, waiting for the moment when the Grand Morrow would admonish her and send her away again.

'You mustn't be cross with dear Cissie,' Sybilla announced, sniffing and trying to recover. 'I can't bear any more unhappiness.' Sybilla bent her head towards Agatha and whispered in her ear. 'Now is the time to tell her the truth.' She smiled encouragingly at her sister.

Agatha Morrow flushed and turned her head away.

'Sybilla is right,' added Edwina firmly, indicating to the maid to leave the tea tray.

Agatha occupied herself by pouring the tea.

'Well?' barked Edwina.

'I will do this in my own time,' her sister replied sternly, motioning for Cissie to approach her.

'What is it, my Lady?' Cissie asked.

The Grand Morrow's face looked haggard. She cleared her throat and continued.

'You have served this family well,' she faltered, 'and you were trying to do what you considered to be right. I know that now and ...' she paused and looked towards the mountains in the distance. 'I-I was wrong to send you away.'

'You must tell her everything,' demanded Edwina crisply, 'or I will.'

Tears came into Agatha Morrow's eyes.

'I'm afraid I made a terrible mistake,' she cried.

Sybilla pulled a handkerchief from her sleeve and passed it to her sister.

'My Lady?' asked Cissie, sounding perplexed.

'Whatever my past misdeeds, I will make you a solemn promise, Cissie.' She hesitated and wiped her eyes 'We will get all our children home again, including Danny.'

'My Danny!' Cissie cried desperately. 'But I-I don't understand.'

Agatha's head sunk to her chest.

'Come, Agatha, you must tell her.' said Edwina.

Agatha gazed down at her lap then raised her head, holding Cissie's bewildered eyes with hers.

'This is hard for me, Cissie,' she said, her resolve wavering as she spoke.

'Come, dear,' Sybilla urged gently.

'The fateful night your boy disappeared, the Dooerlins were able to steal into Winderling Spires because of me and my ill thought through actions.' She stopped and dabbed her eyes. 'I was desperate, you see!' she cried, 'and so I summoned the Grand Witch Kastra to help me find Asenathe – but I failed.' She covered her face and sobbed.

Sybilla took her sister's hand. 'Go on, Agatha,' she insisted.

'Somehow the spell that I cast ruptured, and the Grand Witch Selvistra came in Kastra's place. I could do nothing to stop her,' she wept. 'Then the Dooerlins followed that same night and stole Danny away,' she sobbed.

The colour drained from Cissie's face.

'But why didn't you tell me before?' she murmured, astonished at what she had just heard. 'Why all this secrecy, and for all these years?'

'Agatha was afraid, Cissie. She thought the villagers would take your side and would never forgive her for dabbling in such reckless witchcraft,' answered Sybilla.

Cissie stumbled, grabbing hold of an armchair for support.

'I-I knew in my heart it was those hateful creatures that took my boy,' Cissie faltered. 'But you did wrong not to tell me, my Lady.'

'I'm so sorry,' said Agatha rising and stepping towards Cissie.

But the nurse turned her face away. 'All these years, not knowing the truth!' she cried. 'I tried not to listen to the village gossip that you were all witches and that you were responsible in some way.'

Cissie covered her face. She had given up hope of ever finding her boy again, not after all this time. It couldn't be true, could it?

Edwina bristled and looked rather put out.

'I wouldn't call us witches exactly,' she replied tartly. 'It is true we each have our own special powers but we're no match for the Grand Witches of the Larva Coven. Their magic is old and strong. The plain fact is, Agatha was foolish to attempt that spell on her own.'

The Grand Morrow flushed at her sister's words.

'I have been wrong about a great many things,' she said

forlornly, looking out of the window towards the grey peaks in the distance. 'Forcing Asenathe's betrothal, using that dangerous spell to find her and not listening to Essie and about Tallitha too! I have been pig-headed,' she added.

'And we trusted the Shroves,' said Edwina angrily, 'when all the time they were spying on us, in our own house too! Taking information back to the Swarm! Betraying us …'

'I'm afraid there's something else you should know.' Ruker interrupted, stepping towards the sisters. 'Whilst we're on the subject of spying.'

'Oh no! Who else can't we trust?' asked Agatha warily.

'Snowdroppe,' answered Ruker flatly.

'Snowdroppe!' the sisters cried in unison.

'What do you mean?' asked Edwina, peering at the Skink.

'She's the Thane's daughter. She has tricked and bewitched you all.'

Agatha clutched the arm of her chair.

'I always mistrusted that vain creature,' she cried passionately. 'She entered our lives so mysteriously; there was no one to vouch for her. But Maximillian was a lovesick fool from the moment he set eyes on her. She spun a very pretty lie about having no family!'

'She certainly bewitched Maximillian, my feckless son, but not me, not after they were married at least. She became so heartless. He was a fool to marry her,' added Edwina sadly.

Agatha beckoned to Ruker.

'Who else is involved in their trickery?'

It was all too much to bear.

'I'm afraid Benedict has also betrayed the family,' the Skink replied.

'He's Snowdroppe's nephew and his mother is Queen Asphodel. She is the one who handed us over to the Murk Mowl,' added Neeps. 'Snowdroppe and Asphodel are sisters.'

'The Thane's daughters,' added Ruker.

The three sisters sat motionless. Agatha's mouth twitched involuntarily.

'I feel quite faint,' muttered Sybilla.

'Sickened!' cried Edwina.

'I knew Snowdroppe was a liar. She tricked me about that boy, Benedict – a shameful deception!' Agatha stood up, gripped the table and stared towards the Out-Of-The-Way Mountains. Then she turned to face the assembled company.

'You must go back. Find Tallitha and all our children.' She eyed the Skinks and Cissie keenly. 'This dangerous quest is down to you, now. We are too old to make the journey to Breedoor.' Agatha sighed. 'If I abandon Wycham Elva now the Dooerlins would see it as their perfect moment to invade Winderling Spires and take our lands.'

'But what about the Morrow pact?' asked Ruker. 'We don't know how to destroy it! How we can help Tallitha?'

'Oh, we know about that, don't we, dear?' said Sybilla, her eyes twinkling.

The Skinks watched as the sisters huddled together and began whispering behind their hands.

'We have to tell them,' said Edwina.

They lifted their heads and nodded to one another.

'We have made contact with Septimia Morrow,' she said finally.

Cissie gasped. 'But she's lying in the family mausoleum. She's dead!'

'Of course she's dead, Cissie, but we have our ways,' added Edwina coyly.

'You've never been making contact with the spirits!' cried Cissie, throwing her hands up in horror.

'It's my special gift,' said Edwina proudly.

'What did this spirit tell you?' asked Ruker warily.

The sisters looked gravely at one another.

'About how to destroy that cursed pact and about the Morrow child,' replied Agatha.

'Who's that?' asked Neeps.

'Arabella Dorothea, the child Edwyn Morrow gave to his witch, Kastra, in exchange for helping him escape from Wycham Elva,' answered Edwina.

'But that's the name on the child's coffin! She lies buried in the family mausoleum beside Septimia herself!' cried Cissie. 'I knew there was something fishy about her tomb – it just didn't add up what with the family crest being missing! It was all a hoax – that child didn't die, she was secreted away!'

'Her father was Arthur Edwyn Morrow!' explained Agatha. 'The first Thane of the Morrow Swarm.'

'Oh my word,' said Cissie, muttering an old Wycham saying to herself.

The old sisters began whispering together once more.

'Go on,' demanded Edwina, 'you must tell them what we have discovered!'

'Yes, yes I will,' replied the Grand Morrow.

She stepped towards her sewing box, opened the lid and produced an envelope sealed with wax.

'I have been keeping this safe, hoping that we would find a way of passing this information to Tallitha.' Agatha handed the envelope to Ruker. 'It's all written down in this note,' she said, looking gravely from Cissie to the Skinks.

'What is it?' Ruker asked.

'It's our only hope of getting the children back,' Agatha replied.

'Dabbling with the spirits,' muttered Cissie, 'it isn't right!'

'There is only one way out of this mess. Somehow Tallitha has to find the courage to break the Morrow pact,' added Agatha.

'So you must find Tallitha and Essie, and all the others.' said Edwina

'The note explains what they must do to break the pact and how to make contact with the dead child.' said Agatha.

'Ghosts, you mean, don't you?' whispered Cissie.

Sybilla smiled sweetly and twiddled with her black-headed pins, glancing first at Edwina and then at Agatha.

'If we are right, and if Tallitha can follow Septimia's instructions, then the Morrow ghosts might well be on our side!' added Edwina.

'Then we can be rid of that curse and the wretched Swarm

once and for all!' cried Agatha passionately.

'It won't be easy,' added Neeps

'They'll be meddling with the supernatural, sinister goings-on that should be left well alone!' Cissie cried.

'We have no choice. This dark path seems to be the only hope of saving them from the Swarm,' said Ruker.

But deep down, she knew that the task ahead was full of danger, for the children, for Essie and for them all.

# Eight

Cissie's heart was racing! The enormity of what she had just been told was going round and round in her head. Grand Witches, spells going wrong, the Dooerlins stealing into the Spires and the Grand Morrow's involvement in it all! How had these secrets been kept from her for so long? She feared that her sweet boy was lost forever, yet perhaps there was hope and he was still alive, waiting for her to find him. Did the Grand Morrow's confession shed any light on that fateful night? Was there a chance she would see Danny again?

'What am I to do?' she whispered, running her fingers over Danny's tattered boat.

She was in a terrible quandary. Part of her wanted to hide away in Winderling Spires, to settle back into her old life and forget the dreadful events of the past but another part yearned to travel with the Skinks to find Tallitha and perhaps even her boy.

The journey through the dark tunnel filled her with dread.

What if she didn't have the stamina to keep up with the Skinks? What if she got lost underground in the darkness? What if she never came home again? There had to be another way. Cissie resolved to speak to the Skinks at the earliest opportunity and persuade them to take an alternative route – one that didn't involve the hideous Shrove tunnel.

When she found them, Ruker and Neeps were busy in the kitchen, packing supplies ready for their journey. At all costs, Cissie was desperate to avoid the nosy housekeeper. Spooner and Lince had told her all about Mrs Armitage's tiresome questions and Cissie was in no mood to face her. She sidled up to the Skinks as they joked with the cook, Edna Dibbens, who was trussing up a batch of pheasants and quails for roasting.

The Skinks had made the Cook laugh so much, with their hilarious tales and hair-raising adventures, that she had given them lots of extra special titbits for their journey.

'Seven, eight, ten! Stop foolin' about you two! You're making me lose count of these damned birds,' she giggled, holding her sides. 'Barney!' Edna hollered at the chubby kitchen boy, 'bring some stuffed chicken parcels and woodpigeon pies.'

The kitchen table was covered with goose and chicken pates, golden pies, goose dripping and mounds of feathers from the kitchen boy's reluctant plucking.

'Eh, my sides are splittin',' she cried, laughing and digging Neeps in the ribs. 'You never told me these two were such good fun!' she announced merrily as Cissie entered the kitchen.

The tears were streaming down her plump, rosy cheeks.

Cissie had too many things on her mind to join in their banter. She also failed to notice the figure hovering behind the glass partition in the passageway.

'Well I never!' exclaimed Mrs Armitage, bustling into the kitchen, 'if it isn't Cissie Wakenshaw!'

'Now then, Mrs Armitage,' answered Cissie warily, holding the housekeeper's gaze before turning away and helping the cook to finish packing their bags.

'Well don't just stand there,' the housekeeper added, 'Come into my parlour and take a cup of tea with me.'

'That's kind of you, but I've got a lot to do,' Cissie replied pointing at the food parcels.

But the housekeeper remained undeterred and held open the passage door, gesticulating at Cissie to accompany her. 'Edna has made a bakewell tart – and you and I could have a nice little chat, catch up on everything that's happened recently.'

'Another time, I'm afraid, I'm really very busy as you can see,' Cissie answered awkwardly.

'Well! That's nice,' the housekeeper mumbled, 'try and be friendly and look where it gets you!'

Mrs Armitage put her nose in the air, stomped off into her parlour and banged the door shut.

'Oh dear,' murmured Cissie, shaking her head.

Somehow she would have to make amends with Mrs Armitage. It wouldn't do to get on the wrong side of her. For now, though, she had bigger problems to worry about.

Cissie beckoned to the Skinks to follow her into the shadows of the scullery passageway. They ambled over, munching on succulent chicken legs.

'What's the problem?' asked Neeps, observing Cissie's agitated state.

'I've been thinking,' she whispered, 'now that the Grand Morrow has given us her blessing, there's no need to use that infernal tunnel,' she began, her eyes straying nervously towards the pantry door. 'So I've a suggestion – we could travel across country. My brother, Josh, would be happy to put us up at High Bedders End. Let's forget all about that nasty Shrove tunnel.'

Ruker licked her fingers and wiped her greasy hands down her trousers. Unbeknown to Cissie, the Skinks were eagerly anticipating the prospect of exploring the Shroves' tunnel. It had to be an extension to the cave system that ran beneath the Out-Of-The-Way Mountains.

'Neeps and I have already discussed all the options,' she explained. 'We know that Snowdroppe used the Shrove tunnel to travel to Hellstone Tors. Granted we can't travel as fast but we think it's a direct route to the Startling Caves.'

'Besides, we could discover things about the Swarm down there,' added Neeps excitedly.

Cissie's face fell. The Skinks were set on exploring the sinister tunnel. Her plan had not worked.

'I-I'm not sure I can make the journey, not down that awful tunnel – I'm not as young as I once was.'

'Nonsense, of course you can! We'll hear no more about it. Will we, Neeps?'

Neeps nodded enthusiastically, wiping his mouth on the back of his hand.

So their plan was fixed. They were all going to venture down the vile, black Shrove tunnel.

*

Later, Cissie said her farewells to the Morrow sisters, made her way down the dark steps underneath the pantry and cautiously stepped into the subterranean world of the Winderling Shroves. The candlelight from Cissie's lantern flickered across the tunnel walls, streaked moss-green by the trickling water, and shone into the dark beyond, where the sound of dripping water echoed far away into the distance. As Cissie edged further down the narrow passageway, the light from her lantern landed on a grotesque carving in the rock.

'Heaven preserve us!' she cried, 'what's that horrible thing? It's staring right at me with a nasty pointed beak and beady eyes!'

The Skinks hurried over to investigate.

'Look there!' shouted Neeps, as the light from his lantern alighted on a row of ravens' heads with sharp beaks and piercing eyes.

The intricate carvings stood proud on the rock face. Their heads were cocked to one side in the midst of squawking, their sharp beaks waiting to snap and peck.

'This place gives me the collywobbles!' Cissie shuddered, stepping back.

The tunnel fulfilled her worst imaginings. It was cold, oppressive and dark as the grave; a sinister place where dreadful things could happen at any moment.

Oddly, the Skinks seemed to be thoroughly enjoying their underground adventure.

'This is a great tunnel,' said Neeps, his eyes gleaming with delight, tapping the walls and sizing up the structure.

'Better than the Shrunken Butts,' added Ruker cheerily, 'that was like being in a tomb.'

'Oh my,' Cissie murmured, clutching her lantern.

The ominous birds had unsettled her and she wished that the Skinks wouldn't talk about their potholing adventures. What if the tunnel became narrower, hemming her in on all sides? The hideous darkness was overwhelming. She peered frantically at the roof and imagined the weight of rock bearing down on her. *Stop it! Think about something else …* She tried to fix her thoughts on finding Tallitha and Danny; anything to take her mind off the horrible darkness!

Cissie clutched the toy boat in her pocket and repeated a Wycham saying for good luck, putting one shaky foot in front of the other. But it wasn't easy, the tunnel went on and on, and each step into the inky blackness felt like torture.

'What's that noise?' she called out frantically to the Skinks.

Ruker squeezed her hand.

'Just creatures going about their business.'

'Rats and mice?' she cried, 'oh my, I hate vermin!'

Neeps led her onward, telling her tales of their adventures to take her mind off things, about potholing and cave swimming, climbing up long dark precipices and down steep ravines. But it didn't seem to help one bit.

'So you see, this tunnel is as safe as the old house,' Neeps added.

'Winderling Spires is not a safe place,' Cissie replied uneasily, 'you never know what's round the next corner.'

Huge dancing shadows crowded around her in the flickering light, licking up the walls, fleeting across the roof and making her stomach turn somersaults.

Up ahead, the tunnel seemed to shrink before Cissie's eyes and it sloped ominously downwards.

'I can't go in there,' Cissie wailed, grabbing Neeps arm. 'What if I get stuck?'

'We'll guide you,' answered Ruker, trying to reassure her. 'Get in between us,' she urged.

Cissie held on to Ruker as Neeps brought up the rear, edging down, slipping and sliding down the pathway, to Cissie's consternation. Eventually they reached the bottom of the slope and stepped out into a cave.A waterfall cascaded through the rocks high above them, forming a pool at their feet.

'This must be an underground tributary from Shivering Water,' said Ruker, lifting her lantern to illuminate the way ahead.

'And there's another raven's head,' said Neeps shining his lantern across the water.

On the other side of the pool a bird's head was eerily positioned over another tunnel.

'My hunch is that the raven will lead us in the direction of the mountains,' said Ruker

The pathway snaked by the edge of the pool where the water glistened in the light from their lanterns. Neeps raced ahead to inspect the tunnel.

But Cissie lagged behind.

'Can we stop?' she asked, 'I'm so tired – I knew I'd slow you down.'

Her heart pounded and her legs ached.

Ruker nodded and sat on a boulder, making a space for Cissie beside her.

'Cor, what a feast!' said Neeps pulling out the supplies that Edna Dibbens had prepared. 'Just take a look at these plum pies,' he said biting down on the sweet, juicy pastry.

'Meat pasties,' added Ruker excitedly, breaking the golden pie in half. The thick gravy ran down her chin. The Skinks munched away on the cook's picnic but Cissie had no appetite.

'What's troubling you?' asked Ruker, wiping her mouth.

Cissie's face was pale and she looked worn out.

'How on earth will I get across that pool?' she asked, scanning the breadth of water shimmering before her. 'What if I fall in? I can't swim.'

'Don't fret, it'll be easy,' Neeps replied, 'we'll use the stepping stones.'

He lifted his lantern to reveal a line of flat stones that hugged the edge of the pool. Cissie wasn't convinced.

When they had finished eating, Ruker went first, leaping across the stones and landing at the other side.

'Take my hand, hold it tight,' Neeps insisted.

Cissie took a few steps and wobbled. The thought of what lurked beneath them in the eerie blackness made her body tremble.

'Steady there,' called Neeps as he gripped her hand more tightly.

'Don't let me slip,' she begged, taking another uncertain step as the Skinks encouraged her across.

The reflection from the lanterns danced across the water. Cissie thought about saying how pretty the blue lights were, shimmering across the surface, but she decided against it. She needed all her strength to stay on her feet.

'That's it, right foot here, left foot over there – now, hold on tight.'

'Neeps!' she called out, 'I'm going to fall!'

'No you're not,' he answered, reaching out and steadying her.

Eventually Neeps guided a reluctant Cissie across the pool but it had taken a long time.

She should never have agreed to come in the first place! The Skinks were agile and fit, whereas she was unsure of her bearings, teetering from stepping stone to stepping stone and she ached from head to toe.

'This way,' Ruker called excitedly.

The Skink disappeared down a tunnel that had suddenly opened up before them.

*More tunnels! More darkness!* Cissie thought desperately.

'Be brave, focus on finding the children,' she repeated again and again to herself. 'Maybe even finding my dear boy.'

Cissie took a deep breath, held up her lantern, scanned the entranceway and gingerly stepped into the grim opening. Inside the cave walls were smeared with the familiar moss-green and lined with deep red streaks. Mounds of recently hewn gemstones were piled high against the walls.

'Bloodstones,' announced Ruker.

'I wonder who mines these tunnels?' asked Neeps apprehensively.

'Probably Groats,' replied Ruker scathingly, kicking at a pile of stones.

Cissie shuddered at the thought of the creatures that lived so deep underground.

'If I wasn't so scared I'd think this place was almost pretty, what with those twinkling blue lights back there,' she announced.

The Skinks froze.

'What did you say?' asked Ruker turning swiftly to face her.

'The blue lights that were twinkling in the pool,' she answered.

The Skinks looked about nervously.

'Just look at your faces! What have I said now?' she asked warily.

'Did you notice anything?' asked Neeps.

Ruker shook her head. 'But if you're right Cissie, then the Groats are tracking us.'

'Those lights are the reflection of their eyes in the water,' explained Neeps.

Now Cissie's heart was thumping out of her chest.

'Groats!' she cried, horrified. 'What do they want with us?'

But the Skinks had no time to answer. From out of the darkness, just a little way ahead of them, came a sudden clattering and the sound of creatures hollering to one another.

'What's that?' asked Cissie, desperately.

'Shhhh!' hissed Ruker.

The sound of pounding feet echoed down the tunnel.

'What is it?' Cissie asked desperately.

'I don't know,' replied Ruker.

Cissie held her breath.

'Groats! Quick!' a stranger's voice called out, 'they're coming this way!'

Neeps doused their lanterns. Then everything went pitch-black.

'Ruker! Neeps!' Cissie called out, 'Where are you?'

There was the sound of muffled voices and shushing then a hand went over Cissie's mouth. It was cold and clammy. She tried to scream but only a stifled noise came out.

'Hurry, they're coming!' another voice yelled.

In the next moment, Cissie was bundled down the tunnel by a number of unidentifiable creatures. They were racing ahead, dragging her forward. They smelled strongly of Shrove.

'She's too slow!' shouted a stranger's voice 'Carry her!'

Cissie struggled to get free but it was useless.

Then someone grabbed her around the waist and tipped her upwards, over their shoulder. She bumped about, hanging

113

upside down. She felt dizzy, she was going to faint.

There was a terrible screeching sound and voices shouting, warning them to beware!

Then Cissie blacked out and knew no more.

# Nine

'Wake up, you're safe now,' said a kindly voice.

Pester was busily patting Cissie's cheek.

Cissie anxiously opened her eyes and blinked. She was staring into the face of a Shrove! She could feel the creature's breath, hot against her cheek. The Shrove was going to bite her!

'Get away from me!' Cissie cried, trying to scramble away.

She was still underground, pressed tightly against the rock, but for some reason Ruker and Neeps were grinning at her.

'It's all right Cissie, no need to be scared. This is Pester. She's our dear friend. She's rescued us from many a hair-raising escapade,' explained Ruker.

'But she's a Shrove!' she gasped. 'Are you playing tricks on me?'

The Skinks laughed.

'The Cave-Shroves are distant cousins of the Winderling Shroves, with much nicer manners!' replied Neeps.

It was all too much for Cissie to take in. She remembered the horrible dark caves; the terrifying noise, being up-ended onto someone's back and then fainting.

'Where are we? What happened?' she mumbled, staring at the Cave-Shroves as they bustled about their well-lit cave.

'The Groats were tracking you and almost had you cornered,' explained the cave-Shrove they called Pester. 'So we headed them off and brought you to one of our hide-outs.'

But Cissie wasn't convinced. She couldn't get used to the strange looking creatures. They were definitely of the Shrove variety. They certainly smelled of Shrove, and yet they seemed to have kindly natures. A far cry from the vicious Winderling creatures!

'Don't look so alarmed,' Ruker said, sitting down next to her. 'Let me tell you all about our friends and how they helped us the last time we were in a pickle.'

So Cissie sat and listened, watching the Cave-Shroves out of the corner of her eye as they busied about keeping the cave warm by stoking a small stove in the corner.

As Ruker told her story, Cissie's heart stopped fluttering and she came to realise that these creatures meant her no harm. Quite the contrary, they had saved her from a devilish pack of Groats and they were also responsible for rescuing Tallitha and Tyaas.

'I've still got your old backpacks,' said Ernelle, handing the Skinks their belongings, left behind at the Shrunken Butts.

Inside were knives, ropes and the paraphernalia needed for

survival in the caves.

'Where are we?' asked Neeps, trying to get a fix on their position.

Underground, one cave looked very much like another.

'Just below Ragging Brows Forest and the Holly Pot Ghyll,' replied Ernelle.

'Home,' whispered Cissie softly, tears coming into her eyes. 'I want to go home.'

'But we haven't started yet,' said Neeps, sounding exasperated.

'That's what frightens me. I haven't the stamina for this desperate place and I can't keep up with you. Take me home, please?'

Ruker raised an eyebrow at Neeps.

'Cissie, you'll be fine,' added Ruker.

'No I won't! I'm not cut out for this sort of thing. I've made my mind up. I'll only slow you down or put you in more danger!'

Cissie folded her arms. It was clear she wouldn't budge unless the Skinks accepted she could go home to High Bedders End.

'If you're sure,' said Neeps, 'but you'll miss out on a great adventure.'

'I'm sure,' replied Cissie firmly. 'You can tell me all about it on your way back to Winderling Spires – once you have rescued the children,' replied Cissie firmly.

So that was the end of Cissie's exploration of the tunnels under the land of Wycham Elva.

Once they had rested and Cissie had been persuaded to eat a blindworm pudding or two to get her strength back, the Cave-

Shroves showed them a secret route out of the underground labyrinth. Although the climb exhausted her, when Cissie saw sunlight once more her heart leapt.

'The farm is over yonder,' she called to the Skinks, pointing across the valley, 'come on,' she said excitedly, 'I can't wait to see our Josh.'

After a short trek across country, the Skinks deposited Cissie at the farmyard gate.

'Well now, you're a sight for sore eyes,' said her brother, racing down the path and giving her a big hug.

Sticker and Barney came bounding along the farm track, their tails wagging behind them, jumping up to lick Cissie and make her welcome.

'Bettie!' she cried, as her sister-in-law came happily towards her with her arms outstretched.

'You're most welcome!' Josh said to the Skinks, shaking their hands.

The women cried at the sight of one another.

'You'll never guess where I've been?' cried Cissie, launching herself into her sister-in-law's arms. 'Oh Bettie, it was so awful down there; wet, dark and full of peculiar critters. I don't know how I managed it!'

'I'm sure it was awful! Come on, let's have a cuppa,' said Bettie putting her arm round her sister-in-law and leading her into the kitchen.

'Aunt Cissie!' shouted Spooner, as she raced out of the barn.

'You're back!' cried Lince.

The girls were excited to see their aunt but in truth they were more interested in making a beeline for the Skinks. They wanted to hear the latest news, all about the strange old house and the Shroves and about what had happened after they had high-tailed it out of Winderling Spires. The image of the old sisters, meddling with witchcraft was still imprinted on Spooner's brain!

'Calm down, the pair of you,' said Cissie, 'let's have a pot of tea and I'll tell you all about it.'

That evening, everyone sat down to a delicious farmhouse supper. Bettie had done them proud with roast beef, fresh vegetables and pickles, summer pudding and lashings of custard.

'Neeps and I have been talking,' said Ruker thoughtfully after they had cleared away the dishes. 'That was a close call down there. We only just avoided being captured by those Groats.'

'That was thanks to Ernelle and Pester, and their knowledge of the underground tunnels,' added Neeps.

'We've used the route underground before, from the Startling Caves,' explained Ruker. 'So now that we've broken the journey we've a mind to continue through Ragging Brows Forest instead of going back underground.'

'I guess you know best,' replied Josh, lighting his pipe.

'Changed your mind, Cissie?' asked Neeps, 'because this was your original idea back in the Spires.'

'As much as I want to find the children and my Danny,' she said, her eyes meeting her brother's, 'I've had enough adventures to last me a life time. I'm afraid it's down to you,' she added looking from Ruker to Neeps.

Now she was content to stay with her family in the cosy farmhouse.

Later, as Cissie and Bettie chatted in the kitchen, Josh whistled for the dogs, lit his pipe and strode out of the farmyard and up onto the hills accompanied by Ruker and Neeps. It was a beautiful evening, still and warm, as Josh smoked his pipe and looked back over the misty marshes towards Wycham Elva. Unbeknown to him, Spooner and Lince, desperate to overhear the Skinks plans had sneaked up the hillside, edging through the long grass.

'Penny for them,' said Ruker, coming up behind Josh.

'I was wondering how you were going to get inside Hellstone Tors without being seen,' asked the farmer with a worried expression on his face.

'A Skink will stick out, that's for sure,' said Neeps joining the pair, 'but we've time to plan tactics on our journey.'

'Even if you do manage it, how will you rescue them?' the farmer asked, 'it'll be difficult to get past those guards.'

'Somehow we'll get a message to Tallitha,' continued Ruker.

As Josh knocked his pipe out on the bridling gate he caught sight of his daughters bobbing across the hillside. There was a flash of Lince's golden hair; it had given them away again.

'You two been ear-wigging?' he asked, raising an eyebrow.

He was determined his girls wouldn't get into trouble again, not after their encounter in Ragging Brows Forest.

Spooner grinned at her dad and sidled up beside the Skinks. 'Please tell us about the old house again and about how you saw off those Shroves!'

'Yeah,' said Lince, 'and about Aunt Cissie makin' up with the old sisters and her confrontation with that nosey housekeeper, Mrs what-do-you-call-her.'

Josh laughed at their antics. He knew he was an inveterate worrier and this time he was certain he was worrying for no reason. The girls seemed more interested in the goings-on at Winderling Spires and the Shroves rather than the Skinks' treacherous journey into the mysterious land of Breedoor.

*

'Can you see them yet?' murmured Spooner, peeking through the branches.

Dusk was setting in and Ragging Brows Forest was quietening down for the night in the unsettling way it always did. The birds had stopped singing and the forest light had taken on a hazy, listless pallor. Lince raised her head above a fallen log, her hair now covered with a woollen hat, and peered into the darkening distance. But there was no sign of the Skinks.

'They were here a minute ago,' she replied anxiously, turning to her sister. 'Those hounds will be on the rampage soon. Let's go home and try again tomorrow. We know where the Skinks are headed.'

'Stop frettin'! As long as we use one of the Skinks' burrows, the hounds won't be able to catch us,' Spooner replied with her usual certainty.

All the same, she deftly primed her bow and arrow.

Lince never ceased to be amazed at her sister's bravery, or her stupidity – she could never decide which it was.

'But it's so quiet here, so creepy. It gives me the shivers,' Lince replied, staring fearfully about her.

The hoary, twisted forest was slipping into darkness with every second. Rising mists seeped from the earth and the grey-faced owls hooted overhead, their beady eyes bobbing and watching the two girls as they crept across the forest floor.

'I know what I'm doing,' Spooner grumbled, her hand poised on the bow. 'Who was it that braved it here last time while you babysat our mam?' she snapped.

Lince groaned. There was no point trying to persuade her sister to leave just when it was getting interesting.

'Please sis, let's find that Skink burrow, just in case,' Lince suggested.

'There's one over there,' whispered her sister, pointing towards a tree stump.

Then there was a crack! A branch snapped behind them – the noise ricocheting through the trees.

'What was that?' asked Lince, glued to the spot.

Spooner carefully parted the undergrowth behind them, peering into the gloaming as the mists circled with milk-white tendrils. Then, in the half-light, she spotted a pair of yellow eyes staring straight at her and behind them, another pair, eerily glinting in the gloom. Lince gripped her sister's arm.

'Sis! It's the Black Hounds! I-I can see their horrible eyes – glinting at us,' she whispered hoarsely.

'We'll have to make a run for that burrow,' replied Spooner, desperately searching for the quickest route.

'Will we make it in time?' asked Lince desperately.

'If we're really, really fast – let's make a run for it – NOW!' She cried.

Spooner leapt into the air, grabbed her sister's hand and together they raced through the tangled undergrowth, jumping through bracken and bounding over tree stumps, their arms and legs flying in all directions. The two lone hounds growled viciously and took up the chase, pounding across the forest floor, their paws crunching through the pine needles and their blood-red eyes pinned on their quarry.

'Do something!' cried Lince, glancing behind her. 'They're gaining on us!'

In a split-second, Spooner spun like the wind, took aim with her long bow and shot her arrow as one of the hounds leapt high into the air, drooling with bloodlust. Lince vaulted towards the entrance of the burrow as the point of the arrow sank into the hound's breast. It howled, dropping to the earth with a pitiful yelp as its mate raced to the rescue.

'Get inside – arrrrrr ...,' screamed Spooner as she leapt towards the entranceway.

But her words vanished as they were sucked down into the dark, black earth.

Ruker grabbed hold of Spooner's legs and pulled her through the opening as Neeps shot out of the burrow and captured Lince with one violent swoop.

'Arrrrrggggghhh,' they screamed, as they fell headlong into the peaty burrow.

It smelt of stale vegetation that had been mouldering away in the dark for too long.

'Quick,' shouted Ruker, 'fasten down the hatch!'

Neeps hurriedly battened down the entranceway, latching a heavy wooden door tightly shut against the strong tree roots. On the other side, the growls of a lone hound filled the twilight, scratching and baying into the night, trying desperately to get at them.

'That hound will never get in,' shouted Ruker, squirrelling away under the twisted roots and beckoning to the others to follow.

She lit a taper and surveyed the grubby girls in the meagre light. Her almond shaped eyes shone in the candlelight and flashed with anger.

'What are you two playing at?' she cried, 'Josh and Bettie will be beside themselves with worry. You can't come with us.'

'We want to help find Tallitha and the others,' pleaded Spooner pulling leaves out of her dark hair. 'Just think about it, we can get inside the castle without being noticed.'

The girl had a point.

'But what about your parents?' asked Neeps.

'You can send a message to tell them we're safe, then it'll be too late to come after us.'

'Can't be done,' said Ruker firmly. 'They'll never forgive us.'

'But we can't go back now!' Lince exclaimed, looking uneasily at the hatch. 'There'll be hounds all over the forest soon!'

'Tomorrow, Spelk will take you back to the farm.' Ruker replied firmly.

'Good try though,' added Neeps, winking at Spooner.

She pulled a face and slumped to the ground. Their plan hadn't worked out the way they had planned it.

Later, up in Hanging Tree Islands, the girls enjoyed the delights of the Skinks' tavern. Lince had never tasted Squirrel Scratchings before whereas Spooner played it like an old hand.

'Last time we were here I had a pint,' she said, showing off in front of her sister and grinning expectantly at Neeps.

'That's two pints of Drunken Badger Stout and two halves of Beamish Pear Crush,' said Neeps. He turned to the girls. 'Don't worry, the cider has alcohol in it. Add a cherry for good luck,' he said to the Skink behind the bar.

The Skink behind the bar slipped a slice of pear and two cherries into each glass. The girls cheered up enormously and began sipping their pear cider through twisted paper straws as the Skinks huddled together to discuss the details of their journey ahead.

The girls sat riveted by their side, making a mental note of each cave and of the twists and turns to be avoided.

Spooner smiled, almost a little too sweetly, and then winked at her sister.

Of course, she had another trick up her sleeve.

# Ten

**M**uprid Morrow was sulking. She was in a big fat fug of a mood that only she did best. The petulant girl sat in her dressing room, red in the face and sighing, surrounded by mounds of clothes and heaps of boots scattered across the floor.

'Where are my green riding boots?' she snapped, flinging shoes and boots out of her enormous wardrobe. The discarded items flew across the room and landed at Lapis's feet. Muprid turned her sour face and scowled at her sister.

'Have you been wearing them?' she asked impatiently.

'Why should I wear your silly boots?'

Lapis shot her sister a withering look, turned on her heel and began applying perfume to her smooth white throat.

'But I wanted to wear them today,' Muprid complained. 'They go so well with my riding habit.'

Muprid slumped on the bed with a sullen look marring her perfectly made-up face.

'Get Wince to find them,' Lapis urged. She was bored with her sister's foul temper. She stopped powdering her nose. 'Anyway, where is that good-for-nothing Shrove? I haven't seen him since …' Lapis touched up her lipstick and pondered, turning swiftly on her chair to face Muprid. 'Actually, I haven't seen him for days!'

'I'll ring for him now,' her sister replied eagerly.

But although Lapis rang the Shrove's bell there was no response.

'You can never find a Shrove when you want one,' Lapis moaned. 'Call for that weasel Embellsed, he'll know where Wince has got to,' she announced, brushing her silky tresses.

When the sisters' call came, Embellsed was in his Shrove hole, chewing his fingers and fretting about his murderous act, certain that the Swarm would discover his heinous crime. He jumped out of his skin when the bell rang. But there was nothing for it – he had to obey the summons.

Embellsed appeared at the door to the sisters' apartment and hovered uncertainly.

'Yes, m'Ladies, what can I do for you?' he asked meekly, hopping about.

'Where's Wince?' Muprid demanded, slanting her cold blue eyes in his direction. 'I want my green riding boots now!' demanded the peevish girl.

'Let me help you find them, m'Lady,' offered Embellsed, trotting towards the dressing room.

Lapis leapt to her feet and pinched his arm.

'But we don't want you, dirt-eater! We want *our* Shrove,' she said menacingly, nipping even harder. 'So where is he?'

Embellsed shrank away, warily looking from one evil sister to the other.

They peered at him, their ruby-coloured lips distorted with spite. Their faces held nothing but disdain for the servant. Lapis grabbed him by the ear, nipping his flesh between her fingernails until she left a bright red weal.

'Ouch!' he cried, 'please m'Ladies, let me go!'

'Not until you tell us where he is!' shouted Muprid. 'Spit it out!'

'I-I don't know!' he bleated miserably, 'I haven't seen him …'

'That's a lie!' shouted Lapis. 'You miserable Shroves live cheek by jowl in those nasty Shrove holes.' Her mouth wrinkled distastefully at the thought of their fetid lairs. 'And you know everyone's business.'

The Shrove coloured, trying to wriggle away from their cruel fingers as they nipped and pinched his delicate ears. His stomach heaved and flipped over in a sickening motion.

'You know something, don't you?' said Muprid as she watched Embellsed squirm.

Now he was for it! The awful sisters were onto him and they were cross and cranky.

'We'll take him to the lath stairs and see what the other Shroves have to say,' said Lapis, pushing Embellsed out of the door.

The Shrove was quaking with fear. What should he do now? He would be branded a murderer of his kinfolk and that would be the end of him, banished to who knows where, or worse. Butchered! Garrotted! Slain!

'Come with us, grime-eater!' Muprid shouted, dragging Embellsed along by his earlobe.

'Now we shall uncover what lies the worm has been telling us!' said the heartless Lapis.

The sisters led the struggling Embellsed through the castle to the top of the lath stairs – to the very place where Wince had tumbled to his death. They peered into the dismal shaft as a young Shrove, Croop, scurried past them. He stopped and bowed to the sisters, his eyes darting nervously towards the hapless Embellsed who refused to return his gaze. It was clear that the older Shrove was in a pickle. Embellsed's breathing was laboured and sweat was pouring off his brow.

'You there,' Lapis called haughtily. 'Where's our Shrove, Wince?'

'Have you seen him?' asked Muprid, pinning her eyes on the younger Shrove.

Croop hopped about. He licked his lips and imparted the information that was no longer news in the servants' quarters.

'He's dead, quite dead,' he replied sorrowfully shaking his head, 'dead as a doornail!'

Croop cocked his head at Embellsed, suspicious that the older Shrove hadn't told the sisters.

'Dead!' cried Lapis.

'That's most peculiar!' answered Muprid, eying Embellsed keenly.

'He fell down there,' Croop gesticulated, 'tumbled headlong off the lath steps and landed with an enormous splat,' he said, pointing to the bottom of the gloomy shaft.

'Ooooh!' replied the sisters in grisly unison, 'we wish we'd seen that!'

Embellsed held his breath and shut his eyes. He thought he might pass out with gut-wrenching fear. He experienced a terrifyingly slow-motion moment where everything swims out of control. The sisters turned jerkily, like two painted clockwork figures and nodded knowingly to one another. They bent over the bannister and stared down the shaft to where the Shroves were scurrying about far below them. Lapis arched her eyebrows and Muprid pursed her ruby red lips, then as one, they faced the quivering Embellsed. The accusatory look on the sisters' faces sent Croop scurrying off as fast as his legs could carry him. Muprid and Lapis pounced on Embellsed, tweaked his ears with their sharp nails and pulled him closer, staring into his ashen face.

'I know nowt about it!' he squawked. 'Please m'Ladies, let me go!'

He bowed his head and quivered, shrinking back from their evil glances.

'You protest too much, you grime-licker. You look quite shifty. Doesn't he, sister?' said Lapis.

'He knows more than he is saying about this grizzly business!'

she answered, spitting into Embellsed's face.

'What I want to know, is why didn't he tell us himself?' Lapis gripped the Shrove by the collar and kicked him down the corridor. 'Be off with you! Let us see what Bludroot has to say on the matter!'

'Oh my!' bleated the miserable Shrove as he cowered to the floor.

Now he was in it, right up to his scrawny neck!

The fact that the sisters were bored did not play well for the wretched Embellsed. Had the evil sisters had something better to do they would have quickly forgotten about Wince's demise, replacing him with another eager Shrove, desperate to inculcate themselves into the Swarm's favour. But the day had turned out unsatisfactorily for the spoilt, dissatisfied pair. The sisters had missed their morning gallop because of the misplaced boots and now Embellsed was behaving decidedly oddly. Besides, they didn't like him. He was above himself and had once dared to interrupt them in Caedryl's presence. Now they would get their own back and have some sport at his expense.

Embellsed slavered and shivered. He lifted his pathetic face and searched their haughty countenances for any sign of a reprieve, a bit of softness in their mean mouths and disdainful eyes, but there was nothing but malice.

The sisters sent him packing. Embellsed slunk back to his Shrove hole to await his fate.

\*

Bludroot had been observing Embellsed for many days and the evidence that met his eyes told him that the Shrove was hiding some dark deed. Of course the weaselly Wince had snitched on Embellsed to the High Shrove. The loss of the key and its subsequent replacement was too good an opportunity to undermine Embellsed and to usurp his role as Shrove-Marker. The High Shrove twitched with anger. Not only had Embellsed failed in his duties but he had betrayed his trust and had sneaked into his storeroom to steal one of his duplicate keys. The fact that Wince had broken his neck in mysterious circumstances only added to Bludroot's disquiet.

Later, Muprid summoned Bludroot to their apartment. The sisters sat at their oval dressing tables, braiding their hair, painting their lips and powdering their cheeks with flushing pinks and hot reds. Muprid did not move when Bludroot entered.

'Our Shrove is dead,' she announced coldly, peering into the large mirror to add to the finishing touches to her lipstick. 'We want another one.'

'We want a better one,' added Lapis, painting her nails the colour of lemon peel to match her robe.

'Of course, m'Lady.'

Bludroot understood the self-centred ways of the highborn. The sisters were irritated by the inconvenience of their Shrove's death, but that was all. They were frivolous creatures, egotistical and vain.

'I can recommend Cumberbatch, m'Ladies. A doting Shrove

who will do whatever you require. He has served the Swarm faithfully for many years. Or there's Croop or Flicker, much younger but both keen to progress.'

'We'll see them all,' Lapis replied, 'make the arrangements.' She turned from her mirror and arched one of her perfect eyebrows at Bludroot.

There was something else, he could tell. Her mouth twisted into a nasty sneer.

'That Shrove Embellsed is involved in Wince's death,' Muprid added, her ice-blue eyes flashing. 'Get to the bottom of it, and quickly! See to it that he is dealt with in the worst manner possible.'

Bludroot's eyes flickered nervously then he bowed and left the sisters' apartment. He might be the Thane's High Shrove but he was aware of the precariousness of his position and that all could be lost in a split-second, in a moment of displeasure from either one of these two horrors. The sisters were on the warpath and he must avoid their wrath at all costs.

'I never liked that Embellsed,' Lapis crooned nastily. 'Unfortunately, he didn't know his place.'

'Got too big for his boots,' her sister replied.

Muprid and Lapis giggled conspiratorially and continued to powder and preen, each admiring their garish made-up faces in the looking glass.

*

Embellsed sat hunched and shivering in his Shrove hole, stroking his most precious possessions. He snivelled, wrapping each item carefully and secreting them away at the back of his lair, perhaps for the last time. These were his best snitchings stolen from the Shroves and Swarm alike over the many years he had served at Hellstone Tors. They were small items for the most part, except for one special possession. He clutched a shiny stone in his wrinkled fingers. He couldn't leave it behind. The Shrove tucked the cherished whennymeg he had 'borrowed' down his sock. It felt wonderfully cold against his skin. It was a beautiful bloodstone, earth-green with red, spidery veins.

Embellsed's eyes darted to the entrance of his hovel. His nerves were in tatters. He was expecting the dreaded call to come at any moment – it was like waiting for his own execution as the last precious minutes ticked away before the inevitable finale.

Someone was coming! There was a sound outside! *A cough!* His stomach lurched as the ladder creaked and Croop poked his eager face over the edge of Embellsed's burrow. The young Shrove's eyes were shining and his mouth salivated with the anticipation of gleaning more gossip from the old Shrove.

Croop cleared his throat. 'You're to see Bludroot directly,' he announced. 'The High Shrove is in a real blither about summat,' he cocked his head at Embellsed, 'and well, we wondered, that's me and Cumberbatch and the others,' he nodded conspiratorially to the Shroves huddling at the bottom of the ladder, 'whether it had owt to do with poor Wince's sudden death?'

Croop licked his lips and tightened his grip on the ladder. He could smell the fear emanating from the cringing Shrove before him.

'Mind your business and get out of my way!' cried Embellsed, frantically pushing past Croop and skimming down the ladder.

He darted past the Shroves as they hopped about, searching his face for any inkling as to the true nature of his crime. Embellsed's eyes watered as he scurried off into the Shrove runs. He had to be alone, to think. *THINK!* He slunk into a nook behind the warm kitchens, his legs shaking, his mind awash with foreboding, and considered his fate. He shivered and moaned as he realised that, for all his years of service, he had no one to turn to in Hellstone Tors! His stomach churned with anxiety. He was done for. They would do terrible, gruesome things to him if they caught him. His only chance was to flee, to go far away from the castle and take his chances in the wilderness. He moaned and clutched his precious whennymeg. Oh my! Out in the wilds of Breedoor! Cast adrift from all he knew! But it was better than being skewered and having his warm gizzards strewn to the dogs!

He must calm himself! He counted to ten, and then to twenty. His heart felt as though it would burst out of his heaving ribcage.

'I must find one of the tunnels in the old snickleways,' he whispered finally, 'to escape this cursed place.'

That was the answer! Now he had a plan of sorts. From what he had heard in the burrows, there was a web of secret tunnels beneath the Tors. He shivered as the reality of escape took hold. The Shroves had never set foot in the tunnels before, into the dark underbelly of the infernal castle. But he had no choice.

So Embellsed scuttled through the kitchens, snatched a warm bun and stepped out into the busy thoroughfare, keeping his head down and mingling with the servants going about their chores. But instead of joining the other Shroves making their way up the lath steps he ambled towards the bottling rooms and fruit stores that led to the network of wine cellars. He hovered by the oak door and when he was certain no one was watching, he slipped down into the cool darkness of the cellars.

In that moment, which seemed like utter madness, his fate was sealed. There was no going back! His stomach churned at the realisation that he could never return to his Shrove hole whilst the Swarm ruled Hellstone Tors; never return to the only home he had ever known. But as he crept through the dismal cellars a strange feeling welled up inside him. Suddenly Embellsed felt a surge of excitement powering through his body as the huge weight of servitude was lifted from his shoulders.

Soon he would be free! Never again would he have to clamber up the hideous lath stairs or wait on the dreaded Swarm! Never again would he have to do their bidding!

With a lighter step, Embellsed slipped away into the shadows, vanishing in one deft stroke into the bowels of the Tors, onwards into the chilly darkness of the unknown.

# Eleven

The labyrinth of gloomy wine cellars was located down a narrow flight of steps, lit only by the odd candle placed here and there on the roughly hewn barrels. Embellsed picked his way along the dusty wine racks and peered nervously down the rows of barrels that had lain undisturbed for many years. The air was musty and still, redolent from the heady mixture of rich red wines, and sumptuous whites. As he inched forward, rats and mice scurried away, their sharp claws skittering across the stone floors as they darted out of his path.

Embellsed was on the lookout for an ancient Shrove named Bicker, the Keeper of the Cellars, who had been consigned to the wine stores as punishment for some long-forgotten misdemeanour against his masters. It was well known in the Shrove burrows that the 'old feller', as Bicker was known, had seen some odd goings-on in the cellars but no one knew quite

what. No one had seen the old feller for a very long time.

As Embellsed edged through the dimly lit cellars he felt oddly comforted by the cold bloodstone tucked inside his sock. He would only barter his precious whennymeg as a last resort, in case the old feller wouldn't talk freely. Somehow he must persuade the old Shrove to tell him the whereabouts of the secret tunnels and their destination beyond the castle walls. As he crouched behind the barrels he placed the smooth round stone in his pocket, and then waited in the musty glow.

But unbeknown to him, Embellsed had already been spotted. Bicker may have been old and a little hard of hearing, but he had a keen nose and could smell any strange presence in his cellars. He crept up behind Embellsed and raised his candle. His wizened face resembled ivory parchment in the flickering light.

'What you doin' down 'ere?' said a voice that sounded like a rusty hinge.

Embellsed started as Bicker, shabby and forlorn, appeared before him from out of the shadows.

'I came to find you,' Embellsed whispered hoarsely.

'There's no need to mumble, no one else can hear thee down here,' Bicker replied, eyeing the other Shrove keenly. The candlelight danced between them as the seconds slipped past. 'What are you after? No one ever comes down 'ere. They've forgotten all about old Bicker,' the Shrove muttered.

Embellsed stroked the cold bloodstone nestled in his pocket, rubbed his whiskery chin and put his plan into action.

If he was canny and cajoled the old feller, there might be a way of keeping his whennymeg.

Embellsed pulled himself to his feet.

'I was just studying the names and exceptionally good vintage of these wines,' he replied cunningly, running his finger over the faded labels and watching Bicker's reaction. 'The Thane is having a banquet and wants to serve a range of fine wines. He's wantin' bold reds, fresh sparkling whites, ruby ports and sweet pudding wines. He has especially asked me to consult you, to seek out your expertise and to sample some of your best wines, at your recommendation of course,' he said craftily, the lie tripping off his tongue like honey.

Bicker's crinkly old face lit up and his eyes shone with excitement. Usually the Thane's wine list was pinned to the door of the cellar and Bicker's job was to locate the vintages from the thousands of bottles and leave them by the entrance. No one had ever consulted him before, even though he had studied the art of winemaking - the fermenting process, the corking and the careful storage of the exquisite vintages - over the years.

'Do you really want to try my lovely wines?' he asked excitedly.

Embellsed put his arm around Bicker's shoulder and whispered in his ear.

'Of course, that's why I'm here,' he replied. 'So why don't you pour us some of your finest.' Embellsed smirked, flattering the Shrove.

'Right you are,' Bicker replied eagerly. 'Tell me the dish and I will recommend the wine to complement it,' he replied, his eyes brightening. 'Oooh, there are so many to choose from,' he cried, clapping his hands with glee and hopping about.

'No spitting the wine out, though! We must experience the full impact and nuances of flavour!' demanded Embellsed, winking at the old Shrove.

'Just as you say! Just as you say!' Bicker replied.

The old feller thought he might burst with happiness. The Swarm were starting to take notice of his expertise at long last!

Being the sort of wily Shrove that he was, Embellsed had developed a keen interest in the food that was eaten by the Swarm. He proceeded to reel off a tantalising menu of courses including poultry, game, fish, savouries, cheese and puddings as Bicker ran hither and thither between the barrels, pouring wine and spouting knowledgeably about each vintage. One particular red had a delectable aroma of blackberries and one of the whites had a hint of summer sunshine. But as Bicker became more intoxicated, hiccupping and stumbling along the aisles, Embellsed slyly disposed of his own wine down a convenient drain that ran underneath the barrels. There was no question of him becoming drunk – he needed his wits about him to elicit information from the ancient Shrove. Between glasses and toasts he questioned Bicker about the layout of the wine caves, their history and about who had ventured into the dark, chilly cellars over the years.

'It's a strange old place,' mused Embellsed, gazing at the patterned brickwork in the arched roofs. 'But tell me, old friend, what's so special about the lower levels?' he asked gesticulating towards the cellars below them.

'They house the b-best of the old reds, loved by the Thane, ruby beauties they are, laid down a hundred years ago, locked in their cages like exotic birds. I-I have t-the keys here,' he slurred, tapping his trouser pocket.

'I expect you never see the Swarm this far underground, no reason for them to venture down here,' said the crafty Embellsed, luring the drunken Shrove to reveal more.

Bicker quaffed a glass of shimmering amber liquid in one gulp, hiccupped, and tapped the side of his nose.

'But that's where you're wrong my friend. Let me tell you something,' he whispered, staggering towards Embellsed. He steadied himself, leaned on the barrel and slowly slumped to the ground, patting the flagged floor for Embellsed to join him. 'It's a secret,' he mumbled. 'And I'm the only one that knows it!'

His drunken face peered right into Embellsed's, who momentarily recoiled at the smell of Bicker's wine-soaked breath.

'Go on, dear friend,' encouraged Embellsed, filling Bicker's glass.

'I've watched *her*, spied on *her*, that beautiful creature,' Bicker muttered, 'but she don't come down 'ere from up there,' he gesticulated towards the steps leading back up to the castle. 'No, *she* arrives in the cellars through a secret tunnel from deep underneath the Tors,' he pointed a shaky finger towards the lower levels.

Embellsed couldn't believe his luck! *Another way out! A secret tunnel!* This was the answer to all his troubles! It was his escape route from Hellstone Tors!

'But who do you mean?' Embellsed asked, watching Bicker drain his glass once more.

The old Shrove chuckled. 'Why, the L-Lady Snowdroppe,' he slurred.

*Snowdroppe! Of course it would be her! She often vanished from the castle for many weeks at a time.*

'Where is this secret tunnel? He asked cunningly, gazing down the gloomy interior of the wine caves.

The old feller tapped the side of his nose and licked his lips, holding out his glass for Embellsed to replenish it.

'There's a muddle of twisting snickleways underneath the Tors,' he explained.

Embellsed's eyes widened. 'Go on,' he said excitedly.

'One snickleway winds down to the harbour where the Swarm keep their boats,' he hiccupped, 'and another comes out beyond the castle walls.'

'Where do they lead to?'

Again, he filled Bicker's glass to the brim.

'Everywhere and nowhere,' the befuddled Shrove replied, finishing his wine in one gulp. 'Then my friend, there are those snickleways that lead to the dark, secret places, places you'd never want to set foot in.' He shivered and hiccupped again. 'B-But, *she* comes, like lightning, terrifying and fast as the wind,' he mumbled, putting a finger to his salivating lips. He looked around hastily and muttered a Shroveling saying used to dispel evil spirits. His eyes widened and he licked his drunken mouth. 'Shhhh,' he slurred. '*S-She* might be listening.'

'Don't you fret. There's no one about, old feller. Here, have another snifter,' Embellsed replied, wafting a bottle of wine under Bicker's nose. The deep red liquid glugged satisfactorily into Bicker's sticky glass and flowed even more easily down his throat in one delectable gulp. 'Now, why don't you tell me more about the snickleways and everything you have learned about these dark places,' replied the crafty Embellsed.

*

Once Bicker was snoring soundly lying in his makeshift bed tucked inside one half of a broken barrel, Embellsed seized his moment. He carefully stole inside Bicker's coat pocket and snatched his keys. The old Shrove smacked his lips and rolled over as Embellsed grabbed a candle and began to make his way through the warren of wine cellars, following the route described by Bicker during his drunken babble.

The vaulted wine cellars meandered under the castle in a maze of tunnels, slanting downwards. Embellsed shivered as the air around him became chillier the further he travelled into the dark bowels of the Tors. Just as Bicker had recounted, Embellsed located the door to the lower level. He turned the key and stepped downwards.

The sunken lower vault contained a long stone passageway

with a number of rusted iron gates. Each gated enclosure housed the sumptuous ruby red wines so favoured by the Thane. Bicker had mumbled something about the entrance to the secret tunnel being at the back of the third gated enclosure, *the old '94 vintage, plum-red with a hint of blueberry,* the Shrove had said.

'This must be it,' Embellsed mumbled, placing the candle on the floor and trying a number of keys.

Eventually, the lock clicked and the gate creaked open.

Embellsed crept between the dusty racks, pushing the cobwebs out of his way, spitting grime and webs from his mouth. There, in the shadows, at the back of the wine racks, was a pitch-black hole. Embellsed peered down and reared backwards. It was the blackest, scariest place the Shrove had ever seen. The uninviting entrance had a number of steep steps leading down into the bedrock of Hellstone Tors.

'Oh my,' muttered the Shrove as the candle sputtered in the draught.

The black rocks of the ancient castle engulfed him and his heart began to beat wildly. He clutched at the walls in fright, plagued with indecision. Perhaps he should go back and face the consequences of his crime? Surely it would be better than this cold tomb? But Embellsed knew he could never return. It was madness to go back, but it was madness to go forward! He counted to ten, then to twenty, stayed his pounding heart and stepped into the unknown.

Fear tightened inside his belly. The heavy darkness overpowered him and disorientated his thoughts. He tried to remember what Bicker had told him about the snickleways, but the old feller had been rambling and now Embellsed's mind was racing with a horde of dreadful images, each one more menacing than the last. Was the route to Breedoor to the left or to the right? The Shrove started at his own shadow as jagged shapes jumped across the tunnel walls, marauding through the depths and causing Embellsed to hop about with dread.

'T'was a mistake,' he muttered, wringing his hands, 'to come down here to this grave. Perhaps I'll perish all alone and no one will ever find old Embellsed's bones,' he moaned. Then he stopped deadly still, clutching the candle with trembling fingers. 'Oh my, what was that?' he whined.

In the distance he heard a rumbling sound. .

'No! No!' he gasped 'I've come the wrong way!'

It was the sound of the sea crashing and churning its angry waves against the Hellstone rocks. He was on the route to the harbour! Embellsed hopped about in despair and hot wax splattered over his hand. In a panic, he dropped the candle to the ground.

'Bother and damn,' he cried, shaking the burning wax from his fingers.

Embellsed watched helplessly as the spluttering candle rolled along the ground, struck the wall and the flame petered out.

'My candle!' he bleated, falling to the ground to locate the candle stump. 'Got it!' he cried, snivelling to himself.

Then he reached into his pocket, feeling into all the corners where the fluff had collected.

Then his stomach flipped over. There was nothing there! He was done for! He had forgotten to bring the matches ...

*

At some point, tired and dispirited, Embellsed pulled his jacket around his cold body and dozed off, dreaming of pretty whennymegs, eating warm bread rolls from the Hellstone kitchens, and the noisy chatter of the Shrove burrows ...

'What?' he muttered in his sleep.

His eyes flicked open as he woke with a start. A terrific whirring noise was tearing through the snickleways. Embellsed blinked and peered into the distance. Before his weary eyes a pinprick of light shone in the darkness. Something was moving towards him!

Embellsed darted into a recess in the wall as the noise grew louder and the light much brighter. Then, like an arrow, in an arc of shimmering light, Snowdroppe sped towards him like a whirlwind. The Shrove flattened his body against the wall, stuck like a fly to paper, terrified to move a muscle. He couldn't breathe. He stayed in the same position for a very long time, even after Snowdroppe had vanished. He was terrified out of his wits.

It was Bicker who finally found him.

'Thought you'd outwit me, eh? Get me drunk. Leave old Bicker behind,' he moaned, his flickering candle illuminating his wizened features.

'Oh, how did you find me?' Embellsed cried, throwing himself on the old Shrove.

He was extremely relieved to see the old feller.

Bicker stared into Embellsed's face. 'Told you the wrong direction,' he answered.

So Bicker wasn't so daft after all.

'But why?' asked Embellsed, distraught at being duped by Bicker.

'You got me drunk, but not so drunk that I didn't know what you were up to and what I was sayin'. Besides if you're set on escaping from this castle and from the Swarm, I'm coming too!'

'What! But Shroves don't like company,' Embellsed cried.

'Take it or leave it! I know my way around these snickleways and you don't.'

'Of course you do,' said Embellsed with relief.

'Made it my business to explore these passageways.' The old Shrove scratched his nose. 'Besides, after years alone in the cellars I fancy a change of scene. It's either that or I blow out the candle and you can fend for yourself.'

'No! Not that. Please! I hate this darkness! I-I don't know my way – don't leave me!'

A knowing smile crept over Bicker's face. 'Did you see *her* then?' he asked.

Embellsed nodded. He didn't want to think about *her* – that *demon* of the darkness.

'Aye, she's a rum sight when she's darting through the snickleways. Like a streak of white light! She woke me up when she came up top. She always forgets her key,' he said in a matter of fact tone. 'She's so ungrateful that one. I knew she would have scared you half to death.' he chuckled.

'She was an awful spectacle,' snivelled Embellsed.

'You've got summat that belongs to me,' said the old Shrove and held out his hand. Embellsed handed him the keys.

'I'll take whatever you've got hidden in your pocket too,' said the wily old feller.

Embellsed grizzled and reluctantly handed the bloodstone to Bicker.

'That'll be payemnt for all my trouble,' he muttered. 'Here,' he said , 'I brought us some snacks'

Embellsed fell on the food, devouring it quickly.

'Come on, let's make for the hills of Breedoor!' replied Bicker holding up the candle and making his way down the snickleway. 'I have a hankering for the wild outdoors!'

# Twelve

As Sourdunk repeated Queen Asphodel's message, Snowdroppe dug her violet-coloured nails dug into her arm, leaving a florid ring of indentations.

She sprang from her dressing table, poised like a viper, ready to strike.

'What do you mean Tallitha's gone missing?' she shouted, rounding on the Shrove.

Sourdunk cowered. She had been dreading giving the message to Snowdroppe. Her temper was legendary amongst the Shroves of Hellstone Tors.

'S-She's run away my Lady,' answered the Shrove.

Snowdroppe paced the floor as the abject Sourdunk recounted the tale of how Tallitha had escaped from Stankles Brow. The Shrove wrung her hands and averted her eyes from her tyrannical mistress, trying her utmost to keep out of Snowdroppe's way. One word out of place, one look too many at

Snowdroppe in a fury, would consign her forever to the bowels of Hellstone Tors.

'But how is it possible? How did she escape from my sister?'

'P-Please m'Lady,' the Shrove muttered, swallowing hard, 'T-Tallitha disappeared at night through an underground passageway.'

'Alone?'

'No, my Lady, she was with Quillam – they escaped together,' answered the Shrove nervously.

'With my adopted SON!' she hissed. 'The boy I have cossetted and looked after has betrayed ME! HE was supposed to guard her, not run away with her!'

Snowdroppe's eyes burned with hatred. 'What news of them now?'

'Queen Asphodel fears that they made their way through the Bitter Caves and have escaped across the Northern Wolds.'

Snowdroppe slammed her hand on the dressing table, scattering perfume bottles, sending them spinning and smashing to the floor.

'I will make him pay for this!' she roared. 'Quillam will regret the day he was born!'

The veins in Snowdroppe's neck pumped with anger as she stared out of the window, across the rugged hills, in the direction of the Northern Wolds. She bit down hard on her lip and a trickle of blood oozed from her mouth. She licked it clean as a look of madness flashed in her eyes.

'We will catch them wherever they are! Get word to the Groats – they must begin the search immediately!'

Snowdroppe picked up the fennec fox and stroked his amber-coloured ears. As she did so her hand began to shake. If she failed to recapture Tallitha, all their plans would be ruined. Her father would … she pushed the thought from her mind; the consequences didn't bear thinking about.

'Get word to the Thane to meet me in the Neopholytite's tower, then fetch Tyaas,' she demanded. 'Bring him to me at the foot of the Darkling Stairs.'

Sourdunk slunk out of Snowdroppe's palace, traversing the lath stairs where the unfortunate Wince had perished, gazing nervously down the dizzying drop at the death pit way below. She clicked her tongue and shook her head. Wince's untimely demise was a peculiarly bad business. The Shroves were on edge at the macabre turn of events. Wince had been an ambitious creature, destined for great things in Hellstone Tors, but now he was dead. Murdered, they said, pushed from the late stairs by an unseen hand and if that wasn't sinister enough, Embellsed, the Shrove-Marker, had mysteriously disappeared.

There were strange goings-on in the castle, so bizarre that some even dared to whisper that the power of the Swarm was waning.

*

Sourdunk grumbled away to herself. She disliked children at the best of times, particularly those that belonged to the Swarm.

'You're to come with me, young master,' she barked entering Tyaas's apartment.

'Where are we going?' he asked suspiciously.

He had never seen a female Shrove before and this one was an odd specimen with a shock of red hair, bright beady eyes and a beaky nose.

'We're to meet your mother at the Darkling Stairs,' the Shrove replied.

'Why? What's going on? And where's Embellsed?' Tyaas persisted.

'I cannot answer your questions, so stop going on at me,' she replied, brushing Tyaas away.

So Tyaas followed the Shrove through the dark corridors. All he knew for certain was that the Shrove-Marker had disappeared. Embellsed hadn't collected him as arranged from Aseanthe's palace, which was peculiar given his job as Shrove-Marker. Usually Embellsed took his duties very seriously but it seemed he had forgotten about his charge altogether.

'But you must know something,' Tyaas continued, badgering the frizzy-haired creature.

The boy was a troublesome lad, constantly tugging at her sleeve with niggling questions, wanting to know this and that.

'You're a right nuisance! Do stop badgering me!' Sourdunk sighed, prising the boy's fingers, one by one, from her arm. 'Now, hush! Here's your mother. Look sharpish, you can ask her all about it.'

Sourdunk pushed Tyaas towards the Darkling Stairs and quickly slipped away.

'Mother?' said Tyaas quizzically as she led him towards the Darkling Stairs.

Bludroot hopped about, trying to keep out of Snowdroppe's way.

'What's happening? Why are we here?' asked Tyaas.

'You'll find out soon enough,' his mother said firmly. 'Bludroot, guard the entranceway and let no one up, do you hear?'

The High Shrove bowed obsequiously, hiding his frustration with a bitter smile. A lowly Shrove should have been given this duty! But he stepped aside and did as he was bidden.

Snowdroppe pushed Tyaas through a doorway into a dark stairwell, infused with sulphurous yellow light. The shiny black staircase, carved with a series of menacing ravens' heads, wound up into the garish glow. At the foot of the Darkling Stairs a black cat sat licking her tufted paws with relish. Her swirling emerald eyes settled menacingly on the visitors and she hissed a catty welcome, revealing her blood-red throat.

'Let us in, Caedryl, and get out of my way,' snapped Snowdroppe.

The black cat hissed and stretched her body like a strand of liquorice, springing from the bottom step in one enormous leap. As the dark blur shuddered in the air, the cat transformed into the darkly clad Caedryl with the bloodstone at her neck. She landed nimbly on the ground in front of Tyaas.

'Wow!' he cried. 'That's unbelievable! Do that again!'

'I'm not some circus animal!' she sneered, smoothing down her dress. 'I am from the royal blood of Morrow and I do what I please. Guard!' she commanded. 'Let us up the stairs!'

Caedryl hissed at her cousin then she raced up the Darkling Stairs, taking two steps at a time.

'How did she do that?' Tyaas asked his mother.

'She can change her form at will,' Snowdroppe replied, 'it's a little gift she has.'

She pushed a mystified Tyaas up the dark staircase. Below them, the Night Slopers heaved and snored beneath the stair treads.

'Why have you brought me here?' Tyaas asked guardedly, making his way through the yellow fog.

'That sister of yours has gone missing.' Snowdroppe snapped as they approached the top of the stairs, 'So you better have some answers for the Thane!'

*Of course she has*, thought Tyaas gleefully. Now he was for it.

*

On the other side of the Bone Room the Neopholytite sat in her winged armchair, plucking the threads of her blood-red dress, while the Thane sat hunched in his chair like an angry gnome, his hair sticking out in crazy plaits and his eyes wild with fury. He snarled when Snowdroppe entered, jumping to his feet and snatching Tyaas by his collar.

'What do you know about Tallitha's disappearance? What is she up to?' he bellowed.

'Get off me! I don't know anything about it,' Tyaas answered, struggling to get free.

'You're lying!' barked Snowdroppe.

Caedryl circled Tyaas, smirking with spite.

'I heard them scheming together,' she said savagely. 'No more lies, little boy. Tallitha and Quillam were as thick as thieves on their journey to Hegglefoot. They were plotting and whispering together.' Caedryl announced to the Thane.

It seemed to Tyaas that Caedryl's voice had taken on a strange purring quality.

'Y-You were spying on them!' he shouted but Caedryl only laughed at him.

The Thane's angular cheekbones glinted like a knife in the candlelight.

'Make him talk,' he demanded, throwing a glance at the Neopholytite.

The witch rose and shuffled towards her curse trees, guided by her odious Shrove, Snare. Tyaas shrank away from his great-grandmother, her dark, dead eyes staring vacantly as her bony hands, clutched at him.

'Tyaas,' she crooned, running her wizened fingers across his face.

He shuddered, pulling away from her.

'We need a spell that will creep into all the dark, tricky places,' she warbled, 'where this boy keeps his secrets. He must tell us all he knows of his sister's whereabouts,' she said, snapping at the boy and grinning at Snare.

It was then that Tyaas noticed her blackened teeth and the inside of her dark throat vibrating and pulsing blood-red with every word she spoke.

'Pass me the brown curse. It hangs on a low branch,' the witch demanded

Snare sifted amongst the ancient curse-leaves until he found the right one.

'Smell it!' instructed the Neopholytite.

'It smells of mould and fungus,' Snare replied.

'That's the one, now take me to the whorl-pit!'

'Let me read the curse-leaf for you, Great-Grandmother,' said Caedryl, slipping her arm through the Neopholytite's.

The black-toothed witch and the cattish-girl stepped menacingly towards the pit as Snowdroppe pushed Tyaas towards the cauldron.

'This will be so much fun,' said Caedryl wickedly.

'Let me go! I won't tell you anything!' Tyaas shouted, struggling vainly, but the Thane and his mother held him over the pit.

The witch gesticulated to the Shroves and they emptied a variety of sickly green and bright purple potions into the whorl-pit; wolfsbane syrup and crowsfeet nectar followed by a mound of withered spiders' legs. The brew churned and gulped into a foul-smelling broth as the stinking vapours filled the Bone Room and clouded Tyaas's senses.

'Caedryl stared deep into the cauldron and spoke in a languid, purring tone:

'*Lance and boil the liar's tongue, Slice his belly, jab, jab, jab, Make the weasel moan and talk!*'

'Stir the cauldron!' the witch ordered.

'Let me go!' Tyaas cried, trying to break free.

But they held him fast.

The cauldron bubbled and fizzled as the Neopholytite lowered her head into the steaming pit and breathed in the bewitching potion. Then she placed the palms of her hands together and blew fiercely between her fingers. Suddenly a snaking jet-black curse rolled out of her mouth, pausing and spiralling for a moment before bolting across the Bone Room like a poisoned arrow and darting into the boy's mouth. Tyaas clutched his neck as the curse wormed its way down his throat, its hot tentacles slithering away inside him. Tyaas choked and turned a greenish-yellow colour.

'I feel sick,' he cried, doubling up with pain.

'Then spit out the truth and you'll feel better,' said Snowdroppe.

'Now, little boy, where is your sister? What is she plotting?' asked the Thane.

The stomach cramps came in waves, jabbing at Tyaas's from every angle.

'Make it stop!' he cried.

'Out with it!' cried the witch.

Tyaas tried to resist the power of the spell, but it was useless.

'Tallitha means to destroy the Morrow pact! She can do magic too!'

Snowdroppe pounced on her son.

'She will never succeed!' she shrieked, shaking him violently.

'Stupid, meddling girl,' cried the witch, shuffling closer.

She smelled foul, of rotten eggs. Tyaas reared back at the sulphurous odour.

'Well, father, what do you propose?' asked Snowdroppe.

The Thane eyed his daughter. 'I have a plan,' he said, smiling wickedly. 'Redlevven and Yarrow know the Northern Wolds. They must hunt down my granddaughter. Our betrayer has the Morrow stain upon her so wherever she's hiding, we shall find her!'

'But what of our thirteenth member and the swearing in ceremony?' asked the witch.

The Thane's steely eyes alighted on his grandson.

'No matter – we shall have this boy, if Tallitha cannot be found in time.'

'But I wanted that girl-child. She smelled of the Morrow stain still fresh from Winderling Spires,' the witch answered peevishly.

'The boy will do if we cannot catch his sister. Take him to the Withered Tower and keep him under lock and key,' the Thane replied.

The witch began muttering the spell and the black curse flew out of Tyaas's mouth like a whiplash and dived between the Neopholytite's thin lips. She let out a resounding belch and smiled a black-toothed grin.

'In the meantime, Sedentia can teach the boy spells from the Black Pages,' announced the Thane.

'I'm no good at any of that weird stuff,' Tyaas replied, sounding horrified.

Snowdroppe laughed. 'Then now is the time to learn about the dark mysteries of our family.'

'Can I help train him?' asked Caedryl menacingly, sidling next to Tyaas.

She twisted her fingers into his hair, toying with him like a cat with a mouse. Tyaas shied away from her.

'Teach him your spells and wicked tricks,' the Thane replied and gripped Tyaas's arm. 'You'll be a prisoner until the day you are sworn, unless of course, we catch your sister first.'

'I'll watch him,' Caedryl replied. 'He won't escape from me!'

With that she sprang into the air, her body contracted back into the Wheen-cat and the creature landed on the floor in Caedryl's place. To Tyaas's amazement the cat arched her back and rubbed her body against his legs to mark him with her scent. Then she spat at him and, with her tail high in the air, pitter-pattered down the Darkling Stairs.

'Be sure to make his bed in the high rafters,' said the Neopholytite.

'But who will watch him now that Embellsed has vanished?' asked Snowdroppe.

'One of my Shroves,' said the witch, clicking her fingers. 'Cannisp, you will do my granddaughter's bidding.'

Cannisp appeared from a shadowy corner of the Bone

Room, bowed submissively and scurried away to prepare Tyaas's chamber as Snowdroppe quickly led Tyaas down the Darkling Stairs to collect his belongings.

'I feel sick from that disgusting spell,' Tyaas moaned clutching his stomach. 'In fact, I'm going to be …'

'Eurgh!' cried Snowdroppe looking repulsed. 'Hurry up and get your things!'

Tyaas ran into his apartment as Snowdroppe waited in the hallway. But he wasn't sick at all. He hurriedly located the witch bottle, wrapped in one of his shirts and placed it at the bottom of his bag.

Once inside the Withered Tower, Tyaas was ushered into the strangest bedroom he had ever seen. The large ramshackle bed was built on stilts, high up in the rafters at the top of a long ladder. The room was lined with books and not much else.

'You're to wait here until you're summoned,' said Cannisp. 'I've left food on the shelf behind your bed,' he added, rubbing his hands together.

Tyaas climbed up the shaky ladder to the large bed, tucked up in the rafters, hiding the witch bottle in a gap behind the bedframe.

What was he going to do now? How could he avoid the weird Sedentia Flight with all her spells and potions? He was going to have to do all those weird things. But how could he? He didn't like magic and sorcery. It was Tallitha who could do those weird things, not him.

Then an idea occurred to him. He remembered what Tallitha

had asked him to do.

Somehow, he would get a message to Esmerelda.

*

Slynose's nightly foray into Hellstone Tors followed the same routine. She was a cat after all, as well as being a girl, and she was a creature of habit. Slynose liked to stalk the dark corridors, exploring her favourite hunting spots to catch her mousey-supper. This was usually followed by a visit to the Darkling Stairs to purr contentedly with the Night Slopers, or a trip to the Withered Tower to curl up on Sedentia's soft, warm bed.

The Wheen-Cat licked her paws and purred from deep within her dark throat. '*Tasty treat, tasty, tasty treat*,' she mewed and padded out into the night on the hunt for a Hellstone mouse, or maybe two, the fattest and juiciest ones she could find.

Helter-skelter went the fat brown mice as they spied Slynose, her spiralling green eyes mesmerising them into a state of abject fear, their tiny claws clipping across the wooden floors, fleeing in haste. '*Wee-wee*', they squeaked, '*wee-wee*', they cried, darting this way and that, scurrying for safety with their fat brown bottoms and wriggling tails flashing down the passageways, desperate to escape from the cat's jaws.

In a flash, Slynose pounced and trapped a silky brown mouse in her fangs. She lifted the wriggling creature by its tasty haunch and then in one deft movement flicked it along the corridor followed by a *snap, snap* of her vicious jaws. The mouse tumbled, dazed and confused, and lay in a pathetic heap, injured but alive, attempting to limp away.

This was the moment that the cat loved best! She slunk to the ground with her head resting on her paws, swishing her thick black tail and watched as the terrified creature made a hopeless, stuttering bid for freedom. Slynose's emerald-green eyes swirled with drunken pleasure as she taunted the hapless mouse, batting it back and forth, watching it squirm between her paws. *So much delicious delight in such a little mouse – playtime and snacks in one small package*, thought the evil feline.

Then in a split second she pounced and trapped the terrified creature under her paws '*wee-wee, wee-wee*', the small creature squeaked – but the devilish Wheen-Cat had the tasty brown mouse clamped firmly between her jaws. *Delicious, quite delicious,* she hissed, slinking down the landing with the mouse hanging limply from her mouth. Behind her, a trail of mouse-blood splattered in droplets upon the wooden floor.

But tonight, Slynose's routine changed. She was on her way to see Tyaas.

Cannisp was asleep in an outer room and didn't stir when the Wheen-Cat slipped past his rickety bed. She made a small mewing sound and stared up into the darkness where the tangled rafters embraced the platform bed. Her finely tuned hearing was attentive to the boy's regular breathing. The

Wheen-Cat shuddered, rolled into a black ball, arched her skinny back and, in one agile movement, Caedryl sprang, thin and sombre, from the Wheen-Cat's body. She smoothed down her black hair, straightened her clothes and climbed up the long ladder.

The boy was sleeping soundly with his hair in a tousled mess upon the pillow. Caedryl sat idly on the bed, kicking her legs over the edge, licking the mousey taste from her sticky fingers before braiding her hair into two long plaits.

'Pssst,' she said eventually, nudging him.

Her swirling eyes stared malevolently in the gloom as Tyaas rolled over.

'Psst, wake up,' she hissed. 'Time for tricks.'

Tyaas groaned as he spied Caedryl sitting and watching him. She looked like a demon in the darkness, her green eyes dancing with evil delight. She had a trail of blood by the corner of her mouth, just like a bloodsucker.

'It's the middle of the night,' he protested, sleepily.

'That's the perfect time for what I have in mind,' she replied ominously.

Tyaas slipped his hand under the blankets and felt for the Witch Bottle. It was safe and sound.

'What do you want with me?' he asked.

She climbed down the ladder. 'Hurry up. Get dressed and follow me, little boy – then all will be revealed.'

Tyaas's stomach flipped over at the thought of what might be in store for him.

Unfortunately, when he reached his destination his worst fears were realised. Sedentia Flight was waiting for him.

'Now, Master Tyaas, let us see what you can do,' she said. 'Perhaps you too will have magic running through your blood, just like Tallitha,' she jested.

'I'm not doing any of that weird stuff,' he cried.

'I will be the judge of that,' Sedentia barked. She turned to Caedryl. 'That will be all, my pet,' the governess simpered, smiling sweetly at the cat-girl.

With that, Caedryl leapt high into the air, shuddered and the Wheen-Cat landed in her place. She pranced off down the hallway in her queenly fashion, with her black fluffy tail sweeping madly from side to side.

# Thirteen

Following Flametip's directions, Tallitha and Quillam descended under the mountains, using the entrance below the flat purple stone, skirting away from any path that would lead them in the direction of the Old Yawning Edges.

'When you get to the bottom, follow the tunnel into a grotto filled with yellow stalagmites,' Flametip instructed. 'Behind a small waterfall you will find a raven head carving. Press the beak and a tunnel will be revealed.'

'Where will it lead to?' asked Quillam.

'Far under the Out-Of-The-Way Mountains, to the Raven Stones,' answered the nervous sprite.

Her black eyes darted from one to the other.

'Is it safe?' asked Tallitha, sensing disquiet in the jumpy Flametip.

'Well, yes and no,' she answered cautiously, 'this route will

get you there more quickly but it has its dangers.' The Black Sprite cocked her head to one side. 'It's an ancient tunnel used by the northern tribes, but part of it has fallen into other hands.'

'Whose?' asked Tallitha apprehensively.

'Beware the Groats and the Dooerlins,' she replied. 'The path will pass close to Queen Asphodel's underground kingdom and the deep mines.'

Quillam shot a hasty look at Tallitha.

'We have no choice,' she replied flatly, picking up her backpack.

They said farewell to the sprite, following her directions and coming upon the cave adorned with the jagged yellow stalagmites. They headed towards the waterfall, edging along the slippery ledge and located the stone raven. Tallitha pressed the raven's beak and the stone doorway groaned and swung open before them. Cautiously, they slipped inside the snaking darkness of the secret tunnel.

Inside, the walls glistened and glowed with the unmistakable streaks of the bloodstones. They crept soundlessly along, wary of what may be lurking around every corner, following the narrow tunnel until, tired and weary, they found a place to rest for the night.

They had been sleeping in the small cave, huddled together against the cold, when Tallitha woke to the sound of banging, of hammers and picks raining down upon the rocks with sudden blows and terrifying thuds, smashing them into a thousand pieces.

'What's that noise?' she asked anxiously, shaking Quillam.

He struck a match, lighting a taper in the darkness. It sprang into life, hissing as the light danced across the vivid green and blood-red splashes in the veined walls.

'Come on, let's take a look,' he replied, creeping from their hiding place.

As they inched along, the sound of splintering rocks became louder.

'There's a light ahead of us,' said Quillam.

The sound of groaning ropes and grating chains rumbled from the bowels of the earth like a dragon disturbed from its slumber.

Tallitha and Quillam tiptoed towards the light, where the tunnel abruptly ended at the edge of a sheer precipice.

'What's down there?' Tallitha asked nervously as a red-orange light erupted from the vortex.

'Queen Asphodel's mine,' he said excitedly.

Quillam took her arm, leaned forward and together they peered down into the deep recesses of the Out-Of-The-Way Mountains. A perilous mineshaft was laid out below them, emblazoned with a fiery-golden light that emanated from a series of huge smelting ovens spewing forth metal ore into the darkness. The mine was populated by the Murk Mowl, busily ripping bloodstones from the rock, suspended on perilous ropes, chiselling the rock face and piling the stones onto ledges that ran horizontally along the mineshaft.

'This is where they get their wealth,' said Quillam, pulling Tallitha from the brink.

'Did you know about this?' she asked.

'The Swarm would never speak of the location – it's one of their closely guarded secrets.'

The Mowl clambered like insects across the walls, with their bloodless translucent skin and metal piercings glinting in the light from the huge furnaces below them.

Their leader, a gruesome specimen, was perched haphazardly on a ledge beneath the monstrous troop, hurling orders to his crew over the noise and heat of the mine workings.

'What do they use these precious stones for?' asked Tallitha.

She touched the cold bloodstone at her neck.

'It is said that the stones possess a supernatural power for those who have the gift,' explained Quillam. His eyes swept over Tallitha's face and landed at the bloodstone round her neck. 'The Swarm also use them to barter and bribe, to control the lands around Breedoor and all who live there.'

Quillam nudged Tallitha and pointed towards the ramshackle mine workings that clunked and screeched with the weight of the cages used to transport the Mowl. The ropes groaned as the cages went up and down to the lower levels. It was an old, dilapidated construction. The struts were worn, the ropes were frayed in places and the pulleys were rusted with dripping black water that fell from the roof of the shaft.

'We could destroy the Murk Mowl,' he said eagerly. 'Look there,' he added pointing towards the old mine workings. 'A few deft slices at that old rope would bring the whole thing tumbling down.'

But Tallitha wasn't listening. She was transfixed. She tugged on Quillam's jacket and pointed towards a group that had assembled below them.

Queen Asphodel had suddenly appeared, accompanied by her Shroves and a party of Groats. They had stumbled upon the sunken labyrinthine world of the heartless Queen.

'What's she doing?' asked Tallitha.

The Queen's posture demonstrated her rage; she threw her arms in the air and strode forcefully across a narrow bridge that spanned the deep shaft. Queen Asphodel shouted angrily and gesticulated towards the Mowl leader.

'You must catch them and bring them to me!' she yelled over the din of the mine workings, 'they can't have gone far.'

The grizzly Mowl Chieftain summoned his minions and raised his ugly pierced face, scarred from his chin to his eyebrows, to scour the upper reaches of the mineshaft.

Tallitha grabbed Quillam and they fell to the floor - waiting, breathing, paralysed with fear.

'What's going on?' Quillam asked desperately.

Tallitha peered over the ledge and her eyes alighted on a tall figure. Standing behind the Queen was a familiar face. Tallitha gripped Quillam's arm.

'It's Benedict!' she cried.

He must have heard her. Suddenly the boy looked up and their eyes locked. In a heartbeat, Quillam grabbed Tallitha and they dived back into the tunnel and stood breathlessly against the wall.

'Did she see us?' he whispered desperately.

'I don't know, but Benedict certainly did! Come on,' urged Tallitha.

They raced down the tunnel, as the sound of their footsteps clattered noisily in the darkness.

'She must have seen us!' cried Tallitha, as the sound of the Mowl pounded through the caves.

'This way,' Quillam cried.

They fled up a steep winding tunnel that narrowed and dipped, desperately searching for a place to hide.

'Through here,' urged Quillam pointing towards a dark hole. 'You go first.'

Tallitha bent down on her hands and knees and stared into the menacing darkness. The sound of the Murk Mowl rang through the caves, getting closer. Quillam blew out the taper and crawled in behind her.

'Hurry up!' he shouted, 'they're almost upon us. If you don't move, we're done for!'

Tallitha inched forward into the black, wet hole. They crawled together through the darkness, desperate to put as much distance between themselves and the hideous creatures as possible. The noise of swords clattering against armour, scraping against the walls, and the sound of pounding feet filled their ears.

'They're going to catch us,' Tallitha whimpered.

Then a familiar stench filled her nostrils.

'Just keep going and don't look back!' said Quillam sharply.

He gave Tallitha one last push and she tumbled down a steep

rock face and landed with a splash. Quillam rolled next to her.

'What's that awful smell?' he asked, hurriedly lighting the taper.

'Put it out,' she whispered hoarsely 'they'll see us!'

'Just let me get my bearings,' he answered.

As the light flickered, Tallitha gasped. She had smelt the awful smell at the Throes of Woe.

'We're inside a Murk turrow,' she whispered.

She felt Quillam stiffen beside her.

'We'll have to hide in there,' she said, taking his hand, 'it's our only chance.'

Tallitha's eyes conveyed the horror that would soon greet them.

It was a gruesome sight indeed. A group of dead bodies were preserved in oiled cloths.

Quillam hurriedly doused the taper, grabbed Tallitha and they buried themselves behind a row of mummified bodies and waited for their hunters.

The hammering footsteps of the Mowl moved closer, splashing through puddles, their battle cries screeching in the darkness. Then it all became quiet. The villains were inside the turrow, moving corpses with the point of their swords. Tallitha and Quillam kept as still as the dead that surrounded them.

'Try in there,' shouted one Mowl to another.

He plunged his sword between the shrouded corpses as its shiny point flashed in the darkness and struck the wall between Tallitha and Quillam.

'They must have gone the other way!' A familiar voice called out in the darkness.

Tallitha gripped Quillam's hand.

It was Benedict shouting instructions to the Mowl. Was he leading the horde in the opposite direction?

'Come on!' the Mowl guard shouted, clattering his sword against the rocks. 'After them! This way!'

His thick, booming voice echoed through the caves.

The Murk Mowls' footsteps retreated through the puddles, fading into the distance.

After some time, Quillam eased himself from behind the corpses.

'They've gone,' he whispered.

In the darkness, Tallitha's cold fingers fumbled for the matches. Quillam hurriedly took the box from her and lit the taper. They stared at each other's terrified faces in the flickering light.

'B-Benedict saved us,' whispered Tallitha incomprehensively. 'But why? What does he gain from letting us escape?'

'No time to think about that now,' urged Quillam, 'we have to get out of here!'

He grabbed her hand and they stumbled out of the turrow and raced onwards through the teeming darkness, their tapers licking the bloodstone walls with fleeting shadows.

But Tallitha couldn't stop thinking about Benedict. She was certain he had seen her in the mine. Had he raised the alarm? Yet he had rescued them from the Mowls' clutches and had gone against his mother – but why? *Perhaps the power of the Swarm was beginning to wane.*

Tallitha and Quillam edged through the tunnels, burrowing through dark holes, their bodies shivering from cold and fear. Eventually, after many hours following Flametip's directions, they saw the welcoming light of the Raven's Stones at the bottom of the Cave-Shroves' village.

It was a safe haven in the bitter darkness of the underworld.

# Fourteen

The Skinks were making excellent headway traversing the caverns and caves under the Out-Of-The-Way Mountains. The Weeping Cavern and the Shrunken Butts with its tight, inky shaft was safely behind them. Sour Pit Chimneys was just below and soon they would reach the Raven Stones and the Cave-Shroves village.

At the bottom of the Shrunken Butts, Neeps slunk along the narrow ledge with Ruker close behind him. The roar of the turbulent waterfalls cascaded way beneath them. Neeps suddenly pointed downwards.

'*Groats*,' he mouthed urgently to Ruker, turning quickly and pointing to the motley crew.

Gathering on the northern rim of the Sour Pit Chimneys, a party of Groats was fishing in one of the fast flowing rivulets.

The Skinks slunk back along the ledge and crouched in the entrance to the Shrunken Butts.

'We'll have to sit it out until they've gone.'

They tried to get some sleep, tucking their heads between their knees, and resting on their backpacks.

Some time later, stiff from the cold, Neeps woke with a snore. He wiped his mouth and then froze, listening intently. From up above, a noise echoed down the dark shaft.

'Ruker, wake up,' he whispered hoarsely, shaking his friend and clutching his dagger. 'We've got company.'

Neeps hurriedly lit a taper and shone it upwards. The light bounced against the dark uneven rocks as a pair of feet came into view, moving down the pothole to greet them.

'It's those blasted girls,' he whispered, rolling his eyes.

'Spooner?' Ruker whispered, staring upwards, 'is that you?'

A breathless Lince called down to them. 'Yes, it's us,' she replied.

'What on earth?' cried Ruker.

'Make no noise – there are Groats all around us,' urged Neeps.

The girls slipped between the Skinks and huddled together in the darkness.

'Can you see what's going on out there?' asked Ruker.

Neeps edged out of the pothole to check on the Groats. The northern rim of the Sour Pit Chimneys was empty.

'All clear,' he announced, as one by one they crept along the ledge.

The only sound was the roar of water rushing below them, flowing into the deep shafts.

'What possessed you to come after us again?' growled Ruker. The girls shuffled awkwardly on the ledge.

'We want to help find Tallitha,' Spooner replied tartly.

'We gave Spelk the slip,' added Lince sheepishly.

All Ruker could think about was the anguish of Betty and Josh, worrying about what had happened to their girls. All Neeps could think about was the responsibility of trying to manage Spooner and Lince in the dangerous underworld.

'Well, there's nothing we can do about it now,' Ruker replied gruffly. 'Let's push on to Raven Stones, we'll decide what to do with you when we're there.'

*

Once in the safety of the Cave-Shroves' village, Tallitha and Quillam tucked into a meal of blindworm puddings and grilled rat. The meaty juices trickled down Tallitha's chin as she chatted to Snouter and caught up on the Cave-Shrove's news. Ernelle and Pester were busy bringing more food and a barrel of ale.

'We didn't know whether we would ever see you again,' said Pester with a tear in her eyes, giving Tallitha a warm hug.

'I've missed you all so much,' Tallitha cried, gazing from Pester to the kind faces of the others.

'Tell us about that awful castle,' urged Ernelle, ever-curious about the comings and goings of the infamous Tors.

'Yes, and all about the Swarm,' added Pester, 'are they really as wicked as they say?'

'What was it like?' asked Snouter.

'The Swarm are evil, the Thane and the witch are as rotten as they say,' she hesitated. 'I had to leave Tyaas behind,' she added.

'Will he be all right?' asked Ernelle, 'without you?'

'What will you do?' asked Pester, taking a mouthful of grilled rat

'There's only one thing that I must do,' she answered. 'I must break the Morrow pact.'

Huddled round the table, the Cave-Shroves gazed at Tallitha open-mouthed.

'Tell us everything!' they said excitedly.

Tallitha recounted her adventures – all that had happened since leaving the Cave-Shroves at Melted Water, through her long dark days at Hellstone Tors, the Neopholytite's Bone Room, Sedentia Flight, the Black Pages, their escape from Queen Asphodel and what she had learned about the secrets of the Morrow family.

'The Morrow sisters can explain the mysterious things that I need answers to,' she said finally. 'So you see, we must return to Winderling Spires.'

'We can show you another route to Wycham Elva,' said Pester, waiting for Tallitha to continue with her tale.

Tallitha smiled at the Cave-Shroves. They had never let her down.

'Apparently my grandmother and her sisters know about the pact,' she replied. 'They wouldn't tell me anything at first but now I have found Asenathe, they may be persuaded to help.' She yawned and stretched out her arms. 'I'm so tired – I must get some sleep.'

So Quillam and Tallitha dragged their tired bodies to the soft beds and almost before their heads touched the pillows, they fell into a deep sleep.

*

Tallitha dreamed of Kastra and her bubble shimmering in the dark forest, then of running through the dismal caves and being hunted by the Mowl. She moaned in her sleep, pulled the blankets over her head and rolled over. Then the dreamscape changed and she was flying through Ragging Brows Forest, tree-skimming across the canopy, laughing and joking with Ruker and Neeps …

'Tallitha, wake up,' a familiar voice whispered, breaking her dream.

Someone was shaking her.

'What?' she moaned.

'It's me,' the voice said softly. 'I'm really here and so are you! I-I can't believe it!'

Tallitha opened her eyes. It was no longer a dream.

'Ruker!'

The Skink was squatting before her, leaning back on her haunches. Her almond-shaped eyes shone with delight.

Tallitha blinked. It was true! Neeps stood behind Ruker, grinning all over his face.

'You're a sight for sore eyes,' he cried.

Tallitha flung her arms round Ruker's neck then she leapt to her feet, grabbed Neeps and hugged them both tightly. At her side, Quillam stirred and watched the reunion with suspicion. So these were the famous Skinks!

'But what are you doing here?'

'Looking for you, of course! Although we expected to find you at Hellstone Tors, not sleeping soundly in the Raven Stones.' Ruker smiled. 'It's a long story and will take some telling. First we went to Winderling Spires with Cissie – '

'Cissie!' Tallitha cried, 'where is she?'

Quillam stiffened at the sound his mother's name.

'She came with us but we had to leave her at High Bedders End. The caves proved too much for her and she wanted to go home,' replied Neeps, turning to Quillam. 'And who are you?' he asked a little brusquely.

'This is Quillam, Snowdroppe's adopted child, but that's a long story too,' Tallitha said quickly.

She could feel the atmosphere in the cave suddenly change.

'Snowdroppe! But is he to be trusted?' asked Ruker, bristling.

Quillam reached under the blankets and gripped the handle of his dagger.

'Of course. He's my friend. I wouldn't have made it this far without him.'

Quillam glowered at the Skinks.

Then a movement behind Quillam caught Tallitha's eye.

'Spooner! Lince!' she cried, noticing the girls.

The girls rushed towards Tallitha, pulling her into a big hug, squashing her between the two of them.

'Surprise!' they shouted excitedly.

'They followed us down here, it wasn't our doing,' replied Ruker bluntly.

'It doesn't matter,' Tallitha said, 'in fact it's a good thing they're here.'

'What do you mean?' asked Neeps, 'they'll be nothing but trouble.'

Quillam's eyes narrowed in the candlelight. The sweat trickled down his spine.

'I promised I would find your family,' Tallitha said to Quillam, then beckoned to the girls. 'This is Spooner and Lince. They are your cousins, and Cissie Wakenshaw – your mother – is their Aunt.'

Quillam stared at the young girls. Spooner and Lince shuffled awkwardly, from one foot to another.

'What?' Spooner blurted out.

'Really?' said Lince, half-smiling at Quillam.

Spooner continued gawping. 'Who'd believe it! Our Aunt Cissie –' was all she could muster.

\*

Tallitha's mind was in a whirl with the events of the past few days.

Seeing her dear friends again after so long was a joy, but

there was a strained atmosphere. It was clear that the Skinks didn't trust Quillam, and Quillam didn't trust the Skinks.

Tallitha ignored the tension, for Quillam's sake. Now that he was with the Wakenshaw girls, she could see why the youth had looked so familiar on that first night they had met in the northern tower.

The Skinks relayed their story about sneaking into Winderling Spires and Marlin's vengeful attack on Cissie.

'Did he hurt her?' asked Quillam, his eyes burning with hatred.

'It was a vicious attack, but she's fine now,' replied Neeps.

Quillam's face darkened at the thought of his mother being assaulted by the evil Shrove.

'Then what happened?' asked Tallitha.

'The Shroves escaped through a tunnel beneath the pantry,' replied Ruker. 'Then your great aunt Agatha gave us this,' she said, handing Tallitha the sealed envelope.

Tallitha eyes lingered for a moment, looking at her Aunt's familiar handwriting and wishing she could see her again. Then she hurriedly tore open the envelope and peered at the note.

'Making contact with the Morrow child is going to be harder than I thought,' she said, handing the note to Quillam, 'but it explains what I must do.'

It was a Dark Spell indeed; a thrice-hexing spell that could only be destroyed with the cooperation of a long dead child.

The youth cast his eyes over Agatha's message and nodded gravely. 'This spell will take some destroying,' Quillam added. 'It seems we will need the assistance of many more ghosts!'

'Ghosts!' cried Spooner and Lince together.

'Yes,' replied Tallitha

What Kastra had revealed to her in the strange waking-dream was true!

'Who's Arabella Dorothea?' Quillam asked, looking over the letter.

'She's Edwyn Morrow's child.' explained Tallitha, 'the one who was exchanged for his freedom.'

'Well it seems she is the one who can help us destroy the pact' said Quillam handing the note back to Tallitha.

'But Arabella Dorothea will only come to us under the protection of Septimia and Siskin Morrow and they've been dead a very long time.'

'Grisly,' said Spooner.

'Even if they help us, it doesn't solve the problem of how to get the Morrow child into the tower and at just the right time,' Tallitha explained.

As she looked down at the note, she felt overwhelmed by the task ahead.

*

Spooner and Lince were amazed at everything, the wonder of the Raven Stones village, the curious Cave-Shroves and finding Tallitha. But most of all, they were bewildered by the strange youth from Hellstone Tors. He was their Aunt Cissie's child and apparently their cousin!

The girls sat at the table, grimacing at the weird food, whispering to one another behind their hands.

Spooner lowered her dark head and murmured to her sister.

'Did you even know Aunt Cissie had a child?'

Lince, who was bravely chewing a piece of skewered rat, made a face and surreptitiously dropped the gristle under her chair. She shook her head.

'Do you think our mam knows about *him*?' Lince asked, cocking her head towards the youth.

Spooner glanced quickly at Quillam, studying his hard bony face and the way his sleek black hair glistened in the candlelight.

'I bet they all know,' she added. 'They're always keeping secrets from us.'

Spooner took another peek at the youth. Quillam caught her staring at him and she blushed.

'I'm going to ask him,' she whispered to Lince.

'Don't!' her sister said quickly, giving Spooner a dig under the table.

But Spooner, as usual, ignored her.

'So how come we've never met you, if you're our cousin?' she asked, throwing her chin in Quillam's direction.

Tallitha's face burned on behalf of the youth. He kept his head lowered, circling his plate with his fork. He mumbled something incomprehensible. Tallitha shot a weary glance at Spooner to quieten the girl, but she was on a roll.

'I didn't hear you,' she said cheekily.

Quillam lifted his head and stared glumly at the girls. He was lost for words.

'Anyway, it works in our favour,' she said thoughtlessly. 'Mam and Dad can't tell us off for following the Skinks, now that we've found you. Aunt Cissie will be forever in our debt and will let us do whatever we like,' Spooner chuckled.

Quillam's skin glistened with sweat. He pushed his plate away, rose abruptly and slunk into the dark recesses of the cave.

'What's up with him?' asked Spooner, blushing slightly.

'That was thoughtless,' said Tallitha quickly.

'He's a prickly sort,' added Lince.

'He's had a hard time in Hellstone Tors. He was taken away as a child and never saw Cissie again, so be careful what you say.' She shot a glance at the girls.

Spooner shuffled in her seat and Lince dug her in the ribs.

'Sorry,' she replied, 'I just wanted to know why we'd never met him before.'

'All families have their secrets,' Tallitha replied, giving the girls a hard stare.

*

'You have no reason to return to the Spires now,' said Neeps, watching Tallitha's reaction.

'Then I suppose we must go back to Hellstone Tors' she said glumly, twisting her hair in and out of her fingers.

She felt a longing to be home in Wycham Elva but she knew that joy would have to wait.

'First, those girls have to go home,' said Ruker sternly.

'Spooner is a damned good shot with a bow and arrow. She might come in useful,' Neeps replied.

'Don't we owe it to their parents to send them back?'

'Then who will take them?' asked Tallitha.

'It'll have to be one of us,' replied Ruker.

'That's not possible,' said Tallitha, 'they'll have to stay.'

'Then you'd better explain the dangers ahead,' added Ruker gravely.

When Tallitha told the girls, they were ecstatic.

'Thanks Tallitha, you won't regret it!' cried Spooner, hugging her.

'This won't be easy, there are many dangers ahead. More than just a few bad-tempered Shroves!'

'We can handle it,' answered Spooner, 'can't we sis?'

Lince nodded.

'I promise, I'll make it up to Quillam,' Spooner added sheepishly.

*

Tallitha watched nervously as the Skinks packed their belongings and the girls chatted with the Cave-Shroves, laughing and filling their backpacks with provisions. It was time to leave the safety of the Raven Stones.

'Come, Tallitha,' Ernelle said, taking her hand and noticing the apprehension in her face. 'There is only one way to defeat the Swarm and unfortunately this terrible burden has fallen to you – you must be brave.'

The thought of Hellstone Tors and what she must do made Tallitha's mind race with endless questions.

'What if I'm not strong enough? What if they defeat me?' she asked.

'You have a better chance than most,' said Quillam coming to her side, 'Besides, you will have us with you.'

'We will meet again when it is finished,' added Snouter, putting her arm around Tallitha's shoulders and leading her to join the rest of the party.

The Cave-Shroves led them down a labyrinth of underground tunnels, climbing through dangerous potholes to a hidden shaft way beyond the Throes of Woe.

'It's a long climb,' explained Pester, pointing upwards. 'This shaft will lead you to the tunnels below the Bitter Caves. From there, you will come to the surface near Stankles Brow.'

'We know the place,' replied Quillam, climbing the rope ladder.

Tallitha stared into the gaping darkness. What would be waiting for them up there?

The travellers hugged the Cave-Shroves farewell then they began their ascent up the shaft, stopping on the narrow ledges to rest and drink. It was twilight when they reached the surface. The Barren Edges loomed on the horizon, blotting out the dusky sky.

The Skinks and Spooner foraged for food while Tallitha, Lince and Quillam set up camp by a stream, tucked inside a wooded copse.

Tallitha touched her bloodstone. The necklace felt warm against her skin. She looked up and scanned the heavens. Was Kastra watching her? Was she near?

Before they settled down for the night, Spooner's conscience was pricking her. She sidled up to Quillam.

'Sorry, I didn't mean to upset you earlier,' she said and smiled shyly at him, 'can I sit next to you?'

The youth stared at his cousin. She had messy dark hair just like him.

'It's okay,' he replied, making a space for her. 'This is an odd situation, meeting me.'

'Sure is,' Spooner replied, giving him a cheeky smile and beckoning to her sister.

Lince knelt down beside their newly found cousin.

'Do you want to know about our Aunt Cissie?' Spooner asked tenderly.

Quillam raised his eyes and nodded shyly.

After all the years of being alone, these young girls were part of his family.

He had found them at last.

# Fifteen

The Spell-Seekers were experimenting with their potions when Snowdroppe arrived in their Spell Library unannounced. She clambered over the twisting tendrils that criss-crossed the room like a spider's web, blocking out most of the daylight. The library was a place of fascination and wonder, crammed high with exotic plants, rare herbs and enormous fungi that thrived in the damp atmosphere, spreading their trunks and burrowing into the shabby sofas and cabinets, spitting spores and infusing the room with an array of pungent smells.

The Silver Spell Tower was situated in the heart of Hellstone Tors and it was the domain of Yarrow and Redlevven, the Swarm's Spell-Seekers. Their Spell Library was festooned with grotesque carvings of spiders and spiderlings, interspersed with raven head skulls and paintings of the long dead Morrow spell makers. It was an intoxicating place where the senses were aroused by the magic that abounded within its walls. Spider Orchids, Sneezewort, Hooded Skullcaps and Monkshood burst from their flowerpots, displaying splendid blooms and suffusing the air with overpowering aromas. Towers of fungi with their heavy umbrella heads oozed and spat next to the Dryad's Saddle, Green Spotted Lepiota and the Amethyst Deceiver.

At the far end of the library lay the Spell Archive, a vast complex of shelves and cabinets where twisting tendrils penetrated the drawers like snakes. On one side were the untidy shelves and higgledy-piggledy drawers belonging to Yarrow whilst the neat, cleverly organised cabinets belonged to her brother, Redlevven. They were full of old spells and bewitching potions, collected over the years by the Spell-Seekers.

Snowdroppe perused the new potion bottles with eager anticipation.

'What's this one?' she asked Yarrow, peering at a bottle of green shimmering liquid.

The bottle fizzed and bubbled.

Yarrow, with her stained fingers and mass of blue-black hair, stood behind her bench with a pencil tucked behind her ear, jotting down notes and grinding coloured splinters with a pestle and mortar.

'We stole it from a woman in Much Grovell,' she murmured distractedly, reading her scribbled notes.

Yarrow added citrine shards to her potion vessel and mixed it with garnet-coloured splinters. She shook the mixture until it turned into a bright red sludge. She was covered with smudges of powder and streaks of sticky liquid, red, pinks and orange splodges smeared her apron.

'This is a gem of a spell,' she announced, turning to Snowdroppe. 'It will perk up your complexion. You will feel rejuvenated,' she explained, swallowing a spoonful of the liquid.

As it slipped down her throat her eyes glowed and her skin turned fresh and pink in an instant. Snowdroppe gasped with pleasure, grabbed the spoon and swallowed a good mouthful of the scarlet liquid, smiling at the results in a mirror as her cheeks flushed with recovered youthfulness.

Redlevven was a pale copy of his colourful sister, a peculiar oddity. He was extraordinarily short, with a shock of black wiry hair and a hooked nose – an unfortunate trait of the Swarm. He had strange habits and preferred to blend into his surroundings so that when the time was right, he could slip away unnoticed. Redlevven was a hoarder of spells and a talented weaver of charms, conjured from the collections they had gathered from villages in the Northern Wolds. The Spell-Seekers had nurtured their magical art; it was gleaned from their grandparents, Gravelock and his stern wife, Arcadia, a great concocter of deadly poisons.

Since her childhood, Snowdroppe had adored the mysterious Spell Library, stacked high with ancient spells tucked away in wooden drawers, nestling beside the potions from Breedoor. She explored the library, opening drawers and perusing their contents, peeking into jars and smelling mysterious bottles while Yarrow tempted her with their latest discoveries.

'We came across an old woman in Hegglefoot who was persuaded to part with this fine liquor,' she said, taking the stopper from a jar and wafting it under Snowdroppe's nose. 'Topaz Stargazer,' she trilled, 'used in stunning and immobilising when mixed with frog's vomit and absolutely perfect for ensnaring unsuspecting passers-by in the Stinkwells.'

'Mmmm,' replied Snowdroppe, gazing at the lustrous yellow liquid but carefully keeping her distance. 'What about this one?' she asked.

Snowdroppe unscrewed a jar containing a brilliant blue liquid that oozed a trail of inky blue vapour across the room.

'Indigo Sky Liquid,' Yarrow replied, picking up the jar, 'brewed from the petals of a thousand crushed periwinkles and bluebells, mixed with henbane and used to keep strange witches at bay.'

Redlevven poked his head from behind a cabinet and shuffled between them. In a deft movement, he reached up on tiptoes and whipped the jar from Yarrow's hands.

'Careful sister! As usual you've forgotten the most important ingredients!' He clicked his tongue, admonishing her with a sideways look. 'This potion is not ready yet.' He scurried off and placed the bottle in his spell safe, muttered a few words and it locked with a click. 'It has to be mixed with fresh snakebite drippings and fossilised bats' wings to form the right consistency.'

Redlevven tutted irritably at his forgetful sister; she often misplaced ingredients and stumbled over the words of a spell.

'Do stop fussing, Redlevven,' Yarrow replied, 'you're a worrisome old goat.'

'But sister, you know that each spell is a web of intricate strands. Say a word out of place and it will rupture,' he said curtly. 'Then any nosy witch will be able to sneak in and steal our spells or even worse.'

'I know that! Do stop badgering me!' she hissed and turned to Snowdroppe.

It was a pleasure to have another woman in the Spell Tower. Sometimes being locked away with her brother for days on end was quite tiresome.

'What about this one?' said Yarrow, waving a potion under Snowdroppe's nose.

'A little bitter,' she replied.

Snowdroppe liked to sample the peculiar spells but only under Yarrow's guidance.

'What brings you here today?' asked Redlevven suspiciously, cocking his head to one side.

'The Thane has a task for you,' Snowdroppe explained. 'He wants you to scour the Northern Wolds, to capture Tallitha and Quillam and bring them back to Hellstone Tors.'

Redlevven stared at Snowdroppe's beautiful face with an unctuous leer.

'That sounds most agreeable,' he said licking his lips, his eyes revolving with delight at her soft red hair and pretty lips.

He was an oily toad, thought Snowdroppe, throwing him one of her acid glances.

'My daughter bears the Morrow stain, so finding her shouldn't be a problem. It's just a matter of picking up her trail, from this piece of cloth,' she explained, handing Yarrow the bloodied drape from the Neopholytite's lair. Redlevven breathed in its dark perfume.

'Oh that sounds like fun,' cried Yarrow. 'I love a good chase across country.'

'Yes, my sweet, and on the way we can check our Stinkwells and lace them with our new potions.' Redlevven drooled at the thought of the hideous traps they would set and stared goggle-eyed in Snowdroppe's direction. 'It's always such a pleasure when Yarrow tells me we've caught someone in the Stinkwell's rotting belly,' he replied with sickening glee.

'Where was the last sighting of Tallitha?' asked Yarrow.

Redlevven inched closer to Snowdroppe, twisting his neck to get a more satisfactory view of her radiant face. She reared back at the stench of bitter balms. *Odious worm*!

'She was studying The Black Pages at Stankles Brow when she foolishly escaped with Quillam,' Snowdroppe replied. 'I blame that youth for leading her astray. Asphodel thinks they went through the Bitter Caves and out onto the Barren Edges.'

The Spell-Seekers exchanged a knowing glance.

'But what is your daughter's special power?' Redlevven asked smiling his toothy grin at Snowdroppe. 'Should we be wary of her tricks?'

'Tallitha has developed supernatural powers during her time at Hellstone, but nothing that should trouble you.'

'Mmmmm,' replied Redlevven, 'but she must know some spells or how to fly across the heavens. She is a Morrow girl after all,' he said.

'Only the shadow-flight and time-travel,' replied Snowdroppe curtly. 'But whether she has learned any new magical skills, my sister has not said.'

Redlevven climbed onto a stool and cocked his head at Snowdroppe. He looked unsettlingly like a gnome. Unfortunately, Redlevven only stood as high as Snowdroppe's elbow.

'But if we cannot catch her, who will be the thirteenth?' his voice was trill, like an angry bird.

'If all else fails, Tyaas will be sworn instead,' Snowdroppe answered abruptly. 'But the Thane *insists* you recapture Tallitha.'

'We'll ride out first thing,' answered Yarrow.

Redlevven rubbed his pointy chin. 'The Gross Stumpleback will go with us,' he announced, his expression brightening with the thought.

Yarrow leapt to her feet and clasped her hands with delight.

'Good idea, brother, the creature is well used to sniffing out miscreants,' she replied, 'let her smell the bloodstained cloth.'

'Can that monster behave itself?' Snowdroppe asked sounding alarmed. 'Remember you have to bring them back alive.' she added.

'Of course, Snowdroppe. We understand, don't we, Yarrow?'

'Yes, brother,' she simpered.

The Spell-Seekers smiled wickedly behind Snowdroppe's back.

A day of great sport beckoned, galloping across the Northern Wolds with the Gross Stumpleback in harness.

*

Later, after Snowdroppe had departed, Redlevven made his way to the dungeon beneath the Silver Tower. It was the time of day when the Gross Stumpleback would be clamouring for fresh meat.

'You there!' Redlevven shouted at the drowsy Shrove who watched over the beast. 'Pass me some goat's meat and open the grill to the greedy one's cell.'

Flinter was a Shrove of meagre brain. He mumbled to Redlevven to be careful of the beast.

'She's not had much to eat this day and is in a bad mood. She'll have your hand off as quick as lightening!' the Shrove warned.

Flinter ferreted about in the cold meat store. Mounds of carcasses were laid end to end ready to be fed to the Gross Stumpleback as she slavered and grunted in the depths of her dungeon.

'Skewer the meat and pour this potion onto the flesh,' Redlevven instructed. 'It will stun her fury. Then she will be more malleable when I place her in harness.'

Redlevven climbed on a wooden box, peering through the grill where the Gross Stumpleback reared her horned head, snorted and snarled, then scraped the floor as the smell of flesh emanated from the cold store.

'Quiet, my beauty,' murmured Redlevven, gazing at the fearsome spectacle.

The Gross Stumpleback was an awesome beast, claw-footed, with a hide of silvery-black armoured scales like a dragon, and horned, with ferocious teeth. Her eyes were the colour of jet with a yellow glowing centre. The Stumpleback snorted smoke from her nostrils and chomped on her chains, desperate to set her horrific jaws on the raw meat.

'There, my red-tongued beast, here is your dinner, eat it all up,' Redlevven cried, opening the grill and throwing the bloody haunches into the dank cell.

The carcasses fell on the floor with a sickening thud. The Stumpleback slavered and pounced, tearing the meat as she savaged the goats' legs, swallowing them in a few voracious mouthfuls. Droplets of blood and gore smeared her mouth and dribbled down her scaly jaw. The beast licked her lips and opened her bloody jaws for more, growling and drooling with pleasure.

'Pass me a sheep's carcass and lace it with potion,' demanded Redlevven, pushing the indolent Shrove into action.

Flinter lifted the dead sheep from the meat store, dribbled liquid onto the carcass and pushed it through the grill. The Stumpleback made mincemeat of the animal in a few grizzly seconds. Still, the odious beast panted for more.

'Later, my sharp-toothed fiend! First we have a task for you. Now, listen carefully to my little song.'

Redlevven focused on the beast, hexing the Gross Stumpleback into submission, staring into her eyes, mesmerising her with his lilting tune.

'Catch or slaughter the Swarm Queen's daughter,' he sang with malicious delight. 'Catch or slaughter the Swarm Queen's daughter, you can do that, can't you? You ugly carbuncle – Tallitha is the girl's name! Smell this cloth! She has the Morrow stain upon her!'

Redlevven threw the fabric, unctuous with the Morrow stain, into the dungeon as he hummed his mellifluous tune, hexing the Gross Stumpleback into submission. The beast's eyes rolled back as she lurched forward and breathed in the enticing smell of the bloody fabric. Then she shifted her huge body, trampling the bones underfoot, snorting her way to freedom as Redlevven unlocked the gate.

For Redlevven was a deadly adversary.

For years, he had been hatching his scheme to rule Hellstone Tors.

Now Tallitha and the noxious Quillam were in his way.

This was his opportunity to do away with both of them.

# Sixteen

**E**smerelda waited anxiously for Asenathe's return from her shadow-flight as the hours dragged on with no sign of her cousin. She should never have let her go! Asenathe wasn't used to the physical and emotional exertion that was required to enter the middle plane. If the Swarm should discover her outside the confines of her palace then the game would be up. The Shroves had already been nosing around, entering their apartment under any pretext. They knew something was afoot.

Then, when she had almost given up hope, Esmerelda felt the air pressure drop and the skin on her neck began to crawl as a door suddenly slammed across the landing.

'Attie, is that you?' she whispered, hoarsely.

All at once a *whooshing* sound filled the room and a slick grey shadow slid back into Asenathe's body with a jolt. She shuddered and slumped in the chair. Her face was wretched and pale from the exertion of her first shadow flight in many years.

'Attie? Wake up, you're back now,' Esmerelda murmured. 'Did you find Tyaas?' Did you talk with him?'

Asenathe's eyes fluttered open and she shook her head.

'I couldn't speak with him,' she mumbled, wiping the sweat from her brow. 'But he's being kept in the Withered tower. The bed was a mess and his things were strewn about.' She reached out shakily to her cousin. 'Some water, Essie, please.'

'So where is he?' Esmerelda asked, filling a glass and turning to stare towards the moon-soaked mountains. 'Don't tell me he has fled too?'

'No he's still here,' Asenathe faltered. 'I-I did see him, much later when I was searching the castle. Caedryl was taking him to see Sedentia Flight. I followed them from a distance. They're tutoring him to take Tallitha's place.'

'He won't like that,' replied Esmerelda.

Since Tyaas's visit, Asenathe had used her proximity to the Swarm to find out their plans for the forthcoming initiation ceremony.

'It's dark out there and the wolfhounds will be on the prowl soon,' said Esmerelda. 'Tyaas may be in danger. Please, Attie, you must try and make contact with him again.'

'I can't, it's much too dangerous. I almost collided with Caedryl by the Withered Tower and if they discover I've been using my powers all our hopes will be dashed. They'll realise I'm no longer taking their potions and you'll be thrown back into the Bleak Rooms. Then we'll be no help to Tallitha or Tyaas.'

'But we're running out of time. We must find Tyaas tonight

or it will be too late,' said Esmerelda frantically. 'If we're careful and avoid the guards, perhaps we can slip out after dark.'

'Come,' said Asenathe, rising slowly, 'let me show you something.' She stepped into her dressing room and parted the hanging clothes. 'There's a passageway at the back. We can climb down through the walls.'

'How did you discover this?' asked Esmerelda.

'Arden used to hide things in here. He was secretive about his work with the Swarm. For a long time I didn't want to know what he got up to. Then one day he disappeared into the closet when he thought I was sleeping. The next time he left me alone, curiosity got the better of me and I decided to investigate.'

The wooden panel moved easily. Esmerelda tiptoed into the dingy wall cavity, followed by Asenathe.

'It's so dark,' said Asenathe. 'Do you think we can manage all the climbing?'

'We can help each other,' answered Esmerelda excitedly. 'Is there any rope?'

Asenathe nodded.

'I'll get a lantern.'

*

That same night, when darkness had descended, after Cannisp had retreated to his mattress in the anteroom and the chattering Nooklies were chortling softly in their sleep, Tyaas took his chance to escape. He was determined to find his cousin Esmerelda. He had decided to follow Quillam's route by squirrelling through the walls.

Behind his bed, the plaster was beginning to crumble away. Tyaas picked at it, wriggling his fingers through the warp and weft until a small hole appeared where the draught whistled through. He gouged a hole in the flaking plaster, pushing his hand into the dusty space, tugging until at last he poked his head through the hole. It was stuffy and smelly. The flat dead air was redolent with decay.

'Pooh, what a stench,' he murmured, spitting out plaster dust.

He placed a handkerchief over his mouth to mask the smell of rat, beetle and roach.

When Tyaas was certain that one last push would deliver him into the dark infrastructure of the castle, he put the witch bottle inside his backpack and eased it through the opening. Tyaas squirmed and slithered, snapping off the protruding plaster until his shoulders finally slipped through the hole. His body followed and he landed on the dirty floor in a heap. His hair was full of dirt and his face was white with dust. Once inside, he stuck his hand back through the gap and squeezed a pillow into position to cover the hole. Then it all went black.

As he lit a candle Tyaas found himself in a narrow space that meandered on into pitch darkness. He secured his backpack and wriggled through the dust on his belly, spitting out grime and muck until he found an opening between the planks. It wasn't very big. He peered down the black hole. Slivers of light sneaked through gaps in the lath walls way below him. It was impossible to gauge the drop but he had no choice. Tyaas blew out the candle and tucked it into his pocket.

'Here goes,' he mumbled, lowering his body into the void and holding on to the beam above his head.

Rough wooden splinters dug into his fingers and his knuckles ached as he gripped the beam tightly, swinging his body, his legs flaying desperately in mid air, trying to locate a foothold. But there was nothing there! His stomach lurched. He started to panic. He swung out once more, breathing rapidly, lunging haphazardly in the darkness! Then his boot scraped along the lath wall and he found a ledge with his toe.

'Got it!' he muttered.

Tyaas stretched out his legs as far as he could– then his fingers loosened and he slipped …

'Arrgh,' he groaned, as his body moved disconcertingly and sent him tumbling in the wrong direction.

Tyaas lost his grip and fell with a sickening thud, banged his head and blacked out. As he landed, a million dust motes filled the shaft, swimming upwards in the darkness. A rat shuffled from its hole and sniffed the air, scuttled forwards and eyed the boy. As Tyaas came to, the rat darted behind the panelling and vanished.

His head throbbed and his foot ached.

'Ouch, ahhh!' he moaned, rolling over.

For a moment, stars swam before his eyes. He felt sick. Then he remembered the witch-bottle and hurriedly felt inside the backpack. The heavy glass bottle was still intact.

'Damn it!' he winced as he grabbed the lintel and pulled himself to his feet.

The pain shot up his leg. He had twisted his ankle. Tyaas ran his fingers over the swollen mass, bulging over his anklebone. It felt hot and sore to the touch.

As Tyaas tumbled down the shaft, he had dislodged something hanging on the wall. It lay beneath his leg. He reached down and felt along a long leather casing. It was a knife. Tyaas had found himself in one of Quillam's secret stashes.

'Brill,' he muttered, grasping the knife.

At least something was going right.

Tyaas explored Quillam's hidey-hole, locating hanks of rope and an old sock containing matches and several candle stubs. His hands were shaking from the shock of falling down the shaft and he dropped the two matches on the floor. They fizzed and died in the dust. He steadied his hands, struck another match and the candle finally spluttered into life. Quillam's hidey-hole took shape before his eyes. There was a flask of water that he drank in a few desperate gulps, a row of knives, some hammers and a ball of twine.

Tyaas filled his backpack and limped towards the end of the cavity. He put his ear against the wooden panel and listened. The only sound was his laboured breathing. Cautiously, he prised his body through the gap as shards of moonlight shone through the ivy-covered windowpanes, landing on the worn steps of the Withered Tower. Rats scurried away as he approached and the sound of water drip-dropped beneath him.

Searing pain shot up his leg as he hobbled to the bottom of the staircase. He unlatched the door and peered out into the windswept night. On the battlements, a group of Groat guards were patrolling the walkways. Tyaas waited until they rounded the corner then he crawled along the battlements, keeping beneath their line of sight.

Below him, the courtyard stretched out in the moonlight. Tyaas scoured the lower levels until he spied a scullery window that had been left slightly ajar. He slipped down the steps, pulled himself onto a barrel and wriggled through the opening. He landed on top of a washtub in the warren of sculleries that lay beneath the huge kitchens. Tyaas limped through the passageway towards the servant's entrance leading into the main castle and peered round the edge of the door.

Hellstone Tors was silent and foreboding at the dead of night. A maze of floors and twisting staircases vanished up into the shadows, pierced here and there by daggers of moonlight. Then in the distance he heard the sound that he had been dreading, that of the hounds pounding above him, their claws scratching across the wooden floor. His stomach lurched and he fell to the ground. He heard snarling and the sound of hurried feet as angry voices shouted from the landing above.

'Get those hounds away from me. Fasten them in their cages!' shouted Caedryl to the Groats.

Tyaas swore under his breath, crouching in the shadows of the stairwell, trying desperately to keep out of sight.

*What is Caedryl doing out so late?*

He held his breath and waited, peering up through the moonlight, through the twisting staircases into the dark castle that loomed above him. He could feel the whole weight of the malevolent Tors bearing down, the seething mass enveloping him, waiting to catch him off guard.

Tyaas heard Caedryl's voice and the muffled response of a man. They were plotting together.

'Dear Uncle, at the appointed time, we will strike,' Caedryl replied.

Tyaas pinned his body flat against the wall and listened. The man was Lord Edweard!

'Then Hellstone Tors and all the Swarm's riches will be ours,' Edweard replied.

Caedryl laughed. 'You must leave all that to me. You know what you and the twins must do ... ,' she faltered and stamped her foot. 'Take those hounds away! Do you hear me? Lock them up for the night!' she shouted to the guards.

Tyaas heard the Groats rounding up the wolfhounds as they growled at being denied their nightly prowl. Then the castle became silent once more. The only sound was Tyaas's rapid breathing pounding in his ears.

Then, just above him, the floorboards creaked.

It was Caedryl on the staircase – *she was coming towards him! She was about to discover him!* Tyaas winced and inched further into the shadows, pressing his body up against the wall.

The shadows lengthened, casting their bewitching presence, dancing down the staircase, as Caedryl suddenly leapt in the air.

Tyaas held his breath. A thick purring sound met his ears. A black cat with tufted ears slunk down the staircase, artful and proud, stopping a few steps in front of him to lick her tufted paws. Her claws extended as she flashed her tongue between each talon. Her tail swished and her swirling green eyes scanned the night for her mousey supper. Then an unsettling growl came from deep within her throat. Someone was coming along the corridor.

The cat bristled and leapt into the air and in one deft movement Caedryl landed gracefully in the Wheen-Cat's place. She smoothed down her long dark hair and straightened her sombre dress. Tyaas froze. He dared not breathe.

Caedryl had spied someone. 'You there,' she called.

It was the scullery boy, wandering down the corridor, up before dawn to do his chores.

'Tell that lazy cook to make my breakfast – I'm starving. Bring it to my chamber,' she ordered. 'Then, I fancy a long nap,' she yawned, stretched her arms and licked her lips.

*She mews just like a cat*, thought Tyaas.

His heart was thumping so loudly he felt sure she would hear him.

Had she seen him? Was she toying with him, like a cat with a mouse? Would she turn and pounce?

But Caedryl hadn't seen Tyaas. The artful creature was too preoccupied with her own dark schemes. She touched the bloodstone at her throat, smiled a wicked smile and pranced off into the night. Tyaas shuddered and shut his eyes. He had been a whisker away from the Wheen-Cat's claws!

It was some time before Tyaas dared to move. He reached down to touch his swollen ankle. Gingerly he eased up the staircase, keeping in the shadows.

As he reached the top a hand went over his mouth and a voice whispered in his ear. It was the sweet sound of his cousin Esmerelda!

'Come with us, be quick and make no noise,' she urged.

Tyaas stared at her. 'I-I thought you were one of them!' he said, sounding relieved. 'I've twisted my ankle.'

'Quickly, put your arms around our shoulders!' Esmerelda urged. 'Take his backpack, Attie.'

'Caedryl was here just a moment ago,' he whispered fretfully.

'We saw her antics,' replied Asenathe.

'She turned into a cat,' he added.

'We know, Tyaas. Now try and stand up,' answered Esmerelda.

With their encouragement Tyaas hobbled along the darkened hallway, up a series of narrow steps and vanished with Esmerelda and Asenathe behind the lath walls.

They had him safe and sound, for now.

# Seventeen

In the gloom of the musty wall cavity, tucked behind Asenathe's closet, Tyaas sat nursing his swollen ankle.

'What were you doing wandering about out there?' Essie said sharply.

'Looking for you, of course!' he replied. 'Anyway, I almost forgot,' he said, lifting a dirty bottle from his backpack. 'Not sure if this is any use, but it caught my fancy.'

Esmerelda and Asenathe stared at the grubby bottle as though it was buried treasure.

'It's a witch bottle!' Esmerelda cried, hastily rubbing her fingers over the coloured glass and staring at the macabre contents.

Slivers of the witch met her gaze. The blackened nail clippings and the strands of hair were cocooned like pupa larva, wrapped with silken twine and neatly placed inside the witch bottle. The women whispered excitedly at the sight of the weird contents.

'There's a strand of her hair!' murmured Asenathe.

'Oooh ho!' squealed Esmerelda with delight, 'and her blood too – in that tiny phial!'

'Yuck!' replied Tyaas, frowning, 'that's disgusting!'

'No, this is precious,' answered Asenathe holding the bottle up to the lantern and perusing its contents. 'Now we have this, we may be able to weaken the witch and her hold over the Bone Room.'

'Did you take this from the Neopholytite's tower?' Asenathe asked.

'Yep,' he replied. 'I climbed up and pinched it.'

'Well done, Tyaas! This is like gold dust,' replied Esmerelda.

'The Neopholytite uses these spells to protect her against prowling witches trying to steal into the Bone Room,' explained Asenathe. 'Now we have some power over her at last.'

'Not so fast,' replied Esmerelda. 'If we open the bottle without first disarming the curse tablets, then the curse will attack us and the witch will be able to find us,' she added.

'So how does it work?' asked Tyaas.

'The curse tablet is magical protection against anyone who tries to open the witch bottle and steal a fragment of the witch,' she explained. 'If the curse tablet remains intact when the bottle is opened it will fly back to the Neopholytite to warn her.'

'That's clever,' said Tyaas, staring incredulously at the small bottle.

'The tablets are tricky,' answered Asenathe.

'We can deal with them later,' replied her cousin.

Asenathe wrapped the witch-bottle and hid it for safekeeping.

'Now let's take a look at that ankle,' said Esmerelda, unlacing Tyaas's boot and removing his sock.

'Ahhhh, that hurts,' he winced.

'That's nasty. I'll get some ointment,' said Esmerelda.

But as Tyaas struggled to follow Essie, Asenathe stayed his hand.

'You must stay here,' she insisted.

'Why?'

'The Swarm will come looking for you. If you stay in here we have a chance of keeping you safe. Until – '

Tyaas lookled perplexed.

'Until when?' he asked apprehensively.

'Until you leave and the Swarm recapture you.'

Tyaas groaned.

'It's safer this way,' Asenathe explained. 'Then you can tell them that you didn't mean any harm, you were just exploring and had become lost. They won't hurt you, will they? They need you, now that Tallitha is missing.'

'Can't I stay with you?' he pleaded. 'It's so lonely without Tallitha, and that governess has been trying to make me do weird things.'

'Like what?' she asked, watching the boy.

Tyaas pulled a face. 'To look at an old book and say spooky stuff – but it didn't work. Then she got annoyed and packed me off to bed.'

'That's good. She'll think you're useless at magic and will leave you alone. Trust me,' replied Asenathe darkly, 'it will all work out in time.'

Esmerelda returned with bedding and a basket of provisions. She applied Barrenwort salve to Tyaas's bruises and bound his swollen ankle.

'Here, drink this,' she said, handing him a bottle of liquorice cordial.

He swilled down a few mouthfuls, wiping his mouth on the sleeve of his jacket.

'That taste reminds me of the caves,' he said wistfully, licking his lips.

He began munching ravenously on the chunks of bread and cheese.

'Once you've finished, you can rest. We'll be back later.'

Esmerelda tucked him in and gently stroked his head.

'You're a good lad,' Essie whispered fondly.

Tyaas blew out the candle and snuggled down under the warm bedding.

In no time at all he was fast asleep.

\*

'We must break the curse tablets,' said Esmerelda, pacing Attie's room anxiously.

'We'll have to find the antidote,' Asenathe replied guardedly.

'You mean the Raven Spell?' replied Essie. 'That will be kept in the Spell-Seekers' library. No one can get inside without being caught.'

'I may have an idea,' Asenathe answered.

'But what about Redlevven and his sister?' asked Esmerelda.

'Perhaps Snowdroppe is the answer.'

'Snowdroppe! That scheming monster!' exclaimed Esmerelda, 'have you gone mad?'

'She knows all the comings and goings in Hellstone Tors. Maybe I'll be able to wheedle it out of her,' replied Asenathe mysteriously.

'She won't tell us a thing!'

'Well it's worth a try. Call for the Shrove and tell him to invite Snowdroppe to visit us. You can say you're worried about me, that I've deteriorated and need a remedy from Redlevven.'

Esmerelda pulled a face. 'How will that help?'

'Wait and see,' she answered, smiling.

'I don't know, Attie. It's a risk. It may backfire. She may see that you're better!'

'If I'm right about her, she won't come anyway,' added Aseanthe.

Esmerelda looked unconvinced.

'Trust me Essie, I know what I'm doing.'

So Esmerelda rang the bell for the Shrove. Whatever Asenathe's plan, she was prepared to give it a shot.

\*

Snowdroppe turned on the Shrove like lightening.

'What did you say? Out with it!' she bellowed.

'Please m'Lady, the Lady Asenathe is sick and requires a remedy.'

'What do they expect me to do?'

'The Lady Esmerelda hoped you would visit and advise them,' Croop mumbled, 'she hoped that you may persuade the Spell-Seekers to provide one of their potions.'

Snowdroppe was intrigued at the invitation but she wasn't about to dance to Esmerelda Patch's tune.

*Let's hope Asenathe is really ill and close to death*, thought Snowdroppe nastily.

She pounced on Croop, tweaking his ear with her crimson talons.

'Tell the Lady Esmerelda that the Spell-Seekers are away and won't be back for some days.'

The Shrove scuttled back to Asenathe's and recounted what Snowdroppe had said.

'Very well, that will be all,' Esmerelda replied, dismissing him.

Perplexed, Esmerelda looked to her cousin for an explanation.

'That worked better than I hoped. Snowdroppe has given me the information I need,' said Asenathe, excitedly. 'Tonight I'm going to search the Spell-Seekers' library. I intend to find the Raven Spell, the antidote to the curse tablets.'

'It's too dangerous! I'm coming with you,' insisted Esmerelda.

'No, Essie,' Asenathe replied firmly, 'I must do this alone. Better they discover me than both of us.'

'But if someone should see you,' her cousin said nervously.

'If they should catch both of us wandering about the Spell Library they will separate us again and I couldn't bear that,' replied her cousin forcefully. 'But I have a ready excuse. I can pretend to be befuddled from the sleeping potion, then they will pat me on the back and send me straight back here.'

'But Attie,' pleaded Esmerelda, 'what if you should become ensnared in their spells? The Spell Library is laced with traps, cast by Redlevven and Yarrow to stop intruders. Some say their magic reveals terrible secrets to those who remain there too long – dark secrets best left hidden.'

'I can protect myself,' Asenathe answered quickly.

'Only if you're sure you're strong enough to resist the lure of that evil place,' Esmerelda added.

'I'll leave as soon as I've found the Raven Spell,' she replied.

But secretly, Aseanathe *was* afraid of entering the sorcerers' lair.

\*

Later that night, Asenathe climbed through the wall cavities and edged into the shadowy passageway, hiding in recesses and creeping noiselessly past the guards. When all was clear she sped along the corridors and climbed the rickety black staircase to the Spell Library.

The Library became even more sinister at night. Fleeting shadows leapt up the walls and the room became awash with bewitching aromas that befuddled the senses. The fungus colonies loomed like giant's fingers as they clawed at Asenathe's hair and snagged at her clothes, twisting and turning her until she became disorientated. By the time she had travelled through the forest of tendrils her heart was racing. Now she just had to find the Raven Spell.

As the full moon glinted through the windows, Asenathe spied the Spell Archive, housed in a cluster of ramshackle cabinets and topsy-turvy drawers, interspersed with foliage that wound in and out of the shelves. The drawers were decorated with ornate illustrations and an individual gold letter, identifying the spells contained inside each one. Some had dragons painted outside and others were embellished with toadstools or wild flowers.

"'*Witches and how to ward them off in five easy steps*", said Asenathe, opening a drawer and reading the spell.

Lavender dust, garnet sparkles and silver stars leapt from the dusty drawer and darted into the air, invading Asenathe's senses and making her feel light-headed.

'Concentrate,' she said, trying to shake off the bewitching presence that surrounded her.

She sifted through the spells, entranced by the magic. There were spells for '*instigating illnesses*', '*turning a witch's spell on herself*' and curses for '*bewitching madness*', and '*extremely nasty boiling curses*'.

Asenathe found it difficult to tear herself away. The magic was infecting her.

As she searched the lower cabinets, a sleek black raven came into view, picked out in shiny paint. Asenathe opened the drawer and the words '*Beware*' and '*Dire Warning*' leapt out, written on fine parchment. She had found the Raven spell! The deadly warning was clear – the spell must not be spoken aloud unless the witch bottle was being disarmed.

Asenathe read the words of the Raven Spell to herself.

'*Beware to those who seek to destroy me! Keep stone all around, not a chink of light; remove the stopper and cast the Raven Spell – Anintha, Ravena melliflicant, anintha, Ravena melliflicant - Anintha, Ravena melliflicant, anintha, Ravena melliflicant.*'

She scribbled down the spell, lingering for a moment to trace the outline of the painted Raven with her fingertip. Suddenly, the bird came alive and turned his beady eye on her, transfixing Asenathe, bewitching her to tarry a while. The magic had infected her senses, compelling her to stay and explore the dark spells.

Intense curiosity drew her towards the next cabinet, willing her to peer inside.

'It can't hurt,' she whispered as she opened the drawer with "A" on the outside.

'"A" for Asenathe,' she said, 'perhaps I can discover the drug they used to keep me prisoner.'

There it was. A small white card with her name on it! The words were written in scarlet ink. But this was a love-potion.

Her heart fluttered.

"*Asenathe Morrow – A Spell for Love*", she read the words. "*Mix Lemon Hensbane, three hundred pecks of pollen from crimson sweet-peas, grind the leaves of three arrowhead ferns, crush them to a sweet pulp, add a thimbleful of a young girl's love-sick tears and the ground feathers of a white dove. Rub the salve on Asenathe Morrow's pillow each night for a week and thereafter she will fall headlong for Arden Morrow and the love match shall be made.*"

Aseanthe gripped the drawer. The sharp edge lacerated her finger and blood dripped into the cabinet. She hastily pushed the card back inside the drawer, flying from the spell library, tripping and falling as the words on the card seared into her brain. *Asenathe Morrow, A Spell for Love* – then Arden hadn't loved her! It had all been a terrible trick!

Asenathe stumbled down the rickety staircase, climbed through the wall cavity and back into her palace in a fog of despair.

Esmerelda turned quickly as her cousin burst into the room.

'What's wrong? You're bleeding!' she said, staring at Asenathe's wound.

Asenathe slumped into a chair. 'It's nothing,' she replied, 'I-I stupidly cut my hand.'

'You look pale. I told you not to go in that place,' said Esmerelda sharply, coming towards her. 'Did you find the Raven Spell?'

'Yes,' Attie replied clutching the note.

'What's wrong? Did someone see you?'

Asenathe bit her lip. 'No, but I found something.'

Esmerelda stared at her cousin. 'I told you not to look at anything! That place is bewitched!'

'I couldn't help myself,' she sobbed, wrapping her wound in a handketchief. 'The magic was too strong! I wanted to find the drug they used to sedate me, but I found something else – something so vile!' She burst into tears.

'What? Tell me!'

'An evil spell cast especially for me,' she sobbed, 'to make me fall in love with Arden! It wasn't real, Essie – he didn't love me. It was all a trick! Even our love was part of their cruel scheme!'

Asenathe sobbed in her cousin's arms. The Swarm had tricked her even in that!

Her love for Arden and his love for her was the one thing that made her stay in Hellstone Tors when she knew she should escape.

Now, after all she had been through, even Arden's love for her was a lie.

# Eighteen

'Fresh air!' croaked Bicker excitedly, giving Embellsed a shove from behind.

The rain was sheeting down in waves as Bicker and Embellsed poked their noses out of the rat-infested tunnel and smelt the remnants of the damp, dreary day. Their perilous journey had taken them through the underbelly of Hellstone Tors, through a warren of snickleways, past the tunnel that led to the Swarm's harbour, and out beyond the castle walls.

Bicker scampered across the rain-sodden grass, beckoning to Embellsed to follow him into the wild unknown. The Shroves huddled together under the boughs of an oak tree and stared miserably at their first taste of freedom as the rain dripped off the tips of their noses and soaked up through their shoes, making their feet cold and damp.

'It's not how I remember *the outside*,' announced Bicker downheartedly.

It had been many years since he had seen the light of day and his eyes watered in the gloomy light.

'Where are we?' he asked fretfully.

Embellsed squinted at the sight of Hellstone Tors looming high across the bay as the white tipped waves crashed against the black rocks. White breasted guillemots and hungry seagulls soared on the wind currents, screeching across the pallid skies, searching for food, patrolling the heights with their beady eyes.

'The Castle Keep is over yonder,' Embellsed replied, pointing towards the tavern on the headland. 'But we best keep well away and make for the forest, then no one can betray us to the Swarm. We're on the run now,' he added gravely.

From out of the depths of the forest four pairs of piercing eyes were trained on the Shroves. The Black Sprites had been patrolling the northern perimeter of Hellstone Tors for days, taking it in turns to keep watch for the Grand Witch Kastra.

'Shroves!' said Dipper, urgently pointing at the bedraggled pair plodding aimlessly towards the trees.

'What they up to?' asked Flametip, 'Shroves never venture outside Hellstone Tors.'

'It can only mean one thing,' replied Dipper. 'Something has happened in that castle to force them out.'

Rucheba nodded to the others. 'I'll warn Kastra. You follow the Shroves and I'll be back.'

Embellsed and Bicker scurried into the undergrowth and

onwards through the woody hinterland. The ground dipped and furrowed, and blackened trees festooned with creepers hung down like shrouds, obscuring their route.

'It's so 'orribly cold and frightening out 'ere,' moaned Bicker, staring helplessly into the swirling mists.

'Keep close and don't get lost in the fog' urged Embellsed, taking hold of Bicker's arm as the old feller trotted wearily by his side.

The air was chilly and damp as the wary Shroves trudged over the rugged landscape, the white mists rising from the earth in ghostly patches.

'What about something to eat?' asked Bicker. His mouth hung open and he licked his dry lips. Food had always been available in the Tors and he was unused to having to fend for himself. 'I'm desperate for some grub,' he moaned, 'and we've eaten the last of the bread cakes.'

'I've nowt left either,' replied Embellsed, searching his pockets. 'Come on old feller, we'll catch summat and roast it over a fire. It'll be an adventure,' he added, trying to encourage his miserable companion.

But in reality, Embellsed despaired at their inadequacies when faced with the inhospitable terrain, and their inexperience in surviving outdoors. He stole a glance at the old Shrove bumbling across the muddy earth and muttering away to himself. Bicker may have been useful in navigating their way out of Hellstone Tors, but he was ill-equipped for life outside the castle.

Bicker, for his part, stuck like glue to Embellsed, bleating about this and that, plodding along in the pouring rain, far away from the only world he had ever known. All the while the Sprites followed close behind, always a moment out of sight with just a flicker of a shadow appearing here and there through the mist.

'Did you see something?' asked Embellsed, his eyes darting nervously towards the bushes.

'Only rain, soaking me from head to toe,' answered the old feller.

'Come on, we'll have to get out of this downpour.'

They ferreted amongst the undergrowth and eventually constructed a rudimentary shelter from logs and bracken, covering the structure with moss and sodden leaf litter. Then they sat, like two dejected lumps, hunched and cold, waiting for the rain to stop. The pungent aroma of badger sets and fox lairs laced the air as the Shroves huddled together and listened to the sound of their stomachs growling.

Bicker was in a sorry state, moaning and groaning under his breath. He was fretting about his actions, worried that he had made a terrible mistake. Perhaps it had been the drink that had addled his brain and made him decide that escaping from Hellstone Tors with this mad Shrove was a good idea. But now, sitting in the cold and wet, he wasn't so sure. The outside wasn't as he remembered it from his youth. What would happen to him? Would he ever get anything to eat?

Finally the rain stopped.

Embellsed nudged Bicker and the old Shrove's eyes filled

with tears. 'I'm frit to death out 'ere,' he snivelled

'I'm off to find some food. Coming?'

The old Shrove followed Embellsed out of the shelter and peered into the dusky evening. The birds were singing their last songs of the day and the air was full of the sweet perfume of night-scented stock. Bicker roused himself and tried to put on a brave face. He persuaded himself that perhaps it would all be fine. But it wasn't. Embellsed had no idea how to hunt for their supper. He had no traps and Bicker wouldn't stop moaning about their plight.

'At least in Helltstone Tors I was sometimes warm,' he complained, shivering and hopping up and down.

'Warm? In those cold cellars?' Embellsed snorted.

'Well, I was dry then,' added Bicker, 'and I never thought I'd stoop to scavenging for my supper,' he bleated.

'You were a slave to the Swarm, just like me. Here, stop complaining and hold this leaf steady whilst I pick berries,' Embellsed announced, pulling blackberries from a bush.

Embellsed dropped the ripe fruit into the dock leaf and soon it was overflowing. The Shroves gorged on their pickings, blackberry juice dribbling down their whiskery chins.

'See, it's not so bad after all,' announced Embellsed cheerily, wiping his sleeve across his face.

But Bicker stayed his hand. His old eyes were watering again but this time with fear.

'What's that noise?' Bicker asked, throwing himself into Embellsed's arms.

'Get off me,' cried Embellsed.

'I-Is it wild animals?' asked the terrified Shrove.

The Shroves stood still and listened.

Through the darkening forest they could hear the sound of hooves pounding across the forest floor, of crashing and tearing headlong through the bracken. The sound gathered pace and all at once a herd of rampaging wild boars stampeded through the undergrowth, upending the terrified Bicker and ploughing up the earth in their wake, foraging for truffles and knocking the remaining berries out of Embellsed's hand.

'Ahhhh! Wild beasts!' he cried as he toppled head over heels and landed heavily on his bottom.

But the wild boars were not interested in Shroves. They were on the hunt for acorns, beechnuts and tasty truffles. In no time they had trampled the soil, scarring the earth with deep furrows, and snaffled a mass of truffles, fruit and nuts before disappearing – grunting and squealing – with their hairy-backed family into the undergrowth.

'Oh my, I don't like it out here!' bleated Bicker, sitting up and pulling leaves out of his hair.

'Shut up and let's get those truffles,' shouted Embellsed, pouncing on the earthy, pungent treats.

He dug his fingers into the wet, brown soil and extracted the truffles, ramming them into his greedy mouth.

'Delicious,' said Bicker, stuffing his face.

'Mmm,' added Embellsed.

When their tummies were round and fat, full of the rich

truffles, the Shroves waddled back to their makeshift shelter and nestled amongst the leaves to keep warm. Embellsed smacked his lips and rubbed his lovely full belly. For the first time in their miserable lives there was no one telling them what to do, where to go and how to behave. The feeling of freedom made Embellsed feel quite giddy.

'Goodnight old feller,' mumbled Embellsed, on the verge of contentment.

'G-Goodnight,' Bicker mumbled, wrapping his collar over his ears and thrusting his cold hands into his pockets.

But Bicker couldn't sleep. There were too many noises out in the wild place. Owls hooted high above them and he could hear rodents rummaging about in the undergrowth as the wind whistled through their shelter. Eventually, weary and full of truffles, the old Shrove dropped off – dreaming of his wine cellars and his red beauties …

But the Shroves' freedom wasn't destined to last for long. Suggit was close by, rooting about in the forest, checking his traps in the gloaming light, poaching in the depth of the wood. He had just caught a brace of fat brown rabbits and was tucking them into his knapsack when he came across a makeshift shelter with two snoring Shroves inside. He couldn't believe his eyes.

'Well I never!' he shouted, poking his head under the branches, 'what are you two up to?'

Embellsed screeched, leapt to his feet, hopped about and knocked the shelter onto Bicker's head.

'My brains have been smashed!' shouted the old Shrove.

'Ahhhh!' he bleated, 'get those logs off me!'

Bicker sat bolt upright and screamed his head off at the sight of the huge Groveller leering down at them.

'Shut up you old fool!' Suggit hissed at Bicker. 'You'll bring heaven knows what down upon us,' he growled, grabbing hold of Embellsed.

'Don't tell the Swarm, please,' begged Embellsed shaking with fright.

Suddenly his stomach lurched. He felt sick from gorging on the rich truffles.

'What you two doin' in Sunkwells Bottom?' asked Suggit, scratching his head. 'Strange place for Shroves to be sleepin'.'

He crouched down, wiping his knife and smearing a trail of dark red blood across his thigh.

'Don't hurt us!' yelled Bicker staring from the Groveller to his bloody trousers.

The old Shrove hopped about, twitching with fear.

'You ain't answered my question yet,' Suggit replied, eyeing the two miserable creatures.

Embellsed swallowed hard as his beady eyes watered with fright.

'We've run away,' he whispered desperately.

'Run away,' echoed Suggit incredulously.

'We can't take anymore,' added Bicker, fretfully.

It was a rum turn of events and no mistake. Suggit eyed the pair suspiciously. Hellstone Shroves never dared venture outside the castle unless they were under the Swarm's orders. These two specimens were certainly not on the Swarm's business and they were hard pressed to speak, never mind fend for themselves in the wilds of Breedoor.

'Then you'd best come home with me,' the Groveller said eventually, 'Mrs Suggit will know what to do with you.'

The Shroves looked sick.

'What will she do to us?' asked Embellsed, apprehensively.

His stomach turned somersaults. His nerves were shredded and he hopped about like a Shrove in a blither.

'Cheer up lads, she'll no doubt give you a good feed, maybe even a wash in the tub,' he sniggered, 'then Mrs Suggit and 'er nosey sister will want to know all the goin's on in that castle,' he said, jerking his thumb in the direction of Hellstone Tors.

'Oh my,' said Embellsed at the thought of soap and water.

'Oh deary me,' added Bicker.

He hadn't had a bath in years!

'We'd better go with him,' muttered Embellsed, staring at the ruins of their makeshift shelter.

In the gloom, Dipper and Flametip watched as the Shroves trotted behind the Groveller, following him into the gloomy marshland that surrounded Grovell-by-the-Water, all the while worrying about what was in store for them at the hands of Mrs. Suggit.

*

Close to the Barren Edges the Gross Stumpleback gorged

herself on a sweet young buck, shearing chunks of flesh with her voracious jaws, sucking the blood and gnawing away at the fresh meat. Yarrow grew impatient. The Spell-Seekers had inadvertently veered off course due to the beast's unquenchable appetite.

'She'll be too fat to hunt Quillam and the girl,' Yarrow snapped irritably.

The beast's eyes rolled with pleasure and her lips drooled with gore.

'Not the Gross Stumpleback,' replied Redlevven, stroking the beast's scaly head. He took the fabric, redolent with the Morrow stain and rubbed it across the beast's nose.

'Breathe in Tallitha's scent,' Redlevven instructed. 'She's out there my pretty one. You just have to find her!'

The creature made a snorting noise; steam erupted from her nostrils as she flicked her head from side to side and continued to gorge on the carcass.

'I'm not waiting any longer!' Yarrow snapped at her brother. 'I'm going to see if we've caught any prey in our Stinkwells.'

'Don't forget my potions,' her brother replied, handing Yarrow the jars containing Topaz Stargazer and Indigo Sky Liquid. 'Remember to say the spell when you leave,' he urged.

Yarrow pulled a face at her fussy brother and placed the potions in her saddlebag.

'I know what I'm doing,' she replied curtly.

Yarrow rode off into the distance, galloping past the Barren Edges and out over the lavender encrusted moors of the

Northern Wolds. There she dismounted, tethered her mare and stepped towards the Stinkwells in the hope of finding a hapless traveller, trapped inside.

But as Yarrow approached the well, no heady aromas greeted her. She spotted a dirty mess of sooty footprints smeared around the lip of the pit.

Bundles of sticks and branches had been forced down the shaft to prevent the sun's rays reaching the spells. She raced across to the second and third wells. They were just as dark and uninviting.

'Sprites!' she shouted angrily, raising her fist, 'damn and blast those meddling urchins! They've been tampering with our Stinkwells!' she cried as she hurriedly dragged the branches from the entranceway and climbed down the ladder.

The Stinkwell was cold. Yarrow shivered. The spell pots, usually brimming with aromas and dazzling colours, were dulled by the lack of sunlight.

'Now I'll have to reset these spells,' she muttered bad-temperedly.

Yarrow placed Redlevven's spells with the others and began to recite the magical words.

'*Periwinkle, bluebell, boil the stamens and petals with a young girl's tears, make this Stinkwell a fortress of* ... erm?' she hesitated. 'Bother! That's not right. Calm down and say it again,' she said, trying to steady herself. She was upset by the Sprite's audacity.

Yarrow searched for magical inspiration but the spell had gone out of her head. 'It had something to do with bats' wings and snakes … yes, that's it – *a fortress bold, bind the spell in the bat's black wings and wrap it in the skin of slippery snakes.*'

Yarrow threw in an old Ennish spell for good luck, climbed out of the well and repeated the Periwnkle spell in each of the Stinkwells around the Bitter Caves, seething with anger at the Black Sprites' boldness. Now the Stumpleback would have more work to do – *catching those rotten little Sprites and tearing them to pieces!* Yarrow smiled wickedly, mounted her horse and rode off across the Northern Wolds to reunite with Redlevven.

Unlike her diligent brother, Yarrow was a careless creature and in her fury had not heeded his words. She had cast the spell clumsily and the fragile elements that bound the spell together began to rupture with a *ripple, a puffle* and *a fizz.*

*

High up in Kastra's Unimaginable Palace, the spell-catcher twitched and hummed. The Grand Witch sprang towards the loom.

'Look, Ferileath, there's a ripple,' she cried, 'I can see into the Swarm's web of magic.'

Through a lattice of webs, the Spell-Seekers' magical pots came into view, fizzing and bubbling.

It was the moment Kastra had waited for.

The Grand Witch jabbed her finger inside the tear, dragging the weft of the spell apart, then she arched her body and slid through the silky aperture. She emerged like a slippery fish, swimming through the weft and the weave of the spell, arriving in the depths of the Stinkwell in a hail of sapphire light.

Redlevven and Yarrow's spells sat side by side, some in jars and others in glass flagons, glowing crimson, azure and emerald like precious jewels.

Kastra stole in amongst the jars, opened their sealed tops and breathed in their potencies and strengths.

'Lemon Stargazer and Indigo Sky Liquid,' she murmured, stealing a sample of the spells.

It was the way of all the witches in Breedoor to plunder spells at every opportunity, as a trophy and a means of taking power. Kastra smiled. At last she had discovered a chink in the Swarm's armour of spells. Thanks to Yarrow's clumsiness, she had breached their fortress.

The Grand Witch revelled with delight as the sorcery and the web of magic that protected the Bone Room was finally revealed to her.

Then the Grand Witch turned widdershins in her dazzling sapphire light, moving round the spell pots in a circular motion, disarming the Spell-Seekers' potions.

Now it only remained for the Wycham girl to make contact with the long dead Morrow child, break into the castle and destroy the Morrow pact.

# Nineteen

By the edge of the Bitter Caves, Tallitha moaned in her sleep and flung the blankets from her makeshift bed. She peered into the darkness, towards an unseen presence. Her eyes were glassy, staring dead ahead.

'Where shall I find her?' she asked, repeating Kastra's name out loud.

Tallitha clutched the bloodstone about her neck.

Quillam stirred and shook Spooner awake.

'Who's she talkin' to?' whispered Spooner.

'Kastra,' murmured Quillam.

Tallitha began to shake, her face contorted and she slumped forward.

'Quillam,' she said softly, turning towards him.

Her head throbbed. Her dream, if it was a dream, had seemed real.

'You were talking in your sleep,' replied Spooner, 'wasn't she?'

Lince nodded. 'All about that witch and your eyes looked peculiar.'

'Kastra told me to make contact with the Morrow child and then to find Embellsed. He's escaped from Hellstone Tors,' she said.

'But Shroves never leave Hellstone,' replied Quillam sounding perplexed.

'She also warned me that Redlevven and Yarrow are looking for us.'

Tallitha touched the bloodstone and rubbed her arm. Quillam noticed a trickle of dark blood smeared across her skin.

'Can we come too? We've never seen a ghost. Have we, Lince?' said Spooner.

'Count me out!' replied her sister. 'I'm staying put!'

'You can't come, Spooner,' Tallitha replied firmly 'Too many of us may frighten the child away.'

She turned to Quillam. 'Ask Neeps to take an extra watch and come with me. I need your help.'

*

Tallitha and Quillam crept over the next hill, hiding behind an outcrop of rock.

'This will give us sufficient cover,' she said, peering into the darkness. 'Give me your bloodstones,' she said to the youth, taking them and placing them on the earth

Then she reached inside her pocket and drew out a small object.

'How on earth did you get that?' he asked.

'I stole it from the Dead Room when Queen Asphodel wasn't looking,' she replied, placing the raven's head skull amongst the bloodstones.

They knelt opposite each other as the moon appeared from behind the clouds and stole in upon them, casting an eerie light.

'In order to make contact with Arabella I must say the litany of the dead,' she explained

'It's all here, in Great Aunt Agatha's letter,' she said, opening the note and laying it on the ground before them. 'You must repeat the words after me.'

'Will it work?' he asked.

Tallitha shrugged. 'I-I've only done this once before when I followed Queen Asphodel's instruction, but I have to try.'

She spoke softly into the darkness.

*'Danitha mallecur na tresta,*
*Arabella transcenda, danitha mallecur na tresta,*
*Arabella transcenda.'*

Quillam watched her anxiously. 'I know this is strange, Quillam, but you have to repeat the words,' she whispered, encouraging him.

'Okay,' he muttered, 'if I have to.'

*'Death defy and death decay, come to us we fear no ill, from o'er the grave, from the dank, dark tomb, tell me your secrets, bring them to me, I call upon you Arabella Dorothea Morrow to span the death divide.'*

When they had finished recanting the litany there was silence all around them. It was as if time itself was holding its breath.

'Nothing's happening,' said Quillam.

Tallitha didn't respond but stared dead ahead. Then without speaking she slowly lifted her hand as if transfixed and pointed into the distance.

From out of the night, a chill wind swept past them. Tallitha locked eyes with Quillam.

'I can feel her!' she cried. 'The spirit of the Morrow child,' she said, her mouth trembling as she spoke. 'It's beginning,' she said finally.

Wisps of mist oozed from the earth and curled across the ground like writhing snakes, the milky-white strands wrapping themselves around Tallitha as Quillam watched helplessly.

'I'm so cold,' Tallitha moaned.

The mist swirled amongst the flora and fauna, turning nature into frightening, hoary shapes like frosted stalagmites against the darkness. The night smelt of death, like the clawing stench that oozed from ancient sepulchres and broken tombs.

Suddenly Talitha's body jolted.

'A cold hand, like death itself, just touched me,' she whispered, her voice shaking.

As she spoke a pattern of delicate fingerprints, like frozen petals, appeared across her cheek.

'Tallitha! There's something on your face!' Quillam cried.

Tallitha traced the imprint of the fingertips that had trespassed across her cheek.

'She's here – she's with us!'

Cold breath, like frost, hung in the air and a voice, raw like the biting wind, spoke through the darkness.

'Why did you summon me from my long, dark sleep?' the voice wailed.

A pale, ethereal figure of a wasted child took shape before them, bleached of life, tortured and pale.

Tallitha stared at the frightful spectre.

Arabella Dorothea shuddered. 'SPEAK to me!' she moaned.

'To destroy the Morrow pact,' Tallitha whispered.

The apparition's lips were bloodless, her hair stuck out in brittle clumps and her eyes were red-ringed and as black as coal.

'Will you help me?' pleaded Tallitha.

The ghost shuddered, her form as frail as a moth's wing, flimsy against the darkness.

'My father bartered me to gain his freedom. Septimia and Siskin perished trying to save me, so how can a girl from Whycham Elva destroy the pact?

Frost-white tears trickled down Arabella's cheeks.

'Many strange things have happened to me,' Tallitha replied, 'I've met witches, seen spirits and heard things that I never dreamed possible,' she answered, 'but in one thing I am certain, this is my destiny. I have come such a long way to find you.'

'What can I do from beyond the grave?' the ghost wailed.

'Help me destroy the pact,' Tallitha pleaded. 'Come to the Neopholytite's tower when I summon you.'

'I'm frightened of them,' the apparition cried mournfully.

The Morrow child stepped backwards, looking into the darkness, whispering into the night.

'The Swarm cannot harm you,' said Tallitha, entreating the child to remain, 'if you renounce the words of your father, then the Morrow pact will be broken.'

'They are evil,' the child wailed.

'That's why I need your help, or we are all doomed,' she whispered.

Arabella Dorothea stared into the night, at something beyond Tallitha's vision. Suddenly the wind took up and howled fiercely through the trees. The night grew darker as two spectres swept through the wood.

'Ghosts!' shouted Quillam, jumping to his feet, 'and they're coming this way!'

Two fright-white apparitions – Siskin and Septimia Morrow – with angular shrouded heads, thin and fragile, surrounded by a searing light, swept beside Arabella, engulfing her. The white-light of their ethereal forms glistened and convulsed against the dark sky.

'We have come to protect the Morrow child!' Siskin cried, resting his hand on the child's shoulder.

Tallitha recalled the note from her great aunt Agatha telling her of Septimia Morrow, the seventh daughter of a seventh daughter, and her husband, Siskin, who had died trying to save Arabella Dorothea. The trio of ghostly forms mingled into one.

'We tried to rescue this child long ago but we perished too,' Siskin's voice echoed through the night.

Septimia bent down and spoke reassuringly to Arabella.

'We hoped this day would come, didn't we? When someone who was brave, with a good heart, would try and destroy the Morrow pact.' The child nodded at Septimia's words. 'Siskin and I will come with you to the Bone Room when Tallitha summons you. The Neopholytite cannot hurt you.'

Arabella peered from behind her guardians. 'My father tricked me all those years ago,' she said sadly. 'Selvistra tricked me too!'

'I am not here to trick you, I only want to rid Breedoor of the Swarm and to go home to Wycham Elva.'

'Home, to Winderling Spires,' the child said wistfully, stepping towards Tallitha.

'Then will you come to the tower when I call? Will you help me?' asked Tallitha, reaching out her hand to Arabella.

'Only if you let me see inside your soul,' the Morrow child answered.

'Arabella must see if your heart is truly good,' explained Siskin.

'Will I feel anything? Tallitha asked.

'It will be a curious sensation, like having another entity share your thoughts.'

Arabella focused her black, red-ringed eyes on Tallitha, staring straight at her, penetrating her mind. Tallitha felt her body go limp and she surrendered her will to the ghost.

The Morrow child's eyes brightened and her hands trembled as she absorbed the essence of Tallitha Mouldson.

'She is a wayward girl,' said Arabella, turning to Siskin. 'Yet she is brave and she is determined to succeed.'

'She has fought hard to get this far,' Siskin replied.

'She abhors Hellstone Tors and she despises the Swarm,' added the Morrow child.

'Who does she love?' asked Septimia

'She loves her family – her brother Tyaas, Esmerelda Patch and the old sisters.'

'Trust her,' said Septimia.

'I do,' replied Arabella, letting go of her hold.

Tallitha took a deep breath and opened her eyes.

'Will Selvistra Loons be there?'Arabella asked.

'I-I cannot say,' answered Tallitha.

'I-I came upon her in the Moon Tower,' the child explained, ' she troubled me, but I could fly away into the night. What if she tries to trap me in the Bone Room?'

'We will protect you,' answered Septimia, resting a hand on her shoulder.

The Morrow child shuddered.

'When you call on me I will come but only if Siskin and Septimia can come too?' she replied.

Tallitha smiled at Arabella Dorothea.

'Thank you,' she said, mouthing the words.

The apparitions enveloped each other in a bright white light and vanished into the night.

'You are more powerful than Queen Asphodel,' said Quillam at last.

He had been transfixed by the spirits, and unable to utter a sound during the haunting.

'Why do you say that?'

'You brought the Morrow child here.'

'The thought of the Bone Room frightens me, and Selvistra Loons fills me with dread.'

'The Morrow child believed in you,' he replied.

'And what if I fail? What if the Swarm overpower me? What if SHE overpowers me? Then all will be lost forever.'

But Quillam didn't have a reassuring response.

The task ahead was nigh on impossible.

\*

'Now we must find that dreadful Shrove, Embellsed,' said Tallitha, trudging back to the campsite with Quillam. 'He knows where the underground route is into Hellstone Tors.'

'That Shrove isn't to be trusted,' said Quillam. 'Perhaps the Grand Witch is trying to trick you.'

'Kastra has helped me in the past,' she answered firmly. 'In my dream she took me beyond Stankles Brow and showed me where Embellsed is hiding, but the image was vague, as in all dreams. I have to find him.'

After summoning the Morrow child, Tallitha was reeling from the potency of the supernatural.

'What's wrong?' he asked, 'you look weird.'

'I-I feel peculiar,' she replied.

Tallitha held the bloodstone in the palm of her hand. As she touched it, she could feel it becoming warm. She saw an image of the rolling hills as the Groveller village appeared beyond the dip. Suggit, Rye and Lutch were gutting rabbits and chopping vegetables in front of their houses. They were whispering about the Shroves.

'Lutch,' Tallitha whispered, reaching out.

Quillam's eyes widened. 'What about her?' he asked, sounding alarmed.

Tallitha's eyes turned glassy.

'What is it?' he said, 'what can you see?'

Tallitha smiled. She was looking at something only she could see.

'There! I've found him!' she cried excitedly. 'Tomorrow we must go to Grovell-by-the-Water and find that Shrove.'

# Twenty

The next morning, as Tallitha and the others were eating breakfast, the Skinks raced back into camp, tearing through the bracken, breathless and excited, gesticulating wildly towards the Northern Wolds.

'There's a huge beast out there!' shouted Neeps.

'Roaming across country with a man and woman on horseback! They're coming this way,' shouted Ruker, 'and they don't look at all friendly!'

'A right ugly critter with huge jaws and snorting smoke,' added Neeps, panting.

'Sounds like they have the Gross Stumpleback in tow,' Quillam replied.

'Hide!' Tallitha cried, jumping to her feet.

'Who are they?' asked Spooner as she grabbed her longbow.

'Redlevven and his mean sister, Yarrow – and their hideous beast! Just run,' shouted Quillam.

Spooner and Lince sped after Quillam, high-tailing it through the undergrowth as fast as their legs could carry them. The Skinks fled alongside, pulling Tallitha through the bracken. Branches clawed at their faces and roots tripped them up as they ran helter-skelter through the forest with the sound of hooves pounding across the earth behind them, gaining on them by the second.

Out of the corner of her eye Tallitha saw the charcoal streaks of the Black Sprites leaping through the trees. Dipper bounded in front of them landing on a large purple stone, then the willowy Flametip joined him in a flash. They had fear written all over their faces.

'Quick!' Flametip shouted urgently.

Dipper pushed the stone to one side to reveal a damp pit. Then they tumbled into the dark, musty hole and the stone was scraped back above them.

'How did you find us?' asked Quillam breathlessly.

'We've been on your tail since you since you left the Bitter Caves,' replied Dipper.

'Shhhh,' insisted Flametip, listening intently, 'the Spell-Seekers are above us.'

In the darkness Tallitha could hear horses whinnying, their hooves clipping the ground, circling above them, and then a heavier more unnerving sound – thump, thump, thudding - across the earth. It was the Gross Stumpleback, shaking the ground with her huge body. The earth trembled overhead.

'Keep still,' Flametip growled.

Tallitha covered her head, fearing the roof would cave in, waiting to be swallowed up by the mud and rubble. Seconds passed, and then a strange, shrill voice called out above them.

'Keep that beast on its leash,' shouted Yarrow. 'Any sign of that girl yet? She can't have gone far.'

From their cramped pit, the sound of the Stumpleback grunting and slavering echoed malevolently through the earth. Tallitha gripped Spooner's hand.

'They've fled into the woods!' Redlevven cried. 'After them my scaly one! Let's catch the miscreants! Take another sniff of the Morrow stain!' he insisted, wiping the bloodied cloth across the Stumpleback's jaws.

The creature snorted and growled. Tallitha's stomach tightened. She was being tracked like a common criminal!

Then the horses neighed and galloped off into the distance.

'They won't stop until they've found you,' said Flametip warily.

'Kastra removed the Morrow stain from my hand,' Tallitha whispered.

'It doesn't matter. They're like bloodhounds and that beast will not stop until she's found you,' added Dipper nervously.

When it was quiet, Flametip pushed the stone to one side.

'What you doing?' asked Quillam nervously.

'We have a plan,' replied Flametip.

'Can we help?' asked Ruker.

'Best not,' replied Dipper, 'they can't see us in sunlight and that beast can't smell us. The Stumpleback would sniff you out in no time.'

'We can't just sit it out down here,' added Neeps restlessly.

But Flametip ignored the Skinks' pleas.

'We'll be back soon,' she said, 'so don't move.'

The Black Sprites sprang out of the hole like jack-in-the-boxes, and the stone grated back into place.

'Now what'll we do?' asked Spooner.

'Do as they say,' replied Tallitha firmly.

It was pitch black in the stifling hole and the time ticked slowly by.

Tallitha's legs were numb, the girls were jostling each other irritably and the Skinks were desperate to get in on the action.

'Let's follow them – we have to see what's going on,' urged Neeps, 'they've been gone too long.'

'That's a good idea,' replied Spooner. 'Hey, get off my arm Sis, you're crushing me.'

The girls, pinned into a small space, were busy pinching and nudging one another.

'We should stay put,' replied Tallitha, grabbing Neeps, 'you mustn't go out there, it might be a trap!'

'We could be down here for ages and we've no water,' said Lince

'I'm hungry,' said Spooner.

'Shut up you two,' replied Ruker.

Then there was a heavy thud above them.

'Shhh, what was that?' asked Neeps urgently.

Six pairs of frightened eyes stared upwards into the darkness.

Then the stone scraped to one side. Tallitha shaded her eyes and peered upwards. The light blinded her for a second or two.

'You can come out now,' said a shrill voice.

Quillam gripped Tallitha's arm. The voice didn't belong to Flametip or Dipper. A horse neighed and kicked its hooves against the rock.

'Well, well, and what have we here?' sneered Redlevven menacingly.

He stuck his head into the dank hole, his black wiry hair standing on end and his beaky nose twitching as he ogled the bedraggled bunch.

'Such a dirty lot,' said Yarrow disparagingly. 'Thought you'd be able to trick us, didn't you!' she shouted.

'Get out!' shouted Redlevven, as he reigned in the Gross Stumpleback. The creature snorted plumes of purple smoke. 'Steady my beauty,' he hissed.

As Tallitha edged out of the hole she came face to face with a horrendous beast. Slavering before her were the livid red jaws of the hideous Stumpleback.

'Well I never, it's the Swarm's prize – the Wycham girl!' shouted Yarrow acidly. 'We're taking you back to Hellstone Tors! Climb onto my horse,' she demanded. 'The others can follow on foot.'

Tallitha hovered by the entrance to the hole, waiting for Quillam, trying to avoid the snorting beast.

'Skinks! What a ramshackle crew,' jeered Redlevven, 'and Master Quillam too! Come out, come out, whoever you are!' he sang nastily.

Quillam's eyes darted towards Spooner and Lince as they shrank back into the dark hole, keeping well out of sight of the Spell-Seekers. It was a sign for them to stay put.

Once outside, Quillam pushed the stone back into place with his foot.

'Snowdroppe will be furious when we get back to the castle!' Yarrow said snidely to Quillam. 'You don't betray the Swarm and survive!'

Redlevven slithered down the side of his steed and bound the hands of his prisoners. His beady eyes alighted on Tallitha.

'And you,' he snarled, 'what will the Swarm do to you? Perhaps they don't need you now they have your little brother. Perhaps I should give you to the beast!' he announced, clicking his fingers at the Gross Stumpleback.

Tallitha flinched as the animal licked its voracious jaws.

'Come, my beauty,' Redlevven called as the creature lurched forward.

Quillam was ready to fling his body in its path when Yarrow intervened.

'Not now, brother! Back off! We will have Snowdroppe to answer to if we go against her wishes!' she shouted, manoeuvring her horse between Tallitha and the Stumpleback. Yarrow grabbed Tallitha's wrist, pulling her onto the saddle. 'The Neopholytite still has need of young girls even if the Thane no longer wants her,' she barked.

Redlevven sneered. They would all be fair game for the Stumpleback!

Suddenly, Yarrow's eyes narrowed. 'Sprites!' she yelled, spying a flash in the bushes. 'I will kill them all! They invaded our Stinkwells!'

'But sister, hold fast! We have these prisoners in our grasp.'

Yarrow would not be deterred. 'Follow at your own pace! I mean to destroy every last one of them!'

Yarrow kicked her horse and galloped off, charging headlong through the forest with Tallitha clinging on behind her.

'You there,' Redlevven shouted at Ruker, poking her with the point of his sword. 'Start walking! Disobey me and this beast will gnaw on your bones! Do you hear that Quillam? I would love to watch the Gross Stumpleback rip you to shreds,' he cried, laughing malevolently.

The Gross Stumpleback rolled her great yellow eyes, sniffing at the Skinks as if they were steaks for dinner.

'Now follow me!' Redlevven shouted to the assembled party.

*

The cold ground had soaked right through the girls' trousers.

'Have they gone?' Lince asked.

From up above it was silent.

'I'll take a look,' her sister whispered.

Spooner carefully pushed the stone to one side and peeked out.

'All clear,' she said, scrambling out of the hole and pulling her sister up behind her.

'What'll we do we do now?' asked Lince.

'We have to follow them.'

So they sneaked through the woods, watching all the while for the Black Sprites, but the shadowy creatures were nowhere to be seen.

*

'Those Sprites must be here somewhere,' said Yarrow angrily, surveying the territory around the Stinkwells and climbing down from her horse.

Tallitha noticed a flicker of smoke and a blackened face winked at her from behind a boulder. Then the Sprite put his finger to his lips. In a moment of confusion the charcoal wisps streaked across the ground, pushing Yarrow down the Stinkwell and tipping her from the ladder.

She fell with a thud at the bottom of the well with three Black Sprites landing beside her.

'Got you! She hissed 'These spells will crush the life out of you!' she yelled, her eyes darting towards the spell pots.

'Stargazer!' she shrieked, 'Do your worst!'

But Yarrow's spell jars were cold. Kastra had spiked them all and eradicated their magical powers.

'Ahhh! Yarrow shrieked, hurling her body at the horny black creatures.

They snapped at her fingers, biting her viciously, and then vanished to the darkest recesses of the Stinkwell.

'Vile specimens!' she yelped, 'but I've got them trapped!' she cried gleefully.

'Please, Yarrow, don't hurt them,' begged Tallitha from above.

Yarrow sprang up the ladder, turning her vengeful eyes on Tallitha.

'What's it to you? I'm going to murder the little horrors!' she shrieked, chasing after the Sprites.

Tallitha could hear the sound of flagons being dragged across the floor and Yarrow cursing bitterly. Then there was a blood-curdling scream, the sound of bottles smashing, a tussle, a muffled sigh and then silence.

'Now for the glue!' shouted one sprite to the others.

The three Black Sprites sprang out of the Stinkwell and began sealing the top of the well with sticks and branches, pouring a gluey substance to seal the entrance.

'Make sure you leave no gaps, make it good and fast,' instructed Flametip urgently, 'that ogre Redlevven will be here soon.'

'What have you done with Yarrow?' asked Tallitha, dismounting.

'Trussed her up like a fly in a spider's web! Wound her round and round with Sprite fastenings then laced with her latest spell of Indigo Sky Liquid – we took the potion from Kastra,' replied Dipper, smirking.

'Is she dead?' Tallitha asked.

'No, not dead exactly, just in a state of suspended animation,' replied Flametip, 'if we'd killed her, the Swarm would have found out.'

Tallitha scanned the moors. 'What about Redlevven?' she asked. 'What can I do?'

'See that Stinkwell yonder,' said Dipper, 'stand over there with Yarrow's horse – you'll be like bait in our trap.'

'We'll be back soon!' added Flametip.

The three Black Sprites disappeared in a puff of smoke down the Stinkwell.

Soon Redlevven appeared, trotting over the moors with his prisoners in tow. He reined in his horse and peered down the first well, eying Tallitha suspiciously from a distance.

'What's happened here?' he shouted, pointing at the glue oozing from the well. 'Where's my sister?'

'Killing Sprites,' Tallitha replied gesticulating towards the Stinkwell below her.

'You first, little girl,' he said, prodding her with his sword. Then he turned to the Stumpleback. 'You wait here, my gross beauty, and guard these wretches.'

Redlevven slithered down the horse's flanks and leapt to the ground. 'Move!' he screeched in Tallitha's face, pushing her roughly down the ladder.

At the bottom, the Stinkwell was dark and quiet.

'Yarrow! Where are you? Have you killed them yet?' Redlevven cried, peering behind the flagons and spell-jars.

But the once alluring Stinkwell was cold and dark.

Redlevven sniffed. 'What, no pungent smells to entice me?' he frowned. 'What trick is this?' he gasped 'Sister, where are you?'

Then Redlevven howled.

Quick as a flash, three sprites sprang out from behind the flagons, trussed Redlevven into a cocoon and smeared him in blue sticky liquid.

He screamed obscenities at the Sprites as they glued his arms to his sides and stuck his feet together, winding him ever more tightly into a chrysalis. His voice became a whisper as he slipped into a deep hibernation.

'That should do it!' announced Dipper, regarding his handiwork. 'He won't wake up for a long time.'

Tallitha looked on in amazement. 'What about that beast?'

'Leave him to us,' replied Flametip springing up the ladder with Dipper on her heels, 'Come on,' she urged.

As Tallitha was half way up the ladder, a terrifying howl came from up above. Then there was a snorting and a stamping and a deafening thud.

Tallitha poked her head out of the Stinkwell and stared at the beast. The Gross Stumpleback was lying on her back, kicking her fat scaly legs in the air, madly threshing in the dirt, snorting plumes of purple smoke and writhing in the last ugly throes of death. Her large eyes bulged as the last breath flickered from her body and her mouth oozed a trail of sickening black blood.

In the distance, poised on top of a huge boulder, Spooner stood – legs apart, arms outstretched with her long bow in her hands.

'You've killed her!' Tallitha cried, running towards Spooner and hugging her with joy.

Three of Spooner's arrows were sticking out of the

Stumpleback's crumpled body.

The Black Sprites jumped up and down with delight, darting this way and that.

The Spell-Seekers were vanquished and cocooned.

Now they were prisoners in their own Stinkwells.

# Twenty-one

Esmerelda woke with a terrifying jolt.

The clanging of the midnight bell rang out from the high tower, shattering her dream. She was covered in sweat, gripping the blankets between her fingertips. She peered into the dark corners of her chamber, at the fleeting shadows playing tricks on her, certain that Tallitha was standing, watching her.

'Tallitha,' she murmured hesitantly, sitting up. 'Is that you?'

But there was no answer. Yet the dream had seemed so real – she had heard Tallitha speak to her, telling her what she must do.

Esmerelda flung the blankets from the bed and hurried to Asenathe's bedroom.

'Attie,' Esmerelda cried, shaking her cousin awake. 'Tallitha came to me in my sleep – she's on her way back to Hellstone Tors. It was so real – I could almost touch her.' Asenathe sat up in bed and lit the candle on her nightstand. 'She knows the secret of the

Dark Spell – she wants us to weaken the Neopholytite's power.'

'Then we must break the curse tablets,' Attie replied, rubbing her eyes.

Neither of the cousins had ever attempted to break a binding spell before.

'I'll wake the boy,' said Esmerelda, making her way through the dressing room and stepping behind the wall panelling.

'What is it?' he asked, waking suddenly, rubbing his eyes.

'Tallitha came to me in a dream. She's on her way back to Hellstone Tors. We have to weaken the Neopholytite's power.

Tyaas was out of bed in an instant. 'Great,' he replied, 'how are we going to do that?'

'Destroy that witch bottle,' she replied.

Tyaas was raring to go.

When they reached Asenathe's chamber, she was pacing the room with the Raven Spell clutched tightly between her fingers.

'I copied it down faithfully, but it says – *Beware* and *Dire Warning*.'

'Go on,' said Tyaas excitedly.

He sat hunched on Asenathe's bed, carefully pulling a sock over his bruised ankle.

'This isn't going to be easy, Tyaas,' cautioned Esmerelda. 'If we get this wrong the witch will know we are trying to destroy one of her bottles, then she will scour the castle and take her revenge.'

'We can't just sit here and do nothing!' he cried, looking from one to the other. 'We haven't much time.'

The boy was so excitable. Tyaas, as ever, was keen to embark on the next adventure without a thought to the consequences.

'What if something should go horribly wrong?' asked Asenathe.

Esmerelda crept towards the bedroom door and peered into the corridor to make certain there was no one listening. The Shroves were nowhere to be seen.

'He's right,' said Esmerelda finally.

'Great, let's begin!' exclaimed Tyaas.

'What does the spell say?' asked Esmerelda, giving Tyaas a cautionary look.

'*To open the bottle and spare yourself say –*,' she stopped, 'and it continues with the words of the Raven spell – but we cannot say them aloud!'

'But when will you be able to say them?' asked Tyaas, losing patience.

He was as keen as mustard to spike the witch.

'Not now, Tyaas,' Esmerelda replied, 'we must be extremely careful. We must unstop the witch bottle and say the Raven Spell at exactly the same time.'

'Right,' he said, raring to go.

'It must be in a walled room,' replied Esmerelda.

'Why?' he asked, losing patience.

'These lath walls are not strong enough to contain the power,' answered Asenathe.

'The curse tablets have a tracking spell. If we don't destroy it at just the right time, the curse will alert the Neopholytite. Then she'll be after us with all the fury she can muster.'

'We need somewhere that will protect us,' explained Asenathe.

'What about at the foot of the Withered Tower?' suggested Esmerelda, 'it's left unlocked at night and no one goes there much.'

'Too risky, Sedentia Flight may be about,' added Asenathe.

'What about the old dungeons?' asked Tyaas.

Esmerelda looked askance at the boy. 'Too many guards about.'

'What about the storm drains?' asked Aseanthe, looking excitedly at the others.

'Won't they stink?' asked Tyaas.

'Not the foul drains, silly, the drains that take the rain water from the castle, in the lower courtyard,' replied Asenathe.

'How do we get inside?' asked Tyaas

'Through the round grate, opposite the Bleak Rooms.'

'That's perfect!' said Esmerelda.

*

That same night they laid their plans. The safest route to the storm drain had been discussed again and again. Eventually it was agreed that as the servants would be sleeping and the Shroves would be in their holes, the back sculleries afforded the best route to the lower courtyard.

But by the time they had scrambled through the walls the bewitching hour had already passed and the Thane's wolfhounds were on the prowl. *Pitter-patter, pitter-patter* went the hounds' claws, scratching along the wooden floors, their red tongues lolling as they paced, their yellow eyes piercing the darkness for intruders.

Asenathe snuck out from behind a wall tapestry. The main hallway stretched out before them into the shadowy darkness. Grand heraldic crests and splendid coats of arms hung on the walls, interspersed with paintings of the Morrow clan – of Gravelock Morrow with his eye patch, of Arcadia with her long nose and of Persephone and Pandora, dark sisters from another age.

From a corridor up above them a wolfhound growled.

'The dogs!' hissed Asenathe.

'Run for it!' answered Esmerelda.

'Head for the kitchens,' said Tyaas, grabbing Asenathe's hand.

The night was both a blessing and a curse. The swirling darkness swallowed them up as they sped across the hallway. Outside on the battlements a howling gale battered the castle, shaking the windows and buffeting the high towers, concealing the sound of their footsteps from the marauding wolfhounds. But their scent could not be masked.

'It's as dark as the grave,' muttered Esmerelda, as they raced towards the servants' staircase, edging through puddles of darkness, then inky patches as black as coal.

Then one of the wolfhounds, a beast named Killer, smelt the sweet aroma of flesh wafting in the night air and bared his fangs. The ragged animal darted towards the head of the stairs, let out a terrifying howl, and in the next instant the pack of hounds was giving chase.

'Quick!' shouted Tyaas, pushing the women through the servants' doorway.

Killer and Slayer were almost upon them, bearing their fangs and snarling. The dogs sprang in the air just as Tyaas darted through the doorway and banged the door behind him. He stood panting, trying to get his breath. There had been a split-second between them and Slayer's jaws.

'Hold onto me! Follow the wall,' Esmerelda whispered in the darkness.

They stumbled down the narrow stairway into the pitch-black passageways as the hounds scratched at the door.

'Come away, Killer!' shouted a lazy Groat to the pack leader. 'No more scraps tonight boy! The kitchen's closed. Hey, Slayer! Get down I say, stupid dogs.'

The Groat continued to chastise the hounds as Attie, Esmerelda and Tyaas fled along the servants' passageways. Esmerelda's heart was pounding as she crept beside a warren of rooms. The sculleries were full of washtubs, scrubbing boards and piles of laundry soaking in huge round vats. The smell of rose water and lavender filled their senses. At the back of the scullery she spied a lattice window.

'Is that the way out?' asked Attie.

Tyaas dragged a barrel underneath the window, poked his head into the rain and listened to the water, running away into the gutters.

'All clear,' he said, squeezing his body through the gap and landing nimbly on the other side.

Asenathe came next, followed closely by Esmerelda.

Across the courtyard, the rusted, blackened grate was an unwelcome sight. Esmerelda tiptoed across the flagstones, scanning the parapet for Groats as the moon peeked out from behind the clouds.

'It's stiff,' Esmerelda groaned as she lifted the latch.

'Don't let it creak,' urged Asenathe.

At last she wriggled the latch free and they peered down into a black hole.

'I'm the smallest so I'll go first,' whispered Tyaas.

'Tie the rope around your waist,' insisted Asenathe. 'Pull once if it's safe and twice if there's a problem.'

'And be careful!' warned Esmerelda said as she put matches and candles into his pocket.

Tyaas poked his head into the dark opening, crawling on his hands and knees through water.

'It's grotty,' he called out, 'smelly and sludgy on the bottom.'

In front of him was a chute into murky nothingness.

'I can't see anything,' he murmured. 'Hold the rope tight so I can abseil down.'

Tyaas eased down the slimy wall placing his feet on the uneven brickwork. At the bottom he fumbled for a candle as the sound of water surged down the drain. Tyaas struck a match and as the candle spluttered into life he saw a sloping tunnel with two wide ledges on either side. He tugged on the rope once.

Asenathe went next, followed by Esmerelda. By the time they got to the bottom they were soaked and streaked with slime.

Esmerelda shivered as the huge storm drain came into view. Dark grey stones covered in a green slime formed a dome over their heads. They were in a circular chamber where the confluence of drains met, then ran far underground.

'These walls should be thick enough to protect us,' said Attie, staring at the large dank chamber.

'I'll hold the witch bottle,' said Esmerelda, beckoning to Tyaas. 'You remove the stopper at exactly the same time that Attie says the words of the Raven spell.'

'Sure thing,' replied Tyaas.

He couldn't wait to see what would happen. Tyaas carefully unfastened the seal on the stopper.

'Ready?' he asked looking from one to the other. Asenathe nodded, poised to say the spell. Then Tyaas removed the stopper from the witch bottle. 'Go!' he urged.

*Anintha, Ravena melliflicant, anintha, Ravena melliflicant,*
*Anintha, Ravena melliflicant, anintha, Ravena melliflicant,'*

Aseanthe chanted.

The words fell from her lips and sprang into the air, turning into brilliant yellow shapes, whipping up into the darkness like a swarm of angry wasps. The drain turned brighter as the spell-words hummed and the witch bottle started to shake in Esmerelda's hands.

'Something's happening! Hold the bottle tightly!' Esmerelda cried.

Tyaas grabbed hold of the bottle, his eyes widening, searching inside the shuddering glass as the contents buzzed and fizzed.

'Whatever you do, don't drop it!' cried Asenathe desperately.

All three clutched the witch bottle as it shook and shuddered uncontrollably, making a desperate bid to jump from their hands.

'*Pop, pop, crackle, fizz, zzzzzzzzz, buzzzzzz!*' the witch bottle sang. '*Pop, pop, crackle, fizz, zzzzzzzzz, buzzzzzz!*'

'It's slipping from my fingers!' cried Asenathe as the bottle shot into the air.

Quick as a flash, Tyaas leaped on the stone parapet and lunged as the glass flashed past him fizzing with anger. '*Phewww-zzziinng,*' it sang in a high-pitched rage as Tyaas jumped from the parapet. He grabbed the bottle and fell, rolling to the ground with a splatter.

'Tyaas!' Esmerelda shouted, dashing to his side.

'Are you all right? Is it broken?' she asked apprehensively.

A desperate whirring sound emanated from deep within the glass.

Tyaas shook his head.

'No! It's safe,' he replied with relief.

'*Buzzzz, fizz, wheeeee!*' the bottle wheezed.

The death throes of the Neopholytite's spell spluttered into oblivion.

'Incredible!' said Tyaas, his face glowing with delight.

'It's worked!' cried Esmerelda hugging Asenathe.

'What happens now?' asked Tyaas.

'You must keep these safe until the time is right,' replied Asenathe, removing the contents from the witch bottle.

She wrapped the nail clippings, the phial of blood and the witch's hair in an oilcloth and slipped them down Tyaas's sock. He pulled a disgusted face at the thought of the gruesome contents resting against his leg.

'Tomorrow the Swarm must capture you as planned,' said Esmerelda.

'What will you do then?' he asked, looking crestfallen.

'Watch and wait for Tallitha's return,' replied Esmerelda enigmatically.

'Not long now,' added Asenathe, trying to cheer him up.

'Then all hell will break lose,' said Esmerelda.

With a wicked glint in her eye, she smashed the witch bottle against the wall and kicked the broken pieces into the fast running water.

In an instant the shards of glass disappeared beneath their feet.

*

High up in the Bone Room, at the precise moment Tyaas released the stopper on the witch bottle, the Neopholytite felt a curious shiver. Her milk-white eyes shuddered and her claw-like fingers clutched the arms of her chair, her knuckles turning white through her paper-fine skin.

'Snare!' she bellowed. 'There's something amiss!'

The Shrove scampered to his mistress's side. The witch was troubled. She plucked at the dark red threads of her dress.

'All is well,' the Shrove said soothingly to his agitated mistress.

Snare was all too familiar with the Neophoytite's ill-tempered ways and gently led her to the Emporium of Lost Souls. Bathing in the rejuvenating vapours always calmed her.

Down in the storm drain the words of the Raven spell were trapped, buzzing this way and that, darting up against the walls, pinging into the flurry of fast flowing water, lost and unable to warn the Neopholytite of the chink in her armour. If only the Groats had been more diligent they would have noticed the gap on the lintel where the missing witch bottle had stood. But they had become fat and lazy, and Snare was too busy attending to his mistress to bother with such details. Besides, who would dare climb the Darkling Stairs and tamper with the witch's lair?

The power of the Swarm was waning.

The time was ripe for Tallitha's return.

It was time for the Grand Witch Selvistra to stake her claim on the Bone Room.

# Twenty-Two

As Tallitha and the others reached the outskirts of Grovel-by-the-Water, Buckle, Rye and Lutch were busily gutting rabbits in front of their dwellings.

'Leave the talking to me,' urged Quillam.

He strode over to the women with a beaming smile across his face.

'Morning, Lutch,' he said, greeting her affectionately.

She hurriedly wiped her bloody hands across her apron.

'My lad,' she cried cheerfully. 'Eh, we've been worried about you,' she added, giving Quillam a big hug.

'You look like you've had a rough time of it,' added Suggit, patting Quillam on the back and inspecting the rest of the party with suspicion.

'This is Ruker and Neeps from Ragging Brows Forest and Spooner and Lince all the way from Wycham Elva,' explained Quillam, introducing his companions.

Rye picked her teeth, eyed the assembled crew and hollered out to her raggedy bairns.

'Put the kettle on,' she called out to Archie, 'there's a good lad. Tootles fetch some eggs and that side of bacon from the larder. You look like you need a good breakfast.'

The Grovellers were curious to hear about their adventures, so the villagers gathered round to greet the strangers. But Quillam was wary about revealing too much information in front of the villagers. The less they knew, the safer they would be if the Swarm tried to interrogate them. As they sat around the kitchen eating fried eggs and bacon, Suggit quizzed them whenever their story didn't quite hang together.

'So where did you meet up then?' he asked, eyeing the Skinks.

'In the Northern Wolds,' Quillam replied.

'Seems a bit odd,' he said, cocking his head on one side, 'to go way over yonder and then come back 'ere.'

Suggit sucked on his pipe as the other villagers listened intently, poking their heads through the kitchen window and hanging about the doorway. Tallitha could feel her face burning whenever Quillam stumbled over their story. Spooner and Lince sat awkwardly by the fireplace, eating buttered toast and occasionally staring at the strange Grovellers.

'You look like a fidgety pair,' Rye remarked acidly to the girls. 'Cat got your tongue?' she asked, puffing on her pipe.

Spooner opened her mouth to give a tart response but Quillam gave a sign to shut her up.

Quillam whispered in Suggit's ear. It was time the villagers departed.

'Right then, everybody, our friends need to rest,' announced Suggit to the nosy crowd. 'You can listen to their tales later.'

He shooed them out of the house to a host of complaints. Only Rye, Lutch and Buckle remained – agog at what was to come next.

'Well?' asked Suggit, sitting in his comfy chair. 'There's more to this tale than meets the eye.'

'We don't want to involve you,' answered Quillam firmly.

'But summat happened out there,' added Rye, gesticulating over the marshes towards the Northern Wolds.

'Yes – something did,' said Quillam guardedly.

Spooner kicked her heels against the fireplace. She wasn't keen on the Grovellers giving her nasty looks.

'What then? Don't keep us in suspense, you 'ave to tell us,' argued Buckle, giving the Skinks another unfriendly stare.

Ruker rested her hand on the hilt of her sword. Neeps was ready to pounce should any of the Grovellers turn nasty. He had heard rum things about their association with the Swarm. They were too close by all accounts.

'Have there been any Shroves up here lately?' asked Tallitha, changing the subject.

Ruker bristled at the mention of the cunning creatures. Their enmity went back over many generations.

'Maybe,' said Rye, eying the party, 'what's it to you?'

'Now then Rye, calm down,' said Suggit, trying to placate his irritable wife.

But she'd had quite enough of the prevarication and snapped.

'Well they've a nerve! They comes here, eats our food, takes our hospitality but they won't tell us what they've been up to. All secrets and lies if you ask me! But they expect us to answer their questions,' she replied angrily, folding her arms with a cutting look at the girls.

By this point Spooner could keep silent no longer.

'Well if you must know, something did happen, I – '

'Spooner,' warned Quillam, but it was too late.

'I killed the Gross Stumpleback!' she blurted out.

'And Tallitha met a Grand Witch and …' added Lince.

'Shut up!' shouted Tallitha, glowering at the girls.

An awful silence prevailed in the kitchen. Rye gripped the arms of her chair and Buckle's mouth fell open.

'You what?' murmured Suggit, aghast at their news.

'I shot her!' Spooner announced.

'She's an amazing shot with her bow and arrow,' said Ruker sheepishly.

Lutch turned from one to the other, with a terrified look on her face. Rye looked as though she had been hit in the stomach.

'What did you say, lass – about meeting a Grand Witch?' asked Lutch, turning pale.

'Nothing!' shouted Tallitha shooting a desperate look at the girls.

But Lince was on a roll, recklessly boasting about her sister.

'Our kid killed the Stumpleback! Three fine arrows straight into her hide! She finished the beast off!' she shouted.

'I'll be damned,' muttered Suggit.

'The Black Sprites imprisoned that evil Swarm maiden and her nasty brother, Redlevven, down in the Stinkwells too,' added Spooner.

'Blimey,' said Buckle aghast, clicking her tongue in dismay.

'Oh my,' said Suggit, with a note of trepidation in his voice, 'now you're for it.'

'But only if they catch us,' added Quillam.

Suggit gave him a sidelong glance. 'The Swarm always catch up with you in the end. No matter what you do, no matter where you hide, they have the old magic and will always ferret you out!'

'You'll be sorry you ever set eyes on those Spell-Seekers,' muttered Rye.

'But what about the Shroves?' asked Tallitha again, 'have you seen them?'

'Aye lass, we gave 'em shelter for a couple of nights then showed them to a disused mineshaft out near Cinder's Edge,' replied Suggit.

'What's them Shroves to you?' asked Lutch.

'We need to talk to them, that's all,' added Quillam, as the tension mounted in the kitchen.

But the Grovellers were unconvinced by his story. Rye sat with a cold expression on her face, picking her teeth, whilst Buckle eyed the Skinks suspiciously.

Tallitha could stand the atmosphere no longer.

'Well,' she said, rising from the chair. 'I'm going to find those Shroves. Coming?' she said to the Skinks.

'Count us in,' replied Neeps.

'What about you?' she asked Quillam

But Quillam knew he had to smooth things over with the Grovellers.

'There'll be too many of us. I'll stay here with Lutch and the girls. Come back when you've found them.'

So Tallitha picked up her bag and left the kitchen, starting off for Cinder's Edge followed by the Skinks.

Rye didn't take long to display her displeasure, shaking her head in disbelief.

'You should be more careful who you keep company with,' she snapped, gesticulating towards Tallitha as she walked out of the village. 'Meeting witches an' all!'

The stuffing had been knocked out of Rye. If the Swarm discovered the Grovellers had given these runaways shelter they would wreak havoc in their villages. The Grand Witches were involved too – praise the heavens, they were all for it now!

Rye cast her eye over the youth.

He was a fool to get involved with the Wycham girl.

*

That evening, Grovell-by-the-Water was a hive of activity. The women were chopping wood for the fire; the children were carrying pails of water from the well; mothers were washing their grubby offspring and the men were cooking a communal hog-roast over a fiery pit, all the while chatting about the curious visitors and calling out to one another.

Spooner and Lince had decided that the Grovellers weren't so bad after all. They decided to go along with Suggit and his son, Archie, to set rabbit traps in the woods, while Quillam remained behind, sitting on the front porch with Lutch and Rye. Groveller women never stopped working. Rye was making a patchwork quilt for Tootles and Lutch was intent at her sewing, her eyes screwed up, darning a tear in her second best jacket.

'Put the kettle on, Mossie, there's a good lass,' Lutch said to her daughter.

The girl skipped inside the kitchen as Lutch turned to Quillam. She was determined to get the truth out of him.

'Don't get on the wrong side of the Morrow Swarm,' cautioned Lutch. 'Wherever that girl goes there'll be trouble, I can smell it a mile off.'

'No Ma, you're wrong,' he insisted. 'Tallitha is caught up in the Swarm's evil schemes – but she wants no part of them.'

'She's a Morrow, ain't she?' added Rye acidly, giving Quillam a stern look.

'We don't want you to come to any harm,' Lutch added, nudging her sister to curb her tongue. She continued mending her jacket, her needle flashing, waiting for the right moment to continue. 'The Swarm are mighty powerful and the Grand Witches are a force to be reckoned with. You won't outwit the Larva Coven whatever you do. They're an ancient brood with deadly ways.'

Rye couldn't keep quiet. 'Aye – ways that some of us have witnessed first hand.'

Quillam jerked his head in her direction. Now they had his full attention.

'What do you mean?' he asked, looking from one to the other.

Rye leaned forward and whispered furtively behind her hand.

'Well my lad, I'm not sure you know all there is to know about them Grand Witches.' Rye looked over her shoulder to make sure they weren't being overheard. 'Them Grand Witches roam Breedoor, biding their time, casting their spells, some doing good deeds others doing terrible things.'

'Are they in cahoots with the Swarm?' Quillam asked.

Lutch jerked her head in the direction of Hellstone. 'You never can tell whose side the Grand Witches are on.'

'They're a law unto the Witches' Ways. They have no allegiance except to themselves and even then they're always fallin' out.'

The women continued with their sewing as Quillam gazed towards the northern lands. *Grand Witches and covens – a force to be reckoned with …*

Lutch disturbed his thoughts. 'How come the Spell-Seekers got trussed up?' she asked tentatively.

Rye carried on with her patchwork, pinning the fabric squares while she waited for Quillam's response.

'The Black Sprites laid a trap for Redlevven and Yarrow,' he answered.

'Oh, well you know what that means,' she said, nodding at Rye, 'the Grand Witch Kastra must be involved. The

Sprites do her bidding.' Lutch bit her lip and shook her head.

'Eh, 'tis a sorry day! No good will ever come of meddlin' with them Grand Witches!'

Mossie came back with the tea and Lutch shooed her away to play with her sisters.

'Did you get a good look at Kastra?' Rye asked. 'They say she's a beauty with eyes the colour of hyacinths and raven black hair.'

Quillam shook his head. The women exchanged knowing glances.

'Rye has seen one of 'em, ain't you, my dear?' said Lutch, winking at her sister.

Rye made a warning noise in her throat. It was a sound full of foreboding.

'Aye, I saw a Grand Witch, just the once,' she replied mysteriously, putting her patchwork to one side.

'Go on,' urged Lutch, 'tell us all about it!'

Rye leaned back in her rocking chair, focussing her attention on Quillam.

'When I was a young girl – I saw summat very strange but I was scared and told no one about '*the seeing*' for a very long time. I was frit to death and never told a living soul about them Grand Witches until many years later and then only to my trusted Lutch.'

Lutch smiled, flattered by her sister's kind words and smoothed out her newly darned jacket.

'Good as new,' she said, beaming at her handiwork. 'Now who wants a cuppa?'

'Two sugars,' said Rye, 'no, make it three and add a tot of that black rum.'

'What happened?' asked Quillam.

Rye cut her eyes at the youth and clicked her tongue. 'Why should I tell you?' Rye barked, 'will it make any difference? Will you heed my warning and keep away from them evil sorceresses?'

His face darkened. Lutch gave Rye a nod to continue her tale.

'Come on Rye, don't be gruff with the lad,' she said pouring rum into her sister's teacup. 'Perhaps it will be a lesson to him not to have any truck with them evil witches from the Larva Coven.'

Rye beckoned to them to come closer. Quillam drank his tea and waited.

'When I was a nipper I used to stay with my grandmother's sister, a woman called Wilhelmina Blackstock. She lived in Much Grovell and I used to help her with odd jobs and messages. She was a wonderful seamstress and did intricate embroidery for the Swarm.'

Rye sighed remembering the happy days of her youth and seemed to drift away with her memories.

'Get on with the story,' urged Lutch, watching Quillam's reaction.

Quillam was entranced.

'Aye, well, where was I? Oh yes – one day, when I had been

especially good and completed all my chores, Wilhelmina Blackstock decided to take me with her to Hellstone Tors. It's a day that's etched into my mind,' she said shaking her head. 'Going up to that fearsome castle, I had butterflies in my tummy every step of the way. As nippers we'd been told tales about the sinister place. Anyway, whilst I was there, hanging around in the servants' kitchen, waiting for my great-aunt to return, I peered out through a scullery window and I happened to see one of them Grand Witches float across the courtyard and I mean *float*. She meandered in through the gate, so she did, surrounded by a flaming red light, it made me fair shudder at the sight of her.'

'Who was it?' asked Quillam.

'Wilhelmina wouldn't tell me, she got cross and said I had to get down and mustn't stare at a Grand Witch for fear of falling ill. Then a kitchen boy who had taken a shine to me told me about the Grand Witches from the Larva Coven. They don't get along with each other and have fearsome tempers. Sometimes they fall in with one another for gain but most of the time they play tricks on each other – laying traps and casting spells.'

'Snowdroppe told me stories about the witches when I was little – just to frighten me,' replied Quillam.

'Rye ain't finished her tale yet,' said Lutch, gesticulating at her sister to continue.

'Months later when I was back at Wilhelmina Blackstock's she told me that one of them witches had scorched a poor servant just for looking at her. He became ill, writhing in agony, covered in nasty sores, and the poor soul died a horrible death.'

'That's just an old story you tell children, to scare them into behaving themselves,' laughed Quillam. 'I'm not afraid.'

'Then you should be!' Rye said angrily. 'The same fate could happen to you, if you fall foul of them Grand Witches.'

'Please stay here, boy. Don't return to Hellstone Tors with that winsome girl,' said Lutch, 'it ain't your fight and no good will come of it.'

'She's right. Stay longer – let them do battle with the Neopholytite and the Grand Witches if they have a mind to. It will all end badly. I can feel it in my bones,' added Rye fretfully.

Quillam shook his head. 'I can't do that. I promised Tallitha I would help her. Besides – ' he hesitated and reached for Lutch's hand.

'What is it my lad?' asked Lutch fondly.

'Those girls, Spooner and Lince, there's something you should know about them,' he said, hesitating.

'What then? Spit it out,' demanded Rye.

'They're my cousins,' he answered quietly, 'and Tallitha helped me find them.'

Now the women were hanging on his every word.

'Well I never!' said Rye, 'that's a turn up and no mistake!'

Lutch put her arm about Quillam's shoulders. He was agitated.

'What else is bothering you, lad?' she asked, observing him closely.

'I-I've also found out who my real mother is,' he stuttered, 'not that I don't love you both,' he said quickly, 'you and Rye have always been so kind to me.'

'It's fine, my lad, don't fret. We know you've always been troubled about your birth mother and wanted to find her.'

''Tis only natural,' added Rye, nodding sagely.

'So that's why I must go with Tallitha to Hellstone Tors and then, when it is all over and the terrible pact is destroyed, she will take me to meet my Mother.'

Lutch patted Quillam's hand. 'I'm happy for you, son, of course I am – but promise me you will remember this day and what we've told you. Always beware the Grand Witches,' she said mysteriously.

'Because if you don't watch out, they'll trick you and hex you straight to hell!' replied Rye, with a terrified look in her eyes.

# Twenty-Three

Tallitha discovered the Shroves cowering beneath Cinder's Edge in the disused mineshaft, just as Rye had told her. Embellsed and Bicker nearly jumped out of their skins – spitting and hissing – when they spied their old adversaries, the Skinks, marching into their shelter.

'You! What you doin' here?' shouted Embellsed, throwing a vicious look at Tallitha.

Bicker hopped up and down like a mad thing, swearing and cursing. 'I'll be jiggered, damn and blast, Embellsed! You've got me into a right pickle! I should have stayed in my cellars!' he hollered.

Bicker was always keen to blame someone else for his misfortune.

The Shroves made Ruker's flesh crawl.

'Stay where you are!' she shouted as the Shroves tried to sneak out of the cave.

'Keep those Skinks away from me,' moaned Bicker, shivering behind Embellsed.

'What do you want with us?' cried Embellsed.

'Don't be frightened! We're not here to hurt you. We want you to show us the way into Hellstone Tors,' explained Tallitha, trying a gentler approach.

She could see that the Shroves were terrified.

'Go through the main gate, just like everyone else!' cried Bicker sacastically. 'Tell 'em nowt, Embellsed!'

'How do we know you 'aven't come to trick us?' asked Embellsed.

Ruker put her hand on her dagger. 'You're going to tell us how to get into the castle without being seen. If there's a secret tunnel we want to know about it, or we'll slice you from here to here,' she said, demonstrating a cut from her windpipe to her stomach.

'Oh my poor old bones, we'll be skinned alive, buried and forgotten out here in the middle of nowhere!' cried Bicker, looking for a means of escape.

'We want you to help us,' added Tallitha, trying to calm the frantic Shroves. She shot a glance at Ruker. 'You're frightening them.'

'They're evil good-for-nothings,' she answered.

'Without backbone!' added Neeps.

The Shroves hopped about nervously, keeping their mouths shut. They weren't about to divulge the whereabouts of the secret route through the snickleways.

'Okay, now you're for it!' replied Neeps, holding Bicker by the scruff of his neck. 'Either tell us or we'll garrotte the pair of you and string your gizzards up for the birds to peck!'

'Please, don't hurt me!' begged Bicker.

'You may as well tell us,' said Tallitha. 'You'll never survive out here. Either the Swarm will find you or you'll starve to death.'

Bicker stared miserably at the inhospitable cave. The girl was right. All they had was a bed of leaves and a meagre assortment of nuts and berries.

'Had a hot meal recently?' asked Ruker, teasing the bedraggled pair.

'N-Not for days,' moaned Bicker, licking his feverish lips.

'Shut up,' cried Embellsed, his eyes darting towards the Skinks.

'Lovely succulent meat – I'm so hungry,' moaned Bicker, salivating.

'Then all you have to do is tell us how to get inside Hellstone Tors and we'll cook you a delicious supper,' said Ruker, 'with lashings of gravy,' she added, licking her lips.

'Mmmm,' said Bicker, drooling at the thought of a decent meal and tugging pathetically on Embellsed's jacket.

'Once you help us you'll be free to go wherever you like,' added Tallitha.

'I can show you the way – arrh,' screamed Bicker as Embellsed kicked him on the shin and roughly pulled him to one side.

The Shroves whispered conspiratorially to one another. Bicker nodded enthusiastically at Embellsed and padded over to Tallitha with a look of hope in his desperate face.

'Can we have rabbit stew?' he asked, his eyes popping out of his head at the thought of tasty gravy and juicy pink meat.

'Only if you show us the way,' said Neeps, testing the old rascal.

Bicker nodded.

'Got your knife and traps?' asked Ruker looking at Neeps.

The Skink nodded, handing his traps to Ruker.

'Dinner it is then. I'll be back so get a fire going. Make sure it's at the back of the mineshaft so as not to attract attention.'

With that, Ruker hightailed it across the countryside to catch their supper while Bicker began to describe the snickleways to Tallitha and Neeps.

*

Tallitha was curious about Embellsed's hurried departure from Hellstone Tors. Shroves were forbidden to leave the castle on pain of death, so something serious must have happened for the two miscreants to flee and to remain in the wild under such dire circumstances.

'So Embellsed,' she said, twisting her hair in and out of her fingers, 'I'm curious to know what made you leave the castle?'

'That's my business,' he grumbled, throwing her a vicious look.

'Murder and intrigue,' snorted Bicker, cocking his head at Embellsed. 'He's a killer.'

'Shut up, rag worm!' shouted Embellsed.

The old Shrove was getting on his nerves. He should have done away with him at the end of the snickleways. No one would have discovered his mouldering corpse in the dark passageways. *Kill once and it's so much easier to kill again,* thought Embellsed and shivered at his evil thought.

'Bicker's lying!' he shouted.

'I ain't, you're a bad 'un,' he added, 'tried to trick me too! Don't deny it.'

'Who did you murder?' Tallitha asked.

''Twas that mean old rogue Wince, who was blackmailing him,' replied Bicker, sniggering.

Embellsed kicked the cockroach on the shin.

'Did the Swarm banish you from Hellstone Tors?'

'Nay, never banished! I left of my own accord. I'd had enough of those dratted sisters Muprid and Lapis, nasty pair, punishing me for nowt!'

'He's a villain, heart like stone,' grizzled Bicker.

'I'm nowt but kind, that dirt-stopper fell to his death. 'Twas an accident!' cried Embellsed, wringing his hands and hopping about.

The old feller sniggered as Embellsed looked warily from Tallitha to Bicker. He had no choice. He would have to tell them about the miserable deed, omitting the murderous end.

He sat in a huddle chewing his fingers.

'Wince and Bludroot had it in for me. Bloodroot would have given my job as Shrove-Marker to that maggot, Wince. They were plannin' it! Then he'd have consigned me to the lower

292

levels with the rats and the serfs for all eternity. I couldn't bear the thought of it! I was heartily sick of the Swarm - "*do this, do that, run there, run here,*" - always shoutin' for Embellsed!' he muttered.

'Both brave and foolhardy,' said Tallitha, winding him up 'They'll kill you for sure if they catch you.'

Embellsed's face was ashen. 'Oooh, err!' he bleated.

It was uncomfortable to hear what he most feared from another.

'If you want to survive, show me the secret entrance into Hellstone Tors,' said Tallitha, capitalising on his distress. 'Once I have broken the pact, I promise I will grant your freedom, for you to stay or go as you please.'

The Shroves huddled together. Surely the girl was stark staring mad!

'You'll never destroy their pact,' said Embellsed with trepidation, 'the Swarm will kill you first and grind your bones to dust.'

'You'll be marmalised!' moaned Bicker, hopping about.

'I'll take my chance,' Tallitha replied, twisting her hair in and out of her fingers – but the Shroves did have a point!

'Supper's here!' cried Ruker, strolling back into the mine with four fat rabbits hanging over her shoulder. 'You skin these,' she said to the Shroves, 'while we chop the wild turnips, sage and garlic,' she turned to the others. 'Then we'll roast these succulent fellows!'

'Anyone for gravy?' asked Neeps, winking at Tallitha and Ruker.

\*

After a glorious supper of spit-roast rabbit smothered in lashings of juicy gravy, the Shroves, content with their fat bellies, wiped their greasy mouths and crept to the back of the cave for a long sleep.

'I'll go and get the others,' said Neeps strapping his knife to his belt. 'You'd better watch those Shroves – they can't be trusted and will give us the slip if given the chance.'

So Neeps journeyed back to Grovell-by-the-Water. The next day, with Quillam and the girls, they regrouped by the disused mineshaft.

Tallitha and Ruker had experienced a sleepless night. They had taken it in turns to watch the Shroves from dusk until dawn to make sure they didn't make a move.

'Ready? We'd better get packed,' said Quillam walking towards Tallitha. He turned to the Skinks. 'What about you two?' he asked.

The Skinks were determined to accompany Tallitha to Hellstone Tors and finish the job.

'We're coming too,' said Neeps.

'That's all there is to it,' announced Ruker firmly.

'But what if you're seen?' Tallitha asked, worried for her friends.

'If this tunnel exists then we can sneak into the castle and hide out until we're needed.'

There was no point in arguing with them and, in truth Tallitha wanted Ruker and Neeps at her side in the evil place.

'I can't wait to get inside that spooky castle,' said Spooner excitedly. 'I bet it's even more eerie than Winderling Spires.'

Lince gave her sister an odd look. 'You're just plain weird, our Spoons.'

'Be careful what you wish for,' said Tallitha cautiously. 'Once you see the hideous place, you might feel differently.'

\*

The travellers made their way over the hills of Sunkwells Bottom. They clambered over soggy banks, over dips and hollows, underneath mossy tendrils hanging from blackened trees and across the sandy pathways that fringed the dunes until the dark headland that surrounded Hellstone Tors came into view. In the shadows, just a moment out of sight, leaping to the right and left, Rucheba was on their tail with a small group of sprites, following Kastra's orders to keep watch over Tallitha.

As the travellers approached the Tors, twilight was closing in and a grey mist hung in the air.

'There's a sea fret coming in tonight,' said Quillam, peering into the bleary night. 'The fog is thick in patches so watch your step; there are dangerous crevices and potholes out here

'It's so creepy,' said Lince nervously, taking her sister's arm.

Grey-faced owls hooted to one other as bats swooped, skimming the wind. Then, the moon glinted through the clouds, causing the Shroves to huddle together, whispering frantically to one another.

'What's going on?' asked Quillam observing the twitchy pair.

'We don't like the look of that moon,' replied Bicker pointing into the night sky.

'A waning moon is a warning sign,' added Embellsed wringing his hands. ''Tis a bad omen of things to come,' he said superstitiously.

'Rubbish,' said Ruker, giving the Shrove a cold look, but the sinister sight of Hellstone made her apprehensive nonetheless.

As they climbed the final promontory, the ominous castle loomed high above them, its dark pointed towers rising like a blackened crown out of the ghostly sea fret. The mist hung menacingly over the bay like a dank shroud. The twisted turrets and uninviting towers of Hellstone Tors made a haunting spectacle.

'Crikey,' muttered Spooner, clinging to her sister, 'that castle is creepy!'

'It's horrible! I have an awful feeling,' groaned Lince, staring wide-eyed at the monstrosity erupting out of the headland.

'I tried to warn you,' added Tallitha, sidling next to the girls. 'It's even worse once you're inside, all dark and gloomy, with sinister hallways and never ending corridors, you never know what's lurking round the next corner.'

Tallitha slipped in between Spooner and Lince as the girls whispered an old Wycham saying and clung to one another.

'Which way now?' asked Quillam, turning towards the Shroves.

Embellsed was decidedly shifty, hopping erratically from one foot to another, his beady eyes darting this way and that.

'Over there,' replied Bicker, pointing into the mist. 'There's a boulder next to a clump of trees and underneath the shaft leads down to the snickleways.'

'Come on,' urged Quillam, trudging onwards.

They crept towards the dark hole in the earth, a raggedy group, huddled against the mist, crouching low to avoid detection in the vaporous night.

Slowly and surreptitiously, Embellsed began to hang back, moving assiduously towards the edge of the group, inching away with each step and creeping further towards the forest. The swirling sea fret disguised his treachery. The cunning Shrove had gauged the moment just right. In a split second, he broke free from the others, darted through the trees and vanished like a spectre into the foggy night.

# Twenty-Four

Snowdroppe was lounging in her dressing room, clad in a green velvet gown, dramatically waving her painted nails in the air. Her talons had just been manicured by her ladies-maid and were a soft apple-green.

'Stiggy,' she murmured at the fennec fox, snoozing in his basket. 'Does my darling want her lunch?' she cooed.

The fennec fox pricked up her ears and nuzzled his mistress.

'Get Stiggy her lunch. Roast beef and slivers of ox heart,' she demanded, blowing a kiss at Stiggy and turning abruptly to her Shrove.

Since his arrival from Winderling Spires, Grintley had been at Snowdroppe's beck and call. She relished having her old Shrove to fetch and carry for her. He knew the way she liked things and it meant Snowdroppe could do what she loved most: issue a stream of orders as the Shrove danced attendance to her.

'Throw that one out, pack those away,' she demanded, pointing at various dresses.

'I shall have a new wardrobe of the finest clothes,' she declared, tossing her long red hair with delight, 'to celebrate one of my children becoming the thirteenth member of the Swarm! Which one it will be, of course, I cannot say,' she smirked.

Grintley grunted and set about folding his mistress's discarded garments.

Since their escape from Winderling Spires, the Shroves were settling into their new routines in Hellstone Tors. Marlin had been assigned to Caedryl, and Muprid had been given her own Shrove, Florré, to boss about, while her sister had been allocated a Hellstone Shrove, Cumberbatch, to wait on her every need. Marlin, however, was extremely put out. He grizzled and groaned about his lot. He had been short-changed in the allocation of a new mistress. He had been taken down a peg or two in the Shrove hierarchy.

'Waitin' on nowt but a chit of a lass,' he grumbled. 'In Winderling Spires I had the run of the place and waited on the Grand Morrow!' he sneered, crouching in his Shrove hole.

Florré and Grintley offered their deepest commiserations, tinged with a hint of gloating.

'It's a disgrace! After what you've done for the Thane, you should have the pick of the crop,' added Grintley, observing Marlin's reaction.

Marlin mithered away to himself and pulled a sour face.

'Or even one't Spell-Seekers. Your talents will be put to waste

with that cat-girl,' Florré said, dripping his poisonous words into Marlin's receptive ears.

'What's she like? Does she spit and meow?' asked Grintley, turning the knife once more.

'She's temperamental, spoilt and fussy. Wants this, doesn't like that, can't eat this dish, can't abide that - all day long, I'm at my wits' end,' he moaned. 'There's no good pickings with the likes of her and I have to clear up the mousey leftovers,' he shuddered.

'You know what they're like when they get their first Shrove,' hissed Florré, 'they think they can do what they please. She'll need a good deal of managing,' he suggested.

'Take her in hand, Marlin. Find out her weakness. They all have one, even't Swarm. Then you can play her for your own ends,' remarked Grintley.

'Follow her and make it your business to know everything about her peculiar ways,' offered Florré. 'When she's out prowling the castle at night, see what the little minx gets up to.'

Marlin stroked his whiskery chin. Grintley and Florré were right. He had been so upset by the new arrangements that he'd quite forgotten what Shroves do best! They spy on their mistresses and masters, learning their ways in order to improve their own position – a jewel here, a smattering of food there, stolen pickings to be hidden away.

He chuckled – he would stalk the cat-girl this very night.

*

Caedryl Morrow was beset with a terrible craving for absolute power. Evil had eaten away at her over the years and had changed her from Asenathe's sweet-natured child to a scheming, power-hungry hellcat. Now the desire was so strong she could almost taste victory. Every waking moment was tainted with her duplicitous plans, focussed on one end – to sit on the Thane's throne, to rule the kingdom of Breedoor, controlling everyone in her orbit.

'I must find the Swarm's treasure,' she said, pacing the corridors, looking for her Uncle Edweard.

She would make him tell her everything. Somewhere beneath Hellstone Tors the mysterious deep-green bloodstones were piled high in a sunken crypt. But the precious stones belonged to the Thane and she had waited far too long to see them. Besides, she was the true heir to Hellstone Tors and wanted the bloodstones for herself!

'Your mother has many pretty stones, ask her for one,' said Lord Edweard after a barrage of Caedryl's questions.

'But I want one of the Swarm's bloodstones, not one of my mother's old trinkets,' Caedryl pouted.

'Not possible,' he replied, eyeing his spoilt niece.

'Why ever not? It isn't too much to ask,' she moaned.

How was she ever to locate the treasure rooms? They were steeped in secrecy. She had asked the twins and even Snowdroppe, but no one would tell her anything about their whereabouts or which snickleway would lead her to the Bloodstone Crypt.

'I want to see where they are kept, to choose a stone for

myself. I want it set in my golden locket for my next birthday and it has to be just the right size – large and beautiful.'

'Then give the locket to me and I will see what I can do,' Edweard replied in an off-hand manner.

It was hopeless. She would have to try another tack.

'But it's as I said, Uncle dear,' she wheedled, 'I want to see the bloodstones. I've always been curious about the Bloodstone Crypt. I can't imagine how pretty the stones must look, piled high and guarded by an ancient magic,' she simpered.

Edweard was tired of her endless demands. His heart had turned cold towards Caedryl. At some point he would have to dispense with his troublesome niece.

'The Thane won't agree,' he growled, 'the stones are kept in secret. Besides, it is a dangerous place and neither you nor I will persuade him to let you go there.'

Caedryl folded her arms and shot him a sidelong glance. Her Uncle Edweard was proving useless as an ally. Her darkest desire was to be the Queen of Hellstone Tors and when that glorious day arrived she wasn't going to share any of it with him! There was nothing for it; she would explore the snickleways on her own. She, Caedryl Morrow, would unearth the whereabouts of the treasure!

She loved to wander alone at night. Now she would seek out the Bloodstone Crypt!

Slynose, the Wheen-Cat, was frightened of nothing.

\*

As evenlight descended, Marlin didn't return to his Shrove burrow. He lurked outside Caedryl's palace, hunched in his nooky recess, his beady eyes focussed on the entranceway. The long hours ticked by tediously and he was on the verge of nodding off when the door creaked open and the Wheen-Cat pranced down the steps, her emerald-green eyes swirling in the darkness.

For a moment she surveyed the corridor, licked her paws then in a flash she sped off down the dark hallway, her tail swishing in the shadows.

'Bother,' Marlin moaned as he unwound his creaky old bones and slipped from his hiding place.

The Wheen-Cat minced along in the darkness, sniffing here and pouncing there, after mice, spiders and any other tasty creature that crossed her path.

'She's as annoying as a cat as she is as a girl,' the old Shrove muttered, ambling after her.

He traipsed along the corridors while the cat-girl stalked her supper, pounced in the air, caught a fat, juicy mouse and finished it off with a few rips and tears. She licked her jaws clean and polished her sharp talons, occasionally peering behind her to make sure she wasn't being followed.

But Marlin was a sneaky Shrove, well used to stalking without being seen. He inched along in the shadows, scurrying into recesses as the cat meandered down the gloomy passageways.

*What's she up to now?* He thought as the cat sprang into the air.

The Wheen-Cat shuddered, her black fur rippled and Caedryl landed on the floor in the cat's place. She stroked down her black dress and wrapped her long plaits over her head, pinning them into place.

'Well I never,' Marlin muttered, scurrying after her. 'I ain't never seen owt so weird in all my days.'

Quick as a flash Caedryl slipped through the servant's doorway, down the corridor and into the enormous kitchens as Marlin snuck behind her.

'Where's she goin' now?' he muttered.

The Shrove soundlessly moved through the darkness passing into the servant's thoroughfare that lay beneath the castle.

Like a slippery shadow Caedryl darted down the next flight of steps and into the depths of the chilly wine cellars, edging into a stone passageway containing a series of rusty gates.

Marlin was distinctly uncomfortable. The terrain was unfamiliar. Fat, brown mice scampered this way and that under his feet.

'Blasted vermin!' he croaked.

Gingerly, he picked up his feet, tightly holding on to his trouser legs as though he was stepping through mud – the sound of the mice scurrying away into their dark little holes had unnerved him. Then, in the distance, the hateful girl did her horrid trick again. Caedryl couldn't resist the mousey chase that was on offer that night. In the wink of an eye she shuddered, leapt into the air and landed back on the floor, swished her bushy black tail, pounced two or three times and slid through the iron gates with a fat juicy mouse, *wee-wee-wee*, squeaking away, clenched between her jaws.

Marlin watched helplessly as the cat-girl slid under the wine racks and disappeared into the deepening shadows.

'Bother,' he grizzled and stamped his foot.

He hurried after her, tried the gate, but it was locked.

He could go no further. The damnable cat-girl had outwitted him. Grousing and grumbling, he retraced his steps back through the cellars and out into the castle.

Now what was he going to do?

*

Slynose sped, in slinky leaps and nimble bounds, racing through the twisting snickleways, her tufted paws padding through the dark passageways, her green swirling eyes all-seeing in the pitch black. She sniffed the fetid, cloistered air, at the scents emanating from the damp snickets – a niff of rat, a waft of pungent Shrove and then, something that the cattish creature could not fathom. She stopped and hissed. It was the scent of the sea, salty and wet, that greeted her nostrils. She spat and turned in the opposite direction, meandering down the next twisting snickleway, for the Wheen-Cat hated water of any kind.

Now, she was off to find the Bloodstone Crypt.

# Twenty-Five

'**W**here's Embellsed?' demanded Neeps, circling in the mist.

'He was here a second ago,' said Spooner.

'Double-crossing varmint!' shouted Bicker, 'he's left me all alone!'

'Blast that old rogue,' said Ruker crossly, 'he's done a runner.'

'Which way did he go?' cried Tallitha, 'the fog's so thick.'

'Shhh,' said Quillam gruffly, 'the Groats may be scouting the lower reaches.'

'Let's go after him,' growled Ruker. 'Keep hold of that one!' she said as Bicker tried to wriggle flee.

But the Shrove was old and his joints were stiff from the years consigned to the chilly wine cellars. He was no match for the youth. Quillam grabbed him by the throat.

'No you don't, you're staying here!' he said sharply.

'Please let me go,' he begged, 'I can't go back into that terrible place.' The Shrove shivered and moaned. 'I-I betrayed the Swarm by leaving my post and if they catch me they will surely kill me in the most horrible way.'

'Stop bleating,' whispered Quillam hoarsely, 'make any more noise and I'll finish you off myself!'

'Oh my – I'm just a poor Shrove.'

Quillam squeezed his throat and the old Shrove fell silent, quaking with fear.

The Skinks returned empty-handed.

'No sign of that weasel,' said Neeps, appearing through the swirling fog.

'It's impossible to see anything, the sea fret is closing in,' added Ruker, striding back towards them.

'If he's gone, so be it, we'll never catch him now. Bicker is more use to us anyway,' said Tallitha. 'He knows the snickleways beneath Hellstone Tors.'

'One false move and you'll feel this dagger in your belly,' said Ruker, twisting the hilt of her weapon and staring into the eyes of the terrified Shrove.

'Oh my! I won't run away, I-I promise, please don't hurt me,' stuttered the miserable creature. 'I'll s-show you the way through the snickleways.'

'Make sure you do,' growled Quillam.

So Bicker stumbled on through the fog with Neeps's dagger digging into his back.

'It's this way,' he mumbled, tottering onwards.

Huge black boulders sprang out of the earth, cloaked in

spiralling fog, forming terrifying shapes, momentarily twisting into gnarled faces and horrifying stone creatures.

The bedraggled party edged through the mist whilst the waves crashed against the rocks and the grey-faced owls hooted menacingly across the night.

'This is it,' mumbled Bicker, running his fingers over a jagged rock, 'the entrance is round the back.'

'This better not be a trick,' said Neeps, waving his dagger into the Shrove's face.

'N-No, I swear it,' Bicker replied, cowering.

A steep slope disappeared before them into a dank, dark hole.

'What's down there?' asked Quillam, his ochre-coloured eyes flashing at the Shrove.

'Cold dark snickleways,' murmured Bicker with fear in his voice.

The fog hung in clumps about the entranceway.

'I-I don't like it,' Lince added nervously, 'it looks awful.'

'Shut up Sis,' replied Spooner, 'you can't chicken out now.'

'I'll go first,' said Quillam, climbing down into the darkness. 'Tallitha,' he added, reaching back to take her hand.

She climbed over the lip of the boulder and disappeared down the hole.

'I'll hold this rascal,' said Neeps, 'Ruker, you go next.'

One by one, they edged down the slope. Neeps pushing Bicker down before him and landing with a bump into the darkness.

A blast of cold air caught Tallitha at the back of her throat.

'Here, take these,' said Quillam, lighting a bundle of tapers.

The waxy flames spat and smouldered, bouncing beams of light off the black rocks, illuminating the twists and turns in the maze of tunnels and revealing uninviting black passageways. It was a labyrinth, forged from the underbelly of the Tors, like a bundle of writhing snakes.

'Where do the tunnels lead to?' asked Lince, clinging on to her sister.

Bicker turned slowly, his beady eyes glowing in the light. 'No one knows,' he answered mysteriously. 'Some say they lead further under Breedoor, others that they go under the sea. But I've only explored a few of them.'

'Then how will we find our way?' asked Ruker harshly.

'Just up ahead there's a fork in the tunnel. From there I marked the rock to find my way home.'

So they followed Bicker, stepping through puddles of water, holding onto one another's hands to find their way.

Bicker pointed to a gouge in the rock. It was one of his markings.

'Make sure the varmint can't escape,' Ruker said to Neeps.

The Skink tightened the belt round the Shrove's wrist.

'Lead on,' said Neeps, pushing the hilt of his dagger into Bicker's back.

'No need to be rough,' the Shrove bleated.

The old Shrove sniffed the air and ran his fingers across the rock, feeling for his chisel marks.

'This way,' he said, shuffling onwards with the others trailing behind him.

They crept down the passageways in single file, their eyes scouring the darkness that engulfed them. The web of tunnels spread out beneath the Tors and far beyond, like a maze of buried secrets – a labyrinth of evil. *Drip-drop, drip-drop*; blackened water seeped through the rock and trickled to the ground as the sound of scurrying vermin and the squeaking of tiny cave creatures met their ears.

'Rats!' said Ruker, turning up her nose. 'Watch your footing! The ground is wet and uneven.'

Tallitha took Lince's hand in hers and they crept down the snaking passageways. Suddenly Tallitha's taper alighted on a roughly hewn archway.

'What's down there?' she asked nervously.

Bicker blinked in the meagre light. 'Just darkness and death,' he muttered, 'for thems that are too curious by half,' he warned. 'Thems that will lose their way in these underground pathways, never to be seen again.'

Tallitha peered down the twisting snickleway. As the light from the smouldering taper bumped off the walls, she gasped.

'Look at those hideous birds,' she cried.

A group of carved raven's heads, with their beaks open and their heads cocked to one side, sprand out of the cave wall. Water dripped through their beaks and trickled onto the ground.

'Just like the Shrove tunnel in Winderling Spires,' said Ruker ominously.

'I don't like it,' moaned Lince.

'Shut up,' said Spooner, giving her sister a dig.

'What's down there?' asked Tallitha, staring into the coal-black hole.

Bicker's face twitched in the meagre light. He whispered in a hoarse voice. 'The Swarm's treasure rooms are hidden in the lower crypt but I've never dared look for them,' he shivered. 'Dangerous, guarded by dark magic,' he snivelled and padded onwards.

Spooner and Lince exchanged furtive glances.

'What sort of magic?' asked Tallitha.

'Stuff that Shroves know nowt about,' added Bicker ominously, 'mean curses and nasty spells placed there by the Neopholytite to protect the Swarm's bloodstones.'

'Wow,' said Lince, 'that sounds weird.'

'And exciting,' added Spooner, desperate to explore further.

'We're not going down there,' added Tallitha, giving her a reproachful look. 'It's too dangerous. First, we have to break the Neopholytite's power.'

'We can explore later, once the Morrow curse is lifted,' replied Quillam.

Tallitha and Quillam locked eyes in the flickering light, their faces betraying their fear. The concept of '*later*' seemed such a long way off when they still had the Morrow pact to destroy.

Bicker ran his fingers across the walls, feeling for his chisel marks.

'The Swarm's harbour is down there,' he announced,

pointing towards another snickleway, 'where they keep their sailing boats.'

'Who uses them?' asked Tallitha.

'The Thane and Lord Edweard, and I've see Caedryl and the Morrow twins go down there too,' the Shrove answered.

'How do you know this?' asked Quillam.

For an old Shrove who had spent his time in the wine cellars, he knew a lot more than was good for him.

Bicker tapped the side of his nose. 'I used to watch their comings and goings from behind my dusty barrels, but I said nowt. *Watch and say nowt*, that's always been my motto.'

He traced along the rock face, searching for his chiselled signs.

'This way,' he said.

Black rock upon black rock, turn upon twisting turn, down inclines then up slippery slopes, puddled in black water, they followed Bicker through the cold underground tunnels. Tallitha crept onward holding onto Quillam, listening for any unwanted presence, peering down sinister snickleways into the jet-black bowels of Hellstone Tors.

'Nearly there,' said the Shrove, tracing his marks on the wall. He lifted his smouldering taper and peered upwards. 'Here we are,' he said, pointing towards the steps that twisted upwards into the darkness.

Nervously they climbed out of the pitch-black snickleways and squeezed between the rows of dusty wine racks, inside a gated enclosure that contained hundreds of bottles of ruby red wine.

'Back at the '94 vintage, my red beauties,' sighed Bicker, stroking the dusty bottles.

The gated enclosures lined the vault. Bicker fumbled in his pocket until he found the key and jangled it in the darkness.

'Shhh! Ruker urged hoarsely, grabbing Bicker's hand. 'Someone's coming!'

The Skinks dived behind the wine racks, grabbing the girls whilst Quillam pulled Tallitha and the Shrove down beside him.

'Who is it?' murmured Spooner.

'Keep very quiet,' answered Neeps gruffly.

In the distance, Tallitha heard the sound of scurrying feet, of something darting headlong across the cellar floor. Then there was a plaintive squeak of distress. She gripped Ruker's arm and waited.

From out of the darkness the outline of a cat slipped under the wine racks with a mouse hanging limply from her clenched jaws.

'*Wee-wee-wee*', squeaked the helpless creature as its body flopped between the cat's fangs.

Tallitha stifled a gasp. It was Sedentia's Wheen-Cat, mousing about in the wine cellars. Quillam put his finger to his lips and his ochre eyes flashed danger. Tallitha watched, transfixed, as the cat tormented the mouse, batting the injured animal backwards and forwards until she tired of the game and sank her fangs into the small brown body. *Crunch, crunch,* went the cat and the fat, juicy mouse was no more.

Slynose cleaned her paws, turning her head as her emerald-green eyes revolved with satisfaction then she slunk down into the pitch-black hole, off into the meandering snickleways.

'What on earth was that?' whispered Tallitha at last.

'You don't want to know,' answered Quillam hoarsely.

She tugged on his jacket and mouthed the words: '*Yes I do.*'

He mouthed back one word. '*Caedryl.*'

She stared at him and swallowed very hard. 'Caedryl,' she said softly.

'Did I hear that right?' asked Ruker.

Quillam nodded.

'Someone ought to go after the Swarm's evil daughter and see what she's up to,' added Neeps.

Quillam rose to his feet. 'I'll follow her.'

'No. We should stick together!' said Tallitha.

'You already know the way through the wall cavities. I'll meet you back in the main hidey-hole.'

Quillam touched Ruker on the shoulder. 'Watch out for them,' he said awkwardly, 'I won't be long – I want to check *her* out. See what the evil Caedryl is up to.'

With that Quillam slipped into the snickleways. Tallitha listened to his sound of his footsteps disappearing into the distance.

For a long time they stayed hidden behind the ruby reds. Whenever someone made a move Ruker shook her head – the Swarm's evil daughter could return at any moment and something made the Skink sit it out.

'Okay,' she said eventually, 'let's go.'

'Keys?' Tallitha asked, turning to the Shrove.

Bicker's face was ashen and his hands were shaking.

'I'll give you all my keys, every last one,' he murmured, shaking, 'but please, I beg you, let me go.'

Tallitha regarded the bedraggled Shrove, slavering pathetically, crouched by his precious ruby wines.

'We don't need him anymore, now that he's shown us the way. What do you think?' she asked turning to the Skinks. 'He's an old Shrove who will do us no harm, will you?' she asked Bicker.

'Never,' he bleated.

'Then tell us the layout of the wine cellars and we'll set you free, if that's what you want,' replied Neeps.

'Want! I've no choice but to leave this castle, if they catch me they'll kill me!'

'If you betray us to the Swarm, I swear I will hunt you down and kill you myself,' hissed Ruker.

The old Shrove snivelled. 'I swear,' he moaned pathetically, 'I just want to get out of here.'

So Bicker described the route through the wine vaults and up to the upper levels. He spoke of the wines they would see on their journey, the varieties of *red beauties* and the racks of fine champagnes, laid down in their dusty old bottles.

'Kiss my fine beauties farewell for me,' Bicker called out.

Then he vanished into the darkness of the snickleways.

'Good riddance to bad rubbish,' said Spooner.

'He gave me the creeps,' said Lince, and shivered.

'I wonder if we'll ever see the likes of him again?' asked Neeps, staring towards the winding snickleways.

Then he hitched his backpack over his shoulder and followed the others through the expanse of gloomy wine vaults and onwards into the sinister castle.

# Twenty-Six

The time was right to act. Quicksilver, Frintal Morrow's One True Mirror, had been cloudy all morning. It was a telltale sign that the mirror wanted to reveal something.

'Sourdunk! Bludroot! Darken my chamber!' the Thane shouted, beckoning to Queen Asphodel to come closer.

The Shroves scurried towards the arched windows and closed the heavy curtains.

'Your One True Mirror may tell us the whereabouts of the boy,' said Asphodel.

'The time of the Quickening Ceremony to initiate the thirteenth is almost upon us. Let us see what Quicksilver can tell us,' he replied.

Frintal Morrow slanted his cold black eyes at Quicksilver, peering into the heart of the looking glass.'

'Come, Quicksilver, what do you know?' he asked.

The glassy surface shuddered as a thousand beads of shimmering mercury coalesced and writhed to form a slithering, liquid surface inside the jewelled frame.

Frintal's eyes gleamed with cruel intent. 'Show me, my One True Mirror, where is Tyaas? Where is my grandchild?' he whispered, cajoling the capricious Quicksilver into divination.

A cloudy mass swirled across the surface.

'Is it working?' asked Asphodel, peering over her father's shoulder.

The seeking-power of the One True Mirror could only work inside Hellstone Tors, but even then it was a fickle device.

'Patience,' the Thane drawled, 'my One True Mirror needs time to perform her task. She is searching through the castle for the boy, seeing things we cannot see and peering into all the dark places.'

The Thane poked his face up to the glass and gesticulated towards his daughter to join him.

'Look!' The Thane announced as the misty light cleared.

Asphodel stared deep into the mirror as Tyaas's face appeared, then suddenly the image warped and shuddered as Tallitha's face came into view.

'My One True Mirror has found them both!' the Thane cried, leaping to his feet.

'Tallitha is back!' hissed Asphodel. 'But what is she up to? Where is she hiding? Can the One True Mirror show us?'

The Thane peered deeper. 'The image is shadowy,' he answered, 'but the girl is in Hellstone Tors and within our grasp.'

'And the boy?'

Frintal's eyes shone. 'He's wandering the marble corridor by the throne room.'

The Thane turned to the solitary figure hovering by the door and clicked his fingers. A boy emerged from the shadows and stepped towards the Thane.

'Look, here are your little friends,' the Thane uttered nastily, pointing into the looking glass.

Benedict shuffled towards the Thane and peered into the One True Mirror, catching a glimpse of Tallitha, hiding in a cramped shadowy space. It was a place he had seen once before, when he had spied on Quillam for his mother – Tallitha was hiding in one of Quillam's wall cavities!

The Thane watched Benedict with suspicion. 'Where is she?' he barked.

'I-I don't recognise it,' he replied meekly.

The Thane bellowed. 'Then you must find Tyaas and befriend the boy. Make him believe you have thought better of your treachery, that you are sorry and have turned against us.'

Benedict coloured; he hadn't counted on this! He had painstakingly avoided Tallitha and Tyaas, remaining in his apartments to avoid their contempt. An uncomfortable feeling welled up inside him. He had done terrible things! He had been his mother's accomplice! He had been the instrument by which the Wakenshaws had almost perished. He swallowed hard as the memory of the dreadful day at Snipes Edge came back to haunt him. He hated to dwell on the events by the hideous ravines, particularly the extent of his own duplicity.

'Mother, must I?' he asked beseechingly, turning to Queen Asphodel.

'Do as your Grandfather commands,' she replied, throwing him a stern look.

'B-But Tyaas will never believe me, after what I-I did,' he stammered, attempting to extricate himself from the Thane's plan.

Frintal's bony face darkened. Benedict was a weakling. The boy had demonstrated he had no stomach for the wickedness and guile of the Swarm.

'Then you must make him believe you!' the Thane hollered, snapping his eyes at his grandson. 'Find out whether the boy has seen Tallitha. Tyaas must know something about his errant sister!' he commanded. Lord Frintal clicked his fingers for Bludroot to attend to him. 'Make the necessary preparations. The Quickening time is almost upon us. The days pass quickly and tomorrow night we will swear the thirteenth into our hallowed order.' The Shrove cocked his head, hanging on the Thane's every word. 'Give the order for the Bone Room to be prepared for the ceremony.'

The High Shrove bowed and scuttled from Lord Frintal's presence.

'I will make a potion to bewitch Tyaas. It will loosen his tongue. He must tell us where that girl is hiding,' said Queen Asphodel.

'He won't talk to me,' Benedict mewled.

The Thane gripped his arm.

'Listen and do exactly what I say.' Benedict winced as the Thane squeezed tightly. 'You must stumble upon Tyaas by the throne room. Pretend to befriend him. Make amends for your wrong doings, take him to your quarters and there you will slip him your mother's potion – it will weaken his resolve. He will have no memory of the drug thereafter.'

'B-But Grandfather, he'll never take anything from me,' gasped Benedict.

'Then make him! Dupe him! Trick him. Use the deceptions that your artful mother has taught you,' he thundered. 'Act like a true member of the Swarm and much could come your way,' he added enticingly.

Benedict stared weakly into the Thane's malevolent face. Was he offering him treasure? Was he offering him power?

'I will try my best,' he mumbled, casting a sidelong glance at his mother.

'Make me proud of you, Benedict,' said the Queen, stroking his hair. 'Come, let us make the potion.'

Asphodel instructed Sourdunk to fetch the ingredients.

'Lark's Spittle, Hensbane and Nettle Leaves,' she demanded. 'I will add some sweet cordial to mask the bitter taste,' she said to Sourdunk. 'Bring me blackcurrant and raspberry essences.'

She mashed the leaves, dropping them into the foaming liquid before adding a few drops of the sweet cordial, straining the potion and handing it to her son.

'This time, do a good job on Master Tyaas,' she insisted.

Her son was an enigma. He was fanciful, a bit of a dreamer,

and he had no real magical talent that she had discerned. Asphodel had tried to school him in the ways of the Swarm but Benedict was often in a world of his own. Perhaps this time, with the promise of rich rewards, he would prove his worth.

'Yes, Mother, I will do as you ask,' he replied and kissed her swiftly on the cheek.

*

Benedict headed for the throne room. His emotions were conflicted; his conscious pricked him whenever he remembered what his mother had made him do. Should he throw the vile potion out of the window? He stopped and balanced the bottle on the windowsill, pondering his next move. There were so many options – some that would allow him to make amends for his past deeds and others that would bring him the favour of his mother and grandfather. This was always his abiding dilemma – he could never decide whether to be good or whether to be bad.

'I suppose it can't do any harm,' he whispered.

Benedict persuaded himself that until he made up his mind, there was no harm in convincing Tyaas that he had changed. Part of him wanted to be a good person. He wanted Tallitha and Tyaas to like him again. His stay at Winderling Spires was the one time in his life where he felt he belonged. He had tried once before to make amends, when Tallitha had visited Stankles Brow, but she wouldn't trust him. He tried not to blame her for the rejection but the feeling rankled. Then he had saved Tallitha and Quillam when they were fleeing from the Murk Mowl, so he was a kind person afterall. What had his cousins ever done for him? Called him mean names and made fun of him! And yet, maybe he would stick to his word with Tyaas – he did so want to do the right thing, yet the rewards for being bad were tenfold.

He could be strong, couldn't he?

*

'We must leave you,' whispered Asenathe sadly.

She smiled at the boy before slipping back into the shadows.

'We'll be watching for Tallitha's return,' said Essie fondly, ruffling Tyaas's hair.

'What if it all goes wrong?' he asked.

'We must believe Tallitha can defeat them,' Essie replied stoically.

She squeezed his hand before joining her cousin in the shadows.

'Will he be alright?' asked Asenathe, watching the boy walking down the corridor.

'They won't hurt him, they need him now,' Esmerelda replied flatly. 'We'll stay here to watch and wait,' she added, pulling Asenathe further into the recess.

It didn't take long for the women to hear footsteps. A familiar figure stole past their hiding place, creeping after Tyaas, biding his time.

'But that's …' whispered Asenathe

'Shhhh!' whispered Esmerelda. 'Now what's he up to?'

Tyaas heard a step behind him and froze. He waited for the moment when the Groats would pounce and bind his hands – but nothing happened. He stood glued to the spot as the seconds ticked by. A nasty feeling hit him in the stomach and turned his legs to jelly. Something wasn't right. Slowly he turned to face whoever was lurking behind him. But the sight of the familiar figure took Tyaas by surprise.

It was Benedict. It was his cousin! Their betrayer!

Tyaas's face flushed and his mouth fell open as his emotions battled inside him – hate, fear, shock, betrayal and the awful heart wrenching tug of their old friendship.

'Come with me,' urged Benedict, shooting a fleeting look behind him and reaching out his hand. 'I want to help you,' he implored.

Tyaas stepped backwards. His eyes had the look of a wounded animal as the distrust bit hard. He swore and pushed Benedict's hand away. It was the betrayal and treachery that stung the worst – it tasted like flat metal in his mouth.

'Why should I trust you? You betrayed us!' cried Tyaas, his eyes stinging with tears.

He quickly rubbed his eyes but his face crumpled despite his best efforts. Seeing his cousin reminded him of when they had first met, back home in Winderling Spires. Benedict seized the moment, touched Tyaas lightly on the shoulder and whispered in his ear.

'They mean to turn you into one of *them*. To be their

thirteenth,' he persisted, drawing the boy closer.

Tyaas jumped as though he had been scalded.

'Then I'll be j-just like you, won't I? For you're one of them too!' he shouted, spit darting into Benedict's face. 'I hate you!'

'Please Tyaas, let me make amends, let me help you, I have been – m-misguided,' he added softly, searching for the right word.

'Misguided!' hissed Tyaas, 'that's the least of it!'

'Let me put things right between us, I beg you.'

For a moment, Tyaas didn't know what to do. He was supposed to go along with Esmerelda's plan, to be recaptured and to act as a stool pigeon until Tallitha returned to Hellstone Tors, but he didn't fancy lessons from the Mistress Flight – and now there was this strange turn of events! Perhaps, if he went with Benedict it would turn out better than Esmerelda had planned! Tyaas's eyes strayed fleetingly towards the recess where Essie and Asenathe were hiding. His head inclined towards them.

'The Thane will be watching our every move in his One True Mirror,' said Benedict awkwardly.

'Can he hear us?' asked Tyaas, aware of the danger.

'No, but he can see us,' he explained. 'If you don't come with me the Thane will set the Groats upon you.'

Wasn't that what Essie had planned?

'Maybe I prefer the company of Groats to being with *you*,' sneered Tyaas.

Benedict hung his head, his hair falling across his eyes.

'I-I'm truly sorry for what I did – b-back there in the caves,' he whined, 'but Mother made me do it.'

'Don't blame her, remember I have a mother too and she's just like yours.'

Benedict blushed as his eyes filled with tears.

'B-But the difference is, you have Tallitha,' he whined, the tears welling up and rolling down his cheeks. 'You don't know what it's been like, growing up alone under the shadow of the Swarm.' He swallowed hard and wiped his cheeks. 'P-Please let me help you, to try and make up for what I did.'

For a moment Tyaas almost felt sorry for him.

'So what can you do to help me?' he asked guardedly. 'As far as the Swarm are concerned, my fate is sealed. I don't see how *you* can change that.'

Benedict stooped conspiratorially. 'That's where you're wrong. Tallitha is here, in the castle,' he whispered, luring him in.

'What?' said Tyaas. 'Where is she?'

'I-I don't know exactly but I have a good idea. I saw her face this morning in the Thane's One True Mirror. I suspect she's hiding inside the walls.'

'Why should I believe you?' Tyaas frowned.

'Why would I lie?' Benedict pleaded. 'I promise, I only want to help, I-I swear!'

'Does the Thane know? Did you betray us again?'

Benedict shook his head. 'No, Tyaas,' he answered, looking him straight in the eyes.

Tyaas wasn't convinced but perhaps there was a way of

using Benedict to find Tallitha. His cousin knew about Quillam's warren of shafts and rat-runs. But Benedict was a strange one, and not to be trusted.

Tyaas had learned many lessons since leaving Winderling Spires; that some things were not what they seemed to be. For some reason Benedict wanted something from him. Maybe it was another trick or perhaps he was genuinely trying to change his ways – in any event, Tyaas was determined to get to the bottom of it.

'If you mean it, and truly want to make up for what you did, then you must help me find Tallitha.'

Benedict moved closer. 'Then smile at me, a weak smile will do, to show the Thane that I have won you over, to put him off the scent,' he said a little gruffly.

Tyaas forced his mouth into a thin smile.

'And another thing, I want to know everything about the Neopholytite's tower – and about the secret of the Darkling Stairs. You must promise me or I won't come,' Tyaas growled.

'I promise.' Benedict answered, touching Tyaas's arm briefly. 'My apartment is this way,' he said, gesticulating back the way he had just come.

As they walked down the corridor, Tyaas following on behind, he inclined his head towards the recess where the women were hiding, locking eyes with Esmerelda.

The women pinned their bodies against the wall. As Tyaas passed by he mouthed the word, '*Tallitha!*' and pointed excitedly towards the walls.

Essie gripped her cousin's hand. Tallitha was somewhere in the castle!

'What shall we do?' asked Asenathe desperately.

Essie was certain Benedict was up to his old tricks once again.

'We have to trust Tyaas. Let's hope he knows what he's doing,' Essie replied. 'In any event, whether it's the Groats or Master Benedict, the Swarm have him in their clutches now.'

She began climbing up into the darkness. 'Come Attie, we must make contact with Tallitha, to find out what she has unearthed about the pact.'

*

Tyaas followed Benedict past the black marble snakes that lined the grand stairway and up into the palace he shared with Queen Asphodel. As the oak door creaked open, a cacophony of screeching met his ears.

'My mother's pets,' Benedict explained, 'she has a menagerie of birds and exotic animals.'

He pointed to the caged wildcats that pounded backwards and forwards against the bars of their prison and the vicious birds of prey caw-cawing on their pedestals. 'My rooms are tucked away at the top of this tower,' he added, showing Tyaas the way.

Benedict led him out onto the battlements, up an external windswept staircase to a gated platform. He took a key from his pocket and opened the door into a large untidy study. It was filled with books, manuscripts and maps. Benedict gestured towards a lumpy sofa and Tyaas took a seat while his cousin unpacked his bag, carefully placing the potion bottles on the shelf before him.

'Will the Thane be able to see us here?' asked Tyaas.

'Not in my mother's palace,' he replied. 'The Queen has laid her own spells to protect us from prying eyes, even her own father's.'

Tyaas surveyed Benedict's rooms. There were books on chemistry and mathematics and dictionaries of ancient languages.

'What do you do all alone up here?'

'Study mostly and try to keep out of Mother's way. I avoid the Swarm whenever I can,' he said to curry favour with Tyaas. 'It wasn't my choice to be born into this family, so most days I stay alone up here with my books.'

Benedict cleared away a pile of papers and sat down on the armchair opposite his cousin.

'What is it?' asked Tyaas.

'It's just that we haven't much time until – '

'Until what?'

'You're to be sworn tomorrow night.'

'WHAT?' he cried, 'but it's too soon – Tallitha hasn't …' his voice trailed away.

'Tallitha hasn't what?' asked Benedict, edging closer.

'Nothing – just forget it,' he replied sullenly.

Tomorrow night, he would be sworn into the brood of

vipers. He had to do something!

'You promised to help me find Tallitha,' said Tyaas.

Benedict shuffled awkwardly. 'We must wait until it's dark,' he replied.

'What about the Neopholytite's tower? Is there anywhere to hide in there?'

'Y-Yes, perhaps there is,' he answered, hesitating. 'But how do you intend to get past the Night Slopers?'

'Why don't *you* tell *me*?' Tyaas said disarmingly.

Benedict thought carefully about his answer.

'There's a lever at the top of the Darkling Stairs. Pull it once and the Night Slopers remain trapped beneath the stair-treads,' he replied.

'And if you pull it twice?' asked Tyaas.

'That will set them free. B-But you don't want to do that – they're extremely nasty.'

But that's exactly what Tyaas planned to do.

'What about the hiding place?'

'There's a hiding place tucked away above the fireplace.'

'How did you find it?' asked Tyaas suspiciously.

'I-I used to hide up there when I was small, the witch always frightened me.'

Tyaas realised that the hideout must be close to where Quillam had taken them. Tallitha could hide there until the time was right.

Benedict pushed his hair out of his eyes, stood up and reached for a bottle of cordial.

'Fancy a drink?' he asked, pointing to the bottles. 'I have blackcurrant or raspberry, which one would you prefer?'

'Blackcurrant,' answered Tyaas.

Tyaas drank it quickly. At first the juice tasted wonderfully sweet and then a metallic taste clung to the roof of his mouth, as if … then the room began to spin.

'I-I feel weird,' he moaned, clutching the edge of the sofa and trying to pull himself up.

But he couldn't.

'Lie down and rest,' urged his cousin, sitting beside him. 'It's been an exhausting day,' he said, manoeuvring a cushion under Tyaas's head.

In the confusion, Tyaas agreed. He would just close his eyes for a few minutes …

Then Benedict's face loomed. He was asking him questions, probing him about Tallitha's plans and about Quillam and, try as he might, Tyaas couldn't resist answering – his tongue was loose and his head felt fuzzy.

# Twenty-Seven

**M**arlin was crotchety through lack of sleep. The cat-girl was plaguing him with her errant, unpredictable ways. Caedryl had still not returned from her nightly prowl and the Shrove was exhausted from keeping watch, waiting for her in the hidey-hole outside her apartments. Now, to make matters worse, Grintley had joined him and was getting on his nerves.

'Why not follow her? Go further into the snickleways,' he said artfully, needling away at Marlin. 'You said that's where you left her. Seems like she might need more spyin' to see what she's up to.'

Marlin flashed Grintley a vicious look. 'What's it to you?' he snarled.

'Now, now, you're tired, old friend. I'm just lookin' after my own kind. You can't leave her be, you have to find her weak spot,' he grizzled. 'Besides,' he said slyly, tapping the side of his nose, 'I've heard it said that the crypt is so full of their precious bloodstones that no one would miss a few. Yours for the takin' Marlin – if, that is, you decide to follow her again.'

'But it's cold down there and I'm so tired,' Marlin bleated, 'and besides, I can't get into the lower vaults, they're locked.'

Grintley chuckled. 'But that's where you're wrong,' he said, dangling a large key in front of the Shrove's nose.

Marlin leapt to his feet and grabbed the key.

'Where did you get this?' he asked, his eyes bulging with delight.

'The High Shrove's storeroom,' added Grintley with relish. 'It's such a muddle up there, he can't keep track.'

Marlin's beady eyes were riveted on the key. Grintley sidled up to him, whispered in his ear, dripping temptation into Marlin's shrovish brain.

'Why don't you go after the demon-girl and I'll keep watch for you 'ere. If she comes back I'll take over and spy on her for you,' he grizzled.

Marlin sighed at the thought of the precious stones, just there for the taking. He could bear another foray into that cold, dark place if there were rich pickings to be had.

Grintley cocked his head on one side.

'And while you're about it, you might get old Grintley a pretty whennymeg or two for all his trouble,' said the wily Shrove, eyeing Marlin. 'Anyway, you know that two Shroves are better than one when it comes to this sort o' thing,' he chuckled.

Marlin's greedy nature got the better of him. He skedaddled out of the tower, down the myriad of twisting corridors and through the kitchens, until he found himself edging down the cellar steps and back into the warren of uninviting snickleways, breathless and overexcited.

*

Slynose pranced through the snickleways, her eyes penetrating the darkness, sniffing the air and following the scents and trails leading her as far away from the sea tunnel as possible. She hated the salty smell of the ocean and the lash and splash of the roaring sea!

*Nasty wet place,* she thought and her fur bristled. *Sniff, sniff, old Shroves,* she mewed, their pungent aroma serving to mask other lingering scents in the tunnels.

The Wheen-Cat shivered, remembering the time when her father had taken her on board his boat, sailing away for many weeks to visit a remote island. She had screamed at him and made a terrible fuss – she had an abiding fear of water, even as a child. She hated it touching her in her cattish form. Dry land was her sanctuary.

The underground tunnels were a little damp, with numerous puddles and wet patches. Caedryl minced along, leaping over the water, shaking her legs in case of droplets. She hated her tufted paws getting wet. Any hint of dampness made changing back into her girl-self painful and nigh on impossible; her taut muscles jarring against the tremendous force of stretching and sliding that the transformation required.

Slynose prowled through the meandering darkness, smelling the stale air. *Pad, pad, pad, sniff, sniff, sniff,* she went, exploring the ancient pathways. Apart from the muddy puddles, the snickleways seemed to have been made just for her, with their abundance of mouse holes, full of tasty treats. But Slynose knew she must not tarry and be tempted by a mouse or even a juicy fat rat. She was on a deadly mission to discover the Swarm's secret treasure trove, mounds and mounds of beautiful bloodstones just there for the taking, so on and on she padded.

Just behind her, a moment out of sight, Quillam edged along in the darkness, slinking into recesses in the tunnel wall as the cat bounded along, oblivious to her stalker. Quillam's ochre-coloured eyes, now accustomed to the darkness, tracked the cat's every leap and turn.

Suddenly behind Quillam, the sound of footsteps met his ears.

'Shrove,' he whispered as the stench of Marlin's fetid stench greeted his nostrils.

The youth darted down the next snickleway, hiding round the corner as Marlin hobbled past him, muttering to himself about "annoying cat-girls" and "buried treasure".

*So that's where Caedryl is headed,* thought Quillam, *to unearth the Swarm's jewels.*

In the peculiar turn of events, the cunning Shrove was following his evil mistress, and Quillam was following them both. When he was certain the Shrove was out of earshot, Quillam slunk from his hiding place and tiptoed after Marlin.

Off in the distance, the Wheen-Cat sped down the next

snickleway, going deeper into the heart of the labyrinthine underbelly of the Tors, with Marlin and Quillam on her tail. She darted round corners, leapt over fallen rocks and padded through the maze of intricate tunnels, never putting a paw out of place.

Then Slynose hesitated, her whiskers twitching as a strange new smell wafted towards her. Her eyes swirled in the darkness as she stepped nervously towards the uninviting hole.

Behind her, Marlin crouched in the darkness, waiting for the cat-girl to continue.

*A smell so redolent of witchcraft,* the Wheen-Cat thought, as she sniffed at entranceway, and tried to recognise the aroma.

Tentatively she reached out her paw. Below, the stairwell narrowed and the enticing smell of witches and spells wafted towards her. Slynose slipped down into the deepening darkness with the others on her tail, stalking her, prowling just a few steps behind.

Suddenly the Wheen-Cat stiffened. Her nose twitched as she recognised the mysterious aroma. It smelled of the Bone Room, of the whorl-pit and of the Neopholytite's potions – of sulphur and ash, Banewood Syrup, Wricken Bark and Shrockle Plants. The Neopholytite had cast a spell to protect the Bloodstone Crypt.

At the foot of the steps, a gated enclosure circled the deep opening to the Crypt. The ironwork had been forged into raven's wings, with swooping bats and a macabre crop of ravens' heads mounted at the head of the gate.

*Treasure!* She thought, inching forwards.

The Wheen-Cat was so excited at having found the Bloodstone Crypt that she almost stepped into a muddy puddle.

*Hissss, meeeow!* she spat, leaping in the air.

From the snickleway Marlin watched as the cat spun around in circles. Now he knew her secret. The cat-girl hated water!

Slynose growled and pitter-pattered towards the black gate. Down below, nestled in mounds of deep green piles, thousands upon thousands of precious bloodstones filled every nook and cranny of the enclosure. Slynose purred with pleasure and rubbed her back against the gate. Then she spat, arched her spine and her heckles went up. A powerful spell barred her entrance.

The slippery-bodied cat stretched like a strand of liquorice, sprang into the air, shuddered and reappeared as the darkly clad Caedryl smoothed down her dress and peered into the crypt. Then she spoke the words of a spell – magic long remembered from her school days under the guidance of Sedentia Flight. She began to chant:

'*Tellan sam le nerva manvellus ...*
*Tellan sam le nerva manvellus ...*
*Tenteth, shallam et lucier malam na cora,*'

The gate swung open. The spell was lifted.

Caedryl made a sound deep within her throat, a contented purring as she swished and writhed, stepping down into the treasure trove to plunder her longed for bloodstones. She plunged her greedy fingers into the stones and began to fill her pockets with treasure.

'The little witch,' muttered Marlin, rubbing his hands with glee for now he knew the whereabouts of the Swarm's treasure.

Quillam peered from his hiding place as Marlin inched out of the shadows. The sneaky Shrove was following his mistress, spying on Caedryl. Something wasn't right.

Over and over in Quillam's mind one thought kept reoccurring – things were changing, the balance of power in the Tors was shifting. They were turning on one another.

*The power of the Swarm was waning.*

Quillam hid from the Shrove as Marlin spied on Caedryl, then he slipped into the snickleway and hurried back through the cellars to join Tallitha and the others.

\*

Marlin leaned hungrily over the edge of the crypt as Caedryl filled her pockets, with bloodstones.

'Got ya,' he muttered, 'you're nowt but a thieving wench,' he grizzled.

Now he had her, caught in the act of stealing. Lord Edweard would be keen to hear about this. He may even reward old Marlin for his trouble.

After Caedryl had departed, Marlin checked that the spell had been lifted and slipped down amongst the treasure.

'Just a little keepsake for my trouble and one for Grintley to keep him quiet,' he muttered, running his fingers through the precious stones.

The Shrove chuckled with happiness. He had a pocketful of the best whennymegs he had ever "borrowed" and he had discovered Caedryl's weakness in the process.

The cattish-one was not only a thief – but she hated water!

Marlin scurried back through the snickleways. There was more to be gained from his discovery and he intended to make the most of it!

# Twenty-Eight

'**W**atch your step,' warned Neeps, pointing towards the stairwell that fell away into the shadows.

He grabbed Lince's arm, guiding her along the darkened hallway, trying to keep out of sight. Tallitha crept behind them, darting into recesses and hiding behind curtains, followed by Spooner and Ruker. But as Tallitha gazed upwards, her heart pounded and her stomach churned as the sight of the dismal castle bore down upon her.

'It's late,' she murmured, her eyes darting upwards. 'Those dogs will be out on the rampage soon.'

'We must find somewhere to hide,' replied Neeps, staring wide-eyed at the cavernous hallways.

Onwards they crept, a group of frightened figures dwarfed by the enormous Tors, cowed by the evil that pervaded every crevice of the creepy castle.

'Psst! Over here,' a voice whispered hoarsely out of the shadows.

It was Quillam. He had been following their progress using his hidden rat-runs. One by one they slipped into the recess and disappeared into the infrastructure of the castle. Pitch-blackness, dust and the smell of vermin greeted their nostrils. Quillam lit a taper and directed them through the steely darkness. They climbed ropes, hauled themselves over beams, squirrelled under floorboards, their mouths full of grit and their hands scratched and bloody, until they arrived at his secret hidey-hole.

But Quillam had no time to waste. He immediately began refilling his backpack.

'I'm off to steal some food and to do a little business of my own,' he said. 'Spooner, Neeps – you can keep me company, if you like?'

The girl leapt at the thought of accompanying Quillam into the sinister castle.

'Sure,' said the Skink, 'count me in!'

Tallitha looked quizzical. 'Have you forgotten what we came here to do?' she asked gravely. She observed the tension in his face. 'What's so important that it can't wait?' she asked warily.

'There's an old score I have to settle,' Quillam answered bitterly.

'Who with?' asked Spooner, looking excitedly at the youth.

'Marlin,' he replied coldly, 'he's out there now, sneaking about after Caedryl.'

Quillam was dead set on revenge.

'While you're away I'm going to try and make contact with Essie.'

'Sounds like a plan. I'll be back at dawn,' replied Quillam.

He felt for his dagger and vanished into the wall cavities with Spooner and Neeps at his side.

It was payback time. Quillam had been planning his next move ever since he had heard about Marlin's vicious attacks on Cissie.

The hateful Shrove would rue the day he had ever hurt his mother.

*

In the dusty darkness of the hidey-hole, Tallitha lit a circle of tall white candles. As they guttered in the draught, she slipped inside the circle taking Ruker's hand.

'Hold my pendant and sway it like a pendulum,' she said passing the necklace to Ruker. 'Then say these words – *canya fe-canya fe*. Repeat them again and again, followed by:

*Snenathe ne certhe merl can an le ner …*
*Cerna la bernatha ne tor na lam, berche berche ne cer …*
*Snenathe ne certhe merl can an le ner.*

'Hold on, how will I remember that?' asked Ruker hesitantly.

But Tallitha ignored her pleas and kept repeating the words until Ruker was word perfect.

'What shall I do?' asked Lince, eager to help.

'When my eyes become heavy, repeat these words – *find Essie, find Esmerelda* – marking time with the rhythm of the pendant.'

Ruker knelt before Tallitha, repeating the Ennish words as she dangled the pendant. In the stillness of the hidey-hole Tallitha breathed deeply and focussed on the pendant, moving *backwards and forwards, backwards and forwards*, as the candlelight danced against the gemstones, spinning colours across the darkened space.

Tallitha recalled the time when Essie had hypnotised her in the Great Room, encircling her body, wrapping the flimsy scarves about her face, Esmerelda's bewitching eyes taking her far, far away. Soon, Tallitha was falling under the old spell, remembering the heady smell, lulling her senses.

'*Find Essie, Find Esmerelda*,' urged Lince and Ruker, chanting together.

Before Tallitha slipped into her shadow-flight, Ruker placed the bloodstone pendant around her neck. The gem felt warm to the touch, as Kastra had told her it would – the connection with the Grand Witch was growing stronger. Then Tallitha felt her stomach lurch and her body began to slide – gliding through the middle plane and *whoosh!* – the spell had worked its magic.

Tallitha slipped into the infinite space that stretched before her. Her body whipped up the tunnel with the silver cord flashing behind her. She tumbled – *whoosh!* – out on the other side into the soft grey light in search of Essie. But the way of the shadow-flight was barred – another being was waiting for her in the middle plain – it was Ferileath, the silver-haired spirit.

'I have come to warn you. The Grand Witch Selvistra means to strike you dead! Take me with you to Esmerelda Patch,' she said.

Tallitha took Ferileath's hand and together they hurried towards their destination.

*

In the darkness of her chamber, Esmerelda felt a tremendous tug, as if the breath was being forced from her body. She sat bolt upright.

'Essie,' Tallitha called out.

Esmerelda touched Tallitha's cold fingers in the darkness and called softly to her.

'What is it?' asked Asenathe, hearing Essie's voice and rushing into her bedroom.

'She's here,' replied Esmerelda in a flat voice, 'take her hand in yours.'

In the gloomy half-light, Asenathe could see Tallitha's faint outline and behind her a silvery white face.

Asenathe jerked her hand away at the sight of Ferileath.

'Don't be frightened! She is the one who first warned me about Hellstone Tors,' explained Tallitha. 'She has come on behalf of the Grand Witch Kastra.'

Ferileath shuddered. 'I have come to warn you,' she whispered. 'Selvistra Loons means to take Hellstone Tors.'

'But how will she enter the castle?' cried Asenathe, 'the spells are too strong.'

'That I do not know. Selvistra intends to kill Tallitha once she has destroyed the pact. Then she will take the Tors and Wycham Elva for her own.'

'We have many adversaries,' said Esmerelda darkly.

'What can we do to stop them?'

'There will be a battle between the Grand Witches,' answered Ferileath, her light ebbing and fading. 'If Kastra succeeds in vanquishing Selvistra, she will return to Winderling Spires, to stake her claim on her old home.'

Esmerelda nodded at the silver-haired spirit. "Twas ever thus,' she replied enigmatically.

Tallitha gasped. 'You knew she had lived there?'

'Kastra belongs with us in Winderling Spires,' replied Esmerelda.

Yet again, more secrets were being revealed about her strange family.

'What if Selvistra wins?' asked Asenathe.

But no one wanted to countenance that possibility.

'I must get inside the Neopholytite's tower and summon the Morrow child,' said Tallitha, 'but the witch's magic is so powerful.'

'She's not as powerful as she was,' replied Essie, 'your brother has been busy while you've been away.'

Esmerelda told Tallitha about the destruction of the witch bottle and the elements of the Neopholytite hidden in Tyaas's pocket.

'He climbed the Darkling Stairs without being caught,' added Asenathe.

'Where is he now?' asked Tallitha.

The women looked at one another.

'He's with Benedict,' Esmerelda replied.

'Benedict!' cried Tallitha. 'But he plotted to murder Cissie at Snipes Edge! He almost succeeded in luring the Wakenshaws to their deaths!'

'Then perhaps Tyaas is in more danger than we thought.'

Tallitha shuddered – the power of the shadow-flight was ebbing away.

'Meet us in the northern tower at dawn. Quillam's hiding place is tucked inside the walls on the top floor. I must find Tyaas.'

With that, Tallitha vanished into the night with the silver-haired spirit by her side.

\*

Marlin was a slippery old rogue and had his suspicions that someone had been watching him as he followed Caedryl down to the Bloodstone Crypt. He had smelt a strange aroma, a nasty vengeful smell. It didn't belong to a Shrove and it didn't belong to the Swarm. He would have to watch his step and keep a low profile once he had carried out his plan.

Now he was ready to tell Lord Edweard all that he had discovered about the cat-girl, and maybe get a pretty whennymeg for his trouble.

Lord Edweard's palace was a gloomy affair. The walls were hung with dismal portraits of the Morrow family, and the rooms were littered with mournful statues and huge dark furniture. Marlin met Lord Edweard in his library.

'Why have you disturbed me at such a late hour?' Edweard growled.

'Beggin' your pardon my Lord but there is something that I have to tell you.'

Marlin scurried forward and whispered all that he had witnessed in the Bloodstone Crypt.

Edweard's piercing blue eyes fixed on the Shrove.

'Tell no one else,' he whispered into Marlin's ear.

'There's another matter' the Shrove said moving closer. 'The cat-girl cannot abide water, she hates it touching her fur,' he added.

Edweard's eyes glinted and a wicked smile sailed across his lips.

'Here, take this for your trouble and from now on, report everything you hear about Caedryl to me,' he growled.

Marlin nodded feverishly, his eyes darting over his shoulder in case they were being overheard.

'Yes, my Lord,' he mumbled, gloating with avarice.

He licked his lips and his eyes glowed with delight as Lord Edweard pressed six gold coins into his clammy hand. Marlin bowed before Lord Edweard then he scuttled away to hide in his most secret Shrove hole, high up in an abandoned turret. On his way he stopped at the castle bakery and snaffled enough tarts, pies and bread cakes to keep him supplied for many days. Whoever had been on his tail in the crypt had unnerved him. He had to lie low for a while.

'Going somewhere interesting?' asked Cannisp, eying the jittery Shrove with suspicion. 'Off on an adventure?' he asked, taking one of Marlin's apple tarts and shoving it into his mouth.

'Never you mind, dirt-stopper, be off with you!' Marlin snapped at the young Shrove's audacity.

'Goin' to your special place, eh?' asked Cannisp, nosily.

Marlin seized the Shrove and squeezed hard on his throat. His private bolthole was meant to be a secret.

'You been spyin' on me?' he hissed. 'I'll cut your gizzards out if you breathe a word about it,' Marlin's eyes darted this way and that.

'You're choking me,' Cannisp spluttered, jerking his head away, 'you can trust me, I'll say nowt.'

Marlin pushed the young Shrove to the ground, gathered up his wares and stepped nervously into the noisy thoroughfare, mingling with the Shroves and servants about their chores.

Cannisp straightened his clothes and watched Marlin scuttle out of the bakery. The old Shrove looked as though the Witch of Hellstone was on his tail. Cannisp was anxious to progress within the Shroveling ranks and Marlin could be a valuable ally – but there was something peculiar going on. After his chores, Cannisp decided to make it his business to find out.

Quillam was also on Marlin's tail.

'Where's he going?' asked Spooner, peering after Marlin as he skedaddled out of the kitchen.

They hurriedly squirrelled a bundle of pies and tarts into their backpacks for later.

'We'll follow him,' said Quillam. 'Keep close - Marlin thinks he's clever, but he's not as clever as me!'

Marlin's burrow was well hidden. The old Shrove trudged wearily up the lath stairs leading to a narrow bridge adjoining a turret on the northern edge of the Tors. Every once in a while he peered down the precarious stairwell to make sure no one was following him, sniffing the air and catching a whiff of something that he couldn't put his finger on.

'I'm imagining things,' he muttered, clambering upwards. 'That smell from the Bloodstone Crypt is still lingering in my nostrils.'

He took a tattered hanky from his pocket and blew his nose to get rid of the smell as his eyes strayed nervously into the gloom. The stairwell was quite empty.

But Quillam was a master of ducking and diving and he taught his companions well. They ducked into crevices, creeping stealthily behind the old weasel as he scurried up the precarious lath staircases.

At last, Marlin unlatched the turret door and stepped into the cool interior of his lair, clambering up another flight of steps. At the top he pushed open a small circular hatch as the inviting stench of shrovish clutter greeted him. He burrowed inside his cosy nook and closed the door tight behind him.

'Home and dry,' he muttered, unpacking his fruit pies and placing them on a shelf at the back of his hole.

He had already laid down several flagons of berry juice, which he duly sampled, smacking his lips and slavering with pleasure.

'Now for a well-earned snooze,' he muttered, nestling down under the blankets and wrapping them snugly around his body.

In no time he was fast asleep, dreaming of pretty whennymegs, piles of golden coins and mounds of the bloodstone treasure.

Unbeknown to Marlin, on the other side of the circular door, Quillam, Spooner and Neeps were biding their time, waiting for the moment to strike.

'Wait until he's fast asleep,' whispered Quillam, taking a spiked tool from his backpack.

'What's that for?' asked Spooner.

Quillam and Neeps exchanged a look.

'To make sure he never comes out,' replied Quillam.

There was a sharp intake of breath as Spooner realised Quillam's intention. This Shrove hole was to be Marlin's final resting place.

'Are you going to trap him?' She muttered gravely. 'B-But he'll die in there.'

Quillam licked his lips as he silently screwed the circular door in several places, making sure it was securely fastened.
'And it will be a long, slow death. The kind of lonely, gut-wrenching end that miserable creature deserves.'

# Twenty- Nine

The night sky over Hellstone Tors was threaded with a blood-red-light as Esmerelda and Asenathe tiptoed gingerly through the castle on their way to find Quillam's hidey-hole.

As the cousins entered the dark cavity, they could feel the tension all around them.

'Essie!' Tallitha cried, falling on her cousin.

'You look tired,' said Essie, remarking on Tallitha's grey pallor.

'Where's Quillam got to?' Tallitha asked, throwing them a nervous glance. 'He should be back by now.'

Tallitha was full of foreboding. As if by some magical trick her hand had begun to itch again. She scratched it until it became red and sore.

'It's being near the Morrow Swarm again,' she said apprehensively.

'What's wrong?' Esmerelda asked.

Tallitha twisted her hair in and out of her fingers. Esmerelda touched her tentatively on the shoulder. The girl was a bundle of nervous energy.

'I-I feel sick with fear,' Tallitha replied.

'You must prepare yourself,' Essie said gravely.

'This is it Tallitha,' added Asenathe gently. 'Soon you must face them all.'

In the candlelight they held each other's nervous glances, locked in their fateful conspiracy against the Swarm. Tallitha knew this was the day they had all been working towards – and the day they had all been dreading.

'I keep turning it over in my mind,' she replied desperately, staring at Esmerelda. 'The thought of entering that Bone Room, and seeing the Swarm – ' she faltered. 'Essie, what if something goes wrong? What if I can't summon Arabella and they kill us all?' she cried.

'You can't fail – you've come too far. We all have.'

'But I'm afraid,' she murmured.

Esmerelda took Tallitha in her arms. When she released Tallitha there were tears in her eyes.

'You can do anything you set your mind to.'

'B-But' said Tallitha.

'All this was meant to be, from that day in Winderling Spires when you had the first inkling that all was not as you thought it was. You were determined to unearth the secret about Asenathe and that secret led you here – just where you ought to be to destroy the Morrow pact.'

Tallitha smiled, remembering that headstrong girl of Winderling Spires, desperate to unearth the secret.

'Last minute nerves,' she said, clutching Essie's hand. 'Will you come with me?'

Esmerelda shook her head. There was something she had promised to do.

'I will join you later. In any case, there will be too many of us and our best form of attack against the Swarm is to split up and surprise them. Besides, when the time is right I promised to free Cremola and Leticia from the Bleak Rooms,' said Esmerelda. 'The girls should come with me,' she said, beckoning to Lince.

Lince and Spooner would be a liability in the Bone Room. They had never set foot in such a gruesome place. It would be better for all concerned if they arrived much later when it was all over.

'Sounds like a plan. Once our kid gets back,' Lince replied.

'Attie, whatever transpires today, the Swarm will suspect something if you're not with them,' cautioned Esmerelda.

'I will be there when you need me. I have my own scores to settle,' she replied mysteriously.

Ruker put her finger to her lips. 'Shhh, be quiet,' she whispered, leaping to her feet and listening at the door, 'I can hear someone climbing up the walls.'

The familiar scraping sound of boots against plaster met their ears. Then the door flung open and Quillam appeared followed by Spooner and Neeps.

'Sis, you've been ages!' cried Lince, greeting her sister.

Spooner gave her sister a hug, handing out the meat pies and fruit tarts they had stolen from the bakery.

Tallitha pounced on the youth. 'What happened? Why did you take so long? I was worried!'

'I did what I set out to do,' Quillam replied.

'Did you find Marlin?'

'Yes, I found him,' he answered firmly.

'I'm famished,' cried Lince, falling on the heap of crushed pies and tarts that had tumbled out of Spooner's backpack.

She handed a pie to Tallitha but she shook her head.

'I-I couldn't eat a thing,' she whispered nervously.

All eyes were on Tallitha. Her face was drawn and tired.

'Come on, tell us what happened?' mumbled Lince, her mouth full of pastry.

Spooner sat on her hunkers and surveyed the motley gathering. True to form she savoured the moment for maximum effect.

'We did what we had to do,' she said with a wicked glint in her eye. 'That old rogue Marlin,' she continued, fixing her eyes on Quillam, 'well, you won't be seeing him again!'

There was a sudden intake of breath, then a moment of quiet in the hidey-hole as they looked from one to the other.

'Is he dead?' asked Lince.

Spooner and Quillam exchanged knowing glances.

It seemed that Marlin was no more. Tallitha didn't care – she hated the Shrove for what he had done to her family.

'Whatever you did, he deserved it!' Tallitha replied, hotly.

'He spied on us for years, he betrayed us to the Swarm, and he hurt poor Cissie!'

Quillam blushed at the mention of his mother.

'Any news of Tyaas?' he asked quickly, changing the subject.

'Benedict has him,' Tallitha added gravely.

'They headed in the direction of Asphodel's palace,' added Attie.

'I must find him, to prepare him for what's to come,' said Tallitha anxiously, looking from one to the other.

'Right! Then that's where we're going next – to find Benedict. He's another evil trickster who deserves what's coming to him,' said Quillam hotly. He wolfed down a couple of pies and turned to the Skinks. 'Once we're in the Bone Room we'll need you to provide back-up.'

'Then show me the way to the Darkling Stairs,' said Ruker, grabbing her backpack, 'Neeps, you wait here. I'll be back in a jiffy.'

Now, the excitement in the hidey-hole was palpable.

*

In the feathery light of the new dawn, Tallitha, Ruker and Quillam clambered through the walls, squirrelling away under floorboards guided by Quillam's expert direction and eventually reaching the top floor of Asphodel's palace. Once they had squeezed through an interconnecting cavity they found their way to Benedict's apartment. It was still bathed in sleepy shadows and cocooned behind heavy velvet curtains as they stepped out from the inky darkness.

Tyaas was fast asleep, curled into a ball on a day bed in Benedict's study.

'Wake up, Tyaas,' Tallitha whispered.

She clamped her hand over his mouth to stop him making a noise. He suddenly woke and stared frantically into his sister's eyes. Tallitha held her brother tightly.

'It's me. I'm really here,' she said soothingly.

Tyaas sat up and rubbed his head. It throbbed and he felt sick.

'Tallitha, I have so much to tell you,' he mumbled.

He began gabbling incoherently.

'Slow down, you're not making sense.'

'I-I found all this nasty stuff in one of the witch bottles,' he muttered excitedly, half-dazed. He searched his addled brain, trying to recall the last few hours – but they were a blur. Then he remembered meeting Benedict on the corridor, but he couldn't fathom out what had happened next apart from feeling sleepy. 'They're going to do it today!' he muttered.

'What?'

'The Quickening Ceremony - when they take me into the Swarm!'

Tallitha bit her lip. It was happening.

'There's a secret hideout above the witch's fireplace. Benedict told me all about it,' Tyaas added, 'and you can set the Night Slopers free by pressing the lever at the top of the stairs – but you have to pull it twice.' He ran on, desperate to tell Tallitha everything he could remember.

'We're not taking any chances with him,' she said sharply, pointing towards Benedict's bedroom.

Through the half-open door Tyaas saw Ruker binding Benedict's hands while Quillam held a dagger to his throat.

'It's okay, Ruker and Quillam have him now,' she said, walking towards the door and staring at Benedict. 'Tyaas told me about the fireplace,' she announced.

Then Tallitha stopped dead still. The sound of hurried footsteps and a shrill voice filled the corridor. 'It's Mother!' she called to the others, her eyes darting about the study for sanctuary.

'Hide, Tallitha! Let them take me! They can't capture you or there will be no hope! I'll be the decoy,' urged Tyaas, leaping out of bed and pushing his sister towards Benedict's bedroom.

'B-But will you be alright?' she asked, her eyes shining with tears, 'I've only just found you again.'

'I'm great. Fit as a flea,' he said stoically, 'raring to go, Sis. Now hurry!'

He closed the door and leapt back into bed just as Snowdroppe swirled into the study followed by her grisly Groat entourage. She loomed with a bright light behind her, like a halo of fire, her long fingers drumming on her hips.

'There you are, Tyaas, I hope Benedict has been looking after you,' she said mockingly, striding towards him. 'Now quickly, get up and follow me,' she called, clicking her fingers at the Groat guards. 'Take him to the Neopholytite's tower,' she added, kissing her son briefly on the forehead and stroking his head. For a moment, Tyaas thought that their mother looked happy. 'This is your opportunity to shine! Make me proud of you, Tyaas. Your time has come – the Quickening Ceremony is upon us,' she added menacingly and waltzed from the chamber like an exalted Queen on the day of her coronation.

As Snowdroppe's footsteps retreated, Quillam took his hand from Benedict's mouth.

'Right, you evil monster,' he said, spit flying into Benedict's face. 'You tried to kill the Wakenshaws! You led them like lambs to the slaughter up to Snipes Edge for the Black Hounds to feast on.'

He twisted Benedict's collar tighter and tighter until his eyes bulged.

'P-Please!' Benedict spluttered, gasping for air.

Quillam sliced his eyes at the miserable boy.

'You're choking him,' hissed Ruker, dragging his hand away. 'Quillam! Let him go!'

Quillam loosened his grip and pushed Benedict to the floor. Ruker turned the boy over with her foot and tightly knotted Benedict's wrist bindings. Quillam jabbed the point of his dagger into Benedict's throat. His skin bulged with the pressure of the blade.

'Please, I beg you – you're hurting me!' he bleated. 'Mother forced me to do it! Tell him Tallitha, please, I'm sorry! I-I want to help you, remember I saved you when the Murks were after you!' he snivelled, 'L-Let me prove to you that I'm not as rotten as you think!'

Tallitha yanked Quillam's hand away but not before the point of his dagger nicked Benedict's throat. Blood trickled down his neck and the boy cried out in pain.

'We need him alive,' she said, forcing her way between them. 'Quillam, stop it, he's bleeding!'

Tallitha had never seen Quillam so wired up. His whole body was taut like a trap ready to snap.

'You're going to help us break that pact and tell us everything we need to know!' Quillam spat. 'And if you make one false move, I'll kill you,' he said coldly.

'Don't hurt me,' Benedict moaned, cowering before them.

'You can start by showing us the hideout above the witch's fireplace,' said Tallitha.

'What about the Darkling Stairs?' asked Benedict, fear tearing across his face. 'If those hideous Night Slopers catch us, they'll kill us,' he whimpered.

'We're not going that way,' replied Quillam gruffly.

Benedict looked confused. 'What do you mean?'

'We're going down the chimney,' added Quillam.

Benedict stared at Tallitha. She thought the boy might vomit.

'B-But I hate dark, cramped spaces, they terrify me,' he whined.

'Tough, that's the only way,' growled Quillam. 'Now move!'

He held his dagger against Benedict's throat and pushed the terrified boy into the dark infrastructure of the castle.

*

It took them an age to cajole Benedict through the wall cavities. He whined about the dizzying height yawning way beneath him until Quillam could stand it no longer and stuffed a gag into his mouth.

'The Darkling Stairs are over there,' Quillam whispered to Ruker peering across the disused shaft. 'I'll check it's all clear before we start climbing.'

Ruker scrambled through a gap in the floorboards. It had been agreed she would return for Neeps once she had seen the layout of the tower and the witch's staircase.

'Here,' Quillam said, brandishing a dagger and handing it to Tallitha. 'Use it if he causes any trouble.'

With that, Quillam followed the Skink.

When they had gone Tallitha removed Benedict's gag and held the knife to his face.

'Don't think I won't use it,' she hissed. 'Now I want the truth.' Her eyes shone venomously.

'Y-Yes, of course,' he stuttered, blinking nervously at her.

'Why did you betray us?' she asked, her voice cracking with emotion.

Benedict's eyes were moist. He was trying his old tricks.

'Mother made me do it,' he simpered, 'but I didn't want to. I-I grew to like both of you.'

She pushed her face right into his. 'I don't believe you,' she snarled her heart beating wildly. 'What did you want with my brother?'

'Only to help h-him! We were going to search Hellstone for you but then Tyaas fell asleep and you turned up.'

'Liar!'

'It's the truth! H-How can I make you believe me?' he whimpered.

Tallitha stared deep into his terrified eyes. She twisted his collar tighter until the blood throbbed in his neck.

'Do more than we demand of you, tell us more than we ask of you and help us destroy the Morrow pact. Then, and only if you do all that, I may believe that you've changed – and another thing, stop complaining – you're getting on my nerves.'

'A-Alright Tallitha, I will prove myself worthy,' he answered meekly, giving her a sidelong glance.

The girl had unnerved him. She had become harder and much less easy to fool than he remembered.

Later, after Ruker had returned to the hidey-hole, they climbed the rickety staircase outside the Neopholytite's tower. Benedict was terrified of the sheer drop and the narrow treads.

'Your hands are free,' Quillam hissed, untying the bindings, 'now climb!'

'It's wobbly,' Benedict moaned.

'Put your fingers into the crevices and pull yourself up,' snapped Tallitha.

Benedict's head swam as he struggled to balance on the roughly hewn planks, raising his eyes towards the bat colony.

'I-If those bats swoop, I'll fall,' Benedict snivelled, clinging desperately to the wall. 'I can't go any further.'

Tallitha remembered the time he had made fun of her outside the Startling Caves. He had no sympathy for anyone else's plight – only his own.

'Shut up and MOVE!' Quillam hissed, sticking the dagger into Benedict's side, 'or I'll twist this blade until I see blood.'

Benedict nodded pathetically, his eyes watering with fear as he inched up the satircase.

'Give me your hand,' said Tallitha at the top as she guided the terrified boy onto the rooftops.

When the fresh air hit him full in the face Benedict couldn't believe the wondrous sight before him. The magnificent Tors spangled in copper, silver and gold. The castle's shimmering turrets and burnished rooftops glistened in the dawn light, a majestic forest of towers reaching all the way to the black rocks far below.

'Now follow Tallitha and do what she does,' snapped Quillam.

This time, Tallitha nimbly sped across the narrow bridge.

'I can't do it,' cried Benedict, gawping at the hideous abyss.

The roof of the Neopholytite's tower was bathed in a sulphurous fog that oozed down the walls.

'Best not look down, but if you do and you fall – so be it,' said Quillam, toying with him.

Benedict whined. It was like walking the plank!

Quillam pushed the tip of his dagger into Benedict's back and he stepped nervously onto the small bridge. His legs were shaking. There were no words of encouragement from Tallitha or Quillam – they only mocked his fear.

'Don't wobble. Oh, I wouldn't step there,' sneered Quillam.

'S-Stop it,' Benedict cried.

They hated him. At that moment, self-pity and anger welled upside him, gnawed at his guts and propelled him across the precipice to safety. Quillam swiftly followed and lifted the chimney pot from its housing. He pointed down the black sooty hole.

'Tallitha will go first and you can follow,' he said.

The soupy fog hung about the battlements and slurped down the sides of the tower as Tallitha clambered inside the chimney.

'Watch out Bumps,' she called out. 'It's dirty and dark down here.'

Benedict's face was ashen and his whole body trembled as the detestable nickname echoed in his head. He climbed over the edge of the chimney, gripped the blackened bricks and edged down after her. Quillam's amber eyes snapped at him in the darkness every time Benedict peered upwards, his whole presence pressing down on him – weighing on him, making him feel claustrophobic. Slippery black soot stuck to his fingers, smeared his face and lodged in his hair.

'Where now?' whispered Tallitha as Benedict joined her on the ledge.

'I haven't approached the secret place from this angle. J-Just let me get my bearings.'

Benedict lifted the flickering light and peered into the

soot-filled crevices.

'The fireplace is at the back of the tower – that means to the north and we were facing east from the roof.' He pushed his floppy hair from his forehead. His arm motioned to the left. 'It's somewhere over there,' he said pointing into the flat darkness.

As the light bounced across the brick walls they noticed the chimney base was built in the shape of a letter H. They were standing on the central bar.

'There's another ledge - up there,' said the youth.

Quillam shone the lantern into the darkest section ahead, looking for a way to clamber upwards, but only the sooty walls bounced back at him. He moved closer and scoured the brickwork in the candlelight, but it was a dead end.

'There's nothing here,' he replied, his face glowering at Benedict, 'have you lied to us? If you have, I'll kill you here and now,' he growled.

'N-No, I swear,' Benedict bleated, his eyes pleading with them. 'There has to be a way through. Let me take a closer look,' he said, taking the lantern from Quillam.

'No funny business,' growled the youth.

Benedict held the lantern above his head and searched across the intricate patterns in the brickwork. There had to be something that stood out.

'Perhaps it's like the secret tunnel in Winderling Spires,' he said, turning eagerly to Tallitha. 'Remember when the stones jumped out of the wall? We climbed up and found the Great Room.'

In her excitement at Benedict's deduction, Tallitha forgot how much she hated him – and how much he had hurt her.

'Of course, brilliant! Quillam, lift me up,' she said, clambering onto the youth's shoulders. 'Pass the light, Benedict.'

For a split-second, it was just like old times.

Tallitha scanned every bump and dip in the chimney wall. In the corner, the bricks changed into a herringbone pattern. She nudged the bricks and one came loose.

'Maybe this is it!' she said breathlessly.

Tallitha tugged at the corner and suddenly a series of blackened bricks poked out of the wall.

'Wow!' said Quillam.

'It's a staircase,' said Benedict, smiling up at Tallitha.

In the excitement Tallitha forgot herself again and returned his friendly gaze.

One by one they clambered up the steps.

'There's a ledge ahead of us,' said Tallitha shining the lantern into a hole.

'Where does it lead?' asked Quillam.

Tallitha inched forward on her hands and knees, turned round in the sooty hollow and whispered to them.

'At the end there's a ladder leading down into the witch's fireplace.'

'Are you sure?' asked Quillam.

'Yes,' she said excitedly.

They crouched down, hardly able to breathe in the dirty stillness of the chimney.

At last, Tallitha spoke.

'I guess this is it,' she mumbled, searching their dirty faces. 'Time to call on the Morrow child.'

Benedict stared wide-eyed, terrified at what was about to happen.

'I'll take a look out there,' said Quillam.

He snuck down the ladder and peered round the edge of the fireplace. The hideous Bone Room met his gaze.

In the distance the shrill voices of the Morrow Swarm were chanting, getting louder, more urgent, babbling dark verses into the night.

The Quickening was about to commence.

# Thirty

In the sulphurous hallway of the Darkling Stairs, Ruker and Neeps slunk about in the shadows waiting for the moment when they would climb the bannister to the Bone Room. The sinister staircase, illuminated by a sickly yellow light wound high above them, bristling with the grey-black fur of the Night Slopers. A gaggle of Groats loitered at the top of the staircase with Tyaas trapped in their midst.

'Remember, two pulls on the lever when the time is right,' whispered Ruker.

'Right you are,' replied Neeps, tightening his belt, making ready for the assault.

'They're on the move,' murmured Ruker, as the Groats marched into the Bone Room.

Ruker tiptoed silently across the hallway and sprang onto the bannister with Neeps on her tail. The Skinks edged deftly upwards, moving like crabs, scaling the witch's staircase.

'When I say the word, we'll set the Night Slopers free,' whispered Ruker.

The Skinks crouched at the head of the Darkling Stairs and bided their time as the sound of demonic chanting echoed from the witch's lair.

*

In the candle-lit gloom of the Bone Room, the Swarm were assembled, dressed in their finest clothes, preparing to welcome the thirteenth into their nefarious pact. Asenathe remained in the shadows, propped against a row of cushions on a chaise longue, feigning her stupefied state – waiting for the performance to begin, and for the moment when she would act.

'Where are the others?' demanded the Thane, tapping his fingers against his throne, his grey hair plaited with silver and golden beads.

Bludroot scuttled forward. 'I've searched the Silver Tower, my Lord, but there's no sign of Lord Redlevven or the Lady Yarrow,' he replied with a bow.

'They must be at their precious Stinkwells.'Asphodel scoffed.

'Well, it seems that Benedict is nowhere to be found either,' replied Snowdroppe tartly, smoothing down her crimson gown and slicing her eyes at her sister. 'Perhaps Asphodel can explain her son's absence.'

'Well?' asked the Thane, thrusting his chin in the Queen's direction.

Asphodel stood erect, her jet-black crown glinting in the candlelight and her long charcoal-grey hair covered in a mantilla of black lace.

'He should be here,' she answered sharply, avoiding Snowdroppe's penetrating gaze.

'We will begin without them,' the Thane announced, stamping his staff.

The Neopholytite began casting spells from the curse papers as Snare handed her phials of foaming potions to empty into the whorl-pit. The Morrow twins, Muprid and Lapis, were dressed exactly the same, in an outlandish creation of tulip-pink taffeta and black lace. Their fair hair plaited and curled. Lord Edweard stood next to them, seething with hatred. His dark eyes were fixed on Caedryl, who had wormed her way next to her grandfather. She was determined to stake her claim as the heir apparent of Hellstone Tors. Caedryl pursed her lips with a sugar coated grimace as she stared at her uncle, daring him to challenge her.

'Bring forth the thirteenth,' demanded the Thane.

Tyaas appeared from the head of the Darkling Stairs, flanked by the Groat guards. He quickly scanned the Bone Room, taking in who was present and searching for Micrentor's Cabinet. He discovered it perched by the side of the whorl-pit with one of its small drawers lying open.

'Let the Quickening begin,' said the Thane, gesticulating to the Swarm to gather round.

Then the Neopholytite spoke the Ennish verses to commence the initiation ceremony …

> *'Temenstra, dictatus litha, Tyaas magestica …*
> *Temenstra, dictatus litha, Tyaas magestica!'*

\*

In the sooty alcove above the fireplace, Tallitha listened to the pulsating chants of the Swarm and crouched in readiness, her heart thumping in her chest. This was the moment she had rehearsed over and over again – the moment she had dreaded. With trembling fingers she laid the bloodstone pendant on the dirty, coal-strewn floor next to the raven's head skull.

'Be warned,' she said, lifting her head and staring at Benedict. 'Once summoned, this alcove will turn ice-cold and you will see things that will unnerve you.'

'Like what?' Benedict muttered fearfully.

'Dead people,' she replied flatly.

Tallitha laid her hand on the raven's skull and began to utter the litany of the dead.

'I call upon the Morrow child,' she murmured, nervously. *'Death defy and death decay, come to us we fear no ill, from o'er the grave, from the dank, dark tomb, tell me your secrets, bring them alive, I call upon you Arabella Dorothea Morrow to span the death divide.'*

Benedict stared directly ahead of him, scouring the sooty recesses for any sign of other-worldliness. The enclosed space had the cloistered eeriness of the Winderling mausoleum.

'This place g-gives me the creeps,' he whispered, his breath turning white with cold.

'Wait,' murmured Tallitha, pointing into the darkness. 'Look!'

A blast of cold air whipped through the darkness as Tallitha's face became tinged with an uncanny pallor. Benedict counted the seconds, heavy with foreboding, waiting for the dead things to appear. His blood pounded in his ears and his stomach was awash with trepidation. Gut-wrenching fear got the better of him and he reached out and clutched Tallitha's trembling hand. She didn't push him away.

'It's beginning,' she said faintly. 'I can feel Arabella Dorothea's restless spirit crossing the great divide.'

'I-I don't like it,' Benedict whined.

Tallitha squeezed his hand for him to be silent.

'B-But –' he stuttered, turning quickly towards her.

The look on Tallitha's face silenced him. She had slipped into a trance. Her eyes were glassy and remote, locked in communion with the dark forces. Tallitha was focused on something beyond their reach, that only she could sense.

'Arabella Dorothea's travelling from the other side,' she said in a chilling voice.

Benedict thought he might faint.

Tallitha lifted her finger and pointed towards the sooty brickwork. Wisps of mist seeped between the bricks, stealing through the cracks and curling across the floor like bloodless snakes, wrapping their slippery tendrils around Tallitha's body.

'Save us all,' bleated Benedict as the pearly white tendrils engulfed her. 'What's happening?' he moaned.

'It's the Morrow child,' she said, mournfully.

The tendrils clung to her hair, exploring her dead-white face, as the stench of death pervaded the alcove – it was the smell of decay, of sulphur, pitch and myrrh.

Benedict reared back. 'There's something white and horrible in that corner! It's oozing through the walls,' he moaned.

Suddenly a pattern of snow-white fingerprints trespassed across Tallitha's cheek as a thin voice trembled in the darkness.

'I have answered your call, Tallitha. Septimia and Siskin are with me.'

From out of the coal-blackened walls, Arabella Dorothea's tremulous form took shape, with the bloodless lips and the black eyes, ringed in blistering red. A tiny frail hand reached out, as pale as a butterfly's wing, and touched Tallitha. Septimia and Siskin hovered by Arabella's side as the trio of ghostly shapes mingled into a snow-white blur.

Benedict made a desperate mewing noise.

'Where's the Hellstone Witch?' asked Septimia, her voice

grating like the scratch of a rusty nail.

'In the Bone Room,' Tallitha mumbled.

But as Tallitha pointed towards the Neopholytite's lair she met Quillam's anxious face peering up at her.

'It's time,' he whispered, holding out his hand for Tallitha to descend.

She turned towards the ghostly figures. 'Wait here until I call you,' she said.

As Tallitha climbed down the rickety ladder she could hear the shrill voices of the Swarm getting louder and louder, chanting their evil verses in the Bone Room.

\*

*'Temenstra, dictatus litha, Tyaas magestica ...'*

The Thane raised his hand to quieten the Swarm.

'We are assembled on this night of the Quickening to admit Tyaas into the Swarm,' he announced. 'Step forward, the one who will become the thirteenth.'

Tyaas approached the whorl-pit as Snowdroppe lifted the Morrow pact from Micrentor's Cabinet.

'Our pact!' she hollered, 'written in Edwyn's blood!'

The Swarm gasped with delight as Snowdroppe displayed the ancient cloth, the words picked out in fine Ennish stitching and soaked in the blood of Edwyn Morrow.

Tyaas slipped his hand below his outer robe and deep

into his pocket where his fingers touched the oilcloth. He was ready to act. He watched, waiting for exactly the right moment.

'Anoint the thirteenth in the blood of our pact,' said Snowdroppe, leading Tyaas to the whorl-pit.

Asphodel took a phial from the Neopholytite and handed it to her father.

Frintal Morrow released the stopper from the phial of Edwyn Morrow's blood.

'Take the bottle,' he commanded.

Tyaas wrinkled his nose in disgust as the Thane forced his fingers round the hideous blood-phial.

*Come on Tallitha! Where are you?* Tyaas thought desperately. *Get me out of this mess!*

Tyaas searched the shadows for any sign of Tallitha.

Soon it would be too late and he would be one of them!

The Thane raised the Morrow pact as the Swarm jostled for position to catch a glimpse of the precious relic.

'Let me touch it,' said Caedryl, snatching at the cloth and missing.

'I want it too,' shouted Muprid, elbowing her sister out of the way.

Caedryl, Muprid and Lapis argued about which one of them should touch the pact first, while Edweard tried to keep them apart.

'Get out of the way!' hissed Caedryl, spitting at the twins.

'It's my turn,' squealed Lapis.

In the bickering that ensued, Tallitha seized her moment.

She clutched the bloodstone pendant, stepped from out of the shadows and into the midst of the Morrow Swarm.

'Take me instead!' she shouted. This was it.

Now there was no turning back.

# Thirty-one

'Tallitha!' Snowdroppe screeched.

The Swarm stopped as if a witch's spell had turned them to stone. Only Caedryl reacted, arching her back and hissing like a scalded cat, her emerald green eyes flashing with spite.

'It's her!' Caedryl snapped, pushing the twins out of her way.

The cat-girl was ready to pounce.

Devilish eyes bored into Tallitha as she stepped quickly across the Bone Room, positioning herself next to Snowdroppe. The Morrow twins squawked like a pair of strangled birds choking for breath. In the consternation that followed, Asenathe slipped silently from her chaise longue, unnoticed by the others.

'Well, well, if it isn't my errant granddaughter,' the Thane said sarcastically.

'What's she doing here?' snapped Caedryl.

Tallitha faced them all. 'You chose me first,' she announced.

Her heart was pounding; her throat was dry. 'Well now I'm here! So which one of your children shall it be?' she asked, turning to Snowdroppe.

Her mother's face wavered with indecision.

'Well, Snowdroppe, it seems we can have either Tallitha or Tyaas – so which one shall we choose?'

Snowdroppe gazed from Tyaas to her daughter. *Tallitha, Tallitha!*

'Tallitha!' she cried, 'I choose her!'

Snowdroppe gripped her daughter's wrist, digging her nails into the flesh, and dragged her next to her brother at the side of whorl-pit.

The Swarm were glowering at her!

'So it seems that Tallitha will be our thirteenth!' the Thane announced with a wry smile.

This was her moment! Her eyes strayed towards the chimney. Quillam hovered, ready in the shadows.

Tallitha stepped forward and uttered the words she had rehearsed countless times, the words to confront the Neopholytite.

'I summon the thrice-hexing spell to destroy the power of she who weaves her evil threads of bloody darkness! To crush the Morrow pact forever!'

The Neopholytite gripped the arms of her chair.

'What dark work is this, little girl!' the Thane said laughing. 'You're powerless to break our pact!'

'You don't understand what you're doing!' snarled

Snowdroppe at her daughter. 'You're a wilful creature, always have been! Grab her!'

Tallitha sprang to her brother's side, forming a buffer between Snowdroppe and her son.

'NOW!' Tallitha cried giving Tyaas an almighty push.

Tyaas sprang behind the cauldron, reached for the oilcloth and dangled it above the steaming whorl-pit.

'Do it! Fling it into the pit!' yelled Tallitha, willing him to act.

It was as if the Swarm were immobilised, transfixed by what was happening. They stood, stone-like, staring open-mouthed at the boy.

Then the Thane let out a scream and lunged for Tyaas, knocking Snowdroppe to the ground. In the same moment, Quillam lunged from the shadows, grabbed Frintal and wrestled him to the floor, holding a knife to his throat and attempting to grab the pact from his grasp.

'Stop him!' yelled Asphodel, 'that boy has something in his hand!' she spluttered realising the dark trophy that Tyaas clutched in his fingers.

But it was too late.

'There goes the evil witch!' Tyaas shouted, flinging the oilcloth and its terrible contents into the swirling vortex.

The Neopholytite's dead black eyes snapped in horror. 'What's the boy doing? Grab him!' she hollered across the Bone Room.

The witch began muttering mad curses, conjuring up a spell – it boiled in her gut as she belched and fumes of smoke erupted from her jaws.

'Tallitha! Tyaas!' screamed Quillam, releasing the Thane and pushing Tallitha to the ground. 'Watch out!'

In the commotion Tyaas scrambled across the floor, dragging Tallitha and Quillam behind him as the boiling curse missed its mark, pinging into the cauldron and began winging its way into the rafters, searing the bones with daggers of fire.

Snowdroppe screamed, leaping into the air.

She shuddered violently, moving like lightning towards the whorl-pit but Tallitha flung herself directly in her mother's path.

'No, Mother! You won't stop us!' Tallitha cried, staring into the madness that swirled in Snowdroppe's eyes.

They collided with a terrific thud. Tallitha spun across the room, landing against Micrentor's Cabinet, cracking her head. She felt sick and dizzy.

Snowdroppe let out a blood-curdling howl and lunged for the oilcloth but the pit was too deep and the vapours clouded her vision.

'Grab it!' Asphodel screamed, raving and spitting.

Snowdroppe gripped the edge of the whorl-pit, panting and staring wild-eyed into the abyss as the cloth spun round and round, going deeper and deeper in ever decreasing circles, until it finally disappeared with a tremendous sucking sound.

'My Kingdom!' the Thane screamed, as Snowdroppe came up empty handed.

But it was too late.

The Bone Room darkened. A terrible hush settled on the witch's lair as the Thane bellowed his despair into the silence.

'NO!' he thundered, with a roar that shook the rafters.

The birds screeched whilst the hounds slunk to the floor, cowering and whining.

The Thane lunged for Tyaas's throat but in the same moment Asenathe stepped from the shadows, stuck out her foot and the Thane tripped and fell. The Morrow pact dropped from his grasp.

'You!' he screeched, his black eyes boring into her.

Asenathe stepped on the Thane's fingers, grinding her heels into his flesh as he screamed in agony. All eyes were on her.

'I curse you!' Asenathe shouted as the Thane writhed in pain. 'You tricked me with a love spell,' she added bitterly, 'and for that I seek revenge!' Then she spoke the words of the Raven Spell in a loud and clear voice:

*'Anintha, Ravena melliflicant, anintha, Ravena melliflicant,
Anintha, Ravena melliflicant, anintha, Revena melliflicant.'*

The Swarm stared in disbelief as the Raven Spell fell from Asenathe's lips like a swarm of angry wasps, brilliant yellow and shining black, buzzing and brimming with spite. They darted up to the rafters in angry drones and *ping-pinged* against the witch bottles with unrelenting fury, working the stoppers free, hurtling inside and dive-bombing the curse tablets that protected the Neopholytite's potions and magic.

'My witch bottles!' the Neopholytite cried, as her spells crumbled. *Pop, crackle and fizz* went the noise of the spells expiring in their death throes. 'The Dark Spell is unravelling!' she cried with a pitiful wail.

'Tallitha! Catch!' shouted Tyaas, reaching for the Morrow pact and throwing it to his sister.

As she caught the hideous fabric the tingling sensation of the Morrow stain whipped through her body.

Asphodel lunged for Tallitha as Quillam grabbed the evil Queen, holding her back.

'Run for it!' He cried.

Tallitha sprinted for the whorl-pit, crunching through broken glass as a rainbow of magical ingredients fell all about her. For a moment she was mesmerised by the blood-red embroidery. She was slipping into a trance – it had her in its grasp!

'Tallitha!' Tyaas shouted. 'What are you waiting for? Do it NOW!'

Her brother's voice brought her back to reality with a jolt.

'Let this be the end of the Swarm!' she cried flinging the Morrow pact into the vortex.

In an instant it was sucked down into the vapours and disappeared into oblivion.

'TALLITHA! NO!' Snowdroppe screeched as hoary demonic spectres filled the night.

The ghosts of their long dead ancestors emerged from the dark recesses of the Bone Room, darting across the Neopholytite's lair, howling in despair at the destruction of the Dark Spell. Arcadia and Brimwell Morrow soared across the Bone Room followed by Gravelock and Tollister Morrow, grisly apparitions shrieking at the doom as it befell their descendants. The Thane let out another terrible cry – like the howl of an animal caught in a trap. Snowdroppe pushed Tyaas to the floor and lunged at Tallitha, scratching her across her face. But it was too late. The pact had vanished!

'Bludroot! Croop! My witch bottles – help me!' the Neophoytite wailed.

But the Shroves did not respond. They cowered in the shadows to wait out the storm – Snare and Croop, Cannisp and Grintley, Florré and Warbeetles and even Bludroot were saving their own miserable hides.

'Asphodel. Command the hounds to attack!' shouted the witch desperately.

'Killer! Slayer! Attack them all!' screamed Asphodel, spit flying from her lips.

But the hounds remained cowering on their bellies. The Queen stared helplessly at her father.

'My trusted spells,' she moaned, 'my dark craft is slipping away!'

At the head of the Darkling Stairs the Skinks were poised.

'Now!' shouted Ruker.

Neeps pressed the lever twice and the Skinks leapt onto the bannister.

The Darkling Stairs spewed forth their black-hearted contents, as a marauding pack of Night Slopers sprang forth in a tirade of yowling and spitting. Caterwauling, they dashed across the Bone Room snapping their jaws, brandishing their fangs and flashing their claws in fury.

'Save me!' shouted Snare as the hideous jaws of a Night Sloper discovered him in the shadows and drooled above his head.

She bared her fangs, her red eyes glowing with menace. Tallitha stared on in horror. The Night Slopers had a taste for Shroves!

'Out of my way!' Bludroot squealed.

He shimmied up the ribcage like a Shrove possessed, desperate to escape the pack of feline devils snapping at his heels as the Night Slopers dragged a screaming Snare across the floor, their fangs lodged deep in his neck.

'Help me!' Snare squealed.

But it was too late. His dying screams could be heard, whimpering into nothingness.

The Bone Room was awash with mayhem and madness – a cacophony of baying hounds, roused by the bloodshed, chased the Night Slopers down the Darkling Stairs.

'Get back here! Slayer! Killer!' screamed Asphodel.

But the hounds turned tail and ignored the Queen.

*The power of the Swarm was coming to an end – and now the hateful brood were turning on one another; sister against sister; uncle against niece; father against daughter, in a vain attempt to save their own skins.*

'Get out of my way!' Muprid shrieked as the sisters fought to get out of the Bone Room.

Caedryl threw them a hateful glance, sprang in the air with a shudder, landed in the shape of the Wheen-Cat and slipped beneath Micrentor's Cabinet to wait out the tempest. But Lord Edweard had spied the cat-girl.

'Come back, traitor!' he bellowed, dragging her out by her tail and throwing a flagon of water over her body.

The Wheen-Cat let out a deep-throated yowl. She hissed and sprang at him, sinking her claws into his neck, slashing his flesh. As the blood pumped from the wound he toppled and slumped to the floor. Then the Wheen-Cat, damp and shivering, slunk in and out of the carnage, shaking her tufted paws, spitting and crying out in pain. Now Caedryl was stuck in her cat-body. Her yowls could be heard disappearing into the recesses of the Bone Room as she dragged her bedraggled body into the darkness.

'Do something!' Snowdroppe shrieked, turning desperately to the Thane.

'Quillam! I'll kill you for this,' she spat, flying at the youth.

But Snowdroppe had lost her power. Quillam pushed her away.

Frintal Morrow was transfixed. His breath came in desperate bursts as a grubby youth emerged from the fireplace.

'Benedict, come to Mother,' Asphodel commanded.

But for once her son disobeyed her. He knew that the time of the Swarm was ending.

Then Tallitha spoke the words that Frintal Morrow had prayed never to hear.

'I call upon the Morrow child, Arabella Dorothea, to renounce the blood-soaked words of Edwyn Morrow. Then, and only then, will the dark pact be broken for all eternity:

*Danitha mallecur na tresta,*
*Arabella transcenda, danitha mallecur na tresta,*
*Arabella transcenda!'*

Tallitha cried into the night.

'Not her!' shrieked Asphodel, 'not that child!'

She clutched her father, whimpering.

Frintal hid his face in horror as the Morrow child entered the Bone Room in a ghostly mist, flanked by the spectres of Septimia and Siskin, howling and moaning their words of hatred at the Morrow Swarm.

'Stop that dead child!' the Thane moaned, 'I cannot bear to look at her!'

'It's too late,' Tallitha shouted.

The Thane cowered as Arabella Dorothea uttered the words that would shatter the darkest spell of them all.

'I am brought here by Tallitha Mouldson. So that I, Arabella Dorothea, the Morrow child, renounce the Morrow pact and the blood-soaked words of Edwyn Morrow for all eternity.'

'NO!' screeched the Thane.

Up in the rafters there was an almighty crack. The Bone Room shook as a terrifying roar swept through the skeleton, sweeping aside everything in its wake. The sound of thunder crashed through the witch's lair as the skeleton shuddered and the bones shattered into a thousand pieces.

'Our dark and beautiful world is crumbling!' Snowdroppe wailed.

She spun round in a bright white fury, powerless to stop the destruction.

'My powers …' she shrieked, 'have vanished!'

The Bone Room groaned as the ways of the witch unravelled.

'The Dark Spell is no more!' the Neopholytite croaked. 'My power is gone!'

The sound of the death rattle came out of her throat. The Witch of Hellstone Tors was shrinking. Her dead-black eyes sunk behind her cheekbones and the skin on her neck withered into deep furrows.

'*Lilletha le durna, Lilletha le durna, Lilletha le durna, Lilletha le durna,*' she cried, desperate to rejunvenate her ravaged body in the soul-catcher.

But as she clutched at the Emporium of Lost Souls, it shattered. Alyss Trume, Mattie Burn, Elsie Wood and Grace Eversedge disentangled themselves from the witch's prison. The women from the Emporium of Lost Souls were free at last and fled into the night.

'H-Help me!' the Neopholytite wailed.

But no one moved to save the witch.

With a dying curse, she tumbled headlong into the whorl-pit and was sucked down into the vortex.

The Thane let out a terrible cry. The Bone Room fractured as a thunderbolt shot through the brittle rafters, splitting the ribcage from top to bottom. The mass of bloody drapes fell from the ceiling and burst into a wall of flames.

'Take cover!' shouted Quillam, dodging a shower of shattered bones that pierced the floor.

He grabbed Asenathe's hand as Tallitha dived after them, sheltering behind a cabinet out of the path of molten fireballs. Peels of thunder pierced the night, fires flared up and flames raged. Potion bottles spun out of control and exploded like fireworks, scattering shards of glass across the room.

'This way!' shouted Neeps, taking flight.

The Skinks darted from a hail of broken glass, hiding at the head of the Darkling Stairs. Tyass and Benedict ran for cover, leaping over the scattered bones and broken witch bottles for the safety of the fireplace. The Groats fled down the Darkling Stairs, pushing the Skinks to one side in their desperation to flee disaster. The screams of the Swarm filled the lair as Edweard, lying prostrate, slashed by the Wheen-Cat's claws, was speared by a splintered bone and pinned to the floor.

'Aaarrrggh,' he screamed in agony, grabbing his shattered leg.

The Thane cowered behind his throne, moaning in mad disarray.

The Morrow twins took one final look at their injured father and fled down the Darkling Stairs. Snowdroppe and Asphodel clung desperately to one another and watched, dumbstruck, as the rafters split and fire rained down.

The time of the Morrow Swarm had ended in a hail of brimstone, fire and smoke.

Witch bottles shot from the rafters like cannon balls and

shattered into a million smithereens of red, green and purple glass. Rows of rowan wands snapped and crumbled into dust; black fumes billowed up to the rafters; the curse tablets fizzed in a haze of dust and the spells on the curse trees smouldered and disappeared in a tornado of brilliant firecrackers and trails of acrid smoke. The terrible sound of the Dark Spell imploding roared through the roof of the Bone Room, bursting into the night in a hail of fire.

Tallitha buried her head between her knees as the storm raged on, shielding herself behind Micrentor's Cabinet with Quillam at her side. The evil that had encircled Hellstone Tors and had protected the Swarm from magical attack was no more.

Then, as suddenly as the mad frenzy had begun, everything became deathly quiet in the Bone Room.

Time stood still.

Shards of broken glass stopped in mid air.

The shattered bones hung, poised in the candlelight.

Black smoke dangled in pendulous clumps.

The silence that ensued was as terrifying as the sound of the Bone Room disintegrating.

Suddenly, a flash of crimson light filled the witch's lair.

Tallitha could bear it no longer and tugged on Quillam's jacket.

'What's happening?' she asked.

Quillam peered from behind the cabinet, his ochre eyes searching the witch's lair.

Quillam shot back behind the cabinet.

'Something's wrong,' he whispered hoarsely.

'What do you mean? Hasn't it finished yet?' she asked nervously.

'I-I don't think so,' he answered feverishly.

And it hadn't.

# Thirty-Two

Selvistra Loons swooped over the roaring seas, accompanied by her Hag-Beast, flying in from the remote island of Stack End, armed with powerful spells of twisted magic. The Fire Witch and her beast skimmed the waves in a shock of crimson light leaving a trail of shooting stars in their wake. They flew high above Breedoor on the tail of the Northern wind, sailing straight into the heart of Hellstone Tors. The bewitching hour had arrived and the air reeked of magical havoc and mayhem, of crushed spells and the distinctive aroma of the Hellstone Witches' fear.

This was the night of the Quickening.

'The castle is alight with magic!' shrieked Selvistra, pointing down through the clouds. 'Look, Orgen, the Dark Spell is crumbling.'

Below, the silhouette of Hellstone Tors, shot-black against the moon, was etched against the flames bursting forth from the shattered roofline. Selvistra and Orgen spun down through the darkness, swooping through the turrets, darting into the castle and flying up the Darkling Stairs. Fire and brimstone, smoke and sulphur filled the air. A flash of crimson light exploded in the Neopholytite's lair as Selvistra and her Hag-Beast landed in the Bone Room amidst the carnage. All around them, the room was disintegrating.

'Widdershins!' shouted Selvistra,

The witch spun round, casting the spell to reverse the damage that the destruction of the Dark Spell had wrought.

Immediately fragments of bone shot into the air, flying back into rafters and reformed into ribs. There was a terrific groan and the broken ribcage snapped back into place. Coloured glass smithereens melted back into witch bottles and the bloody drapes danced across the floor and surged to the rooftop.

'Now for the Swarm,' Selvistra cried, 'Find them Orgen, I know they're hiding, cowering before me!'

She commanded the Hag-Beast to attack.

The half-man, half-wolf – a vengeful creature, with a hideous lupine jaw – stood on his hind legs and sniffed the air. His nostrils quivered and he licked his fangs, searching for the scent of the Swarm.

The Thane, shaking with fear, cowered behind his throne.

The Hag-Beast scented him first.

'You!' Selvistra bellowed, spying the Thane's mop of hair as he tried to slip away. 'Your time here is finished!'

Orgen pounded across the Bone Room, his jaws aching with bloodlust.

Frintal Morrow froze and closed his eyes in terror. He felt

the beast's foul breath, hot against his cheek; smelt his wolf-man sweat; felt saliva dripping down his neck.

'I'll give you anything! Whatever you want, take it!' He snivelled, squeezing his eyes open and coming face to face with the Hag-Beast's ferocious fangs. 'Save me,' he whimpered.

The Hag-Beast's black eyes bored into the Thane's petrified face.

Selvistra savoured her moment of victory.

'You thought the Dark Spell would protect you!' she jeered, her red eyes drilling into him.

'Anything, take it all!' he wept. 'Take the bloodstones, take my Kingdom!' he begged.

'YOUR KINGDOM IS ALREADY MINE!'

Frintal Morrow began to whimper and whine.

With hatred in her heart, Selvistra nodded to the Hag-Beast. Orgen opened his jaws and sank his fangs into Frintal Morrow's throat, dragging the once arrogant and invincible Thane behind the whorl-pit to finish him off.

His terrible screams echoed through the night.

'What's that?' asked Tallitha, holding tightly onto Asenathe in the shadows.

'Don't move a muscle,' Quillam whispered. 'Selvistra is out there.'

From the depths of the Bone Room the Thane's unholy screams unearthed Snowdroppe and Asphodel from their hiding place.

Snowdroppe shrieked as she spied the Fire Witch and the blood-soaked Hag-Beast.

'*Cressillita mentol mori, Cressillita mentol mori,*' Selvistra

chanted, swallowing the phial of shiny black liquid.

Out of her mouth a trail of festering smoke shot across the room.

'Black Drop!' Asphodel screamed.

In their haste to escape, the sisters collided with one another. Snowdroppe pushed Asphodel out of her way and fled towards the Darkling Stairs as the spell zipped across the Bone Room and caught her like a whip, reeling her in.

'Ahhhh,' she screamed, clutching her neck.

But there was nothing she could do.

Then the Black Drop lashed out at Asphodel, hooking her with its tendrils and immobilising her to the spot. The evil sisters were caught in mid-stride, like a pair of waxworks models. Asphodel's face had the look of a hunted dog and Snowdroppe's mouth hung open with fright. They had been stilled by the spell. Selvistra laughed menacingly and sucked the black smoke back into her mouth.

'The Black Drop tastes of liquorice and dandelions,' she said, licking her lips and inspecting the frightful sisters.

Selvistra Loons took a black-headed needle from her gown and viciously pricked Snowdroppe on the arm. A trickle of blood rolled down her pale white skin as the slightest hint of fear flashed across her eyes.

'The Hellstone witches are petrified!' she laughed, calling out to Orgen.

But the Hag-Beast was preoccupied with Lord Frintal.

'Now for that girl!'

Selvistra scanned the Bone Room for any sign of Tallitha, but only Lord Edweard, injured and pinned to the floor, reared his head and groaned.

Selvistra clicked her fingers. 'Dinner,' she said wickedly to Orgen.

The Hag-Beast didn't need calling for a second time.

Edweard Morrow's awful screams sent shivers down Tallitha's spine. She reached out and clutched Quillam's hand.

'What'll we do now?' Asenathe asked desperately.

'Make a run for the fireplace!' Tallitha replied.

But the Grand Witch had the nose of a bloodhound and the eyes of a hawk. She spotted them the moment they slipped from behind the cabinet.

'Like rats scurrying for cover!'

Selvistra lunged at Tallitha, grabbed the girl and swiftly knocked Asenathe unconscious.

'I've caught the Winderling girl!' Selvistra hissed, dragging Tallitha by the hair.

'Let her be!' shouted Quillam, raising his fist to strike the witch.

Selvistra caught his arm, twisted it behind his back and flung him to the ground. The Black Drop poured from her lips and she stilled him to the spot. Try as he might, he could not move.

'I have the meddlesome child!' she screeched, hauling Tallitha up to the rafters and dangling her above the carnage like a rag-doll.

'Let me go!' Tallitha screamed.

'Shall I drop you?' Selvistra crooned, a devilish smile dancing across her face.

It was a terrifying drop. Tallitha held the bloodstone in her fingers – it was warm to the touch.

*

'What'll we do now?' whispered Neeps, crouching at the head of the Darkling Stairs. 'That witch is going to kill her!'

Ruker kept her eyes fixed on Tallitha, hanging precariously from Selvistra's grasp.

'I'm going in,' she growled.

'No you're not,' said a voice behind her.

It was Esmerelda, accompanied by the women from the Bleak Rooms as Spooner and Lince brought up the rear.

'Will that witch drop her?' asked Lince, craning her neck to get a better view.

'We must help her,' said Ruker gruffly, abruptly pulling away from the others.

Esmerelda grabbed his arm. 'This fight is beyond us. Selvistra has stilled Snowdroppe and Asphodel with Black Drop and she'll do the same to us. Step back into the shadows and wait until the time is right. If we enter now, that witch will kill Tallitha.'

'But we have to try!' Ruker insisted.

'No, not yet.' Essie said firmly. 'We must wait.'

So they hid at the head of the Darkling Stairs, biding

their time, watching as Selvistra squeezed Tallitha's limp body between the rafters.

*

Selvistra's eyes alighted on Tallitha's bloodstone.

'What's this?' she cried, grabbing the pendant. 'What do you know about that witch, Kastra Micrentor?'

Tallitha refused to answer.

'Let's try a little magic,' she called. 'That is before I kill you!' Selvistra teased, as Orgen the Wild prowled below and licked his fangs.

The witch bored into Tallitha, hexing her so that her head grew heavy.

'*Calamistra, navar shenine malancthon deit,*' Selvistra shouted. 'That will drag the truth out of you!'

'Tell me!' The Grand Witch repeated, hitting Tallitha across the face. But the girl still refused to answer. 'You have more magic inside you than I thought, Wycham girl!' Selvistra cried.

She held a dagger up to Tallitha's throat, pressing the blade into her flesh.

'If you won't speak, this dagger will send you straight to hell!'

Tallitha held her breath and closed her eyes. She was going to die … she willed the Morrow child to help them, again and again.

In the depths of the Bone Room the Hag-Beast began circling and snarling as a frosty- white mist whipped across the room in icy blasts.

'Stop!' a thin voice wailed. 'I won't let you kill her as you killed me.'

'What mischief is this?' Selvistra snapped, removing the blade from Tallitha's throat.

Selvistra swooped across the Bone Room, searching the shadows for the owner of the thin voice. She landed on the floor, her black dress billowing about her.

'Will she find us?' whispered Tyaas, turning to Benedict in their sooty hiding place.

'S-She's sure to, she's a Grand Witch.' Benedict shuddered.

'There's someone in there!' Selvistra taunted. She sniffed the air. 'Boys! I can smell little boys!' she cried, moving steadily towards for the fireplace.

Benedict buried his head between his knees. 'She's going to catch us!'

Selvistra muttered a curse, swooped up the chimney, and dragged Benedict and Tyaas from their hiding place.

'It's the boy from Winderling Spires and his little friend,' she crooned, jabbing a sharp nail into Tyaas's cheek.

'Get away from me!' he cried.

Selvistra dragged Benedict before his mother. 'Watch as I make him squirm! *Tellas callenta sellis!*' she roared.

'Mother! Help me!' he cried.

Then Benedict was catapulted across the Bone Room. He landed with a sickening thud, smashing against the ribcage walls. His body hung like a limpet, snagged on the bones.

'*Tellas callenta sellis!* Selvistra cried.

The bloody drapes flew across the room and encased Benedict, muffling his cries for help.

But there was nothing anyone could do.

Benedict had got his comeuppance at last, sealed like a mummy in a shroud.

Selvistra rounded on Tyaas. 'Now it's your turn,' she said, raising her dagger.

The thin voice spoke once more. 'You cannot hurt him.'

'Who dares thwart me?' Selvistra bellowed.

Then out of the mist the Grand Witch Kastra sprang before her.

'You dare to come here!' Selvistra cried, flashing her molten-red eyes.

'I have come to do battle with you,' cried Kastra as the ghostly apparition of the Morrow child appeared by her side.

'Y-You!' Selvistra shrieked, pushing Tyaas to the floor.

The boy scrambled across the Bone Room and scaled the ribcage, climbing towards Tallitha.

'Not only me,' Arabella wailed, 'but the others you murdered that day!'

Septimia and Siskin slipped into view. Their faces were a deathly grey pallor and their woeful black eyes peered out of their angular skulls. The smell of decay and death rose up all around them.

'The Dark Spell is no more.' As Arabella spoke her breath was frost-like. 'I will protect the Wycham children from you.'

Her bloodless lips puckered and her hair stuck out in brittle clumps. Red-ringed eyes stared at the fiery witch with hatred.

'Orgen!' Selvistra screamed. 'Attack that creature!'

The Hag-Beast's lip curled and his fur bristled, but he cowered, powerless against the dead things.

'Set Tallitha free and leave this place,' moaned Arabella.

'Never!' Selvistra hissed.

Selvistra darted away from the ghostly trio. 'Get that dead child away from me!' she shrieked.

'Arabella Dorothea comes to take her revenge,' answered Siskin.

The dead-ones were untouchable. They had slipped beyond the realm of witches and their magic.

High up in the rafters, Tallitha clung to her brother as he tried to untangle her from the bones.

'Arabella died because of you,' announced Kastra. 'I swore revenge that day.'

The Grand Witches faced each other across the Bone Room, circling in their magical light – sapphire and red sparks danced and flew about the room.

'You can't outwit me!' Selvistra cried.

'Yet I have played a witch's trick on you,' Kastra replied devilishly.

'You won't beat me!' Selvistra roared.

Selvistra lunged at Kastra, sending a hail of fire towards her.

Tallitha and Tyaas watched from their vantage point as Kastra leapt out of the fiery blast, darted up the ribcage and into the rafters, retaliating with a thunderous blue orb that shattered into a thousand pieces around Selvistra. In the ensuing battle the Grand Witches hurled fire and brimstone, spells and curses until the Bone Room glowed with magical light.

'You have forgotten the power of my cabinet,' cried Kastra at last. 'The one you stole from me!'

Selvistra dived towards Micrentor's Cabinet, flinging the drawers wide open. 'There are no tricks in here!'

'Arabella, look inside my cabinet,' instructed Kastra.

She swooped down from the rafters as the Morrow child stepped towards Micrentor's Cabinet.

'What am I looking for?' she asked

'You will know when you find it,' replied Kastra, 'then say these words – *Examina la durna, figurine Arabella.*'

'No!' Selvistra howled, flying round the Bone Room in a fury, but her magic was useless against the dead-ones. She clung to the rafters, her eyes blazing with madness.

Arabella prised open a secret drawer at the back of Micrentor's Cabinet.

'*Examina la durna, figurine Arabella,*' she announced as a doll tumbled out. 'It's the poppet I embroidered with you in Winderling Spires – but then Selvistra stole me away,' murmured Arabella sadly.

'Now show the poppet to the witch!' demanded Kastra.

Abrabella held the poppet for Selvistra to see. The Grand Witch howled, rearing back, spitting at the sight of the rag-doll. The poppet had flame-red hair.

'That poppet is me!' she screeched.

'Hex the Grand Witch Selvistra. Remember the spells I taught you and take this!' said Kastra, handing Arabella a black-headed needle. 'Your power from beyond the grave is stronger than all her magic. Speak the truth and have done with her!'

Tyaas struggled to free Tallitha. He untangled her clothes and untied her hair and together they climbed down the ribcage.

'Do as Kastra says,' Tallitha said breathlessly, stepping towards the Morrow child.

Arabella twisted the needle in the poppet's side.

Selvistra doubled up in pain.

'I take revenge on Selvistra Loons!' Arabella wailed, '*Examina la durna, figurine Arabella*,' she cried again. 'I reverse your spell,' she stabbed the poppet once more.

Selvistra clutched the side of her body where the pin had entered the poppet.

'Orgen!' screamed Selvistra, scouring the room for the Hag-Beast.

But the beast was nowhere to be seen. He had flown from the Bone Room when the ghosts arrived.

Selvistra spluttered a stream of obscenities and spun round in a hail of flaming light, circling the Bone Room one last time. Suddenly, she spied a pair of emerald-green eyes peering up at her from the gloom. Selvistra swooped down and grabbed Slynose by the tail, whisking her up into her arms. The Wheen-cat spat and scratched, attempting to turn back into her human form, but it was useless.

'I curse you all!' Selvistra shrieked. 'Be warned, one day I will return to stake my claim on Hellstone Tors and then I will kill you all!'

Then Selvistra fled from the Bone Room hollering and screaming into the night.

'She's got Caedryl,' Tallitha whispered to Tyaas.

He smirked, 'Well, a witch always needs a cat!'

'Has Selvistra really gone?' Arabella asked guardedly.

Tears dropped like frozen petals from her coal-black eyes.

'That witch is finished. You have reversed the spell. She has no power here,' answered Kastra triumphantly.

The Grand Witch wrapped her arms around the Morrow child.

'Remember when I was your teacher in Winderling Spires,' said Kastra fondly. Arabella's doleful eyes rested on Kastra's face. 'I taught you magic and kept you safe while you learned the ways of the witch, preparing you for the Larva Coven.'

'But Selvistra stole me away,' murmured Arabella.

'She always wanted you. You embroidered the poppet during your last days with me,' said Kastra.

'I remember,' whispered Arabella.

'Now say the Ennish words embroidered on the poppet,' said Kastra, pointing at the doll.

Arabella did as she was asked. '*Splenunnatha feyned, castor resillinda*.' She whispered.

Suddenly a beam of light began travelling through Arabella's body from the tip of her toes to the top of her head. As it moved, her frozen outline began to melt, the hardened edges of her face softened and her ice-white pallor faded. Suddenly Arabella lurched forward, clutching her stomach, her body jerked and she took in a huge gulp of air. When she lifted her face the dark-rings of her eyes and the bloodlessness of her lips had begun to fade.

'You've come back to me,' whispered Kastra, lovingly.

With their work complete, Septimia and Siskin enveloped each other in a bright white light. They kissed Arabella on the cheek and the spectres vanished into the night.

'I-Is she alive?' asked Tallitha incredulously.

'She isn't as dead as she was, but it will take time for her to return to the living. Arabella must learn to live again,' explained Kastra.

'But what is she, exactly?' asked Tallitha, staring at the pale child.

'She's a deathling,' answered Kastra, 'she still has one foot in the dark reaches from whence she came.'

'Like the women from the Emporium of Lost Souls?' asked Tallitha.

Kastra nodded. 'But they haven't been dead for as long as Arabella.'

'Can I stay with you?' asked Arabella, searching Kastra's face.

'Come home with me to Winderling Spires and I will teach you everything I know about spells and witchcraft. Then, once you are a Grand Witch, you need never die again.'

'B-But how can she be alive and dead at the same time – and how will she live forever?' asked Tyaas, scratching his head.

The Morrow family never ceased to amaze him.

'Magic and sorcery,' replied Kastra enigmatically. 'Arabella Dorothea will be a Grand Witch one day.'

Arabella tucked herself inside the folds of the Grand Witch's cloak.

'Selvistra Loons has fled,' said a jubilant voice from the top of the Darkling Stairs.

Essie strode into the Bone Room with the Skinks behind her and the girls at her side.

'I knew you could do it!' shouted Ruker.

'Essie! Neeps! Ruker!' shouted Tallitha, running into their arms.

'This place is so creepy!' said Lince, staring up at the bone-rafters and hanging onto her sister.

'Worse than the Winderling mansion,' replied Spooner.

The girls wandered through the Bone Room, followed by Esmerelda and the women from the Bleak Rooms, awestruck at the sinister remains of the witch's lair.

Later, when the power of the Black Drop had diminished, Quillam and Asenathe emerged from the spell, amazed that the Swarm were no more and that Selvistra had been vanquished.

Against the odds, Tallitha had won – she had destroyed the Dark Spell with the help of all her friends.

They were safe at last.

*

'It's all yours, Tallitha,' said Asenathe, taking her arm. 'So what will you do with Hellstone Tors?'

Tallitha didn't know how to answer that question. The castle - with its accursed secrets, its dark history and untold stories - was a burden, and too much to take in.

'I haven't decided yet,' she answered in awe of the responsibility that had befallen her. 'But I know what I must do now. I'm going home,' she replied, 'back to Winderling Spires – to Great Aunt Agatha and the Morrow sisters. They'll know what to do with this castle and besides, I want to see Cissie again,' she sighed, her eyes straying towards Quillam.

He smiled and stepped awkwardly to her side.

'We'll look after everything until you return,' added Esmerelda. 'Now we can really start to explore this sinister place and begin to unearth its treasures.'

'And its dark past,' added Asenathe solemnly.

A muffled sound came from the rafters.

'What about Benedict?' asked Tyaas, 'someone should let him out.'

'All in good time,' added Esmerelda, 'he'll come to no harm in there.'

'What about mother?' Tallitha asked.

But Snowdroppe and Queen Asphodel had vanished too.

'Where have they gone?' asked Tyaas.

The Swarm who had survived Selvistra's vengeance had disappeared.

'They will be headed to the secret harbour. There's a ship moored there,' explained Asenathe.

'Good riddance,' replied Ruker.

'Perhaps Caedryl will be safely on board,' said Asenathe knowing she had lost her daughter, perhaps forever. 'She wasn't always so wicked,' she added sadly.

'What about Selvistra?' asked Tallitha.

'She will have fled to the island of Stack End to lick her wounds. That witch won't be back for some time,' Esmerelda replied. 'But rest assured, when she returns we'll be waiting for her.'

'Are you ready to leave this dismal place?' asked Tallitha, staring around the hideous Bone Room.

'You bet!' Tyaas replied.

'Soon, we'll be home in Wycham Elva,' said Tallitha excitedly, hardly able to contain her joy. 'Coming?' she asked Quillam.

'I can't wait!' he answered, beaming at her.

'Hey, wait for us!' shouted the Skinks, laughing as they caught up with Spooner and Lince.

So in the stillness of the night the happy band of friends stepped down the Darkling Stairs and away from the dreaded Bone Room, far away from the Dark Spell that had exerted its evil for so long, far away from the power of the Swarm and onwards towards freedom.

# Thirty-Three

Tallitha's last few days at Hellstone Tors passed in a whirlwind of frantic activity. Esmerelda was keen to start exploring the Swarm's palaces, so Asenathe and Quillam led the party up into Redlevven and Yarrow's deserted tower and into the labyrinthine quarters of the Thane's inner sanctum. The interconnecting chambers of Frintal's catacomb contained a fabulous library with bundles of old manuscripts and room upon room filled with magical artefacts.

'This castle will take years to explore,' said Tyaas, climbing onto a high platform in one of the dusty chambers. 'Look, there's a secret room back here.'

Spooner and Lince clambered up the ladder with Tallitha following behind them. Through the dark passageways the chattering Nooklies could be heard making their presence felt to the unwelcome visitors. It was a treasure trove of delight with potion archives and spell rooms. Spooner crawled out of the small opening and called down to Esmerelda. She was covered in dust.

'You know what?' she said cleaning her hands down her trousers. 'Now the Swarm have gone, I really love it here. Can I stay with you, just for a while?' she asked.

'What about Lince and your parents?' asked Asenathe. 'Won't they miss you?'

'Yeah, what about me?' her sister teased.

'You're fine with me staying here, aren't you, our kid?'

'Suppose,' answered Lince, 'but our mam won't be happy.'

'Just for a few weeks and then I'll be home, promise.'

Asenathe turned to Esmerelda. 'I'll be going back with Tallitha and the others, to see my mother,' her voice faltered.

Esmerelda nodded and squeezed her cousin's hand.

'I know Attie, it will be an emotional reunion.' Then she turned to Spooner and brightened. 'Well if you're staying I have a job for you – I have a yearning to see if there are any plans for this castle. And if not, we ought to draw some ourselves.'

'Brilliant!' answered Spooner, 'when can we start?'

'Soon as you like,' added Esmerelda. 'We have to map out the cellars and all the snickleways too.'

Spooner's face glowed with excitement.

So it was decided. Spooner would stay on with Esmerelda and assist her in mapping the floors, towers, turrets and the underground passageways of the great castle.

Kastra had left behind a group of Black Sprites, including

Flametip and Rucheba, to guard Hellstone and patrol the surrounding countryside for any intruders. The Black Sprites had news too – Redlevven and Yarrow had escaped from the Stinkwells and were hiding out on the Barren Edges. There had been rumours that Grintley and Florré had set them free.

Once the Swarm had escaped, the Shroves and servants who had always spent their days confined to the lower levels of Hellstone Tors, gingerly crept up to the castle to survey the eerie edifice. Flinter, the Shrove who had fed the Stumpleback, crawled up to the castle for the first time in many years. The sunlight pierced his rheumy eyes and he gasped at the opulent feasting halls and the rich pickings that could be had "upstairs".

In time, Bicker and Embellsed returned, a tad more humble, and begged to be forgiven. The Shroves had experienced difficult times in the wilds of Breedoor and now that Hellstone was free of the Swarm, they wanted to come home. As for the Groats, those at Hellstone Tors sided with whoever was in power and so for the time being they pledged their allegiance to Tallitha.

There had been many searches of the castle but Marlin could not be found anywhere. No one ever spoke about the Shrove's entombment in his turret. But as the weeks passed by, rumours began to circulate that he had been seen up at Stankles Brow with Bludroot.

As word spread across Breedoor about the demise of the Neopholytite, and the gruesome deaths of Lords Frintal and Edweard, the Grovellers began to arrive at Hellstone Tors to see for themselves.

'It's all true then,' said Rye, agog, surveying the sunlit gallery.

Her brood of bairns clung to her side, overawed by the splendour and majesty of the huge castle.

'Mam! Look at me!' squealed Tootles with delight as she climbed onto the Thane's throne, like a princess over all she surveyed.

The Grovellers had never been allowed inside the castle during the Swarm's reign, so Rye and the others were keen to see the riches that adorned the formal rooms.

'That night it 'appened, we all stood in the moonlight and watched the Grand Witch flying 'cross the skies – we was all terrified,' said Lutch, nodding at Buckle.

'Look at these tapestries,' said Buckle, touching the wall hangings as the sisters nosed about the grand hall with the children at their heels.

Even though the Swarm had vanished, there was still the problem of the Murk Mowl. Before leaving Hellstone Tors, Tallitha heard that Queen Asphodel and her entourage had fled across Breedoor to Stankles Brow. The bloodstone treasure still lay undisturbed in the castle crypt and in the mines worked by the Murk Mowl. But finding the treasure and exploring the mines would have to wait until another day. Tallitha was homesick and desperate to go back to Wycham Elva – *home* to Winderling Spires!

Once released from his cocoon, Benedict, who had fulfilled his promise to Tallitha, wheedled away and eventually persuaded her to take him back to Wycham Elva.

'I-I did as you asked in the Bone Room,' he whined, 'so please take me with you Tallitha. I won't let you down.'

'I don't trust him, never have,' replied Quillam, eying Benedict darkly.

Benedict scowled at Quillam and pushed his floppy hair out of his eyes. The animosity between them was mutual.

'I'll keep an eye on him,' said Tyaas, 'just to make sure he doesn't get up to anything.'

So Benedict joined the group as Tallitha, Tyaas, Asenathe, Quillam, Lince and the Skinks travelled across Melted Water and through the Tear Drop Tarns. They rendezvoused with the Cave-Shroves who had heard of their victory at Hellstone Tors and were waiting for them on the high pastures by the Out-Of-The-Way Mountains. Ernelle and Pester were delighted to see their dear friends again and guided them safely through the underground tunnels, avoiding the Old Yawning Edges and the Throes of Woe.

Over dinner at the Raven Stones, Pester told them news of the Swarm.

'Some of them have fled across the Viridian Sea to the Far Islands,' she said, passing round a platter of skewered rat.

'We've heard that the twins, Lapris and Muprid, are with Sedentia Flight, staying with Queen Asphodel at Stankles Brow,' added Snouter. 'Some of the Shroves are there too by all account.'

Pester carried a tray of blindworm puddings to the table to a roar of enthusiasm from the diners.

'They can't do much harm though.' Ernelle shrugged. 'They have nothing – no treasure and no power.'

'We must never underestimate them,' added Asenathe gravely. It would take a long time for her to recover from the torment of Hellstone Tors.

Tallitha twisted her hair in and out of her fingers. She looked pensive. 'What about our mother?' she asked guardedly.

'We've heard nothing about Snowdroppe,' said Pester, handing out the treats, 'but rumour has it that Redlevven is up in the Northern Territories.'

'What about Yarrow?' asked Quillam tucking into skewered rat, the juices dripping down his fingers.

Ernelle shook her head. 'Not a squeak out of that one.'

Over the next few days the Cave-Shroves gave them safe passage over the Sour Pit Chimneys, up through the Shrunken Butts and finally into the Weeping Cavern. The travellers were constantly on their guard, waiting for any sign of the azure blue eyes to appear on the cavern roofs or the sound of the Murk Mowls' battle cries to reverberate through the caves. But the Groats and the Mowl were nowhere to be seen. Perhaps the creatures were tucked into their lairs, biding their time, waiting for Queen Asphodel to return. At last the travellers reached the Startling Caves, and made their way across Hellsnip Pass and into Wycham Elva.

'Nearly home,' shouted Tyaas excitedly, running helter-skelter down the steep meadow.

Tallitha breathed in the flower-scented air. *Nearly home*, she thought blissfully and had to pinch herself! The undulating hills and sweet meadows buzzed with insects and were a beautiful sight to behold after the darkness of Hellstone Tors and the Out-Of-The-Way Mountains. At the edge of Ragging Brows Forest, they said their goodbyes to Ruker and Neeps.

'We'll visit Winderling Spires soon,' Neeps promised, 'and this time we won't be working in the kitchen garden.'

'Or sleeping in the tree houses! We expect royal treatment. Feather beds and sumptuous food for us!' joked Ruker.

'Nothing is too good for you,' said Tallitha, hugging Neeps.

She turned to Ruker. 'Watch out for the Black Hounds,' she teased.

Ruker laughed. 'Those critters can't catch us. We're much too clever for them.'

Tallitha turned to Benedict. 'You can't come with us to High Bedders End,' she told him firmly. 'You're not a favourite with Josh and Bettie.'

Benedict pulled a face.

'You'd better come back with us then,' said Neeps.

'W-What?' moaned Benedict. 'But what about the Black Hounds?'

'We'll guide you back through Ragging Brows in a day or two. Then you'll be able to find the way back to Winderling Spires by yourself,' added Ruker.

Benedict glowered sulkily at his companions, but he knew he had no choice.

'Ready?' asked Quillam, tightening his backpack.

In the morning sunlight Quillam exchanged glances with Asenathe. The excitement of the day ahead beckoned. After so long and so much heartache, they were about to meet their mothers again.

It was time to embark on the last part of their journey, stopping off at the Wakenshaw's farm at High Bedders End. Quillam's stomach felt tight. He was going to meet his mother. *His Mother!* The words sounded unreal – he couldn't take it in. He had yearned for this for as long as he could remember.

The farmyard chimneystacks came into view through a dip in the hills. A trail of smoke billowed upwards as Barney and Sticker, alert to the visitors, began barking.

'You okay?' asked Tallitha as they tramped down the hillside.

Quillam still felt queasy. 'I'm scared,' he answered, meeting her gaze. 'What if she doesn't like me? What if I'm not what she imagined after all these years?'

Tallitha regarded the youth who had been by her side through all the bad times. He was just like Cissie, brave and loyal to the end. But on this occasion his fearless spirit seemed to have deserted him.

'Of course she'll like you, Quillam,' she replied gently.

The dogs bounded up to them, wagging their tails and running round in circles with excitement.

'Hello boys!' shouted Lince laughing. 'Have you missed me?'

As she bent down to stroke them, the dogs knocked her over, licking her face and rolling on top of her.

'Barney! Stop it!' she cried with exasperation. 'Sticker! Get off me!'

Tallitha laughed at their antics and helped Lince to her feet.

'Well, they're pleased to see us!' Asenathe announced, giving Quillam a meaningful look.

The dogs ran about in a frenzy of delight.

Then from out of the farmhouse they heard Bettie scream.

'Lince! It's Lince! Josh! Cissie … oh my goodness,' she cried, rushing towards them. The tears were rolling down her cheeks. 'You're home!' Bettie cried shooing the dogs to one side and hugging her daughter. For a second or two they clung to one another. 'But where's our Spooner?' Bettie asked quickly, pulling away. 'Has something happened to her?' Her eyes looked frantically from one to the other.

'She's fine, Mam. She decided to stay on at Hellstone Tors,' replied Lince sheepishly.

'Why would she want to stay in that terrible place?' Bettie answered gruffly, giving a sideways glance at Asenathe.

'It's safe now. The Morrow pact has been destroyed,' explained Tallitha, 'we're all home now, including Attie'. She said pointing towards her cousin.

'The Swarm have fled. Spooner's safe with Essie. She wanted to explore the castle,' added Lince.

'That girl will be the death of me!' said Bettie shaking her head.

'My dear lass!' Josh called, his voice breaking with emotion.

He stood with his arms outstretched and his face beaming from ear to ear.

Lince rushed into his open arms.

'Dad,' she murmured, her voice muffled by his enormous hug.

Josh chuckled happily and nodded a warm welcome to the rest of the party. Then he noticed the youth standing behind the others. He observed the stranger keenly.

'How do?' he called.

Quillam muttered a gruff response.

'You'd best come in, all of you,' said Bettie at last, nodding towards Asenathe. 'I'll put the kettle on.' She ran towards the farmhouse calling for her sister-in-law. 'Cissie, Cissie! Just look who's turned up!' she shouted excitedly.

As Tallitha walked towards the farmhouse her beloved Cissie appeared on the doorstep, drying her hands on her apron.

Then she cried out and ran towards them.

'I thought I'd never see you again. It's been so long,' Cissie sobbed, burying her head between Tallitha and Tyaas.

She kissed them over and over again. They grabbed her, holding on to her, hugging her desperately.

'Cissie?' whispered Asenathe.

'Oh my lass, you're a long time coming home,' replied Cissie, hugging her tightly. 'Your mother won't believe it!' Then she burst out laughing. 'You did it!' She cried, hugging them all – Tallitha, Tyaas and Asenathe. 'I knew you could do it!'

'I've missed you so much,' Tallitha cried.

'There, there, my chicks, you're home now! All's well!'

As Cissie raised her head she noticed a young man hovering uncertainly by the farmyard gate. She studied his serious face and the way he held himself. He was a little awkward and a bit out of place. But somehow he looked familiar.

'Who's this young man then?' she asked, gazing down at Tallitha and running her fingers through Tyass's dishevelled hair. 'Did you pick up this waif and stray on your travels?' she joked.

For once in her life Tallitha couldn't speak. She had a huge lump in her throat. She thought she would burst. Tears fell down her cheeks as she tried to speak, swallowing waves of emotion.

'Oh Cissie …' she murmured. 'It's …'

At once, the expression on Cissie's face changed.

Something clicked and everything fell into place.

He was here at last. It was her Danny.

The miracle had happened.

'Oh Tallitha! I-I –' was all that Cissie replied.

Then she ran towards her boy and hugged him for all her life was worth.

# Thirty-Four

Tallitha Mouldson sat by her window with her nose pressed against the glass and gazed out over the rich green fields and sludgy brown hills of Wycham Elva to the place where the rolling countryside met the dark grey mountains in the distance. So much had happened, out there in the wilds of Breedoor, way beyond the snowy peaks and dark caves of the Out-Of-The-Way Mountains, to Stankles Brow and beyond to Hellstone Tors. Yet here she was back home again, safely tucked up in her bedroom at Winderling Spires. Her fine clothes, now somewhat small for her, still hung in the wardrobe and her powders and perfumes remained as Cissie had left them all those months ago, laid out in a pretty semi-circle on her dressing table. The strange events that had happened seemed like they had taken place in a dream and to a completely different girl.

The Skinks, Ruker and Neeps, were back home in Ragging

Brows Forest and the Swarm, or what was left of them, were dispersed with their Shroves across the Northern Territories or way over the Viridian Sea. Kastra had returned to Winderling Spires to stake her claim on the Raven's Wing, much to the delight of the three Morrow sisters. There was now a Grand Witch living in the big old house again who could perform fantastic magical spells. The Morrow sisters observed the sorcerous goings-on from their balcony, bewitched and enchanted by Kastra's magical abilities. Of course, Arabella Dorothea was with her; a frail, colourless being who retained her death-like quality but who was getting stronger every day. Kastra kept her in seclusion in the Raven's Wing. Even the Grand Morrow had not been able to visit the sickly deathling.

'When she's fully recovered and can do a little magic of her own you will be allowed to see her,' Kastra had informed them.

Tallitha was curious about Arabella Dorothea. She wondered what it was like to be a deathling, half-living and half-dead.

A knock at her bedroom door disturbed Tallitha's thoughts and Sophie, who had been promoted to Housemaid to replace the Shroves, entered and bobbed her knee.

'Please Miss, the Grand Morrow would like to see you in her sitting room.'

The maid smiled shyly and left.

Tallitha pulled her clothes into some semblance of order and made her way along the shadowy corridors of the old house, resonant with the familiar smell of beeswax and lavender. Across the landing, Edwina and Sybilla came towards her chattering away together, with Licks and Lap mewing about their feet.

'Morning Tallitha, beautiful day,' trilled Sybilla sweetly, her face highly powdered and rouged-pink. 'We've just seen Maximillian, he's taking coffee in the library.'

Tallitha smiled, she would see her father later.

Sybilla picked up the cats and handed Licks to Edwina. She stroked the creature before her eyes strayed over her granddaughter's attire and she frowned.

'If you're on your way to see your great aunt Agatha, tidy your dress and tie your hair up,' she added stiffly.

Her face was set like a porcelain figurine – freshly painted in garish reds and pinks.

'We've been chatting to that nice boy, Benedict. Such a studious young man,' said Sybilla. 'He's pouring over the family histories in our library.'

'He was asking after you, Tallitha. He seemed a little lonely,' added Edwina.

Benedict! What to do about Benedict? Tallitha opened her mouth to say something but thought better of it. He was a conundrum. He had helped them in the Bone Room, had done all he was asked and more, and yet she still didn't trust him. Benedict had pleaded to come to Winderling Spires and on seeing him, Great Aunt Agatha had agreed that he could stay. She wanted to make a proper home for the boy and to improve him. She was especially fond of improving young people. After all, he was another of the children that had been affected by the hateful Swarm.

'I'll see him later,' mumbled Tallitha, as an excuse.

She bade the sisters *good morning*, trundled down the staircase and into the grand hallway of Winderling Spires. She knocked at the sitting room door, shuffled her feet and waited.

'Enter,' her great aunt's familiar strains echoed across the room.

Agatha Morrow was sitting in her armchair inspecting Tallitha's sewing, turning it round in her hand and clicking her tongue in dismay.

She flashed a disapproving look in Tallitha's direction.

'This just won't do,' she said sternly. 'Why can't you sew in a straight line? I despair! Yet again your embroidery has managed to get into such terrible knots!'

Tallitha waited, unsure what was coming next.

Agatha Morrow lifted her face and beamed at Tallitha. The girl laughed and ran to her great aunt's side laughing, kissing her warmly on the cheek.

'One day, dear Aunt, I might learn to sew properly.'

'There's still time,' answered Agatha fondly, patting Tallitha's hand. 'You see, Tallitha, there's more to this humble craft than meets the eye,' she added mischievously.

'But Aunt Agatha, even you have to admit that I learned a lot of useful things out there,' she said longingly, gazing towards the mountains, a lump developing in her throat. 'About how to survive in dire circumstances, about who to trust and who not to trust in this strange world of ours, and about the value of true friendship.'

Agatha turned to her great niece with a new softness in her

face. A tear came into her eyes as she remembered how close she had come to losing all the children.

'And about your family in Winderling Spires, you came to realise how much they meant to you and that they have always loved you,' Agatha replied sweetly, dabbing her eyes.

'It's true,' Tallitha replied.

Yet a shadow crossed Tallitha's face. She stepped towards the window, opened the lattice and stared towards the Out-Of-The-Way Mountains, yearning for the heavenly scents that came off the meadows at Sweet-Side Pasture and the delicious taste of Bettie's farmyard tea. The dark peaks were at once threatening but also enticing, forever beckoning to her to return like a moth to a flame.

'I wonder how Cissie and Quillam – I mean Danny – are doing. I miss them so much. Every day I wake up and expect to see them and – well, they're not here,' she said sadly.

'Danny has been through a great deal. He needs time to adjust, my dear, to get to know his mother and his family at High Bedders End. Then he'll come home to Winderling Spires with Cissie.'

But Tallitha felt lonely without them all. She missed them.

'And Attie, where's she today?'

A warm smile played over Great Aunt Agatha's face each time her daughter was mentioned. To have her dear child back home in Winderling Spires was a dream come true, and more than she had dared hope for.

'That's what I wanted to speak with you about,' she said

mysteriously, ringing the servant's bell. 'Asenathe has something she wants to discuss with you.'

In no time Attie had joined them, kissing her mother warmly on the cheek. It was such a pleasure to see them so happy together, reunited at last and enjoying each other's company. Asenathe patted the sofa for Tallitha to join her.

'I've been exploring the South Wing where Sir Humphrey Morrow used to live. It used to be a beautiful part of the mansion in days gone by.'

'I remember, it's where we went exploring – where we weren't supposed to,' Tallitha replied casting her eyes towards the Grand Morrow.

'Now, sadly, the wing is a little tired and has fallen into disrepair, but I want to redecorate it and to make it my home.'

'What about the Great Room?' Tallitha asked, twisting her hair in and out of her fingers.

'There are too many sad memories there,' Asenathe replied. She hesitated for a moment. 'But perhaps you would like to have the Great Room? It's time you had a bigger apartment.'

Tallitha's face lit up. She thought of all the changes she would make to the maze of higgledy-piggledy secret rooms.

'Oh, thank you!' She said. 'I'd love that – but …'

'What's wrong?' asked Aunt Agatha, regarding the girl. She looked distracted. 'I thought you would be excited at the prospect of the Great Room.'

'I–I am,' she replied, 'well –'

Try as she might, Tallitha couldn't resist the lure of the grey mountains, where the mist swept high into the clouds and new adventures awaited her. It was then that the strange unsettled feeling that she hadn't been able to put her finger on became clear.

'It will be wonderful to have Attie's room a-and please don't think I'm being ungrateful,' she paused, 'but I must return to Breedoor and to Hellstone Tors.' She took her great aunt's hand. 'There are things I must do – secrets I still have to uncover, and besides I promised I'd return to help Essie.'

'She has Spooner for company,' added Great Aunt Agatha.

'And the Shroves, Embellsed and Bicker,' giggled Tallitha, remembering the bedraggled pair. 'But those two old grouches are hardly a barrel of laughs and Essie needs me.'

Tallitha knew in her heart she could never stay in one place for long, even if it was her beloved Winderling Spires. She had adventure running through her core and magic in her blood.

'I have always known you would return to Hellstone someday. You are my kin after all – but don't go just yet.'

Tallitha's eyes strayed towards the mountains.

'Not yet,' she replied hesitantly, 'but maybe in a little while once I've settled into the Great Room.'

Then it will be time, she thought excitedly, to step out on another glorious adventure.

Tallitha kissed Asenathe and her great aunt goodbye and skipped off to find her brother. He wasn't in any of his usual places but she had a good idea where he'd be hiding, up in their tree house or perhaps chatting to one of the Skinks in the potting sheds.

The day beckoned, full of endless possibilities for daring exploration. The sun was high in the sky and Tallitha Mouldson had the beginnings of another plan, the stirrings of an idea, perhaps another amazing adventure, whizzing around in her head. Of course, she loved Winderling Spires with its hidden rooms and secrets turrets but the lure of Breedoor was too strong to resist for long.

As she stepped out of the conservatory, a cheerful blackbird sang out, whistling its beautiful song for anyone who cared to listen. Tallitha breathed deeply and gazed at the languid summer's day, the mesmerising sound of the bees, the heady smell of honeysuckle and rose-blossom wafting through the air. The lilting sounds of the feathered chorister mingled with the delicious perfume took her breath away. It was the start of another magical day, the sort of curious day that always gave her ideas. Her heart skipped a beat. That was it!

'Tyaas! Tyaas, where are you?' she called excitedly as she raced across the expanse of verdant lawns, her hair flying in all directions.

Tyaas poked his head through the branches of their tree house. As usual he was in a bit of a mess. His face was dirty with smudges of paint and he had leaves sticking out of his hair.

'I'm up here,' he shouted, grinning down at her.

Tallitha couldn't wait to tell him. She climbed up through the lower branches and pushed open the small trapdoor.

'There you are, at last!' she cried, clambering up into their secret place and flopping breathlessly on the floor. 'I've been looking everywhere for you,' she said feverishly.

As usual Tyaas was busy making something gluey, sticky and nasty. He was sitting amongst an array of paint pots, fastening makeshift arrowheads onto long shanks of wood; managing to get glue all over his fingers in the process. He grinned and wiped his messy hands down the front of his shirt.

'I'm making weapons,' he announced excitedly, intent on the job in hand, 'we can use these to –'

But Tallitha had more important things on her mind than Tyaas's latest project.

'Yes, I see,' she replied quickly, moving the paint pots to one side. 'We can talk about that later – this is much more important,' she replied.

Tyaas lifted his paint-splattered face and frowned at his sister. There it was again, that urgency in his sister's voice. She had that distracted look on her face too, and she was twiddling nervously with her hair. That was always a sign that Tallitha was up to something.

'What's going on?' he asked guardedly, putting down the glue.

She smiled expectantly at him. Now she had his full attention. She was brimming with eager anticipation.

'Oh Tyaas!' she cried happily, 'I can't wait to tell you. I've had such a wonderful idea, in fact, many wonderful ideas!' she announced, almost bursting.

'Tallitha?' he asked with trepidation. 'What are you up to now?'

'Just listen. It all became clear to me this morning when I was talking to Great Aunt Agatha, we were looking at the grey mountains,' she gabbled on breathlessly and grabbed her brother's hand. Her eyes shone brightly and she could hardly get the words out. 'I-It's about this idea I've had. Well, really, it's a sort of plan that I've been mulling over, a-about another adventure to all the amazing places we've been to and some of the places we haven't even see yet. It will be so exciting, I can't wait, and of course you have to come with me!'

And in Tallitha's mind it was all settled.

Their next amazing adventure was beckoning!

'Come on,' she said excitedly, climbing down the ladder.

'Where are we going now?' asked Tyaas, scampering after her.

'Just you wait and see!' she replied grinning up at him.

## About the Author

Susan McNally's love of books and strange make-believe worlds began in her childhood in the North of England. Her parents were great storytellers, recounting ghost stories and fairy tales that ignited her lifelong love of the fantasy and mystery genres. Susan wanted to recreate this world, to take readers on a magical adventure and so began the idea for The Morrow Secrets, a dark spellbinding trilogy of intrigue, magic and suspense.

Susan lives with her husband in North London.

**Susan invites you to visit her at:**

http://www.themorrowsecrets.com
https://www.facebook.com/MorrowSecrets
https://twitter.com/SMcNallyauthor

# In Conversation with Susan McNally

*How do you feel now that you have completed the trilogy?*

I loved writing *The Morrow Secrets Trilogy*, creating the plot lines and developing the characters gave me immense pleasure. Every time I sat down to write I loved entering the fantasy world of witches and the supernatural, it was as if the characters and the mysterious world of Wycham Elva and Breedoor took over and the story wrote itself. Undertaking the mammoth project of writing three books has its challenges and although I miss Tallitha, and even the sinister Shroves, I have ideas for my next book.

### What do you plan on doing next?

The wonderful thing is that once you begin writing you always have a place where you can create your own world and that's what I love about storytelling – you can enter this magical realm whenever you choose. My next book could be a horror story or I may stay with fantasy, but whatever the genre, the plot and the characters have to grip me. I will know that I have found my next story when I can't wait to get back to my desk and start writing. At the moment I am working on a number of different book scenarios.

### What have you learnt about yourself as a writer during this process?

I have learnt a great deal. When I started, as with any new skill, it was trial and error, but I am never deterred by complex problems and that's what narrative creation is all about, particularly when you have a strong story like *The Morrow Secrets* where multiple sub-plots are happening simultaneously. I am like a magpie, gathering snippets of information, being inspired by a single word and I enjoy the research phases of the writing process. I would say that

I am driven, visually imaginative, and willing to rework my writing until I get right.

### *Is there anything you would change about the trilogy?*

In answering that question I am gazing at the walls in my study at the 60 illustrations that were created for the three books. These Gothic drawings encapsulate the progression of the story and I cannot imagine it unfolding in any other way. The trilogy evolved during the writing process and, although I planned aspects of characterisation and plot, the narrative tumbled out as though it was just waiting to be written.

### *What advice would you give to young aspiring writers?*

Write the book that you want to read, the book that inspires you and not what is currently in vogue. The process of creating a story, rewriting it several times to get it as perfect as you want it to be, finding a publisher and editing is hard work. You need to persevere and never give up; only stop writing every day when you know how the plot moves forward, then it will be easy to pick up the writing again.

Treat writing as a job. Don't wait for inspiration to occur, you have to create it. Sometimes you will write rubbish and other times the words will flow just the way you imagined it.

Read from many different genres and notice how authors use dialogue and employ their craft. Watch movies and notice how directors and scriptwriters build suspense, dialogue and tension. I love the visual arts and am motivated through art, cinema and photography as well as the written word.

### What writing habits do you have?

I don't have a daily schedule that adheres to set times but I do like writing at night. When I am in the grip of a new idea or a scene I never find it difficult to write. My method is to get the idea down on paper and refine the writing later.

I create index cards on every character - their attributes and physical characteristics - and key plot decisions otherwise I would be continually searching the script to check facts.

### You initially self-published The Morrow Secrets, are you glad you decided to work with a publishing house?

Of course. It provides greater exposure especially to foreign markets. *The Morrow Secrets* has now been translated into Czech and it's very exciting.

Working with an editor provides an author with an external view that is extremely helpful particularly with complex plot lines.

Of course, this is obvious and is perhaps special. Either way, both ...